PENGUIN B

Australia Street

Ann Whitehead was born in Sydney and now lives beside Lake Illawarra at Berkeley in New South Wales. Ann has won awards and is a published author of plays, short stories, and novels for children, young adults and adults. Her previous novel, *Blackwattle Road*, was written under the name of Ann Charlton.

Australia Street

ANN WHITEHEAD

PENGUIN BOOKS

PENGUIN BOOKS

Published by the Penguin Group
Penguin Group (Australia)
250 Camberwell Road, Camberwell, Victoria 3124, Australia
(a division of Pearson Australia Group Pty Ltd)
Penguin Group (USA) Inc.
375 Hudson Street, New York, New York 10014, USA
Penguin Group (Canada)
90 Eglinton Avenue East, Suite 700, Toronto, Canada ON M4P 2Y3
(a division of Pearson Penguin Canada Inc.)
Penguin Books Ltd
80 Strand, London WC2R 0RL, England
Penguin Ireland
25 St Stephen's Green, Dublin 2, Ireland
(a division of Penguin Books Ltd)
Penguin Books India Pvt Ltd
11 Community Centre, Panchsheel Park, New Delhi – 110 017, India
Penguin Group (NZ)
67 Apollo Drive, Rosedale, North Shore 0632, New Zealand
(a division of Pearson New Zealand Ltd)
Penguin Books (South Africa) (Pty) Ltd
24 Sturdee Avenue, Rosebank, Johannesburg 2196, South Africa

Penguin Books Ltd, Registered Offices: 80 Strand, London WC2R 0RL, England

First published by Penguin Group (Australia), 2008
This edition published by Penguin Group (Australia), 2009

1 3 5 7 9 10 8 6 4 2

Copyright © Ann Whitehead 2008

The moral right of the author has been asserted

All rights reserved. Without limiting the rights under copyright reserved above, no part of this publication may be reproduced, stored in or introduced into a retrieval system, or transmitted, in any form or by any means (electronic, mechanical, photocopying, recording or otherwise), without the prior written permission of both the copyright owner and the above publisher of this book.

Cover design by Jo Hunt © Penguin Group (Australia)
Text design by Anne-Marie Reeves © Penguin Group (Australia)
Cover photographs – slums, Woolloomooloo image: Hood collection, State Library of NSW; neighbourly chat image: Bert Hardy/Getty Images; 1940s woman portrait: H. Armstrong Roberts/Classic stock
Typeset in Fairfield Light by Sunset Digital Pty Ltd, Brisbane, Queensland
Printed and bound in Australia by McPherson's Printing Group, Maryborough, Victoria

National Library of Australia
Cataloguing-in-Publication data:

Whitehead, Ann.
Australia Street / Ann Whitehead.
9780143009535 (pbk.)

A823.3

penguin.com.au

In memory of my parents, Jimmy and Tom

The Beginning of a Bad Day

Chance had nothing to do with the fact that life for the Gordon family took a sudden turn for the worse on Hannah Gordon's thirty-sixth birthday. Her daughter Allie's birthday was on the same day, February 13, and this year it fell on a Friday, the first of only two Friday the thirteenths in the whole of 1948. Added to all that, it was the day of a full moon, and if the moon could push and pull at huge oceans and cause tides to change, it stood to reason it would affect air in much the same way. No one could feel this pushing and pulling, but it had to influence people's moods. More fights and arguments happened during a full moon. That was common knowledge. More murders took place; more people went missing or mad. Hannah didn't need Grandma Ade's warning, 'Bad luck's coming, I can feel it in me water,' for her to realise the odds were against them.

Hannah was determined not to give herself time to start making guesses on what might happen. She drove a taxi all week, but Fridays and Saturdays were her days off, so she had mapped out this day hour by hour with chores like window cleaning, floor polishing and whittling down the pile of mending stacked on the Singer treadle. Added to all that, Grandma Ade had a few jobs lined up that would take most of the afternoon. Not that this was the kind of birthday Hannah would have chosen if she had any say in it. A salon visit would be the preferred option. A professional cut to bring out the curl in her long dark hair, and a beautician to shape her too-thick eyebrows and massage away the crow's-feet that were just beginning to appear. Even a pot of good commercial face cream to replace the rose water, lemon juice and rain water she blended herself. But those things cost money she didn't have, and wasn't likely to get in the near future. At least the bonus of a housework-free weekend would sweeten the sour.

Reviewing the list for the third time that morning, she wondered if she'd been too ambitious. 'There's not enough hours for all of this,' she told Tom while picking up his yesterday clothes off their bedroom floor.

He grunted something the pillow over his head made unintelligible, but it would have contained more than a few oaths. Hannah was heading for the laundry when he tossed the pillow after her and repeated the oaths loud enough for everyone to hear.

'A hangover is self-inflicted punishment so you get no sympathy for it,' she shouted in an effort to drown out his curses.

Time was a whip cracking at her heels, urging her through the housecleaning ritual at full speed: quick flicks with the feather duster over the furniture, half-circle sweeps across the wood-panelled walls, and brooming through each room without bothering about hard-to-reach places. Every one minute and ten seconds she'd race into the kitchen and take out the toast, then thrust two more slices of bread into the toaster. All this while a mixture of oats, water, honey, butter and a dash of salt simmered on the wood stove. She knew that in another three minutes, the porridge would start catching on the bottom.

'Janet, you'll be late for work,' she called, wiping down the linoleum-covered tabletop with lunging sweeps of the dishcloth. 'And, Allie, you said you'd be responsible for getting Hal off to school this year.'

'Don't know why you have to get us all up at sparrow-fart because you can't sleep,' Tom griped as he stumbled past, bleary-eyed, on his way to the bathroom.

He hadn't buttoned his pyjama top, and a stream of light through the kitchen window highlighted the pallor of his skin. It also showed a stomach beginning to pot and a slackening of his muscles. Yet even with his fair hair sticking up in greasy clumps, courtesy of yesterday's Californian Poppy hair oil, and the morning glare diluting the deep blueness of his eyes, he would turn most women's heads. But Hannah preferred the tanned, wiry body and angular good looks he'd brought home from Darwin when his role in the war ended. She thought he was still handsome, but the rest had gone: the tan, the wiriness, eighteen years of marriage. Like the passion, the loving glances, the long foreplay. Now it was the beer-smelling wham-bam like last night. She hated nights like last night.

'There's no reason for *you* to get up,' she said, 'But the rest of us have things to do. I promised Grandma I'd help with an inventory of the herbs, seeing as she won't be open for business today, and I have to make up some cod-liver oil emulsion before herb day on Sunday.'

'Ten ounces of cod-liver oil, six ounces of glycerine, a little tin of condensed milk, and one and a half gallons of lime water,' Hal chanted as he entered the kitchen. 'And Allie won't have to be responsible for me. See?' He indicated his grey shorts and shirt, the long socks held up by elastic bands, and the well-polished if rather shabby shoes. 'I can get ready by meself. I'm nine now, remember.'

'Of course you are, love. It's just that you usually need a bit of prodding to get you out of bed and moving along. And you get an excellent for the emulsion recipe,' Hannah told her foster son, and leaned down to receive a good-morning kiss on the cheek when he stood on tiptoe and lifted his face. She kissed his forehead as she straightened, but her action was a little too quick, trying to gloss over an initial hesitancy. She didn't want to hurt his feelings, but she was still trying to get accustomed to these demonstrations of affection – something Hal had started after spending a few days with Cousin Maria and her tribe of kids.

Hannah considered herself to be affectionate, but she showed it with a smile, her eyes, words. She wasn't, never had been, a kissy-huggy kind of person. That, she believed, was through no fault of her own. Growing up, she'd had no role model as far as that sort of thing was concerned. Her parents had rarely done either; her grandmother never. 'It's the English coming out in us,' Grandma Ade once said, and Hannah could see the truth of that. The only demonstrative member of her extended family was Cousin Maria, whose mother's ancestry was Italian. Maria and her greeting and farewell hugs tended to make Hannah feel awkward. Though thanks to Hal, she was learning to overcome this inherited reserve.

Tom had paused at the door to watch the exchange. His expression altered from annoyed to what seemed to be wistful, and Hannah wondered if he wished she'd greet him like that of a morning.

As if that would happen, she thought. Though maybe if he stayed out of the pub for a week I might think about it.

'Seeing as ya got a day off, I reckoned we could do something for yer birthday,' he said when she raised an eyebrow at him. 'You know, just the two of us like we used to. The zoo maybe, or a picnic. I'll even do the museum if yer twist me arm.'

His offer caught her unawares, and he looked so vulnerable standing there with both hands bunching the front opening of his pyjama pants together, that her tongue caught behind her teeth, holding back a quick-smart answer about having no money for those things. Mainly because of his unwillingness to find another job. He'd walked out on the last one four weeks ago. But what would be the use of bringing that up now?

'I promised Grandma,' she said instead.

'I can make the emulsion,' Hal offered as he slid onto a chair at his usual spot closest to the wood stove. Nobody else wanted to sit at that end of the table. Not in summer anyway.

I'll get an electric stove one of these days, Hannah promised herself, smiling at Hal's pleased as Punch look when Tom crossed to his side and said, 'Good on ya, mate,' as he ruffled the boy's hair.

Hal looked up, matching his grin, and Hannah paused in the middle of setting the table, struck by a sudden realisation that the older Hal grew, the more he resembled Tom. Hal had lived with them since the age of two and she'd almost forgotten that she and Tom weren't his birth parents. She knew his mother but not the identity of his father, and most of the time she couldn't care less. But at times like this she couldn't help wondering if it was someone from Tom's extended family. If he hadn't been away in the army around the time of Hal's conception, she might have started asking questions.

'What?' Tom challenged as she continued to stare.

'Nothing.' Placing the rest of the plates and cutlery on the table, she slopped a large spoonful of porridge into a bowl and handed it to Hal. 'The emulsion ingredients have to be blended in the double boiler. You're too young to be handling things on the stove, Hal love.' Too short, she almost said. Not that Hal seemed worried by his lack of height. Which was just as well. He'd read her thought.

'I can stand on a chair,' he told her.

'Let the kid 'ave a go,' Tom said.

'Oh, Dad, do you mind? Go and put some clothes on,' Janet ordered before Hannah had time to answer. One hand covered their eldest daughter's eyes as she staggered in from her bedroom, pretending to be blinded by his bare chest.

Hannah shook her head, feigning disgust, but couldn't hold back a snort of laughter when he flicked the opening wider.

'Garn, yer won't see a body like this too often,' he said, dropping the shirt back onto his upper arms. Adopting a female model's pose, he winked at her over his shoulder.

'Idiot,' Janet said, and burst out laughing when he jutted a hip and fluttered his eyelashes. 'Yer dad's mad,' she told Hal, bending to plant a kiss on the top of his head before adding, 'Good day to you, gorgeous one.'

'Gorgeous back to you,' Hal answered, grinning when Janet kissed him again as a thank you. This was their usual morning greeting to each other, and had been since Hal declared that apart from their age difference, they could be twins. True, they both had blue eyes and freckles, and the same ginger-blond hair – though Janet mostly wore hers in a pinned-up plait while Hal's was short back and sides when it didn't needed cutting, as it did now. The main difference was in physique, Hal being thin as well as short while Janet liked to call herself well-built.

Curvaceous is what she is, Hannah thought, looking her up and down.

'Why are you staring at me like that?' Janet asked.

'That uniform has seen better days. Where's the other one?'

'In the wash.' Janet grimaced a refusal when her mother held out a bowl of porridge. 'It's a factory uniform, isn't it? They're all BBB.' She winked at Hal. 'Blue, button-through and bloody awful,' she added before he could ask. 'Anyway, you should talk.'

'It's a housecoat. I don't wear it outside the house,' Hannah protested.

'Looks as if ya dug it outter the rag bag. It's gotter be ten years old.'

'Don't be silly,' Hannah said, not wanting to admit that the floral cotton housecoat was closer to fifteen.

I suppose I have been getting a bit lazy about the way I look, she thought, but it still fits, so that means I'm not putting on weight like Tom.

'And I always dress nicely and wear make-up at work,' she added, reassuring herself more than Janet.

'I work in a factory full of women. Nobody looks twice at me,' Janet told her. 'And if they did, they wouldn't be able to tell me apart from everybody else.'

'I'd hate that,' Hannah admitted. Frowning at Tom, who had slumped in the chair next to Hal and grabbed the bowl refused by Janet, she pushed the billy can of milk aside. 'No, Tom, not until you're properly dressed.'

'Who made you the dress police?' Tom asked. 'And talking about getting dressed, when are ya gunna get Hal his long pants?'

Hal sat up straight, looking hopeful.

'Soon as I get a few shillings to spare,' Hannah promised. 'Be a love and wake Allie for me, will you, Jan?'

'I already did, and her majesty reckons she's got a right to lie in, today being what it is.'

Hannah heard the note of sourness but didn't comment. Except for their ages, the girls were as far apart as sisters could be, and seemingly growing further apart every day. Allie resented the fact that Janet usually got the new clothes while she had to wear the hand-me-downs. Janet hated the idea of Allie still being at school while she'd been working since she turned fourteen. Yet there was a lot more to it than that. Very different natures for a start. And Allie insisted that her sister came first in more ways than birth. Janet hadn't forgiven Allie for being born.

Janet had been born during a baby-free couple of years as far as the local kin were concerned. Until the age of two, she'd had the extended family to herself. They gave her presents almost weekly: home-made dolls, knitted bears, sugar treats, stories invented especially for her. She was their all until Allie stuck her bib in. Though even at that early age, Janet must have guessed something was about to change. She should have known by the way people exclaimed over that stomach growing bigger every week, the bulging thing emptying out in the middle of the night and growing into Allie of the lustrous dark hair, brown eyes and pale olive skin, so lovely that she made her cute big sister a plain Jane by comparison. Still did for that matter, though looking at Janet here and now, she was more than average pretty despite the multi-freckles.

And, Hannah thought, it's vain of me to think Allie's lovely when people say she looks just like me, though she's more lanky than I've ever been. Sometimes I wonder if she's ever going to fill out.

'Mum, while you're daydreaming the toast is burning. And I'm already up, thanks to all the noise,' Allie said from behind her.

''Bout time too,' Janet said, one hand switching off the toaster, the other grabbing the slice of toast Hal had just smeared with Vegemite. 'Thanks, lovie. I'm off.'

A peck on his cheek, a touch on Hannah's shoulder on the way past and, giving a quick wave to her father, she vanished through the back door.

'And so long to you too,' Allie called after her. 'Hullo, Hal sweetie.' She dropped a kiss on the top of his head. 'Morning, Mum. Dad, shouldn't you get dressed before coming in for breakfast?'

'We can't all be chirping with the birds and looking spick-and-span like you,' he retaliated, but patted her cheek when she wrapped her arms around his neck from behind. 'Hullo, me darling. Yer look and smell beaut as usual.'

When Allie grinned and said 'I know,' Hannah cut in with, 'A little modesty is always nice,' though she knew it to be true. The smell was courtesy of a birthday gift from Grandma Ade, a tiny vial of rose oil, and Allie shined her shoes and ironed her uniform and blouse every night. Her socks folded just so, a snowy handkerchief tucked into her belt, and her long hair tied back in a neat ponytail completed the picture of a girl, a sixteen-year-old young woman now, who took pride in her appearance.

'Sorry, Mum,' Allie said, then, 'You haven't forgotten you know what, have you?' she asked her dad.

'I haven't forgot. Now sit yerself down and get a feed. Yer need to fill out like yer sister. Not that yer aren't a knockout looker anyways,' he added when she placed a light slap on his shoulder.

'Mum, do you want me to help Grandma?' Hal asked hopefully. 'I can check what herbs have to be ordered and I can write the list.'

Hannah considered his offer while tossing aside the burnt toast and slotting in another two pieces of bread. 'You can't miss another day, Hal,' she finally said. 'You took too much time off last year and I promised your teacher that would change. I know you don't much care for school, but you have to go.'

'So do I,' Allie said. 'Right now. I'm supposed to meet Roma and the others in ten minutes. Her dad is going to shout us a milkshake at his cafe for breakfast.'

'At least have something to eat. And a very happy —' Hannah began.

'A milkshake will be enough and Mr Tomasi will have them ready by now and the others will be waiting,' Allie told her, and was through the door before Hannah could argue.

'— birthday to you,' Hannah finished.

'Janet says we're not to say anything about birthdays until this afternoon. We'll all be together then and nobody in a hurry,' Hal said.

Allie's head reappeared around the door. 'Same to you, Mum. And a taxi's just pulled up out front. Your boss is driving,' she said before disappearing again.

'Darn, I bet he wants me to work.' Hannah pulled a face. 'Someone must be off sick. Guess it can't be helped.'

'Well, that puts an end to a day out with me, don't it?'

Not waiting for an answer, Tom shoved his chair back and shuffled into the bathroom, slamming the door behind him. Hannah stared after him for a few seconds, then glanced at the Hal-made calendar. Beneath a collage of flower pictures he'd thumb-tacked onto the wall, the oblong of brown paper – ruled in twenty-nine squares for the days of February – showed a thick red line circling the number thirteen.

'It's started already,' she muttered, placing a finger on a white-coloured circle just above the line. 'Full moon, and Grandma's right. It's going to be a mongrel of a day.'

As it turned out, the day wasn't too bad after all. Not until early evening after Hannah had been driving a taxi for six hours while Tom spent his afternoon at the pub.

Not even Grandma Ade could have predicted what happened then.

Most People

Along at the corner terrace house, Hannah's grandmother kept her front door closed all day. This was to let people know that if they wanted one of her herbal remedies, they would need to come back tomorrow. Grandma Ade knew better than to try evoking her healing powers on a Friday the thirteenth combined with a full moon. A knowledge of timing had been passed down her line through many years. If her maternal ancestors hadn't fled to Germany four hundred years ago, back to England a few centuries later, then on to Australia, they would have been called witch or gypsy, depending on country and era, and drowned on ducking stools, incarcerated for life, or gassed in crowded ovens. If her ancestors hadn't been prudent enough to leave each place at the right time, that line of healers would have ended long ago.

Grandma Ade could cure almost anything with her herbal concoctions, or so the local women said, and they preferred her to hospital when their time came for birthing, despite the gossip of backyard chicken sacrifices. Most people believed old Doc Howe had planted those rumours. In truth, when Grandma wanted a hen for her healing chicken broth, she killed, plucked and gutted it herself, talking soothingly all the while. A distressed chook sours the soup, she would say. It had been the Methodist minister and not the doctor who interpreted this as her way of placating the spirits. Which happened to be true enough, except for the fact that it was only the chicken's spirit she intended to placate. 'Still and all, it's a pagan practice,' the minister said when one of his parishioners gave him the facts. 'Perhaps even sacrificial.'

Hannah knew about the minister and the chickens, just as she knew that when Grandma advised her to tie pink ribbons around every door knob, the old girl believed Luck to be a lady. But then, most people did. Hannah had decided long ago that Luck was definitely male: one of those blokey males who preferred the company of men to women, young or old. Men were for mates, women for mating. And he'd be an alcoholic male, so you'd never be able to predict what kind of a mood he'd be in by the time he arrived at your door. Tom was lucky at cards and the horses. At least, lucky enough to keep him from finding a job or getting too sober too often, which proved to be unlucky for his family. They had to watch him change from good-natured to disagreeable when he ran out of money for grog.

At five o'clock that afternoon, Hannah stood by her gate, waiting for Tom to show. Everything pointed to him being in an unpleasant mood when he finally staggered home. He had money, and when he had the means he usually switched from beer to spirits. A few beers made him the life of any party, but two shots of whisky or rum on top of those beers threw his shoulders back, his head up, and he'd be spoiling for a fight.

I'm ready for him this time, Hannah thought, straightening her shoulders and planting her legs apart, unconsciously adopting the stance he used when readying himself to fight. She'd never been as angry with him as she was right now. She'd hurried home, intending to hand Allie an envelope with cash tucked inside the moment she arrived. With it would be a promise that they'd go shopping in town on Saturday morning for a birthday present. But the money had disappeared. The money she'd been saving for months. She knew Tom had taken it. He considered any cash that wasn't in her purse or the 'bills drawer' as spare, even though she'd told him countless times that there was no such thing as spare money. Not in their house anyway. Not till he found a job and pulled his weight. He'd have spent it all by now, but at least she'd have the satisfaction of telling Tom what she thought of him before Allie got home, which wouldn't be for another half hour or more. Earlier in the week, Roma's mother had sent a message that her daughter was throwing a surprise party for Allie when school had finished for the day.

Most people who saw Hannah idling at the gate would have supposed she was waiting for her youngest daughter, though Allie often hung back at one of her friend's houses for a few hours after school. For the past year it seemed she'd rather be anywhere than at home, though who could blame her for that? Who on God's earth would voluntarily spend more time in the shadow of the biscuit factory wall than was absolutely necessary? For that matter, who would spend more time than necessary in Australia Street?

It was a narrow, bitumen-clad street, bordered by footpaths just wide enough for one person to stroll comfortably, two arm-in-arm if they pressed their elbows together. A small primary school with bitumen play areas, and not a skerrick of grass, let alone a shade tree, took up the northern corner. Alongside the school, a biscuit factory spread its reddish-brown brick wall to the next corner, which made for an interesting clash of odours: the unmistakable smell of children enclosed in hot classrooms all day, squashed bananas, Vegemite and peanut butter sandwiches, wet pants on some of the littlies, and the waft of baking biscuits. After a few weeks of inhaling the mixture, the school odours always came out on top. As far as Hannah knew, no adult in Australia Street had eaten a factory-made biscuit in years.

A row of houses clustered along the southern side: six two-bedroom cement-rendered terrace houses at one end, five larger by an extra bedroom at the other. All were painted in pastels of pink or cream and had arrowhead iron fences, and gates opening onto steps leading to tiny porches and recessed front doors. The middle row of homes, three weatherboard houses a matching off-white colour, boasted their stand-alone status by being separated from the street and each other by lawns, shrubs and a few stunted trees. This green boast was spoiled a little by the grass's struggle to stay alive in the shadow of the wall, and all the houses needed a coat of paint. Yet to most people who lived there or somewhere nearby, they looked respectable enough.

Hannah never let a day pass without glaring her hatred of that wall. In winter when the sun rode low in the sky, the wall shaded the front of her house and tunnelled the cold westerly winds. In summer it captured the humidity and barred the cooling nor'-easterlies. In dreams it collapsed onto her, or slowly crept forward and swallowed the house room by room. She suspected random daubs of dark patches across its middle area as being blood, the lower blotches as semen stains. But she knew for a fact that heads had been banged against that wall, both accidentally and on purpose, and with only two street lights along the length of it, an occasional prostitute chose the pools of darkness as a workplace. Not that one would make much of a living in this area of the city. Any forward-thinking whore would leave long before the local women chased her away.

If some of those stains are semen, it isn't only because of the prostitutes, Hannah thought as she stared at a dark patch opposite her gate. The black shadows under the wall were more private than a front porch or one of the pocket parks. In this part of the city, where else could a couple go when they got past the point of kissing and touching? Not home – most parents were too watchful to allow young couples more than a few minutes alone. And not to one of the parks – too many families went there to sit around on blankets, socialising while they caught any stray breezes during the warm weather, and who would want to lie around on cold grass during winter? There were no cows to kick up and steal their warm dry spots in the inner city. Luckily, most boys had enough sense to withdraw before the baby-making deed was done. The ones who didn't were married a few months later.

Like Tom and me, Hannah thought. I still don't know if he did it on purpose or if he was just too slow. Or too excited. Maybe too selfish. I'd like to bang his head against the bloody wall.

'And when a drunk pees against it,' she said aloud to take her mind off Tom, 'it has to be scrubbed with lye soap to get rid of the beer-piddle stink. As if the women in this street don't have enough to do.'

Hearing the back screen door bang, then the sound of running feet, she composed herself enough to say reasonably quietly, 'Isn't that right, Hal?' when he joined her at the gate.

'Is what right?' he asked, looking up into her face, his own creased in a troubled frown.

'Nothing.' She curved a hand around his head and pulled him close. 'Don't look so worried, love. I'm just rambling on. You're allowed to do things like that on your birthday.'

Reaching down, she caught hold of his wrist to prevent him from pulling on the side pocket of her skirt. She'd had it for years and that was beginning to show, but it was a slimline skirt and she liked the fact that it still fitted. Granted, it had seen more washes than she'd seen birthdays, but it was still good enough to wear while driving the taxi.

She'd put her hair up in a French roll and worn her good rose-patterned pink blouse as a birthday celebration.

Hal had moved close enough to be really crowding her, something that had happened far too often over the past few weeks. Except when he was at school, or she at work, he'd be right there beside her or behind her, so near that she'd be stumbling over him if she didn't watch out.

What had happened to make him want to be so close? Was he being bullied? That wasn't likely. As small as he was for his age, Hal knew how to stick up for himself, and he had lots of mates. Besides, not much bullying went on at the Australia Street Primary School. Half the kids there were related to each other.

Staring down at him, she tried to read his expression. He seemed anxious. Maybe he thought she'd disappear if he didn't keep an eye on her. As if she would! She wanted to reassure him but didn't know how. Words always let a person down at times like this. They were either too much or not enough. She'd just have to hope he'd grow out of it.

While she tried to think of something encouraging to say, one of those eardrum-splitter whistles lifted her head and the corners of Hal's mouth.

'Here comes your big sister,' Hannah said. 'I think she's early.'

'I quit me job,' Janet said before Hannah could ask.

'And a good afternoon to you too,' Hannah told her.

'Sorry, Mum, but I'm fed up to me teeth.'

'Seventeen's too early in life to get fed up to your teeth or anywhere else,' Hannah pointed out as she opened the gate, closing it again when Janet entered. 'I tried to tell you about working in a cigarette factory when you hate the smell, didn't I? But what do I know? Anyway, there's plenty of other jobs. Meantime, see if you can do something with Hal. He's been hanging onto me since I got home from the depot.'

Watching Janet crouch low, pretending to be sneaking up on Hal, fingers wriggling in a tickling action, she added, 'And don't tell me it's because he doesn't like staying next door with Franny Peters after school. I know that.'

Janet gave a witch's cackle that sent Hal running away in pretended fright.

'He's got a thing about Mr Peters,' she said to Hannah. 'That bloke gives me the creeps too.'

'Since when?'

'Since he started staring at me every chance he gets and telling me I shouldn't be wearing lipstick. As if it's any of his beeswax.'

'I suppose you remind him of Maisie. You were her best friend. Must be as hard on him as it is on Franny, not knowing where their only daughter got to. Or if she's still alive after being missing all this time. It's two years this September since she vanished.'

'Missing her doesn't give him the right to follow me home from the dances,' Janet said, pretending not to see Hal sneaking up on her.

'He follows you?' Hannah asked.

'A few times now I've been coming home on me own and heard someone behind me. I turn around and it's him.'

'What does he say?'

'He doesn't say nothing. Soon as I see him, I run. He can't keep up because of his bummy leg.'

Hannah frowned. 'Come to think of it, I remember one of your cousins saying he followed her one night. Gave her a hell of a fright. I'll ask Grandma to speak to him. She'll soon tell him what's what. That way, Franny won't get upset with me. It's best to keep on good terms with your next-door neighbours.'

'Good idea,' Janet answered and swung around, crying out, 'Aha!', then grabbing Hal under the armpits and lifting him high.

Chuckling low in his throat, his version of a laugh, he hugged her head when she tried to lower him. 'I wanner stay up,' he ordered into her hair.

'You're too old now for Janet to be lugging you around,' Hannah admonished.

'And you're getting too big anyway,' Janet said into the side of his neck, rubbing her nose sideways, trying to bring out that infectious chuckle again.

'Dad says I won't always be a shrimp. He says I'll be bigger than him one day,' Hal told her.

'Bigger and better,' Janet agreed. She glanced at the house. 'Is he home yet?'

Hannah scowled. 'The pub's not shut, is it?'

'He promised to be home early. And he promised Allie he'd buy her a birthday present.' Janet added a humphing noise that was half sneer, half grunt of disbelief. 'He won't do either of those things, will he?'

'He found the money I've been putting aside for months. I hid it in the tea canister because he hardly ever drinks tea, and when he does he never makes it himself so I thought it would be safe. That man has second sight when it comes to money.'

Hannah bit down on her lip when she saw Hal staring at her. She shouldn't talk about Tom like that when Hal could hear, but sometimes she couldn't stop herself. Hal and Allie thought the world of him despite his drunkenness, his hangovers, his bludging. Most of the time he was playful and loving with them. He was a two-faced mongrel and she'd never forgive him for taking Allie's money. Sometimes she wished he'd go off to the pub and forget to come home. They'd all be better off without him.

Janet allowed Hal to slide to the ground. 'You should've bought the present soon as you saved enough.'

'I wanted to get Allie a new dress, and I wanted to take her with me to try it on and make sure of the size. She has really sprung up this year. I noticed this morning that her school uniform is too short now.'

'One of the cousins might have grown out of theirs,' Janet said. 'Allie's pretty skinny.'

'She's probably taller than all of them.' Hannah stared up the street, frowning. 'I think it's time we had a talk, Allie and me. The boys are starting to gather around her like flies to honey.'

'Bully for her,' Janet stated peevishly.

Hal jerked his elbow into her side and gave her a reproachful look. Picking him up again, she hugged him hard, then placed a smacking kiss on his cheek. He lowered his head and grinned, pretending to be embarrassed.

'Allie doesn't get many new dresses,' Hannah said.

And you'd be able to knock me down with a feather if Tom spent money on buying one, she thought.

Hal held out his arms again as she stared up the street and added, 'Here comes the mongrel now.'

'Please, Mum, don't start in on him.' Janet flicked a quick look towards her father. He had paused to regain his equilibrium after turning the corner into their street. 'You do and you'll still be yelling at each other when Allie gets home.' Giving Hal another kiss, this one briefer and quieter, she lowered him onto the pathway. 'And what sort of a birthday's that?'

'Since when did you start worrying about upsetting Allie? And what about my birthday?'

'That's the one I'm talking about. Me, Hal and Allie got you something, but you can't have anything till she gets home.'

Hannah's face brightened. 'Fair enough.'

'Come on then, I'll make you a cuppa. I bought some vanilla slices to celebrate. Just ignore him when he gets here, okay?'

'Easier said than done,' Hannah said, scowling as she stared up the street and leant against the gate as though intending to hold it shut, refusing him entry until he apologised for taking Allie's birthday money, for drinking again when the refrigerator was almost empty, for a few years of happiness that had turned into one plodding day after another. What had happened to the life they should have had?

'Why did it all change?' she muttered.

'I can't remember it ever being different,' Janet said. 'If yer talking about Dad I mean. He doesn't even look any different to the way he's always looked.'

Hannah's eyes narrowed as she peered at him. He still walked tall. He always had, which was unusual, a tall man walking tall. Most tall men slouched. Well, maybe six foot one wasn't all that tall. Shoulders back, head held high, showing the world he was happy enough with his place in it. Or was he? Would he drink so much if that was the case?

'Come on, Mum,' Janet said, nudging her shoulder.

He wouldn't leave the house if he couldn't see his reflection in the shine of his shoes, if his shirt wasn't ironed to perfection – always a long sleeved shirt with the cuffs rolled back twice. He usually had stubble, said it matched his short back and sides haircut, and he usually had a self-rolled cigarette hanging out of the side of his mouth, not always alight. None of that had changed in eighteen years. Yet she couldn't help remembering the morning light emphasising his frowzy look.

Hal yanked on Hannah's arm. She glanced down. He wore that anxious expression again.

'All right. I'll try not to argue. I know how you hate it,' she assured him, and allowed them to lead her inside.

'I probably should've found another job before I chucked it in at the fag factory,' Janet said as she closed the door behind them. 'Maybe I could get one with you driving taxis. Out seeing the streets. Meeting people. I'd love that.'

'You'd better learn to drive first,' Hannah said, shutting the door firmly behind them.

Gordon Territory

Tom Gordon clamped a hand on his hat and danced a jig around the corner into Australia Street. Australia Street, his street, his territory, and he loved it as he would have loved his father if he'd had one. One that hung around and watched him grow, that is.

'You look out for me and I'll take care of you. Gotter keep the place tidy,' he mumbled, and lost his balance while trying to pick up an empty cigarette packet and check along the footpath for more litter at the same time. Stumbling sideways, he almost tripped on the gutter's edge, managing to regain his balance by launching himself in the opposite direction and grabbing the school fence. Turning to lean his backside against the twin rows of pipe topping four rows of bricks, he flipped the packet over his head into the schoolyard and grinned widely – a proud grin as he stared along his street. To him, the factory wall was as much a part of the street as strong arms were to a father. Familiar and solid, it was his security. He'd been looking at it for all of his life. Sometimes, like now when he'd had a bit too much to drink, he thought of it as a living thing, like trees or the ocean.

'My wall,' Tom said, sliding along to rub his back against its brickwork, scratching an itch. Or maybe marking his territory in the way of a cat. The day had been warm, and beer-smelling sweat had soaked his good blue shirt.

Though when he thought about it, the wall didn't belong to just him. Or any one person for that matter. The biscuit factory owners might have built it, but the neighbourhood believed that wall belonged to everyone living in its vicinity. Many of the locals from age fourteen up worked behind it, male and female. The factory provided their bread and butter, and its manager was one of those rarities: a good boss, hard but fair. The factory and its walls set this neighbourhood apart from other house-crowded inner-city suburbs. It was their difference, and the local kids were proud of it for that reason. 'We've got the biscuit factory. What have they got?' they asked each other when kids from one of the posher neighbourhoods looked down their noses. The posher streets might have trees, and the houses might be bigger, but they all looked the same. You could easily get lost out there. Here, the stove pipes leaking the smell of baking biscuits gave newcomers a point of reference when they were looking for a particular street. Directions always began with, 'You see the chimneys over there?'

Almost all the local kids excelled at handball, at throw-cards (a game played with flattened cigarette packets up against a wall – more difficult than it looked to the casual observer) and their version of squash played with warped tennis racquets unearthed at the Tempe tip. The very skilled played with the pot-sticks their mums used for hauling out sheets boiled in their coppers on wash day. And besides being the base for a compendium of games, the wall provided a perfect surface for drawing love hearts, arranging trysts and leaving insulting messages to friends and enemies alike. For the artistic – meaning those with coloured chalks – it provided an area large enough for the creation of a diverse range of characters and scenes.

Opposite the wall and in the exact centre of the stand-alone houses, the Gordon residence, number 19 Australia Street, was famous for being the only house for miles around built on a double block. It was also famous for a towering stink pipe that had been erected in the south-west corner of the backyard when sewerage came to town. Captain Richard Macy, who owned the house, had given his permission to have it built there. He lived on the North Shore, so what was it to him if a stink chimney spoiled the look of the place?

Tom's grandfather, Harry Gordon, had met Captain Macy during the Boer War. Served under him and saved his life, as it turned out. Old Harry confirmed this himself. 'The cap'n got himself shot and I drug him to the medics was all,' he'd boast to anyone who cared to listen. 'Didn't do it for money 'cos I didn't know he had none, but it turned out his family owned a couple of 'ouses over t'other side of Sydney, plus a few in my neck of the woods as well. Can't live in 'em all, he said.

So as long as I take care of the place, me and me family can stay on here till kingdom come and the rent won't never go up.'

And he had taken care of it. A coat of paint when needed, repair or renewal of water pipes and electrical wiring, the fowl pen at the bottom of the yard kept clean and smell-free. He turned the second block, which was a few arm-spans less than full size, into a flourishing vegetable garden, thanks to the baker's and milkman's horses. 'Can't get nothing better for growing vegies than horse dung,' old Harry used to say, and made himself popular by sharing what produce his family didn't eat or bottle with the rest of Australia Street. They confessed to missing him like heck when he died.

'Missing a free feed more'n likely,' Tom Gordon muttered now as he stared along the houses, remembering which neighbours had attended the funeral and which ones hadn't.

The senior Gordons saw the birth of two granddaughters before leaving this dimension for the next. Old Harry went first. Couldn't get his breath no matter how hard he tried. 'Some sort of lung trouble, and I blame the bugs in that horse dung,' his wife said after the funeral while giving away all the bottled vegetables from her pantry. She didn't seem to care a damn when the garden withered and died, probably because the same thing was happening to her. She passed on six months after Old Harry. 'And glad to be going,' were the last words she spoke to Tom.

The house gradually became shabbier. The roof sagged, the guttering began to rust, the paint slowly peeled in scrappy strips. The chooks remained, renewed every few years by broody hens with batches of chickens, but people complained about the chook-poop stink. And except for one patch where Grandma Ade grew herbs, the vegetable garden was long gone, replaced by a weedy lawn.

Guess it don't look its best, Tom thought uneasily, rubbing his back along the wall again, taking comfort from its warmth. Not like it did when Pop was around. Still, Hannah needed to think herself lucky that they had the house. During those bad Depression years, she'd never had to shift into the tunnels like other families did, those who had no money for rent. She'd always had a roof over her head, and he had always managed to find work. Small-paying jobs for sure, but she'd never had to line up for handouts like a lot of their friends. Yeah, she should think herself lucky instead of nagging at him all the time.

At the age of two weeks, Tom had arrived at number 19, sent to live with his grandparents Harry and Grace Gordon when his mother died in childbirth. A bastard, the neighbourhood dubbed him, though never to his face, and never where the elder Gordons might hear. Grace and old Harry were too well-liked for that. Later, if any of the local lads openly hung the tag on Tom, they ended up with a black eye, and were shunned by the local girls until they apologised and sounded as though they meant it. He was handy with his fists, the young Tom, and his good looks, easygoing manner and face-lighting smile made him popular with the girls. At the age of sixteen, Hannah basked in their envy when he began hanging around her every chance he got.

After eighteen years of marriage, Hannah informed him time and again that it was only the envy-basking that had persuaded her to accept when he proposed. She would shout that marrying him had been against her better judgement and the wishes of her family, despite the fact that she'd been four months pregnant at the time. Being handsome and likeable didn't stack up to all that much, she said. Not when it was measured against a preference to spending his days at the pub rather than earning a living for his family.

At the age of nine, he had started earning money weekends and afternoons after school and the odd days wagged from classes, working as a block boy. Once the men had cleared and levelled a street with picks and shovels, he and dozens of other kids would lay the blocks of wood ready to be covered with bitumen. From the age of fourteen, he'd worked at the brickyards, first off handing half his pay to his grandparents, then, after marriage, most of it to Hannah. As a soldier, he learned that life could be snuffed out in the blink of an eye, so he didn't want to go back to the hard slog of manual labour after the war. Not with the measly wages the bosses paid their unskilled workers. What was the point of it when a man could fall off the perch at any moment? Maybe there was nobody shooting at you any more, but you could get hit by a car, a truck, a heart attack. Best to do something you didn't mind doing, and for the shortest possible time. He tried the boxing tents for a while. Good money, but he soon grew tired of being a punching bag for the younger and better-trained fighters. He reasoned it made more sense to be a layabout at the pub than live in misery doing a job he hated. Better for him anyway.

'Seems like he's bone lazy, and a bit of a squib as well,' Hannah's Grandma Ade stated if anyone asked for her opinion. And if they didn't.

Remembering this, Tom's mood began a descent. Aiming a two-fingered scowling salute at Grandma Ade's corner house, he pushed himself off the wall and made his reluctant way home.

Hannah's sour look hit him like a rotten tomato the moment he entered the kitchen.

'Don't start,' he warned, feeling his temper rise, wanting to knock that superior expression off her face. He'd never hit her, but God how he wanted to when she looked at him like that, like he was dirt, a nobody. It wasn't his fault he couldn't find a job that suited.

'It's all right, I'm not saying anything,' Hannah replied as Hal scrambled under the table. Janet gave her father a dirty look and stalked off to the bathroom.

'If ya got something to say, then say it,' Tom challenged, standing with his legs apart, his chest out.

Hannah picked up the magazine she'd been reading and started flicking the corners of the pages, sliding her middle finger across the edges. It was a habit that really irked him. And she knew it. He could tell that by her expression.

'The first thing I need to say is that you'd better come up with a job, and soon,' Hannah stated. 'The boss told me today that the government's passing a law that stops women from driving taxis. Of course it's to give our jobs to the men, so maybe you should get your licence and apply for mine.'

He'd got his licence in the army, driving trucks, but he wasn't going to let her know that. He didn't want to drive bloody taxis. Because he'd been in the army and that was supposed to make him tough, he'd be sure to get the late shift. A bloke would have to be off his rocker to go driving around Sydney half the night.

Before he had time to say anything at all, she came up with the next whinge.

'And the second thing is this letter I found waiting for me when I got home.' She tossed it onto the table.

He lifted it up gingerly, as though it might explode at any moment. Whatever was in it, it had to be bad. Slipping the single page out, he slowly picked his way across the printed words. Printed to make it look more threatening, he thought.

'All right.' He slipped the page back, noting that it was his name on the envelope. 'So this Claude Macy bloke has inherited this joint and he's gunner put up our rent because he reckons I haven't been keeping my part of the bargain. You tell me why I should spend good money on sprucing up a place that don't belong to me. And that's my name on that there envelope. Since when have you been opening a bloke's private mail, eh?' Before she had time to answer, he added, 'I s'pose ya want me to go labouring at the brickies. Breaking me bloody back for a few lousy bob.'

'I don't care what you do as long as it stops you from taking what's mine. You took the money I saved for Allie's present,' she said, her voice rising on the last two words until they were a spit in his eye.

His heart plummeted. Allie's birthday money? 'How was I to know that?'

'Well what did you think it was for?' Janet called from the bathroom.

He felt like crawling back outside on his belly. But who did she think he was? His kid talking to him like that. How come she always stuck up for Hannah?

'You keep out of this, missie,' he said. 'And Hal, don't go sitting under that table as if I'm gunna bite yer.'

He hated seeing the boy scared, even while he knew that Hal wasn't afraid of him. It was the loudness he didn't like. 'The anger in the air,' Hannah once said. Like she knew about anger in the air. Pity she couldn't have spent some of his time up there in Darwin when the Japs were dropping bombs, then she'd know what anger in the air looked like.

'Leave him be,' Hannah said. Or commanded, it sounded like to Tom.

'For Chrissake, Hannah, what d'ya want from me?' he asked, his voice rising to a shout. 'So I had a few beers. I need something to help me forget what you got up to while I fought for me bloody country.'

'Don't start in on that old moan again,' was Hannah's answering scream. 'I went out a bit, so what? I worked all day every day to feed my kids, which is more than you do. I'm tired of you shoving it down my throat because I went to a few dances and didn't sit at home waiting for you. I didn't do anything wrong and I'm sick to death of you making out I did. You're just bringing it up to change the subject. You took Allie's birthday money!'

'I didn't know, I told ya. I went to make meself a cuppa and the money was there. I thought it was tips you was keeping from me like ya always do, and I was thirsty.'

'Then get a job!'

'I'm sick of this,' Tom said and strode off to their bedroom, slamming the door behind him. Lucky Hannah didn't know he had a bottle hidden away in there, in the old fireplace they never lit any more. He'd been keeping that beer for emergencies like this when he got so mad he felt like punching walls. A beer would calm him down, even if it was warm and would probably give him a gut ache and the runs tomorrow morning.

Five-thirty

By five-thirty, the corner primary school had emptied out a couple of hours ago, but a dozen boys and girls had returned to play cricket along Australia Street. The game had been started by four high-school lads, and they were happy for others to join in. It meant that nobody batted long enough for fielders to get restless and find something better to do, and more catching hands meant fewer balls landing over fences. When that happened, doors had to be knocked and permission sought to retrieve the ball, even though it was sitting in full view.

The early chores had been done – shopping, messages to kin, riding bikes if they had them, on shanks's pony if they didn't. Blocks of ice were fetched for the ice boxes, clothes brought in from clothes lines, shoes cleaned, wood chopped for bath heaters and wash coppers. The chore list was endless, but many of the jobs could be put off until after dark when there was nothing else to do except homework, or listen to the wireless if you were lucky enough to have one.

The Trilby sisters – one married without children and one spinster who ran a boarding house – were at their usual meeting place opposite the school. They pretended to be studying the contents of their brother's Corner Shop window while giving away secrets that didn't belong to either of them. Most of the local women were preparing the usual Friday night tea of sausages or lamb chops, potatoes mashed with pumpkin or turnip, and peas. A few slices of bottled fruit with jelly and junket if you were lucky. What time they ate depended on how far the man of the house needed to walk home from their local hotel. The men downed their last beers for the day when the Golden Barley publican called, 'Time, gentlemen please,' at 6 p.m. on the dot.

Franny Peters occupied her usual place on her porch next to the

Gordon house. For the past eighteen months, Mondays to Saturdays between the hours of five and seven, she waited for a daughter who never arrived. Maisie Peters at age sixteen had left home one morning for her job at the hosiery mill and never returned. 'Gone off for a night out with her boyfriend and too scared to come back,' was the general opinion. Foul play had never been considered.

Franny's hair had transformed to silvery grey during the first few months after her daughter's disappearance. She'd lost weight and developed more lines on her face than was usual for someone under the age of forty. Now her fear was not only that Maisie wouldn't return, but she might not recognise her mother when she did.

'Some people just can't be pleased no matter what,' Clara Paterson from number 23 had admonished her on several occasions. Yet the two women were great friends, brought together by the fact that neither one was part of the large extended families who abounded in that area of the inner city.

Most locals who happened to be passing by during the hours of Franny Peters' vigil were embarrassed by her foolishness. They would stare straight ahead or look the other way. Though Clara Paterson usually stopped to chat. A tall, thin woman with a straight back and a way of holding her head that made her look haughty – something she definitely was not – and iron grey hair always caught up in a loose bun, Clara Paterson was a new chum in Australia Street, having lived there for just fifteen years. Even so, there was little about the street or its community she did not know. On this day she was sweeping the footpath outside the row of terraces facing the school, as she did every afternoon.

Clara lived alone, so the sweeping gave her something to do, besides being an excuse to observe what time the man of each house returned to his family after work. During the past week, Gandhi had been shot, the Brits were scampering out of India, and Jews and Arabs still killed each other for no good reason she could think of. She knew about those events from the newspaper, but to her, what happened on the other side of the world was on a par with what happened on the moon. Problems did not interest her unless she could place them in the life of someone she knew. When she wasn't sweeping the footpath or washing down her front steps, which she did twice a day despite the fact that they were rarely trod by anyone except herself, she'd be sitting on the homemade chair on her front porch keeping a check on Australia Street's daily life. So it was that both her and Franny Peters were on the spot to bear witness that what happened wasn't really Allie's fault.

Happy Birthday

If anyone had mentioned the bad karma caused by a full moon combined with the number thirteen to Allie Gordon, she'd have laughed them to scorn. At 3.35 p.m., the exact time of her birth, she was officially sixteen years old.

'You're bound to become a woman sometime this year. Soon as you get your you-know-whats,' her best friend Roma Tomasi had said. Roma had thrown an after-school party for her at the Tomasi house in Marrickville. A surprise party, where it seemed that the only surprised person was Mrs Tomasi who, judging by the amount of food laid out, had been expecting a small army of guests. Allie was dismayed by such extravagance until Roma pointed out that with eight children in the Tomasi family, her mother had cooked enough to make sure there'd be leftovers for dinner.

It was Allie's first time at being the star of a party, and half her old classmates attended. Females only at Mr Tomasi's insistence – though Roma knew her best friend would want it that way. Most of the girls had been showing an interest in boys for some time, but to Allie, all males under the age of twenty had been put on this earth just to annoy, like flies.

Most of Allie's long-term friends had left school the previous year, but still, eight girls arrived at the party with eight gifts: a homemade beaded bag, screw-on plastic flower earrings, see-through scarves, lace-trimmed handkerchiefs, and a pale pink lipstick which had to be a tester by the look of it, but that was all right because Allie knew the giver couldn't afford the real thing. Roma gave her the most excellent present of all: a brassiere. Small like Allie, but a brassiere nonetheless. Her pleasure at getting it, her first one, made her temporarily forget that she really didn't have much in the way of breasts to fill it.

She left at five without taking any of the presents, except the bra of course, so Janet couldn't grab a few for herself. The sisters shared a bedroom, and Janet, being the first to sleep in that room, had decided that everything in it was hers. 'What's yours is mine and what's mine's me own,' was her clarification of the situation. But the bra was safe, the sisters being as diverse in size as they were in looks and temperament. Janet was a D cup, with plump hips and a small waist. An hourglass figure like Dorothy Lamour, she insisted when Allie called her chubby. 'You were supposed to be a boy,' she liked to tell her tall, slim sister, 'but God ran out of what-d'ye-m'-call-its at the last minute.'

With no money for a bus or a tram, Allie had to walk home. Usually she wouldn't have minded – her house wasn't all that far from Roma's. She just had to hope she wouldn't get another one of those horrible stomach pains she'd been getting for the past hour. Oh hell, like the one happening now. A sharp, jabbing thing taking her breath away. She doubled over, gasping for air while it slowly receded.

She must have eaten something she shouldn't, not being accustomed to the sort of food Roma's mamma cooked: lots of tomatoes and onions and pasta and olive oil. Allie had never had pasta as an afternoon snack before. Her mum cooked it occasionally, but they ate it for breakfast with milk, a dob of butter and a sprinkling of brown sugar. Maybe she should go to Grandma Ade's before she went home. Grandma would give her something to settle her stomach. The trouble was, Allie didn't like Grandma Ade.

It was a terrible thing not to like your own great grandmother, but she couldn't help it. Grandma was so big, so harsh. Hard-handed, like a working man, and not backwards in using those hard hands to lash out if she decided that a child (anyone from eighteen months to voting age) was misbehaving. Bad behaviour, in Grandma's opinion, was cheekiness, not instantly jumping to do her bidding, eye rolling, fibbing (lying was a major sin earning a harsher punishment, though only Grandma Ade could spot the difference), pulling faces – the list went on and on, and it seemed Allie was guilty of at least one of those sins every hour of every day. She had always been afraid of those hands and their long fingers with the squared-off, blunt nails that poked and prodded without caring about the pain they inflicted. She was even more afraid of the knife-like eyes, steel-grey to match Grandma's hair. No one could keep a secret from Grandma Ade. One of these days she'd find out about Allie not liking her and there'd be hell to pay. Yet Allie had a sneaking suspicion that the aversion was mutual. Janet was Grandma's favourite.

Anyway, the pain had faded. Going home would be the thing to do.

Jogging the rest of the way, she turned the corner into Australia Street as the cricket game started to break up, but the kids (males and females from Kitty Donahue at eleven to Charlie Lenahan at seventeen) decided that seeing as today was Allie's birthday, they'd stay long enough for her to have a bat.

She tried to say no. She didn't feel too good. No pain now, but a weighty, heavy feeling, as though her stomach was about to drop down out of her private parts at any moment.

'I ate too much at my party,' she told the kids – part boasting, part apologetic.

Larry Lenahan pulled a face and told her to get on with it. Being a girl, she wouldn't last long anyway. Cricket was a man's game. Grabbing the bat, she thumped the end of it on the ground a couple of times and warned them to get ready for a sixer, their interpretation of that rule being over any fence without breaking a window. A broken window meant all the kids had to put in for new glass, and the money had to be taken from pocket money earned by collecting bottles and newspapers. Bottles were sold back to the corner store, newspapers to the butchers and fish-and-chip shops. Parents recognised those earnings as Saturday afternoon-at-the-movies money and usually left them alone.

First hit, Larry Lenahan caught her out when the ball bounced off the factory wall onto Charlie's chest, then into his brother Larry's hands. An argument on the fairness of the dismissal had almost reached the fisticuff stage when Mr Lenahan arrived. He was seated on his baker's cart, which resembled a large box on wheels. Feet firmly planted on the footboard, he hauled back on the reins, mumbling a few oaths when his horse danced sideways before stopping.

'Enough now you kids,' he shouted, 'and git out of me way before Jessie tramples the lot of youse to smithereens.'

The baker's grey mare was considered to be too old, too gentle and too streetwise to be a danger to anyone, though she did snort and take a few steps sideways when Allie ducked under her nose. Not like Jessie at all.

'What's wrong, girl?' Allie asked softly, stroking the grey neck with her knuckles — an action which usually had Jessie stretching out her head, begging for more. This time she shrugged Allie away by taking a few steps forward.

'You're running late today, Mr Lenahan,' Clara Paterson said as she walked over to fetch her usual Friday high-top half loaf.

'Had a bit of a fire at the bakery,' he answered in a voice made croaky by a bout of influenza. 'And some tomfool's been feeding Jessie something she shouldn't be eating. She's colicky and didn't want to be hitched to the cart. Trod on me foot and I reckon me big toe's broke.'

Clara grimaced sympathy. 'Two accidents, eh? You had better watch yourself then. Accidents always come in threes. And you need to use a saltwater gargle for that scratchy throat. A eucalyptus rub or a mustard and linseed poultice might do your chest a lot of good, and I'm sure Mrs Ade could fix you a draft that would have you feeling better in no time.'

He nodded. 'Me wife says the same, but time's me trouble. Whenever I get a bit to spare, something happens to fill it in. And I didn't make it to church last Sunday, so what with the fire, this rotten chest-cold hanging on, old Jessie mucking up and me heartburn giving me heck because I'm running late and buzzing round like a blue-arsed fly, pardon the French, I suppose I'm paying for me sins.'

'We all know what a fine man you are, and I'm sure the good Lord knows it too,' Clara answered soothingly, also knowing on which side her bread was buttered. Mr Lenahan would often hand out day-old loaves for free when times were hard.

'Kind of you to say so, Mrs Paterson,' he said, and turned to his sons. 'Charlie, you and yer brother can give me a hand, lazy buggers that youse are. I've got seven streets to go.'

The brothers had been up since four that morning helping with the baking, but if they objected to the 'lazy' tag, neither one protested. The mildness of his tone didn't fool them for a minute. Their dad could be quick with his belt if his sons didn't do as they were told when they were told. Opening the back doors of the cart, they shoved their bat and ball inside, grabbed a couple of loaves each and ran ahead. They helped out often enough to know where to go. The rest of the kids put the garbage-can stumps back where they belonged in Franny Peters' yard, then headed for their respective homes, yelling a 'happy birthday' and 'you were out fair and square' to Allie as they went.

'Here, lass, take this.' Mr Lenahan tossed a loaf to her. 'Tell yer mum I'll collect me money when I bring her order tomorrer. And tell 'er this week will be me last Sunday delivery now us workers got a forty-hour week.' His grin looked a trifle sour as he added, 'Though sixty or even seventy hours sounds pretty good to me.'

Allie caught the bread and hurled a few insults after the disappearing kids before crossing to her side of the street, her gait made awkward by the way she folded her arms across her chest as though the loaf of bread was a secret hugged into herself so no one else could see.

'Hello Mrs Paterson Mrs Peters it's my birthday today I'm sixteen,' she called breathlessly.

'Then I hope this day's a better one for you than it is for Mr Lenahan,' Clara called back while climbing the steps to her porch.

Franny Peters smiled down at the upturned face. 'I'm sure it will be, Allie me love. Many happy returns.'

'Thanks. I had a party at my friend Roma's house and Dad's promised to buy me a dress,' Allie blurted out. 'Brand-new, too.'

'Fancy that,' Franny Peters said absent-mindedly, her face drooping in its usual lines of sadness as her memory flashed back to her missing daughter's sixteenth birthday.

Allie read the look. She'd seen it many times. 'Maisie's sure to be back any day now,' she said with the same confidence she always said it.

Her sister and Maisie Peters had been best friends since their baby days. 'If she was going to run off with her boyfriend, I would've known. It wasn't all that serious anyway, her and him. Something terrible has happened. Maybe murder,' Janet had said in a melodramatic way a few days after Maisie's disappearance.

'Maisie's not the kind to go round getting herself murdered. She wouldn't know anyone who'd do such a thing,' Allie pointed out scornfully.

'Then she's been kidnapped by white slavers,' Janet stated positively.

Allie flat out refused to believe that, chalking it up as wishful thinking. Everyone knew that white slavers captured beautiful women to present them as wives for handsome Arabian princes. Maisie was just average looking and anyway, things that exotic never happened to people you knew.

'You'll hear from her on her next birthday,' Allie insisted now, as she'd been insisting for the past eighteen months.

Franny's drooping mouth turned upwards. 'You're right of course, me love. I seen your dad come home a while ago so you better hurry or he'll give that dress to your sister.'

'Wouldn't fit. She's fatter and shorter,' Allie said, but she whirled around and raced through her gate and onto the back veranda. Her voice grew to a shout as she burst into the kitchen.

'Dad! Dad! Did you bring it?' she called, dropping the bread onto the kitchen table.

Her mother looked up from a much-thumbed women's magazine. It and others were passed along from Grandma Ade, Hannah being third in line.

'Bring what?' Hannah asked.

Allie skidded to a halt, made wary by the sight of Hal under the table, his knees pulled close to his chest, his eyes pushed into his knees. Hal always scrunched into the smallest space possible when something scared him, and raised voices frightened him more than anything else. Glancing up the hallway, she noted her parents' closed bedroom door and knew her father was home and that they'd been fighting again. He would have shouted the usual horrible things, hurling accusations left and right at whoever got in his way, then stamped off to his room and slammed the door before anyone had a chance to answer. That meant her mother would be tense and scratchy and looking for an argument to let off steam. Janet would be almost as bad.

Straightening her shoulders, Allie said defiantly, 'I thought he might have bought me a birthday present.'

Hearing Allie's voice, Janet opened the bathroom door and glared around the kitchen. Hal always used the space beneath the table as his refuge. Janet preferred the bathroom. Then she could pee, look at herself in the mirror or have a shower and hide at the same time.

Neither her nor Mum has worked out that if they leave Dad alone he's fine, Allie thought, scowling at her sister. He just hates being picked on when he's had a few drinks. If I didn't stick up for him, he'd probably go away somewhere. Mum should know better. She gets all sad-faced when she talks about how her dad went off and left her. I should tell her to think about that when she starts in on my dad.

'Your father wouldn't part with a penny of his beer money to buy a present for either of us. All I got from him was a mouthful of abuse,' Hannah said gruffly.

The look on her mother's face belied her tone and Allie realised that her feelings had been hurt. Dad should know better too, she thought.

'I thought he might have got us something,' Allie mumbled. 'Not that I'm worried.'

'I'm sorry, lovie.' Hannah's voice softened. 'I didn't mean to be so sour. You know I'd have had something ready for you if I could have, don't you?' When Allie nodded, head down and refusing to meet her mother's eyes, Hannah added, 'I'd give you a choice of anything of mine if I had anything worth choosing. Anyway, come payday we'll go to the shops and lay-by something you like, no matter what. That okay by you?'

'Yeah. Sure,' Allie said, moving one shoulder forward in a don't-care-don't-believe-it kind of shrug. Turning slowly, she glanced up the hallway again. It divided the L-shaped house, two rooms on one side, one on the other, until it reached the large kitchen. Her parents' room was on the right side of the hall. It looked out onto the veranda, Australia Street and the wall. She wanted to go up there and bang on the door, but she knew better than to go near her dad when he'd been arguing with her mum after spending time at the pub. Scuffing into the room she shared with Janet, the one leading off the kitchen, she closed the door behind her, flopped onto her bed and stared around, trying to dredge up her usual fantasy of how she would change it, given half a chance and a purse full of money.

As it was, the two beds were narrow and uncomfortable, the mattresses worn and lumpy over wooden slats. The coverlets had been hand-sewn by old Grandma Gordon and were warm but plain. The wardrobe, tallboy and chest of drawers were large, chunky and old, the mirror above the drawers dull and spotted. The walls were identical throughout the house, tongue-and-groove timber panels freshly kalsomined late last year after Tom had a good win at the races. Kalsomine being a pale cream colour, the walls were bright and cheerful enough, but what Allie loved most were the loop rugs given to her and Janet by their Great-Aunt Florrie – three made from leftover dress material, bright and colour-coordinated – and the collages: pictures cut from magazines and pasted onto opened-out brown paper bags, created by Hal and framed by one of his uncles. Country scenes and massed flowers dominated the side walls. Using a paste of flour and water, montages of film stars had been stuck straight onto the walls at the head and foot of the beds. Usually, they never failed to comfort her. Today, they and her mood were darkened by disappointment. She hadn't expected an armful of gifts from her family, but one would have been nice.

'Any spare money, you make sure it goes on you,' she said, mocking her mother's voice, but careful to keep her tone too low for Hannah to hear.

To make matters worse, the stomach-ache was coming back.

'What's up with you?' Janet asked as she burst into the room. She'd washed her hair and it hung almost to her waist. Water had deepened the blonde tones in it to a dark honey.

Much like the colour of her thousand freckles, Allie thought, but kept the thought to herself. Janet hated being reminded of those freckles. Allie wasn't sure why. She thought they looked good. In her opinion, everything about Janet looked good. I'd give my right arm to have a figure like hers, she thought. Not that I'd tell her so.

'There's nothing up with me,' she said instead.

Janet paused. 'Happy birthday anyway.'

'Thanks.'

'I didn't get you a present 'cos I spent everything on Mum's.'

Allie shrugged. She hadn't bought Janet a present on her birthday either. 'We never do, do we?' she said, momentarily wondering why. They saved up or made presents for Mum, Dad, Hal, Grandma Ade and Great-Aunt Florrie, but never for each other.

'Do what?' Hannah asked from the doorway. Hal had attached himself to her skirt again.

'Talking about birthday presents, here's one from me,' Janet said.

Opening a drawer, she took out two parcels and, handing the small one to Hal, gave the other to Hannah along with a rather tentative stiff-necked hug. 'Open mine first,' she instructed her mother.

Carefully removing the butcher's paper covered in crayoned flowers to make it more birthday-like, Hannah stared down at a soft and shiny blouse the colour of red delicious apples. A perfect complement to her lightly tanned skin and dark-chocolate coloured hair.

'It's absolutely gorrrrgeous.' She breathed out the last word. 'Ab-so-lutely perfect.'

Janet shot a triumphant glance at Allie. 'Now open Hal's.'

'Pearls!' Hannah exclaimed, as though the little white paper bag held the real thing instead of mother-of-pearl buttons. 'They'll be exactly right on this blouse.'

Allie noted the brightness of her mother's smile as she looked at Hal, at the way she bent down and kissed the top of his head. Something she'd never done to Allie. Or Janet either, for that matter. What did Hal have that they didn't? It wasn't as if he'd been born to her. Was it because he was a boy? Not that I care, she thought. Dad gives enough hugs for two people.

'What is it?' Hannah asked. 'Why are you looking at me like that?'

'When did you start kissing and hugging?' Allie couldn't help asking.

Hannah's smile was self-conscious as she replied, 'Hal's been teaching me, haven't you, love?'

'Where's my kiss and hug then?' Allie demanded of Hal. 'Just because I had a couple this morning before we went to school doesn't mean I can't have a couple more, seeing as it's my birthday too.'

Hal almost flung himself at her, grabbed her around the neck and planted a half-dozen kisses on her forehead.

'You're strangling me,' Allie gasped, but managed to hug him back.

Hannah laughed aloud when Janet flopped onto the bed beside Allie, placed an arm around her shoulders and kissed her cheek.

'Happy birthday, sis,' she said when Allie stared at her in amazement.

'God, it's contagious,' Allie yelled and, leaping off the bed, she opened a drawer and took out a brown paper parcel. It was also decorated with coloured-in flowers.

'They took all the white paper,' she said apologetically. 'Janet helped me pay for it, but I chose it,' she added as Hannah unfolded a multicoloured scarf.

'It feels like silk,' Hannah murmured while placing one side of the scarf under the back of her below-shoulder-length hair. Tying the two ends in a knot at the top of her head, she drew the other ends together and tied them loosely, enclosing all but the top of her head.

'A perfect snood. Thanks, love. It'll be just the shot in the taxi. Keep all that smelly cigarette smoke out of my hair.'

'The colour looks good,' Janet said.

Hannah looked searchingly at Allie. 'I really did mean to buy you a present, love. I've been putting aside a few pennies for months and I feel terrible that I can't have something for you here and now. I know you don't want to hear this, but I'm tired of taking the blame for him where you're concerned. Your dad found the money this morning and I don't have to tell you what he did with it. We'll just have to hope there's a little left. Enough to lay-by something that I can pay a bit off each week.'

'That's okay,' Allie mumbled, not believing a word of it. Her dad wouldn't do such a horrible thing.

'At least we'll have a cake. Chocolate with chocolate icing. Your favourite,' Hannah said huskily.

'Mum, it's not your fault.' Janet directed a glare at Allie.

'I didn't say it was,' Allie protested loudly, feeling a stab of guilt when she saw the shine in her mother's eyes. 'I'm not worried. Truly, Mum.'

'Right.' Hannah straightened her shoulders. 'I'll go take a squiz at myself in the bathroom. Your mirror's too dark. I'm one very lucky woman today.' Pausing at the door, she added, 'I guess you tried the scarf on. What suits you has to suit me. We'll share it, eh?' Her look pleaded. 'You can borrow it whenever you like.'

Nodding, Allie watched Janet and Hal follow her mother out.

I still didn't get a kiss or a hug from her, she thought resentfully.

Closing the door behind them, she peered into the dull glass of the dressing-table mirror, hating the knowledge that she looked more like her mother than her mother did. Or so Grandma Ade always said. 'Alma, don't complain about Hannah to me. You're the spitting image of her in looks and in nature,' Grandma had told her at least a hundred times. Allie hated knowing that was true almost as much as she hated being called Alma.

Long, dark, slightly curled hair, eyes brown enough to seem black when she was in a bad mood, oval face, skin she thought looked too white most of the time, but luckily took a tan with ease and without pain. All inherited from her mother's father who had come to Australia from Quebec at the age of eighteen. Leaning closer, she looked for anything inherited from her dad's fair to reddish complexion. Janet had taken all that with her sandy hair and blue eyes. Even little Hal looked more Gordon than Allie did. She was about to turn away when she saw it.

'A pimple,' she whispered, glancing down at Janet's bottle of witchhazel. That was Grandma's remedy for blackheads and pimples, usually getting rid of them in two or three days. But this pimple was at the side of her face and hardly noticeable. She'd keep it until the girls at school had seen it.

To her undying mortification, every girl in class except her had started getting pimples and periods sometime during the years between eleven and thirteen. She hated that. No doubt they had lots of underarm hair as well, though of course she didn't know for sure. They would have shaved it off and anyway, the girls wouldn't talk about underarm hair and menstruation or sex and boys in front of her. Roma said that was because she always made fun of them when they did. But they all let her know when they got their curse. They all knew she was still a child. Who ever heard of being sixteen and still no period? It was almost freakish. Something else she'd inherited from her mother.

'It's a family peculiarity. My mum and Grandma Ade were the same,' Hannah had told her. 'When it does happen, you'll be glad it took so long.'

'I don't think so,' Allie had protested.

Now she had a pimple. Definitely the first sign. She rubbed it gently with the pad of her finger.

The next sign will be hair on my private parts to match those few little soft underarm ones, she thought, and considered going into the bathroom, the only room in the house with a lock, to check it out. The idea was instantly forgotten when a loud scraping noise grated through the house. Her parents' door had been slammed so often the hinges were bent. The curved groove across their floor grew deeper every day. That scraping noise was the sound of the door being opened.

Jumping up, Allie stumbled into the kitchen, almost falling over her own feet in her haste to catch her dad before he left. He always went out after an argument. Skidding to a halt outside her door, her expression grew sullen when she saw her mother and father, one on each side of the table, their expressions hostile while each waited for the other to speak.

'Dad, did you?' Her voice faltered when she noticed the dull glitter in his eyes. He'd been drinking again. Her shoulders sagged.

Tom's ugly stare fell away. A teasing grin replaced it as he pulled a parcel out from the front of his shirt. 'This what yer after?' He held the parcel high when she made a dive for it. 'Gotter give yer old man a kiss first.'

'What is it?' Hannah asked.

'A dress for me youngest daughter. New like I promised.' Tom's eyes narrowed. 'That all right by you?'

'Please, Mum. Dad. Don't fight. It's my birthday. It's Mum's birthday,' Allie said, even while knowing the plea was useless. Her parents didn't seem know how to talk to each other without snarling.

Tom threw the parcel onto the table. 'Go try it on,' he ordered, turning his back on his scowling wife.

Grabbing it up and ripping off the newspaper wrapping as she went, Allie ran into her room. Janet followed.

'Oh look. Look.' A froth of blue leapt out of the paper. Allie held it up against her chest. 'It's beautiful. Beautiful.'

Within seconds, her school uniform lay in a heap on the floor. Slowly, almost reverently, she pulled the blue dress over her head and stared into the mirror, close to tears of joy at the way she looked, the way she felt.

'And it's new,' she told her sister triumphantly.

'That colour looks great on you,' Janet said grudgingly. 'But the dress is a size too big and it's too sort of, you know, dressy. Youngish too. More for a twelve-year-old. Where would ya wear it? Would've been better if he'd got ya something to wear on afternoons and weekends. I'd like to see ya playing cricket in that.'

'I'm never taking it off,' Allie stated fervently.

'You'd better show it to Dad before he leaves,' Janet said, adding in a sour voice, 'He reckons he's going to live at Miss Trilby's boarding house.'

'Liar! You're just trying to spoil everything.'

'Oh quit it,' Janet ordered. 'He's all talk anyway. He'll go walking around the streets for a while, then he'll come back sober and sorry when we're in bed like he always does.' She scowled. 'He'd never have the money to stay at a boarding house and he'd never have the guts to leave here.'

'I'm going to tell him you said that!'

Janet shrugged. 'Tell him what ya like.' She looked past Allie. 'And while ya telling him, ask him where he got the money for the dress.'

'You're getting as bad as yer mother,' Tom said from the doorway. 'And you look a million quid,' he told Allie.

'You're not really going, are you? Not to Miss Trilby's,' she said.

'Yer mum's kicking me out.'

Hannah appeared beside him. 'That's a barefaced lie.'

Janet glared at her father. 'You're always trying to blame Mum for everything.'

Allie stared from one to the other. She could see determination in her father's expression. At least, as much determination as his drink-slack face could show. Pity was Hannah's expression. Pity for her, for Allie.

'You want him to go, don't you?' she accused her mother.

'I don't know what I want,' Hannah said wearily. 'But I did hope this one day would be about you and me for a change. Not about him like most days are.'

A bolt of pain shot through Allie's stomach. Clamping her forearms across it, but keeping her face straight so no one would know, she told her dad, 'If you're going, I'm going with you.'

He shook his head and walked away. When Allie tried to follow, Hannah grabbed her arm. 'Don't be silly. It's getting on to dark.'

'He'll be back,' Janet said scathingly.'

'That's enough now,' Hannah warned. 'As your father, he deserves your respect. I won't have you speaking of him in that tone of voice.'

'You do,' Allie said sullenly.

'I'm not his child,' Hannah stated.

'Anyway, it's the truth,' Janet answered defiantly. 'Look at the dress. Ya can see it isn't new.'

'Stop it, Janet,' Hal yelled from under the table.

Ignoring him, she grasped the back of the blue dress and pulled out the tag. 'See? He got it at the seconds shop, ya can tell that by the pen mark and the newspaper wrapping. Dress shops use bags or coloured paper. Probably conned it too. The money you saved would've all went on his grog. Probably shouted his mates. Big-noting hisself.'

'I hate you!' Allie shouted, and ran.

Tom Gordon was already across the street and heading west. Striding along with only an occasional stagger. Not looking back.

'Dad! Wait!' Allie screamed, and almost ran into Mr Lenahan's bakery cart as it came down Australia Street. Jessie was close to trotting. The old mare knew she was on her way home, finished her daily grind at last.

'Watch it, girl,' Mr Lenahan shouted. He was standing on the foot board at the back of the cart, counting his leftovers.

'Dad!' Allie screamed again, ducking under Jessie's nose as Hannah ran to the gate. Hal and Janet were close behind.

The mare reared, snorting loudly. The cart jerked upwards with her, tossing Mr Lenahan onto the road. He landed flat out on his back, and Allie's third scream caught in her throat as his head hit the bitumen with a dull thump. Tom Gordon turned as Jessie pranced sideways like a filly half her age, then walked on.

'Jesus, Allie! Lookout. Look at what you've done,' he shouted.

Allie watched, not able to move as her father ran back, squatted down and placed two fingers on the fallen man's throat. She felt a warm trickle down her leg and thought she'd pee'd herself. Didn't really care when she saw her father shake his head and stand, staring down, then turn as though he was about to walk away as Mr Lenahan's blood seeped onto the bitumen from the split in the back of his skull.

Death and Dying

He didn't want to stay. Didn't want to see this. He'd seen enough blood to last him a lifetime. And this time he had grog in him and his head wasn't right. It felt strangely light, while his stomach felt as if he'd swallowed a hunk of lead.

'Dad? Dad!'

That was Allie calling him back. Of course she was right. He had to do something. Had to go back. Oh Jesus, look at him.

'Christ, Bob, mate, just look at ya.'

'Oh, Dad.'

Allie's voice slid downwards into her shoes. He could hear the grief in it, and the guilt. What could he say to her? He couldn't think of anything. Couldn't look at her standing there biting her fingernails like she always did when something had her whipped. So much like her mum. But with Hannah it was just the little fingernails that got bitten to the quick. She'd be doing that now, chewing on her pinky fingernail. He couldn't look at them. Couldn't take his eyes off Bob Lenahan's face with its purpling lips, its glassing eyes staring up.

'Hal, get yerself up to the shop and tell 'em to ring an ambulance.'

He thought he'd shouted, but the words were barely more than a whisper as he squatted, placing his fingers against Bob's throat again. When he couldn't feel the flutter of a pulse that would have told him Bob was still fighting for life, he lurched backwards and fell, landing on his tail bone.

Luckily, Hannah heard him and repeated the words to Hal. 'And hurry, love,' she added.

Tom had seen death and dying before. He'd been in a war, '41 to '43. Training at Dubbo, then on to the Northern Territory. People laughed when they heard Tom Gordon had never left Australia. Sat out the war in Darwin, they'd sniff. But he got there the day before the Japs dropped the first bombs in '42 and flattened just about everything in the harbour. He was still there when they dropped the last one. Most of the people in Australia Street didn't know much about those bombings, and he wasn't about to tell them. Not because him and his army mates were told to keep mum about it at the time – to save people from panicking was the drill. And not from being shy about the part he'd played. Not from being disinclined to hit those ignorant civilians with the truth neither. He just couldn't talk about it. He saw the bombs drop, saw just about every ship in the port wiped out. Houses flattened. People killed. Death and dying. Soldiers and civilians. Women and kids. Babies and old men. He couldn't talk about it without being asked things he didn't want to even try answering. How he felt about what he'd seen was the favourite question. That's what Hannah had asked a dozen times, then got her feelings hurt when he wouldn't answer. Couldn't answer. That's what the army doctors had wanted to know.

Forcing himself to sit upright, he watched Hal running like blazes up the road, saw old Mrs Paterson coming down her steps, Franny Peters down hers. Janet just stood there by the gutter, gawping, not wanting to go away, not wanting to stay. Hannah was leading Allie back through their gateway. Looking down at Bob again, he wanted to cry but he held the tears in. Doesn't do to let women see a man cry. Grunting with the effort, for that lead weight had spread right through him now, he got onto his knees and straightened Bob's head, his legs, and pulled the edges of his cardigan together. He didn't know what else to do. Didn't have a clue as far as first aid was concerned. Far as he knew, nobody else around here did either.

The bleeding had stopped. That meant Bob was dead. Dead people don't bleed. He'd seen it before, this oozing of blood slowing to the full stop of death. He hadn't expected to see it again, the death and dying; yet here, right here in front of him now, here it was again. But this, oh this, this was very different. This was in his street, Australia Street, and there, lying on the bitumen in a pool of blood was his old mate Bob Lenahan. Been mates for years, him and Bob.

'Is it bad, Tom?' old Mrs Paterson asked. She was kneeling beside him now. Her and Franny Peters both.

'Think he's gone,' Tom said.

Struggling like an old man to get to his feet, he fell back once more before finally managing to stand. Turning aside from the all too familiar face of death that he'd been trying for years to forget, he turned and leaned his forehead against the wall.

How the hell did they think he felt when they asked about Darwin? Every time he'd seen a wrecked house, smashed furniture, walls and clothing and toys mixed with body parts and blood, he'd seen Hannah and the girls among the wreckage. He didn't want to see them, but he did, and it drove him nuts. A lot of the blokes were the same. It ended up making him sick. Chest pains. Headaches that wouldn't go away. Night sweats. Waking up crying. One time the nightmares got so bad he walked out into an ocean filled with poisonous jellyfish, sharks and a saltwater croc or two. Funny thing that, because it was the same ocean he'd been swimming in since he was a nipper, though a lot further north of course. Luckily, Serg Bates realised what was happening and wrestled him out before he hardly had a chance to get himself wet. That's when the brass gave him a choice. He could leave, a discharge on medical grounds – hypertension was the name they gave it – or he could have a promotion to sergeant, go to Cowra and guard the Japanese prisoners of war. 'Extra money and your family would be proud of the promotion,' the brass told him. Proud of a prison guard? He didn't think that bloody likely. And he knew that every time he looked at one of those Jap prisoners, he'd see it again. The destruction. The chaos. The death and dying. He'd want to kill them. Shoot them. Bash their heads in for killing his mates; and in his imagination, Hannah and his kids. No, he'd seen enough of death and dying.

'Tom, what's wrong with you?'

He turned. Hannah was on the footpath, one arm around Allie who looked as though she'd throw up at any moment. Even from across the street he could see the dark stain on his daughter's legs. At first he thought she'd somehow got Bob's blood on her. Then he noticed her hanging on to her stomach. Saw her cringe and blanch as a spasm hit her. Bloody hell, she'd got her monthlies at last. Poor bloody kid. But Hannah would take care of her. Hannah takes care of everything.

He never told her how he felt up there in the Darwin heat. Hot enough to boil your brain. Even the rain felt hot. Sweating all the time. Hard to breathe when you came from the cooler weather down south. A lot of his mates got crook with malaria. Ulcers and sores. Dysentery. He never told her how helpless he felt. Them bastards up in the sky dropping their bombs on families just like his, him down on the ground, them up there, too far up for a man to fight. What could he do? Helpless, that's what he was. Helpless and bloody hopeless. He thought when he got home, Hannah would take that away. When they were young, kids together then courting, Hannah used to make him feel like Superman.

'Dad? Don't just stand there staring at that wall. Do something,' Janet shouted at him.

'Hush now, Janet. There's nothing for him to do,' old Mrs Paterson said as she stroked Franny Peters' arm.

Franny was crying now. Sobbing as though her heart would break. She couldn't have been that fond of Bob. Thinking about her own loss, that's what she was doing. Thinking that something like this might have happened to her Maisie.

'Nothing to do but wait for the ambulance to take Mr Lenahan away,' Mrs Paterson went on. 'And there's grieving to do. Your father and Mr Lenahan are old friends.'

He'd gone to school with Bob. Worked weekends with him in his father's bakery. They'd knocked around together. Bob had been keen on Hannah at one stage. Offered to toss a coin to see who'd ask her out. Showed he didn't know Hannah too well. If she'd got wind of that, she'd never have gone out with either of them. That was before Bob met and fell for Madge. Her father got sent to work at the local school and her family moved into a house around the other side of the factory. He, Tom, had been a bit keen on Madge at first. But Bob got her and he got Hannah. That's how they'd wanted it.

What's wrong with me, paying attention to this crap flashing through me mind when I should be doing something, like Janet said. Gotter stop thinking. Gotter do something. But what? Too late for poor Bob.

The biscuit factory wall was cold against his face. He'd turned to its solid comfort so he wouldn't have to see how the life had drained out of Bob's face, making his old mate into a stranger. He wouldn't have to see Allie's face gone just as white, or the horror on Janet's, the blame in

Hannah's eyes. Or little Hal who had skidded to a stop on the footpath when it happened, staring around at them, his face blanker than the wall. Most kids his age would have chucked a fear tantrum. But not Hal. Hal had seen death before. Years ago, when he was just a little kid. Was it a lifelong haunt, like Darwin? Christ only knows what goes on in Hal's mind. There he goes, racing up there. He's got to the shop. They'll ring the ambulance. Nothing more to do here. Franny and Mrs Paterson there on either side of Bob, sitting on the road next to him as if they were guarding him, ready to fight off death. Too late for that. The cops will come with the ambulance. They'll want to know what happened. Nothing he could tell them because he didn't rightly know. It all seemed like a dream, even while he was standing there seeing it all. Hannah will take care of things. She always does.

She should've known how much it tore at his guts when he came back and found out how well she'd managed. Didn't need a husband. Got on pretty good without him, thank you very much. So what did that make him? A big fat zero, that's what. What had he ever done for anybody?

'Tom, you'd better get word to Madge Lenahan,' Mrs Paterson said. No doubt she could see how useless he was here. 'Hurry now!' she added.

I'm going, he meant to say, but the words wouldn't form. Turning away from her, from all of them, he plodded up the street.

Look up there, Bob's old mare waiting at the corner. Waiting for Bob before she crossed the road. Madge and the kids would be waiting too. Waiting for Bob to come home, to put the old mare away, feed her, brush her down, put the leftover loaves into a bin ready to sell cheap as day-old bread. The ovens would need to be lit early tomorrow. The bread had to be baked and delivered. Can't take days off when people are depending on you for their bread.

Madge and her three boys could do the baking, no worries. But somebody has to do the deliveries. Kids can't do that. Kids aren't allowed to drive carts around the streets. Well, maybe young Charlie could, but he's going right through school and on to university. Gunna be a teacher like Madge's father. That's what Bob had wanted. It's my fault Bob's lying there dead. Wouldn't have happened if Allie hadn't been chasing after me.

It's up to me now.

Allie's Curse

'Oh God, Allie, what have ya done?' Janet asked from beside her.
'Shush up, Janet. Come on, Allie darling.' Hannah placed an arm around Allie's shoulders, tugging her away, leading her to the house. 'It's all right, love. Cuts on the head always bleed a lot and look worse than they are. Come on now, let's get you cleaned up. I'll fetch a hot water bottle, that will ease the tummy-ache.'

Allie looked back at Mrs Paterson and Franny Peters gathered around Bob, at more neighbours on their way down the street as though someone had rung a bell to summon them, at Tom walking up the street like a zombie.

'What about Mr Lenahan?' she asked in a dazed, out-of-it voice. 'Where's Dad going? Where did Hal go?'

'Up to Trilby's shop to phone for an ambulance, lovie. That's where Hal went. They'll be here in a flash and they'll help Bob. See, Hal's on his way back already. And your dad would be going to tell Madge.'

'But this shouldn't be happening, Mum. Not on my birthday. Not on our birthday.'

'I know, love. I know.'

But I don't know much of anything, Hannah thought. Allie knows even less, poor kid. She's grown up in this suburb and everyone around her is either kin or friend of kin. All looking out for her. She's more protected than a rich kid would be. Rich kids travel. They socialise with all kinds of people from all over the place. My poor Allie knows nothing outside her own little world. Look at her now in that frothy blue dress a size too big and five years too young. A little girl trying to be a woman. But she is a woman now.

'Everything's changing,' Allie said. 'I know it, Mum. I can feel it. Everything's going to be different.'

Hannah's shoulders drooped. Allie was right. Everything was changing, she could feel it too. But she said, 'Hush now, it's just you getting your curse. It plays hell with your body, and with your mind. Especially the first few times. I've been expecting this and I've got just the right herbs to help you feel better.'

Stopping at the front door, Allie placed one hand against the jamb, bracing herself as though she expected to be forced inside. Turning her head to rest her chin on her shoulder, she stared after her father.

'Is he going to leave us, Mum? Is he really going to Miss Trilby's boarding house?'

Hannah felt a swelling sensation inside her chest – love for her daughter, and pain because no matter what she did to demonstrate that love, Tom would always be first in Allie's affections. Even with everything that had happened – Allie's periods coming on like this, Bob lying there in his own blood – all Allie could think about was her father and whether or not he might leave. What had he ever done to deserve such devotion? She and Hal thought the world of him.

'Of course he's not going anywhere,' she assured Allie, reaching out to Hal as he raced onto the veranda. 'Why would he?'

'We're his family, aren't we, Mum?' Hal said as he slid his hand into Allie's and held on tightly, tugging her towards the hall.

Allie looked down at him, leant forward and kissed the top of his head, then burst into tears. Hal followed suit.

'Is she all right?' Janet asked from the veranda steps. 'Are you okay, Allie? I didn't mean anything. It's not your fault.' She looked imploringly at Hannah. 'I didn't mean anything. I just opened me mouth and them stupid words came out. It's not Allie's fault that Mr Lenahan fell off his cart. Why is Hal crying? Is he all right?'

'I guess we're all feeling the shock. Come inside, Janet. I'll mix us a soothing draught.'

Janet backed up a few steps. 'I should wait for Dad, stay till the ambulance gets here. And the coppers. They'll want to know what happened exactly.'

Hannah glanced at the crowd of neighbours gathering along the street, at Clara Paterson and Franny with Bob, and knew Janet wasn't needed. Yet she obviously wanted to stay. Perhaps to witness what would happen next, but it was more likely that she didn't want to be a part of an emotional scene with Allie. Janet always disappeared when emotions ran high. 'Just wipes you out and doesn't change a thing,' she'd say later. So much like her father.

Hannah nodded. 'Okay, Jan, you wait out here.'

As she guided Allie into the house, one hand on her shoulder, one hand on Hal's, Hannah glanced back and up. A full moon on a Friday the thirteenth. Allie getting her first period on a day of such bad omens. Bob Lenahan dead or dying. Tom going off with that funny look on his face. No, she didn't need Grandma Ade saying 'Trouble's coming, I can feel it in me water' to know that this birthday would be a day to remember. Or one to try to forget.

Hero

By the time Tom reached the bakery, Madge had heard the news. He expected her to be either numb or grief-stricken. Having returned home from the war a year or two before most blokes around here, he'd seen it as his duty to talk to the newly made widows. Some of those women seemed to be without any feelings to speak of, as though they didn't believe death could take their husbands when they weren't around to see it happen. Of course they knew men were killed in war – that's what war was all about – but it wouldn't happen to their men. They continued acting out their daily routines until either a man or a body came home. Some got neither. Now, three years after the end of the war, they were still waiting. The others, the grieving ones, seemed to have known of their loss before the telegram arrived telling them their bloke was either dead or missing in action. They'd felt the bullet or the bomb. They'd heard their man crying out to them.

Madge, she wasn't like any of those women. She seemed more confused than anything. No sign of tears. Her red hair just combed, and she'd left it hanging down around her shoulders, Veronica Lake-style. She'd put make-up on to hide the freckles, and coloured around her green eyes with more green. Matter of fact, that floral dress had to be one of her best, even though it made her look a little pudgy. Looking at her now, she had put on a bit of weight over the years. Why had she gone and got herself all done up? But that was Madge. He remembered Bob once saying she put on make-up and corsets the moment she climbed out of bed, even when she wouldn't be doing anything except housework. Some women were like that. Wanted to look their best all the time. Hannah didn't worry. But then, Hannah looked good in rags.

'I been walking around for an hour or more,' Tom said. 'Been thinking about what I should say to ya. How I could say it.'

'I already know. The police were here.' Madge blinked tiredly. 'But before they got here, Miss Trilby came and told me what happened.'

So that's it, Tom thought. After old nosey-beak Trilby left, Madge spruced herself up knowing the coppers wouldn't be far behind. Next there'll be a mob coming to pay their respects. Most people thought the world of Bob. Madge would know that.

'Where's yer boys?' he asked.

'Young Bobby stayed at a mate's place last night and Larry's gone to fetch him. Bobby don't know about his dad yet.' She sighed. 'Charlie's out back settling Jessie down.'

'Yer old horse is not doing too good I heard. Want me to fetch a vet?'

Madge waved that aside as if Jessie was the last thing she wanted to think about. 'I don't know what to tell the boys,' she said. 'They're grieving for their dad right now, but come tomorrow they'll be getting scared about what will happen to us. I've never been on me own and I don't know that I can do what I'm supposed to do. Don't know what that is. What I'm supposed to do. Bob always did, you know? And my mum and dad before him. One of them always told me.'

She thrust her hands out to either side, palms up. What any of it was supposed to mean, the gesture or the babble of words, he didn't know. He suspected she didn't either.

'I'm not good at thinking, Tom, just at doing,' she explained when his expression must have told her that he didn't have a clue what she was going on about. 'I can do anything once I'm shown or told. But who'll do the telling now Bob's gone?'

'Did the coppers let on to ya how it happened?'

'I don't for one minute blame Allie. How was she to know Jessie would carry on like that? The old mare was playing up on Bob when he hitched her up this morning. It's one of those horrible accidents that come at us out of nowhere. No good thinking about it. I've got to get this fog out of my head. I've got to think about how I'm going to manage without him. I guess I'll have to sell up.' Covering her face with her hands, she added in a mumble through the vee between her two palms, 'But then what will we live on? How can I raise three boys by meself?'

'That's why I've come. To do what has to be done till ya can find someone better.'

He pried her hands away, which turned out to be easier than he thought. It seemed like she wanted him to do something, anything, to put her mind at rest. Seemed like she was expecting it from the moment he walked in the door. But that was all right. Made it easier for him. That was something Hannah would never do. Make things easier for him.

'I reckon I could take Bob's place in the bakery till yer get sorted,' he said gently. 'You know, do the delivering. Help out. I've done it before when Bob and me were youngsters.'

Madge didn't ask any questions, nor did she ask what Hannah thought about that. She bowed her head and cried. Tom recognised it as a relieved kind of cry, not a sorrowing one, but he couldn't hold that against her. She was that kind of a person. Needing help. Needing someone to take over the thinking.

'I'm so lucky to have you here,' she said after he rubbed the back of her hands for a while, then made a cup of tea. 'I guess we'll need to talk about wages, but I don't know how much to offer. For that matter, I don't know how much money there is. I just know how to keep a house and bake bread.'

'We won't worry about wages for a while.' By now he'd gone from patting her back to placing an arm around her shoulders. It seemed a natural thing to do. 'And I don't know much about the money side of things neither, but I can learn.'

When she nodded gratefully, he couldn't help thinking how Hannah would have reacted. She'd have done her crying, showing respect for the dead, then she'd have taken over the account books, the buying, everything. Then again, she would've been doing all that in the first place. But not Madge. To Hannah, he was a burden, to Madge a champion.

That's you all right Tom Gordon, a bloody hero, he thought, and almost laughed aloud. But still, his head went up and his chest seemed to expand as his arm tightened around Madge's shoulders.

'Tell yer what. I can doss down on yer back veranda if that's all right by you. That way I can get an early start,' he said.

He hadn't meant to say it, hadn't thought it out. Didn't realise till he said the words that he had no intention of going back to all the fighting and rowing. That's what had cost Bob his life.

Staying Put

The Lenahan house was similar to most others along the street. Except for nine terraces at one end, the rest were 'stand alones' built close to the front fence line, with small porches and arrow-head fences. A mixture of weatherboard or cement render, all were painted in pastel colours with dark green, brown or red roofs and trims. The bakery house was a dull pinkish beige with a red corrugated iron roof. The windowsills were brown, the eaves, fence, four steps and concrete floor of the small porch were painted dark green. The bakehouse out back couldn't be seen from the street, but Hannah had visited many times in the past and she knew it was a square brick building. Inside, two walls were lined with cupboards and benches, one wall held two large gas ovens. Two large tables and a mouth-watering smell of baking bread were the other fixtures.

Hannah tried to block out the memory of a flour-smattered Bob smiling broadly, beckoning to his best friend's wife, gesturing with a broad sweep of his arm – Bob was like that, couldn't talk without using the whole of his body – inviting her in to taste a loaf fresh out of the oven. Until he realised he couldn't afford to do it, or Madge realised it for him, he'd often give away a loaf of bread to his friends, and to anyone who he deemed to be in need of a free loaf. There was no doubt that the world would miss Bob Lenahan. And now here she was, trying not to think about him, blocking him out so she wouldn't start crying again.

The front door to the bakery house was shut and it seemed as though all the visitors had gone, though the porch light was on. Hannah knew it was after nine but still, in most cases after a death, family and friends would drop in to pay their respects until all lights out indicated a wish to be alone. She could leave, come back tomorrow, but Tom hadn't been home and she wanted to know what he planned to do. Okay, he'd broken the news to Madge and her sons, but that was hours ago.

Lifting her fist to knock, she hesitated, not wanting to intrude, until the decision was taken out of her hands when Charlie Lenahan opened the door. His face was blotched red, his eyes swollen.

'Thought I heard someone open the gate,' he said huskily. 'How are you, Mrs Gordon?'

'I'm fine but Allie's not the best,' Hannah admitted. 'How are you?'

'You know.' Giving a one shoulder shrug, he stepped back into the hallway, inviting her in with a wave of his hand. The heavy shuffling of his feet, the droop of his head and shoulders told of his devastation. Bob was much loved by his three sons.

'I'm truly sorry, Charlie. Your father was one of the best and I know how much you'll all miss him,' Hannah said softly. 'But I want you to know that it wasn't Allie's fault.'

Charlie cut in before she could elaborate. 'I know that. Tom told us everything. And we knew Jessie had been acting up. Larry and me had left Dad when we finished the deliveries to help Mum clean up in the bakery. There'd been a bit of a fire you see.' His lip trembled. 'We should've been with him. Then it wouldn't have happened.'

'Oh, Charlie, you don't know that.' Tears filled Hannah's eyes and she stepped into the hallway and hugged him hard. 'Don't blame yourself,' she whispered in his ear. 'It wasn't anybody's fault. It's one of those horrible accidents that happen for no reason that we can see.'

Charlie didn't show surprise, though he must have known that Hannah wasn't usually so demonstrative. He hugged her back before pulling away.

'That's what Mum said.'

Hannah nodded. 'I need her or Tom to tell that to Allie. She's blaming herself. I've never seen her cry so hard and for so long.'

'I could tell her,' Charlie suggested hesitantly.

'Best not to wake her now. Grandma gave her a valerian potion and I'm hoping she'll sleep until tomorrow. How's your mum?'

'Dr Howe gave her sleeping pills,' Charlie answered as he led the way down the hall. 'She's been out like a light for the past half hour.'

'And Tom? Is he still here?'

'He's out on the back veranda having a smoke. Mum doesn't like anyone smoking in the house.' Halting in the lounge room, Charlie turned to face her again. 'You know, Mrs Gordon, I don't know what we would've done without Tom. Don't think I could've settled Larry and Bobby down on me own.'

It was Hannah's turn to hide her surprise. Tom settled them down? It would be more his nature to go the rounds of his mates looking for a drink. She frowned. That was unfair. He was Bob's best mate and he'd be feeling rotten.

'I hope you don't mind me calling him Tom,' Charlie added. 'He suggested it.' When she shook her head, he asked, 'Can I get you a cup of tea?'

'Thanks, no. I won't stay.' She glanced at the mantel clock. 'It might be best if you ask any other late visitors to come back tomorrow. Let your mum sleep.'

'That's what Tom said.'

Hannah looked around for Tom, expecting him to come inside when he heard her voice. He was nowhere to be seen. But then, he was much more familiar with the house than she was. Although she'd known Madge since her family moved to Sydney from the country twenty years ago, she'd only been here a dozen times since Madge and Bob were married. He and Tom were lifelong mates, but their wives had never really hit it off. Madge had always irritated her. She was a gushy person, lavish in praise for the least little thing, and Hannah had never trusted her. In her experience, gushy people usually had a knife ready for the moment you turned your back. Though come to think of it, she'd never heard anyone complaining about Madge being two-faced. I'm being unfair again, she thought.

'If you'll fetch Tom for me, we'll leave you to get some sleep.' She touched Charlie's arm. 'Or not sleep I should say. I imagine you'll spend most of the night watching over your family.'

'Probably.' He looked uncertain. 'I think Tom said he was staying.'

'The whole night?' Hannah asked, sure Charlie must have misheard something Tom had said.

'Well, yeah. I'm not sure. I'll fetch him and he can tell you what's going on. I haven't fed the dog yet and I'd better check on old Jessie so I'll say goodnight.'

'Thanks, Charlie. Goodnight.'

He looked worried, she thought, as he hurried out. But then, he has a lot to worry about. Madge isn't the brightest spark around, a bit of a ditherer really, so he'll have to start making all the decisions around here now. But I don't think that's what he was worried about. What has Tom been up to I wonder.

Not wanting to be alone in the room, she walked back up the hallway and onto the front porch.

'How's Allie doing?' Tom asked as he joined her there.

'Best you come and see for yourself,' Hannah replied tersely, annoyed that she had to come looking for him and he hadn't bothered apologising.

'I thought ya said she was sleeping.'

'You were listening to me and Charlie,' she accused. When he didn't bother to deny it, she walked down the steps, not looking back to see if he followed. He did, but stopped at the gate when she continued onto the footpath.

'Allie needs you to tell her it wasn't her fault, Tom,' she said without turning.

'I'm staying put,' he said bluntly.

She swung around. 'You're staying here the night?' Surely he didn't mean that! 'Don't you realise the kind of gossip it will cause?'

'Why are ya so pissed off with me, Hannah?'

Hannah studied his face, wondering if he was trying to be smart, needling her. 'Well there's the business of our rent going up and Allie's birthday money for a start,' she said, keeping her voice level. 'And you should have come home sooner. After you told Madge.'

'I mean all the time. No matter what I do or say. Ever since I got back from the war.'

His tone was as unreadable as his expression. She moved a step closer.

'You can ask that?'

'I'm asking.'

Her hands tightened to fists and she thrust them into her skirt pockets.

'Tom, you came home from Darwin a different man. We never have a conversation unless it's an argument. You take ages to find a job and when you do, you don't stay for more than a month. Do you want me to go on?'

'Do ya care anything at all for me, eh?'

She'd expected him to get angry, as he usually did when she threw accusations at him, but he stayed maddeningly calm.

'We don't need to have this conversation here and now.' Her voice rose. 'What are you trying to tell me? You're not coming home at all?'

'Keep yer voice down. You'll wake Madge.'

'Madge is not your worry, Tom.' She wanted to hit him.

'Yair she is. Her and the boys. It's my fault what happened and she needs someone to take care of her. She's not like you, Hannah. She can't just pick up and carry on, do better than she ever did with a man around to get in her way.'

The bitterness in his tone shocked her. He meant every word of it. Okay then, if he wanted a clinging vine, a bloody featherbrain, let him have Madge Lenahan.

'Then you'd better stay and take care of her,' she snapped.

'Just tell me one thing, Hannah. Just look me in the eye and tell me you give a shit whether I come home with you or not.'

'You're imposing conditions?' she asked incredulously. 'Know this, Tom. If you don't come home with me now, don't bother to come home at all.'

'Fair enough. I'll pick up me clothes on Sunday while yer at work.'

Slamming the gate between them, he swung around and strode inside. Hannah stared after him, knowing she should follow him, apologise for saying those words. For Allie and Janet and Hal if not for herself. Unless she did, Tom might never come back.

She knew she should feel bad. Aggrieved. Hurt. Angry. Any one of those. Instead, she felt relief.

Everybody's Leaving

Two days later, over the usual afternoon cup of tea, Janet dropped her bombshell.

'You're doing what?' Hannah asked, sure she hadn't heard right. Hoping she hadn't heard right.

Janet stared into her cup. 'One of the girls I used to work with at the fag factory told me about it. I bumped into her at Trilby's shop yesterday. She left the factory ages ago and she's got this job and she said they were looking for someone else.' Her voice grew steadily more defiant as she looked up, finally meeting her mother's eyes. 'So I went there this morning and Mrs Best, she's the lady who owns the joint, she said I could start right away.'

Hannah pushed her own cup across the table as though it were to blame for Janet's bad news. 'And you're going to live in? It's on the other side of Sydney. A boarding house.'

'A guesthouse. A flash one. They have people staying there from all over the place. France even. And Mrs Best will supply me uniforms. They're not like that daggy fag factory thing that makes ya look like a grandma. Mrs Best's uniforms look better than this floral dress and ya know it's one of me good ones. She showed me a black skirt with a white blouse for when I'm waiting tables, a maroon high waister for when I'm cleaning.' Janet made a show of looking Hannah up and down. 'Really nice. Smart.'

Conscious that her own dress was a size too big, Hannah smoothed it down over her hips. Not that it helped. The dress, a hand-me-down from Cousin Maria and now a washed-out blue, fitted where it touched, and that was nowhere. After she finished work at 4 o'clock, she'd been at Grandma Ade's, cleaning out the herb shed. The dress was good enough for that. Still, she promised herself to throw it in the ragbag this very night.

'Oh, smart. That makes a great deal of difference,' she said, leaning her elbows on the table and sinking her chin onto her clasped hands.

'Mum, don't make a fuss about it, and don't be so flaming sarcastic.' Janet banged her cup onto its saucer, slopping milky tea onto the table. Jumping up, she grabbed the dishcloth and wiped up the spill using twice as much energy as needed. 'You must've known I'd be leaving one day,' she added, keeping her eyes down. 'I'll be in a really swank place and I'll even get a room of me own. Two things I've always wanted.'

Hannah pulled the cloth out of her hand and tossed it into the sink. 'You've never worried about swank, and you're not just living there, Janet. You're working there, cleaning up other people's messes. Waiting on tables and making their beds. Pulling a forelock. Yes, sir, no, sir, three bags full, sir.'

'You're just being silly,' Janet said sulkily, flopping back into her chair. 'And mean.'

'It isn't the greatest time to be leaving. Not now. Not with your father . . .' Hannah left that hanging, reluctant to voice the fact that Tom had said he wouldn't return. She still hadn't told Janet, Allie or Hal about her last conversation with him. She hadn't shown them the letter from Claude Macy either. Either Janet hadn't heard Tom talking about it or she'd forgotten, for she'd made no mention of it. And it wouldn't be fair to hit her with it now. She had to live her own life without being made to help support her family. That was Tom's duty, though he apparently didn't think so. Not for now, anyway. She had no doubt he'd come crawling back sooner or later. Would she have him back? She didn't want to think about that. Right now, the answer was no.

'He won't be coming home,' Janet stated in the same sulky voice. 'And you should be glad. Now youse won't be fighting all the time. Ya won't have to be screaming at him to get out because he already has.'

Hannah looked shocked. 'Did I do that?'

'Mum, ya know ya did. All Australia Street knows it.'

Of course Janet was right, yet Hannah felt as though she'd been slapped. 'I couldn't help it. He made me scream. Not working. Drinking. It's a lousy marriage and I'm glad it's over.'

'It's not over just because he won't come home for a couple of days.'

'And nights,' Hannah said angrily. 'Everybody's talking about it. I did everything I could, Janet.' Making an effort, she softened her voice. 'It's like they say. It's always the kids who suffer most when a marriage breaks down.'

'Is that what happened? I thought he left us to go live with Madge Lenahan and her tribe of boys. That's not a breakdown. That's a walk out. He got tired of us like I got tired of that fag factory.'

'It isn't the same thing!' Hannah was shocked by the venom in Janet's tone. 'He feels responsible for what happened to Bob, and our marriage was falling to pieces. There was nothing left to keep him with me.'

'What about me and Allie and Hal? Don't we count for anything?'

'Of course you do. You shouldn't need me to tell you that. But Jan, none of us have been happy with all the yelling and fighting, and it's been getting worse with every passing day. I can't remember when your father and I sat down and had a conversation.'

'Would you have him back if he wants it, Mum?'

The intensity in Janet's stare was almost palpable. Hannah hesitated before answering. 'If I'm to be honest, I'd have to say that it's been a long time since I cared about what your father did. Except when it hurt us.'

'His going hurts Allie and Hal.'

'And you?'

Janet nodded slowly. 'I do still remember what he was like before the war. It changed him, Mum. It turned him into a drunk and I've seen too many of them around here to have one for a dad.'

Hannah lifted her cup and took a gulp of the now cold tea, more to give herself time to think than for reasons of thirst. She didn't like Janet talking about her father like that, but she didn't feel like defending him either. The way he'd walked into the Lenahan family as if he was a part of it made her wonder if something had been going on between him and Madge for some time. She wouldn't forgive either of them if that was the case.

Janet seemed to read her mind. 'Mum, if something was going on, you would have heard.'

'Well, yes. Something physical.' But maybe they had a yen for each other, she thought, then gestured impatiently. 'It doesn't make any difference to the fact that I don't want him here any more.'

'So that's it then?' Janet asked. 'All over, red rover.'

I can't answer that, Hannah thought. There's been too much anger and hurt between us to ever go back to what we were, but it isn't easy to turn your back on eighteen years.

'Is it all over?' Janet persisted.

'Your dad and me have to be better apart because we weren't any good together,' Hannah said. Smiling ruefully, she added. 'Meantime, you're not going to change your mind about this job, are you?'

Janet shook her head.

'Can you wait until after Bob's funeral then?' Hannah slumped back into her chair. 'Allie's going to stay home and mind Hal along with some of the other kids.'

Janet's hesitation was momentary. 'Of course I will. I wouldn't not go to the funeral. I've known the Lenahans all me life. And I know you're going to feel rotten, Dad being with her, so I'll stick by your side every minute.'

'Thanks, Jan. You're a doll,' Hannah said gratefully.

Janet stared down at her, frowning. 'Aren't ya even a bit sorry he's gone?'

Hannah was about to confess that what she really felt was a sense of freedom. The words stayed unsaid when Hal made his presence known.

'Course she is,' he said angrily.

'Ya should have told us you was there,' Janet said, grabbing him by the feet and hauling him out from under the table.

'You and Mum was fighting and you're going away like Dad and and . . .' He sniffed, wiping a hand under his nose.

'And you think Allie and I will go too and you'll be alone. Oh, darling, that will never happen. Come here.' Hannah opened her arms, almost going backwards off the chair when Hal threw himself into them. She held him close, her arms tightening as he took deep, short breaths. She knew that as his way of preventing himself from crying. 'I promise. Cross my heart and hope to die,' she whispered into his ear.

'Ohh, I should have known how he'd take it,' Janet said. Kneeling at Hannah's feet, she put her arms around them both. 'I'm not going far, Hal,' she promised, 'and I'll be back lots and lots of times to see ya. You'll hardly know I'm gone.'

'Is Dad ever coming back?' Hal asked, turning to look into her face.

'That isn't likely,' Hannah said before Janet had a chance to answer. She felt sure that whatever her eldest daughter said, it would be a lie. Something, anything to stop Hal from feeling bad. But what was the point of putting off what had to be said sooner or later? 'Now stop crying, Hal. Allie will take you round to see him any time you want.'

'Go wash ya hands and ya can help me peel vegies for tea. You can do the caulie while I'm doing the peas and Mum crumbs the lamb chops,' Janet said with forced cheerfulness.

'And can I do the spuds too?' Hal bargained.

'You're a strange one,' Hannah said. 'I don't know any other boy who likes peeling potatoes.'

'I like cooking them better,' Hal told her.

'Yes, I know you do, and there should be more very special boys like you,' Hannah said, reeling back again when Hal threw his arms around her neck.

'What's going on here? What's with all the hugging?' Allie asked as she entered the kitchen.

'It's Hal, he's upset about, you know,' Janet told her.

'No, he's not. He's upset because you're leaving too. I was just in the bedroom, Janet. I'm not deaf you know.'

'God, it'll be good to get away from you,' Janet shot back.

'Feeling's mutual,' Allie snapped.

'Stop it! Just stop it!' Hal yelled.

Both girls stared at him, open-mouthed. Hal never yelled.

'See? We're still the same fighting family even without your dad,' Hannah told him. 'Enough of the sad stuff now, and enough arguing. Allie, you can make us a cup of tea. Janet, you can start packing your things if you like.'

Janet grimaced. 'What I've got will take five minutes to shot into a bag. I'll have a cup too. You make it, Allie, and I'll butter the scones. Great-Aunt Florrie dropped some off early this morning.' She climbed to her feet. 'And Hal, we won't fight any more, okay? Will we, Allie?'

'Not today anyway,' Hannah stated. 'Hopefully.'

'Fight? Us?' Allie said, wide-eyed.

'Never,' Janet added.

They looked at each other and grinned.

Black Hats

Hannah paused at the doorway. The church was crowded. She'd expected that. Generations of Lenahans had been delivering bread around this part of the city for as long as anyone could remember. Old folks said the first Lenahan had sailed to Botany Bay in chains, an unwilling member of the first fleet. Whether that was true or just a sly dig at the Lenahans' habit of rounding up accounts to the nearest penny in their own favour, she didn't know. But of course their customers would be at Bob's funeral, though she could only count seven bare heads. Row after row of black hats proclaimed a majority of women mourners. Funeral hats. Funeral clothes. All black. Everyone had them, including herself, and they only wore them to funerals.

Being a Wednesday, the men would be at their place of work, those who had a job. Those who hadn't would have chosen to stay at home and perform the unfamiliar task of minding their kids. Children didn't go to funerals until they were of an age where they could conduct themselves with the proper amount of decorum. Of course they and all the jobless men would turn up for the wake. They'd start arriving at the Lenahan house at any time from now on, though most would wait until after the burial. Except for Tom. He was in the church, but not in the back half where friends of the family sat, leaving the front rows to relatives. The mongrel was sitting in the second row, right behind Madge Lenahan. He might as well hang out a sign.

Sensing someone's stare, Hannah looked around for its source. Over to her right, Janet had placed herself up against the wall. Her face was lowered, her head covered by a black shawl borrowed from one of the aunts. She'd left home early to fetch the shawl and must have bumped into Grandma Ade, who no doubt insisted that Janet accompany her.

Waiting for Janet to return had almost made Hannah late, which would have been inexcusable. Hannah would be expected to keep up appearances by acting as though it was completely natural for her husband to move into the bakery an hour after Bob died.

After all, there is such a thing as pride, Hannah thought, stiffening her face to hide a surge of bitterness.

Next to Janet, Grandma Ade glared at Hannah as though it was her fault, Tom sitting where he didn't belong. Next to Grandma sat Great-Aunt Florrie Gatley, Grandma's sister-in-law who had moved into the corner house when her husband was killed in the Boer War, who had slept in the same bed with her since Great-Grandfather died. On a few occasions, rumour tried placing something into their relationship that didn't exist; that couldn't exist, Grandma being the narrow-minded bigot that she was. Colin Gatley sat next to Great-Aunt Florrie, who was his grandmother. Behind him, a number of aunts, uncles and cousins surrounded them. In fact, there were six rows of relatives if she included the honorary kin who were really long-term friends of the Ades, Gatleys and Gordons.

Were they there to show support for her, for Hannah, or was it a mark of respect for Bob Lenahan? Perhaps both. Whatever it was, they shouldn't have made Colin come along. The poor man looked absolutely miserable. Since coming home from the war, he couldn't bear anything to do with sickness or death. He would have seen enough of it in that prison camp. But Grandma wouldn't leave him at home on his own because of the time he tried to hang himself in Fat-Auntie Jean's shed. An appropriate place, he was reported to have said at the time. The Treasure Shed was the kin's storehouse for all kinds of paraphernalia they regarded as no longer useful. Yet as Grandma pointed out, it was really a swap store, one man's junk being another man's treasure. Hence the name. Luckily for Colin, the shed beam broke and he fell onto a stack of clothing. Or was it so lucky? Colin probably hadn't thought so. But then, he was miserable drunk at the time. He still drank a lot from all reports, but not so much since he'd moved in with Grandma.

Why am I thinking about Colin Gatley right now? Hannah asked herself, and immediately knew the answer. Because I don't want to dwell on Tom being down there with Madge Lenahan, that's why. I don't want to think about the gossip it will cause. As if there isn't enough already. He wouldn't care, but you'd think she would. She has her three boys to consider. Tom has always wanted a son. I'd thought that taking in Hal and raising him as our own would make Tom happy. No one can doubt that he loves the boy, even if they aren't of the same blood. But apparently one isn't enough.

Someone touched her back. A signal for her to move forward. Knowing most of those black-hatted heads would turn the moment she entered the church, Hannah stepped reluctantly into the aisle. She was right. The gossip radar was working well. More than half the women turned to stare. They avoided eye contact by pretending to look for someone behind her. Ignoring the sudden buzz of whispered conversation turning more heads, she moved into the centre of the second row from the back and made room for herself next to Colin. Sitting in the back row or the far end seat would make her look as though she was trying to hide. This one could be just as bad. But why should she worry about what people might say? She'd done nothing wrong.

Standing suddenly, she side-slid back to the aisle and marched to the second row of pews, head up, shoulders squared, and stopped beside Tom. The back of his neck turned red, showing that he was aware of her, but he didn't look up.

'I'm sorry about your husband, Madge, but Allie can't eat or sleep and what happened to Bob wasn't her fault. I need Tom to tell her that and I need you to tell everybody else,' she said to the top of the woman's head, not bothering to lower her voice. That way, the report of what she'd said wouldn't get too twisted.

Noticing a horrified look on the minister's face, she added, 'After the funeral of course,' for his benefit.

Striding back up the aisle without waiting for an answer from Madge or a look from Tom, she glanced at Grandma Ade, who appeared more thunderous than before, then at Colin. His eyes begged. She stopped at the end of his pew, held out a hand and pointed with a sideways nod of her head. He jumped up and beat Hannah through the door.

The black hats turned again. She snatched hers off and crushed it into a shapeless mess. Colin reached in, grabbed her sleeve and dragged her outside as her black-gloved hand began to rise, thumb extended.

'That's kid stuff. You'll just make things worse,' he said.

She knew he was right, just as she knew that if someone else's husband had been down there with Madge Lenahan, she'd have been one of the gawking and gossiping black-hatters. Knowing that didn't make her feel any better, while thumbing the lot of them would have given her a few seconds of satisfaction, even if it was childish.

'Do you want to go to the Golden Barley or to my place?' she asked when they reached the footpath.

Colin hesitated for a moment before avoiding the question by saying, 'You're not trying to rope me in as payback on Tom, are ya, Hannah?' The gleam in his eyes denied the mock seriousness of his tone.

Looking him up and down, she nodded appreciation of his dark navy double-breasted suit, the impeccable white shirt, starched white pocket handkerchief (real, not fake) and the navy and red diagonally striped tie. Holding the smile in his eyes, he raised his eyebrows in question and hitched up his trouser legs at the knees to reveal navy socks and highly shined shoes for her inspection, giving a half-bow of acknowledgement when she nodded again. None of it surprised her. Since his return from the war, she hadn't seen him in anything but a suit. He owned three. He'd bought them with his severance pay the day he came home, and she knew from Grandma Ade that he showered, shaved, and dressed in one of those suits the moment he got out of bed each morning.

He was a half-head shorter than Hannah in her three-inch heels, as thin as a rail, and his blotchy skin had a yellowish tinge. The only healthy-looking thing about him was the thickness of his hair, and that had started going grey. At age thirty-six, he looked closer to fifty-six.

As children, they'd been best friends and fiercely protective of each other. His father had been too worried about where his next drink was coming from to bother with his kids, and her mother was coldly uncaring. He'd been a cheeky, happy and energetic boy, always shorter than most other boys his age but sturdy, and liked by everyone. There was no sign now of that boy who used to be, though from all accounts he was still popular with people of all ages.

She felt a sudden, deep, aching regret. They had drifted apart for no good reason she could think of. He'd left Sydney, gone to the country looking for work and had stayed away until after the war. When he returned, he spent a long time in hospital, then lived on the western side of the city until he moved in with Grandma. He hadn't tried to renew his friendship with Hannah. She didn't know why.

'Gunner answer me or just keep on staring?' he asked. 'Not that I mind. Most women can't take their eyes off me. So what d'ya say? Your place or mine? Better make it yours. Grandma's place is like Central Station most days.'

'I'm tempted,' she said, keeping her face straight, 'but Allie, Hal and a half-dozen of the kin's kids are at home so I think you'd be safe.'

He winked. 'I thought I might be. No harm in hoping but.'

She laughed suddenly. 'You've been living at Grandma's for weeks now, yet we've hardly talked, have we? Not since we were kids. We were such good mates then.'

A memory flashed of her sitting on Grandma Ade's porch, sobbing so hard it made her physically ill, Colin holding her head while she vomited, pulling her face onto his chest when she'd finished, not caring about the sick, the smell. They were fourteen when her mother ran off with the man with the ginger beard and her father dumped her at Grandma's house. More than half a lifetime ago.

'I should've stayed out bush.' He looked curiously at her. 'I would've been able to dodge the draft out there.'

She shook her head. 'I bet you volunteered.'

'Yeah, chump that I am.' He frowned. 'Why are ya looking at me like that?'

'I'm wondering what happened to us. When Mum then Dad took off . . .' She looked away. 'It was you who held me together. Yet when you left, you never said goodbye. You never wrote. We never kept in touch.'

'We grew up,' he said. His voice had a rough edge as he added, 'You were going out with Tom.'

His tone puzzled her but she decided not to comment on it. 'Now all we say to each other is good day. My fault. I stay away from Grandma's as much as I can. Though that mightn't be for much longer.'

He nodded, as if they'd made some sort of agreement. 'Why's that?'

'I stay away because I get tired of her continuously finding fault with Allie, but we had a letter from a Claude Macy last week. He's inherited our house and is putting up our rent because Tom has let the place go to pot. I'm about to lose my job because the stupid damn government's making my boss sack me, and Janet is leaving home for a live-in on the other side of the Harbour Bridge. So my only option is to move in with Grandma until I find a better job or cheaper rent.' She smiled wryly. 'Or a man with money now Tom and I are going our separate ways. Anyway, let's not talk about those things. It's either my place or the pub. Unless you want to get a couple of milkshakes, take them to the park and catch up on years of talk. That would be nice.'

'I've never been invited to your place,' he said slowly.

Hannah started walking. 'I see you at Grandma's and anyway, you don't need an invitation. You're welcome any time.'

He caught up. 'You've never invited me because you're afraid I'll go off in front of your kids.'

Same old Colin, she thought. Always trying to stir.

'You do get a bit violent at times,' she stated calmly.

'Only if I'm well and truly pissed, which doesn't happen all that often. Or when I'm woken up too sudden from one of me dreams. Never during the day. And you should know that I'd never hurt a kid.' He stared up at the sky. 'Not that I'll ever have any.' When Hannah didn't answer, not knowing what to say to that, he stopped her with a hand on her arm and stared into her face. His eyes were hard as he added, 'Maybe you'd like to part with Hal.'

Hannah's smile faded as she realised he was serious. She jerked her arm away. 'I couldn't do that, Colin, as you very well know.'

'He's Lily's kid, and her dad and my mum are brother and sister. Hal's no relation to you.'

'He's been with me for seven years now,' Hannah pointed out. 'I think of him as mine and he thinks of Tom and me as his parents. We've brought him up since Lily left. He considers us to be his family. Allie and Janet are his sisters.'

'But you're not family, and I can't help wondering why you took him in.'

Though he seemed determined to goad her, she kept her voice even. 'We were best friends as kids, Lily and me.'

'If I remember right, you ended up hating each other's guts.'

'That was a long time ago, Colin. You can't be serious about wanting Hal. He hardly knows you.'

'He could get to know me.'

'And you could be his favourite cousin and visit him whenever you like,' Hannah said firmly. 'Maybe take him to the beach and football now that Tom's busy somewhere else. But you haven't answered me about where we're going. My place, the park or the pub?'

'All right, I get yer point. Subject's closed. Knew I wouldn't win anyway.' He grinned suddenly. 'You should go to the burial. They'll think you're running away.'

'I am.' She grimaced. 'Running from the stares and the gossip really.'

'Then it's the pub, seeing as we're heading in that direction anyway. Saves the effort of turning round.'

'It'll be noisy. We can't talk there.' Hannah decided that's what she wanted to do – talk with Colin for a while.

'Talk about what?' he asked, sounding wary now.

'Not Hal.'

'And I'm thinking you're not interested in talking about me. About you then?'

It was her turn to grin. 'That would be nice.'

'What makes ya think I want to hear your problems?' he asked. 'Got enough of me own.'

She felt as if he'd shoved her. 'What makes you think I'd tell you?'

'Memories,' he stated brusquely, and strode away at a pace closer to a jog than a walk, not once looking to see if Hannah was keeping up.

'Not so fast,' she said. 'I'm not used to heels any more.'

'Then take 'em off,' he answered without slowing down.

She did. They reached the Golden Barley together.

Pulling the shoes back on at the doorway, she looked inside and was surprised to see so many men, most of whom she'd known all her life, though a few strangers stood at the bar.

'Why aren't those men at work?' she asked Colin.

'Some because they don't wanner work, some like me who can't, the rest because they haven't got a job. It's not so easy now all the blokes are home from the war. Women are doing the work they used to do.'

'My boss said the government has decided that driving taxis is too dangerous for women, even though we've been doing it for years,' she said sourly. 'Of course we all know they're creating jobs for the men by taking them off us.'

'Better for the man of the family to be working than the woman,' Colin stated.

Detecting the note of bitterness, she said, 'Sorry, Colin. I guess it's a sore subject for you.'

'What, being a kept man? 'Specially when it's ya grandma doing the keeping? Come on, let's get a drink. A bloke could die of thirst out here.'

She glanced in at the dozen or so women seated around tables in the lounge. A blowsy looking lot, she thought. Boozers, like Tom. He'd know all of them. She knew some from her school years, and some were kin. These were the pub women. This is where they spent their days, drinking and gossiping and eyeing off the men. Probably hopping into bed with a few for the price of a beer, if the truth be known. Or because they were too blotto to think about what they were doing. Or maybe because they just enjoyed a little variety, she thought, half-jokingly, half-disparagingly, instantly dismissing a jolting thought that Tom might have been with one or more of them. After all, he'd shown that faithfulness wasn't one of his virtues.

Do I stay or go? She glanced in again. They'll make me the butt of their jokes if I join them.

'Why can't you work?' she asked Colin to buy time.

'Because I'm too crook to do a hard day's yakka. Me lungs and kidneys are shot, me ticker's heading there in a hurry, and I get dizzy spells. There's too many blokes looking for work for a boss to take me on. But Grandma must have told you that.'

'Grandma won't let anyone say a word against you. She says she couldn't manage without your board money.'

'She would say that, wouldn't she? It's the money she gets for her snake-oil remedies that props that household up. And me. And all the rest of our kin who come to her for help.'

'Snake-oil remedies?' Hannah frowned. 'Does that mean you don't believe —'

Colin interrupted. 'I'd probably be dead by now if it wasn't for her remedies. Or at least one hell of a lot sicker. Me and half this suburb. How did we get onto this subject anyway?'

He looked around when someone called, 'Hey, Hollywood, what are ya doing out there chatting up Tom's missus?'

'Hollywood?' Hannah smiled. 'Of course. The way you dress. You weren't always so particular. As a kid, you were just as raggy as the rest of us. What happened to change that?' she asked, still stalling for time, trying to decide whether to stay or go.

Expecting a light-hearted answer, she was surprised when he said, 'Three years of wearing nothing but a bit of rag to cover me privates, and getting around filthy because the only time I had a wash was when it rained. I reckon that's what makes me particular now.'

'I'm sorry,' she said, not saying whether she meant sorry for him being a prisoner of war, or her asking a question that reminded him of it.

He let it pass. 'There's a few of me mates.' Four men standing at the bar raised their glasses in a salute. 'What'll ya have to drink?'

She turned. 'I'm going.'

'Aw, hang on. I'll just say g'day to those blokes, then I'll be back.'

'I'm not allowed in the bar and if I went into the lounge, those women would give me a hard time. I'd get worse from Grandma and the aunts. You know she'd find out.'

'So?'

'So Lottie Nelson is in there. I went to school with her. She was a friend, and now I cross the street to avoid bumping into her. I don't want people to know I know her because she spends most of her days in a pub.'

He gave a wondering shake of his head. 'When did you sprout the bloody halo?'

'When I became a respectable married woman with kids.'

'Jesus, Hannah!'

'I know. I know. Holier than thou. Don't rub it in. But it's easier to be that way than to put up with Grandma's nagging. I'm not a drinker. Seen too much of it with Tom.'

'Just because you don't do it doesn't make having a few beers wrong ya know,' he said.

'You didn't think that when your dad staggered home drunk most nights,' she retaliated, and instantly regretted it. 'Sorry, Colin, that was below the belt. You go in and have a drink with your mates. I'm going back to the funeral. I've known Bob all my life and the least I can do now is to show my respect by attending his burial.'

'You reckon I should go too, don't ya? Him and me were mates before I took off for the bush.'

She hesitated for a moment before saying, 'I know terrible things happened in that P.O.W. camp. I don't know what they were, but I've heard enough about those places to understand why you'd want to stay away from death and grieving.'

'Thanks,' was his answer, and his expression told her not to ask questions.

Giving in to impulse, she leaned forward, kissed his cheek, then turned aside before he could show a reaction. Smoothing her hat into shape, she pulled it on, took a deep breath, and headed for the church without looking back. Once there, she ignored Tom and surrounded herself with her black-hatted relatives until they reached Rookwood cemetery. It wasn't until then that she noticed Bob's three sons: young Bobby, Larry and Charlie.

Charlie was a year older than Allie. That made him seventeen. A man now, some would say. Tall and solid without a skerrick of fat, wavy sand-coloured hair, blue eyes, and features that were still puppy-rounded but would turn square in years to come. Much like his father, but more handsome. Allie wouldn't admit it now, but she'd been keen on him for years. At age ten, she had sworn to marry him one day. They'd be a good match, both being intelligent and ambitious as well as good-looking, though Allie probably wouldn't forgive Charlie for Tom's decision to live with the Lenahan family.

Not that it's Charlie's fault, so don't glare at him like that, Hannah told herself, switching the glare to Tom before turning her attention back to the boys.

They were fine-looking lads, standing as stiff as soldiers alongside their mother by the grave, hiding their pain so as not to upset her; though grief was etched on their faces for anyone to see, if she cared to look. Even nine-year-old Bobby had that stiff upper-lip expression. No doubt his older brothers had coached him. Yet Madge seemed more bemused than grief-stricken, as though she didn't understand what any of this was about.

Well, it's about you taking my man because you lost yours, Hannah wanted to say, but had the grace, good sense and enough pride to keep to herself.

'A ditsy woman, that Madge. I don't know why I ever supposed she was a friend,' Hannah thought, not realising she'd said it aloud until Grandma elbowed her ribs.

A ditsy woman who needs someone to take care of her. Well I don't. 'So good luck to you, Madge,' Hannah said as she filed past the Lenahan family, then walked away. It wasn't until she reached home, until she stood staring at herself in the bathroom mirror, her black hat battered and slightly askew, holes in her gloves, her face devoid of cosmetics – not even a touch of lipstick – that she realised she'd grown into the wrong woman.

This person looking back at her wasn't who she was meant to be. She and Colin had that in common. What had happened to the boy who hated even the smell of alcohol, whose future was to work hard, get married and have half a dozen kids one day – or so he had always vowed. What had happened to that girl who was near top of the class every year, more than passable pretty, popular with girls and boys alike, ready to become rich and famous? How could she possibly think she was superior to Lottie Nelson and Madge Lenahan? Lottie hadn't started drinking until her man was killed in a desert some place she'd never heard of, and Madge had lost her husband through a terrible accident not of her doing. She, Hannah, had lost hers through lack of care, and she didn't even feel the loss. What she felt was this niggling, guilty feeling of being free, of room to move. But move to where?

'Why are you standing there looking at yourself?' Allie asked.

Hannah turned to see her and Hal staring from the doorway.

'I'm wondering who I am,' she said. 'Do you know?'

Allie shook her head, mystified.

Hal grinned and nodded. 'You're Mum,' he said.

'Who else?'

He frowned. 'Nobody.'

'Exactly,' she sighed.

'Who do you want to be?' Allie asked.

'That's the problem. I don't know. Somebody important.'

'How do you know when you're important?'

Hannah grimaced. 'I'll let you know when I get there.'

With a shake of her head to show that the conversation was a lot of nonsense as far as she was concerned, Allie grabbed Hal's hand and pulled him away. 'Come on, I've make you a cup of tea,' she tossed back over a shoulder.

Hannah nodded, but she'd gone back to studying herself in the mirror.

Whoop De Do

Plonking down on the kerbside without bothering to check if it was smeared with the usual gutter grime, Allie hugged her knees, propped her chin on them and fixed her stare on the corner where her dad was due at any moment. She was prepared to sit there for a week if that's what she needed to do. He had managed to avoid her yesterday, throwing her a loaf of bread – she'd caught it without thinking – then calling out, 'Take it to your mum,' before running on.

'Well whoop de do,' her mother had said. 'He gives us bread for free. Wonder what the poor little widow thinks of that. Wonder if he tells her.'

He'd been delivering bread for six weeks now. Six weeks with Mum and Janet still not able to talk about him without getting angry, Hal still sad about him leaving. For Allie, the days passed quickly enough as school took up the weekdays – school work and school friends, afternoons working at the fruit shop. Weekends were the same with the fruit shop on Saturdays, doing Janet's share of the housework as well as her own on Sundays. Missing Dad all the time, especially nights when they used to be all at home together listening to plays on the radio, reading books – sometimes aloud but usually to yourself with everyone having different tastes. The reading and listening only happened after she'd finished her homework and study. But it all seemed different now. The familiar routine of her life had changed since Mr Lenahan was killed.

Not killed. Died, Allie told herself. Mrs Paterson and Mrs Peters said it wasn't anybody's fault. Mr Lenahan fell backwards off his cart, hit his head on the road and died. Mrs Lenahan said it was a dreadful accident that could happen to anyone, or so Charlie had told Janet. Charlie might have told Allie himself if she'd been speaking to him, which she wasn't. Janet had played Australia Street cricket on her afternoon off from work last Monday. She hadn't called in to see Grandma Ade, and Grandma was taking that out on her, on Allie.

Mum vows she's not, but I reckon she is, Allie thought. Why else would she keep nagging at me to leave school? She knows that's the last thing I want to do.

Glancing across the street to the opposite corner and Grandma Ade's house, she wondered if anyone in there had seen her yet. Grandma couldn't know she was sitting on the opposite gutter's edge or the old girl would have come out and ordered her home.

Grandma's good at giving orders. 'Sit like a lady, don't talk so much, speak when spoken to, mind your manners, children should be seen and not heard,' is just a few of the ones she goes on about every time she sees me. Round and round like a record. Yet I'm always old enough to know better in her opinion, and she doesn't see that she's arguing with herself.

If Great-Aunt Florrie saw her there in the gutter, she wouldn't tell. Allie wasn't so sure about Colin. He was close to being mad. Maybe not completely bonkers, but really strange. While she was walking down the street a few minutes ago, he drag-footed towards her, all dolled up in his suit as usual, but with a bowed back and his shoulders slumped as though he carried the weight of the world. He reminded her of one of those zombies she'd seen in a movie. His face looked as though he'd dragged his hands down his cheeks and they stayed that way. She couldn't help staring, and when he noticed, he did that weird thing: jumping around, scratching his armpits and 'Ooh oohing' like a monkey, then laughing like a jackass when she crossed to the other side of the street. Then he had the hide to wink as if it was all a big joke between them. When she glanced back, he was going through her gate again.

He'd been visiting a lot these past six weeks. She wouldn't go home until she saw him leave. Maybe she didn't have a sense of humour because she couldn't see the funny side of Colin. Not funny ha ha anyway. Funny strange definitely. She couldn't bear to live in the same house as him. She'd be too afraid to sleep. Everyone knew he went berserk in the middle of the night, running through the house yelling blue murder, then crawling under his bed and lying there shivering like a wet cat. She'd heard Grandma Ade telling that to Mum. Yet Mum's talking about moving in with Grandma and him and Great-Aunt Florrie. Living in that house didn't bear thinking about. Dad had to do something.

Where are you, Dad?

As if on cue, the bakery cart rumbled down the street. Her father sat on the driver's seat, totting up the day's takings in a small blue book, not worrying about holding Jessie's reins. The old mare knew the day's work was done. She didn't need to be guided home.

She's a good old horse, Allie thought. It wasn't her fault, Mr Lenahan falling off the back of the cart. Not Jessie's fault, not mine. He should have been hanging on. I'd love to live in the country and own a horse like Jessie.

Caught up in a daydream of riding through leafy lanes like the ladies in English movies, she almost missed her father. He'd gone past by the time she called, 'I have to talk to you, Dad.'

It was then she noticed Charlie Lenahan standing on the ledge at back of the cart. That was the same place Mr Lenahan had been standing. Her stomach gurgled at the memory. She had stood when she saw the cart, but her legs weakened now and she sat back on the gutter's edge.

'Whoa, girl,' Charlie called, stepping down onto the bitumen when old Jessie stopped.

'G'day, Allie.' He stared into her face with a look on his that dared her not to answer.

Blowed if I will, she thought, and firmed her lips. She knew Charlie Lenahan was keen on her, and had been since she was ten and him eleven. She'd decided long ago that she'd marry him when she was ready to settle down. Now she couldn't forgive him for taking her father away. Him and his two brothers.

'Mind your manners, girl,' Tom Gordon said.

Drawing her knees up to her chin again, she wrapped her skirt around her legs and turned her face aside.

Charlie continued to stare. 'If she wants to act like a two-year-old, then let her.'

Allie screwed up her face and poked out her tongue, as any two-year-old would.

'The wind will change and you'll stay that way,' he said.

He didn't smile, but she could hear the laughter in his tone. Laughing at her. It suddenly occurred that she hated the way he'd sailed through his fifth year at high school when he wasn't half as smart as her. She knew he'd wanted to quit after gaining the Intermediate Certificate, but his mother was determined he'd be a teacher because her father used to teach at high school.

'You think you're clever,' she couldn't help saying, though she knew she was being silly. Childish, even. But she hated the unfairness of it.

'I don't think. I know,' he said, laughing aloud now and looking at her in a special way that begged her to laugh with him.

'Not funny,' she snapped.

'That's enough, Allie,' Tom said, picking up the reins as though contemplating urging the old mare on. 'There's no need for that sort of behaviour. You've been taught better.'

Allie looked up. 'I'll follow you to Mrs Lenahan's house and stand at the gate and yell your name fifty times if you don't stop and talk to me.'

He knew she was pigheaded enough to do just that. 'Okay then, hop up here,' he said, and the note of reluctance was easy to read.

She shook her head. 'You come down here.'

'Want me to take Jessie home?' Charlie asked Tom, though he was still watching Allie. She darted a glare at him then looked away.

'It's not me, Allie. What did I do?' he asked, and strode off down Australia Street without waiting for an answer. Not that she had one to give.

Tom squatted beside her and lit a thinly rolled cigarette. 'Okay, what is it?'

'Is that all you can say when I've hardly seen you for ages? You are my dad you know. Mine, not Charlie's.'

'What d'ya want me to say?'

'Something a bit nicer than that.'

'I'm tired, Allie. I been working me innards out since three o'clock this morning and I'm not in the mood for your shenanigans, and not those bloody word games ya learnt off yer mum. If yer got something to say, come out with it.'

'Dad, we haven't spoken to each other since the day Mr Lenahan died.'

'I know, and I'm sorry about that. I can't come and see ya without a yelling match starting up between me and yer mum. But you can come see me any time ya want.'

'Then Mum would think I'm taking your side and I have to live with her, even if you don't.'

'What's this business about sides? There's no sides. Only difference now between me and yer mum is we don't fight any more.'

'You can't truly believe that!'

'We can be mates like we used to be as youngsters once she wakes up to herself.'

Allie rolled her eyes. Did he know he was talking nonsense and was trying to soft-soap her?

'Of course there's sides,' she stated.

'Have it yer own way, Allie,' Tom said tiredly. 'But tell me now why you've bailed me up at this particular moment. What is it ya want of me?' He frowned, adding, 'An' make it something I can give ya.'

Leaning forward, she stared up into his face, forcing eye contact. 'I want to come and live with you.'

His answer was immediate, as if he'd been expecting her to say exactly that. 'Can't be done. Especially if yer gunner treat Charlie like ya did just then. He's a decent bloke. Anyhow, there's no room. I'm on the back veranda and that's no place for a girl. No privacy, and ya know there's three boys in that family.'

'Well whoop de do,' she said sullenly, pulling back from him. 'I suppose that makes it better than ours.'

'Not better, just different. And just because ya look like yer mother, ya don't have to talk like her. That's the kind of thing she would say.'

Allie almost said, 'She already did,' but decided that would only push her father further away. 'You always wanted a boy,' she accused him instead. 'I heard Mum say that.'

'I've got Hal, haven't I? I'm happy the way it turned out.'

Her tone was a plea. 'Then why are you at the bakery and not at home with us?'

'They need me, Allie. Madge's trying to get enough money together to buy a van so she can retire that old nag.'

'I need you too,' she wanted to scream at him. Instead, she said, 'Then what will happen to Jessie?'

He looked surprised. 'I dunno. I guess she'll go to the knackery.'

She jumped to her feet. 'You don't care about anybody or any thing.'

'What else do ya do with an old horse?' He gestured helplessly. 'It's not as if we live out bush and can put her in a paddock somewhere.'

That 'we' felt like a slap in the face to Allie.

'It's bad luck your proper family can't be sent to a knackery too,' she said fiercely. 'Then you wouldn't have to worry about any of us. Not that you do.'

'It's no good carrying on, girl. Things are what they are. I'll be staying at Lenahan's until they get on their feet and that's that, and there's no need to take it out on young Charlie.' He cut off the lit end of his cigarette with a thumbnail, dropped the ember into the gutter and the butt into his shirt pocket. Standing, he added, 'Now off ya go home. I've got work to do.'

'How come you never worked when you lived with us?' she demanded, knowing that would sting him.

'Don't smart-mouth me, missy,' he warned.

Or you'll do what? she almost said, but knew that would get her exactly nowhere. 'Please, Dad,' she begged, her tone desperate now. 'I won't be in the way. I can sleep on the floor.'

He kissed her forehead. 'I'll see you again soon.'

Allie grabbed his arm. 'Mum got the sack from the taxis and she has to work in the shirt factory and she hates it and she only gets half as much pay. Janet doesn't help Mum out now she's not living with us and the rent went up and she can't pay the extra. She told them we'd leave and now we've got to move Grandma's because you let our house go to wrack and ruin,' she said with hardly a pause.

He ignored that last bit. 'Why don't you see if Janet can get you a job with her?'

'It's waiting tables and cleaning up other people's messes and I'm only sixteen, Dad.'

'What's the point of staying at school now ya got yer Intermediate? Janet didn't sit for that exam and didn't stay at school. She was working at fourteen. So was yer mum.'

She clenched her hands. He didn't understand. He never had. 'That's them. That's not me,' she cried out. 'I want to go right through. You know that. I've told you that a hundred times.'

'Ya get through high school, pass yer Leaving Certificate then what?' He glanced down at his watch.

'Well if you don't know, I'm not going to tell you.' She jabbed at his wrist. Spitefully. Digging her fingernail into the back of his hand. 'And you can go now. I'd hate to keep you away from your bloody girlfriend.'

'Don't curse, and she isn't my . . .' he began. Allie had already walked away. 'Get a job and work for a while. Get yer own money to buy clothes and that sort of thing. Then, if in a couple of years ya still want to finish yer schooling, things will be different and I'll be able to help ya out,' he called after her.

Ignoring that, and refusing to look back when he shouted her name, she walked slowly, waiting for him to catch up. Waiting for him to apologise and say he'd be home that night. Waiting for something, anything that would tell her he hadn't swapped families for good.

Well that's it, she thought, her heart sinking when she heard him tell Jessie to gee up. I'll stay on at school until they make me leave, then I'll find a job and work for a few years, then go back and finish. Next stop after that will be university.

'And I will get to university no matter what anyone says,' she shouted to him as he went past, not looking at her, to Grandma, to the whole street. To anyone who thought she couldn't do it.

Well Met

The back veranda's tin roof had rusted away long ago. As it disintegrated, Hannah replaced each sheet with chicken wire and rows of climbing plants. Now an intertwining of runner beans, pumpkin, choko and banana passionfruit vines provided shelter, fresh vegetables, various foods swapped with neighbours for the fruit of the roof, and a screen from the smelly fowl pen and weed-ravaged yard. Her favourite place for reading and daydreaming was under this tangle of greenery, sprawled on one of the lounging chairs made by Tom's grandfather, old Harry Gordon.

She'd been sitting for an hour at a Grandfather Harry-made table, pencil in hand, trying to figure out ways of earning more money than her new job at a clothing factory provided. It was a job she had hated from day one, but her only skills were sewing, cooking, cleaning, and driving a car, so she needed to grab what she could get, even if the idea of bending over a sewing machine for the rest of her life sickened her. As she sewed collars onto an unlimited pile of shirts, her mind filled with a desperation that continued far into the restless nights. Instead of a taxi and the Sydney streets, she was surrounded by dozens of other women who needed to work because of failed marriages, or lazy or alcoholic or war-dead husbands; and in the case of the younger ones, lack of education or ambition. Instead of multifaceted conversations with men and women from all walks of life, the talk around her now was either domestic, complaints or commendations on families and family life, or advice/revelations regarding men.

Working overtime shifts at the factory and casual nights cleaning at the Golden Barley to pay the usual bills meant she felt constantly tired, constantly heavy-hearted. Of course she had the satisfaction of knowing she was independent, not a clinging vine like Madge Lenahan, and she was proud of the fact that she could allow Allie to stay at school. But days that used to race by when she was driving a taxi now dragged on and on into weeks then months. The sameness was excruciating. For three months now it had been get up, go to work, come home and fall into bed, with housework and helping Grandma with the herbs filling in the between times. Life would be unbearable without Allie and Hal. But was this to be her destiny, this head-down, bum-up existence, her face drooping with wretchedness, her body sagging with age as the months and years crawled by? And was her only company to be those other head-down, bum-up women? She'd grown out of the idea of being famous one day, but what had happened to the dream of seeing the world? Paris, Vienna, Egypt. The idea of streets with names in languages other than English had once filled her with excitement. Now she just felt sadness at the loss.

'I did what I swore I'd never do when I was in my early teens,' she said aloud. 'Pregnant and married young, a dead-end husband and now a dead-end job.'

I'd be better off dead, she thought miserably, not bothering to turn and look as the screen door banged behind her. It had to be Hal. He was the only other person at home on this Sunday afternoon.

'I made you a cuppa tea,' he said, carefully placing it at her elbow.

She sat back and stared at him. His oval face with its multitude of freckles, large eyes and longer than usual lashes, the pigeon chest that was a result of malnutrition before he came to live in Australia Street, the thin but wiry build, all these masked a determined and independent nature. The only hint that he was a lot tougher than he looked showed in the mass of curly blond hair, impossible to tame. But he was also shorter than most kids his age. Now they were into the colder months, she kept the fuel stove in the kitchen fired up night and day. A kettle sat on one side, ready for tea-making or dish-washing, but Hannah always made sure it was pushed back out of Hal's reach.

'How did you make the tea?' she asked, shuddering at the thought of him manoeuvring that hot, heavy kettle.

'I got a chair and I put the teapot on the stove, then I put on the stove glove, then I tipped the kettle.' He used his hands to help the explanation. 'Warm the teapot, a spoonful of tea leaves for each person and one for the pot, and don't let the water boil or you kill all the oxygen,' he said in a singsong voice, 'and you have one sugar and no milk.'

'That's pretty clever, Hal love, and you've got a good memory. But the stove glove must be lots too big for you.'

'It didn't fall off. I'm getting big now,' he said proudly. 'Great-Aunt Florrie said I'm the man of the house.'

Putting an arm around him, she drew him close and kissed the top of his head. 'Oh, darling, yes you are. But hot things are very dangerous.' Sitting up straight, she raised the cup to her lips, sniffed, sipped, then nodded appreciation. 'Though I have to admit it's perfect.'

His smile was bliss. 'I'll get you a bickie.'

'You mean biscuit.'

The correction was automatic. Hannah was determined that her children would speak proper English, or as proper as being Australian would allow, though she'd given up on Janet, who had taken on the inner-city idiom from the day she first put two words together. Which, by the way, were 'Git orf' when she grew tired of the kin wanting to kiss or cuddle her. Janet had been a cute kid, rosy and plump with white-blonde hair, but definitely not an affectionate one.

'I don't think there are any biscuits,' Hannah added.

He smiled again. 'Mrs Paterson gave me some in a tin with birds on it. She said someone gave them to her and they're too rich for her stomach because she gets a bit sick if she eats too much sweet things.'

'Do you like Mrs Paterson staying with you while I'm at work?' Hannah asked, studying his face for the telltale blush of a lie. Hal would usually say what he guessed people wanted to hear.

After thinking for a moment or two, he said, 'Mrs Paterson is all by herself and she gets lonely sometimes.'

A neat evasion for a nine-year-old, Hannah thought. He was much too stoic for a small boy. She knew Hal didn't like being left with anyone outside of close family, even at home, though he tried to make the best of it. Though he liked school, had plenty of friends – including a few of the 'big boys' who made sure he was never bullied – and did well in class, he was never happier than when he could be with his 'best family'. This was Hannah and Tom, Janet and Allie. His second best was Grandma Ade and Great-Aunt Florrie.

'Would you rather stay next door with Mrs Peters? I know she'd love to have you. She likes you a lot, Hal.'

'An' I like her. But not if Mr Peters is home,' he said darkly.

There must be something very wrong about that man, Hannah thought while Hal ran inside for the biscuits. And something wrong with me to be such a misery guts, was an added thought as she sipped the hot, too-sweet tea, shuddering again at the idea of Hal wrestling with that heavy kettle. And doing it so proudly. How would she be able to forbid him from making tea again without hurting his feelings? She could learn a lot from Hal. Not being sorry for herself would be a good start. Okay, getting pregnant and marrying young wasn't a good idea, especially marrying Tom, but Grandma Ade would never have placed Hal in her care if she'd managed to attain that dream of fame and fortune. She couldn't imagine a life without Hal. Or Janet and Allie. Tom was a different matter.

There were times when she felt as though he'd left a large hole in her life, but those times were becoming rare. Daily life was so much less stressful without him. She felt more at ease, no longer having her stomach tying into knots when she heard his footsteps on the veranda. As a matter of fact, when she was being completely honest with herself, she was happier with him gone.

Forcing herself to focus on a positive, she rearranged the mental picture of herself at the factory being a mirror of other sad-faced women. It wasn't like that. They worked hard, sure, but while they worked they sang along with the wireless. They shouted jokes, laughed, waved to friends during a favourite song, played all kinds of tricks on each other and the two male mechanics. Especially the mechanics. Before and after work and during lunch breaks, they chattered continuously – joking around, describing days or nights out, boyfriends, husbands, kids, families, often in a tongue-in-cheek way. During the warmer months, and with the boss's help, a group would scrape up enough money to hire a bus on Sundays. They'd take their families to the National Park: boating, hiking, swimming. The bus was always crowded.

'We could be a part of that,' she told Hal when he reappeared with two biscuits on a plate.

He nodded solemnly, as though he had knowledge of her thought process.

'Thanks, honey, for more than you know,' she told him. 'Now I need to finish doing my sums. Janet brought some magazines from the guest-house where she works. They're in the middle kitchen cupboard with the paper bags, scissors and glue if you'd like to make one of your wonderful collages for me.'

When he ran back inside, she picked up the pencil and frowned down at the writing pad.

Five minutes later, the sums had turned to doodles at the realisation that she couldn't afford to stay in this house, not without Janet's help, and now Janet had that a live-in job on the other side of the harbour, she could hardly be expected to continue handing over half her wages. Of course it should have been Tom helping out, but he hadn't offered and she would cut off her tongue rather than ask. It was mid May now. He'd been gone for three months and the rumours still flew thick and fast, though the Lenahan boys swore he slept alone on the back veranda. They had no reason to lie. Well, to avoid gossip could be classed as a reason, but those kids had adored their dad. They'd transferred a lot of that regard to Tom, speaking of him in glowing terms to anyone who asked, and surely they wouldn't do that if he'd taken their father's place in his bed when Bob was barely in his grave.

But enough about Tom. Time to start planning. The trouble was, her furniture wouldn't fit into Grandma's house and she didn't want to sell it. Surely the day would come, and hopefully not too far into the future, when she could afford to rent again. There must be reasonably priced houses around Sydney somewhere. Although moving to a suburb away from her kin was a daunting idea.

How ridiculous is that, she thought. One minute I'm moaning to myself about not being able to visit foreign lands, the next minute I'm shuddering at the idea of living in another suburb. Though if I could go across to the other side of the world, I'd be coming back sooner or later to the kin. But I'm already behind in the rent so I should move soon. And instead of whining about my fate, I should be grateful to Grandma for offering to take me in as she did when I was fourteen.

'Time to be up and doing. I need to finish cleaning this house and get out before I get kicked out,' she muttered.

'I beg your pardon?' a male voice asked.

He stood at the entrance to the veranda. Tall, well-built and good-looking, though she preferred a rugged look and he didn't have that. His skin was too pale, his dark hair too well cut. Definitely not a working-class man. Perhaps a salesman? He had that body-shine look of one. She continued to stare as his gaze took in her surroundings before he fixed his eyes on her again, his expression politely grave.

'So you should beg my pardon,' she finally told him, but softened the words with a smile. 'It's bad manners to listen in to other people's conversations.'

An answering smile flickered. 'You were talking to yourself.'

'And?'

She liked the look of him, and the deep, low voice. He exuded a quiet confidence. What impressed her even more was his clothes. Years of driving a taxi had taught her to know quality when she saw it, and she knew the grey slacks, dark blue pullover and blazer would have cost her six months' wages. He definitely wasn't a salesman. Thank God she was wearing one of her old taxi-driving outfits. A cream blouse that underscored her light tan and dark hair teamed with the A-line maroon skirt looked good on her, she knew.

'I . . . ar . . . I did knock at the front door,' he said.

'And nobody answered so you though you'd have a wander around?'

'A boy with a voice bigger than his body said I'd find you on the back veranda.' He took a step forward but stopped when she held out a hand, palm up. 'I told him he shouldn't open the door to strangers.'

'And did he?'

'No. He shouted at me through a closed window.' That sudden smile again. 'I should introduce myself. I'm Claude Macy.'

She blinked surprise. 'The landlord?'

'Guilty as charged.' He extended a hand, palm up. 'May I come in?'

She stood. 'It's your place.'

He stayed at the entrance. 'Not while you're paying the rent.'

Hannah stared at him, not knowing what to say, and he seemed to mistake her silence for a refusal.

'I'm sorry for intruding. I should have made an appointment.' He began to turn away, then stopped. 'I did overhear what you said about getting kicked out. I have no intention of forcing you to leave before you're ready. I know you're on your own with two children and —'

She interrupted. 'How would you know that?'

'From Clara Paterson, an old friend of my family. She remonstrated with me for daring to ask you to leave when my grandfather said the Gordons could live here forever. Yet there was a condition.'

'I know of the condition, and I'll be leaving at the end of the month.' Hannah grimaced. 'Or perhaps July if I can hang on long enough. You'll have your house then, Mr Macy.'

Hal stormed onto the veranda, his face puckered in temper. 'You can't live with us,' he shouted. 'Only my dad Tom is allowed.'

'I'm not going to live with you,' Claude Macy said, holding out his hands, palms up. 'Though when you leave,' he looked at Hannah, 'and in your own good time, I will be moving in.'

Hannah placed an arm around Hal's shoulders to quieten him.

'You'll live here in Australia Street?' she asked, not attempting to hide her surprise. The Macy family were known to be rich, and people with money did not live in this area. It was a working-class neighbourhood. Claude Macy must know that.

'My grandfather was a carpenter and I inherited his love of working with hammer and nails,' he explained. 'I'll live here while I'm renovating this house, and I hope to have it looking like new by the end of the year.'

Hal looked to be on the verge of tears. 'Where are we going to live then?'

'At Grandma's house with me and Grandma and Great-Aunt Florrie,' Colin said from behind Claude Macy. 'And you, mate, can nick off till this house is empty.'

Hannah held back a smile. Colin had fronted up, chest out, his eyes hard. Like a bantam cock trying to bluff a full-sized rooster, she thought. Claude Macy turned towards him but didn't back away. Which wasn't surprising. He was a head taller and much broader. Altogether not a bad-looking man. And with money, she couldn't help adding to the appraisal.

'And you are?' he asked, looking above Colin's head, then lowering his eyes.

Colin's eyes gleamed. 'Short I am, and a staying-at-home bloke looking after the missus and kids if I had a missus and kids. You can call me Mr Gatley.'

'Mr Colin Gatley?' At Colin's brief nod, Claude Macy added, 'I've had you described to me. A cousin of yours, Chris Gatley, is a cleaner at my car dealership. She calls you a war hero.'

'Yeah, that's me. A bloody hero all right. That's what they call ya when ya go through a war without getting shot because ya sitting it out in a bloody prison camp.' Colin grinned and extended a hand when Claude Macy winced. 'Glad to meet ya, mate, though it don't change nothing, you being me cousin's boss. Half the people round this neighbourhood are kin. And I'm still asking ya to leave and not call in unexpected.'

'Fair enough.' Claude shook Colin's hand before turning to Hannah. 'Please take your time moving out. I assure you I'm in no hurry. I just wanted to look around to see what needed to be done so I could order supplies.'

Hannah smiled. She liked this man: his looks, his smile, his warm personality. He was obviously genuine in his desire not to put her out, in his want or need to work with his hands. Walking towards him, she said, 'If you'd care to come back for an inspection next Saturday afternoon, I'll show you around inside.'

Taking her outstretched hand, he held it for a moment, smiled from Hal to Colin then walked away. She felt Colin's eyes on her but she continued watching Claude Macy. He disappeared around the corner of the house. A few seconds later, he reappeared walking up Australia Street. Just as he reached the side fence, he stopped and looked directly at her. Their eyes met for a few moments before she lowered her head.

'Fancy what ya see, hey?' Colin asked. When she ignored him, lifting her head to watch Claude disappear from sight, he added, 'The size of his wallet wouldn't get in the way. Except ya might trip over it.'

Keeping her back towards Hal, she muttered, 'You're such a fathead, Colin.'

'Course I am,' he agreed.

'Of course you are and always were.' She couldn't help laughing. 'Come on in and I'll give you a cup of tea and some of Mrs Paterson's sweet biscuits.'

'Only two,' Hal warned.

Colin held out a hand. 'How ya going, Hal? We've been seeing each other here and at Grandma's for months now, but we haven't had much of a good natter, have we? You know, good day, Colin good day, Hal and that's about it. We should've been saying a lot more, seeing as we're blood kin. We're second cousins, ya know. My mum and your actual mum's dad are sister and brother. Ya can't get much closer than that. Plus we need to be mates if we're going to look out for this mum here.' He darted a knowing look at Hannah. 'Can't let blokes like that last one wander around wherever they want.'

Hal studied Colin's face for a few moments, then took the outstretched hand. Their eyes met and held until Hannah spoke.

'That says a lot for you, Colin. Hal doesn't like strangers, and strangers are people he hasn't known for longer than a year. Especially men, cousins or not.'

'Then we're well met, aren't we, Hal mate?' Colin said.

Hal clung to his hand while leading him inside.

What's a Man to Do?

Tom glanced over at the small clock standing on the banana crate that passed as a bedside table. Quarter past eight. Christ, was that all? He felt as though he'd been lying there for half the night. Madge had made dinner at five o'clock. That's what time Bob had eaten. Then he'd go to bed at half-past seven, or so Madge said, because he had to get up at three. No pub and late afternoon rush to throw back as many as possible before six o'clock closing for Bob. Not after he married Madge anyway.

Lucky bugger, Tom thought. Wish I'd always been a teetotaller, then me tongue wouldn't be hanging out for a beer like it is now. And it's too early for sleeping, even if I do have to get up early. Nothing else to do but. If I go hanging about in there with Madge, I'm likely to end up in her bed and I don't want that. Or do I?

His loud sigh brought Blue Dog, the Lenahan family's blue heeler cross, up the veranda steps and onto his bunk. Starting at Tom's feet, the dog crept up the bed, belly low to the blanket, and stuck a cold nose into his neck.

'That's the trouble with sleeping out here,' Tom grumbled. 'Brass monkey weather now so I got you wanting to bunk in with me. Oh well.' He rubbed Blue Dog's head. 'Guess I took yer spot, eh, feller?'

The answer was a wet lick along the side of his face.

'That teaches me for having naughty thoughts about Madge,' Tom said, laughing as the animal interpreted the spoken voice as an invitation to play. Grabbing a mouthful of blanket, Blue Dog backed up, then jumped off the bed, taking the blanket down the steps and onto the back path, where he sat, waiting to see what would happen next, obviously hoping Tom would join in the fun.

'Yeah, tug o' war,' Tom said. 'Not bloody likely, mate. The blanket would get shredded and I'd be to blame.'

When Blue Dog wagged agreement, Tom nodded towards the front of the house. 'Come on, drop it and I'll take ya for a walk.'

Minutes later they were on the footpath, the dog unfettered, Tom dressed in shorts, a well-worn Newtown Blues football jersey, long socks and work boots. Without actual intention on his part, they headed for Australia Street.

'It pulls me back like it's got a rope around me,' he said when he saw the wall. Stopping under the light across the street and down a little from number 19, he added in a mutter, 'But maybe it's them.'

He felt the pull of his family as if it were a physical thing, an actual rope drawing him closer to the lit windows, the faint sound of a radio playing 'A Slow Boat To China'. He knew that as a recent hit song, and Janet's particular favourite.

An all-pervading sadness overwhelmed him, making his body feel heavy, his eyes burn. What the hell was he doing sleeping on the back veranda at the bakery, taking care of Bob's wife and kids when he should be looking after his own? If he hadn't walked out, spitting the dummy like a big kid the way he always did when he got on the booze, if it wasn't for that and for Allie chasing after him, Bob would be alive today. Bob would be alive and he, Tom, would be flat out on his back, pissed again. He wouldn't be getting the respect he now got from Madge and the boys. He liked being there with them. He bloody well liked the way they made him feel. They looked up to him. He was a somebody as far as they were concerned. But he missed Janet's digs at him, her constant efforts to reform him. He missed warring with Hannah, he missed Hal and Allie's blind devotion, he even missed the feeling of guilt when he looked into their upturned faces and saw those eyes, blue on Hal, brown on Allie, those eyes filled with enough love to satisfy a dozen dads.

Jesus wept. What was a man to do?

'Dad, why are ya hanging round here? It's freezing. Don't tell me ya finally come to ya senses and are waiting for Mum to invite ya in.'

Janet stood in front of him, hands on hips, eyes accusing.

'That's a nice outfit ya got on,' he said, not able to think of anything else at that exact moment.

She gave him a start of surprise before saying, 'It's me uniform. But look at you. Not ya usual going out outfit. Won't she iron ya a shirt? Ya look like a navvy.'

'Well that's what I am. It's me working gear anyway. This is what I wear while I'm hosing out the bakery and brushing down old Jessie and suchlike. Didn't get round to getting changed. Anyway, how ya going?'

'I'm all right. But never mind changing the subject,' she said aggressively. 'Ya still haven't said why you're hanging round here. If ya thinking about strolling in like ya never left, ya just might be too late.'

'I'm just taking Blue Dog for a walk,' he stammered.

She nodded. 'Mighta known. Getting it too good at the bakery, eh?' Her voice and expression were scornful. 'Madge Lenahan keeping ya in the style you're not accustomed to.'

'I been busting me gut in that bakery,' he protested, 'and I'll have yer know I ain't touched a drop since I been there.'

'Oh yeah, what've they got that we haven't? That we never had?' Her blue eyes darkened to the colour of a storm out to sea. 'We're ya blood, me and Allie. And Hal thinks he is.'

'You're not home anyway,' he blustered. 'I heard about ya working over the north side. Why aren't ya here helping out yer family?'

Her chin went up. 'Not my place, Dad.'

His shoulders sagged. 'Yeah, yer right.'

She softened at last. 'You never even told us why.'

'Somebody has to look out for Madge and them boys.'

'There's more to it than that.' She shook her head in disbelief. 'Gotter be.'

'Yeah, I suppose there is. But none of it's your business, me girl.'

'Mum's doing all right. She can look out for her kids without no bloke coming in to take over the job.'

He nodded. 'Exactly. She don't need me. She never did.'

Janet stared at him. He could see by her expression that she could see the truth in that.

'Look, Janet. Me and yer mum were bound to call it quits sooner or later. Once she gets used to the idea, there won't be no difference except I won't be living here. Won't be fighting with yer mum every second I'm home. You and Allie and Hal can come see me whenever youse want.'

'Try telling Allie and Hal that.'

'They'll come round to it,' he said, trying not to reveal his uncertainty.

'Then you're never coming home?' Hal asked, his voice breaking halfway through the sentence.

They had been so intent on each other neither had seen him walk up behind Janet.

'Aren't you ever?' he added, and his eyes and tone were filled with tears.

'Ah jeez, Hal,' Tom said miserably.

'You had to face him sooner or later,' Janet said. 'Gotter tell him something, Dad. Better make it good or Hal will be up bawling half the night. I'll leave ya to it.'

'Yer not going!' His fingers slipped off her arm as she pulled away from him before he had a chance to close them.

'I'm not staying here holding your hand. I'll miss me ferry. Just been to see Mum. Catch ya later.'

Before he could voice another protest, she was running up the street. He watched her disappear around the corner before turning back to Hal.

'How's it going, mate?' he asked, trying for light-hearted, but knowing a smile would look more like a grimace, he kept his face straight.

'Allie's been sad for a long time,' Hal said, and bit down on his lip to stop it from trembling.

'And yer mum?' Tom asked, glancing at the house, hoping Allie would come out and rescue him.

Hal gave a half shrug. 'She's just cranky.'

'Yer mum's always cranky with me.' Tom grinned, wishing he could lighten the mood. He wasn't up to this. Nothing worse for a man's chance of sleeping at night than his boy's face looking up at him, accusing, trying not to turn on the waterworks.

'Listen, Hal.' Kneeling, he held out a hand. 'I know it's hard, mate, but it just has to be. You can come see me at the bakery any old time ya want.'

Hal backed up a step. 'Why can't you come here?'

'Because me and yer mum would just start fighting again and I know how much ya hate that, don't ya?'

Hal nodded slowly. 'But we're all by ourselves now, me and Mum and Allie.'

'You got all the kin,' Tom said encouragingly. 'Grandma, Great-Aunt Florrie, all the rest of them. And me. I won't be far. In fact I'll come round at night, often as I can, round about your bedtime, and I'll stay till I know yer sleeping. That way, you'll know I'm still yer dad, still around, and yer mum and me won't be fighting.'

''Cause you won't be here,' Hal said.

'Ah, mate.' Tom reached out, meaning to pull him close.

'You won't, will you?' Hal said, backing away again.

Tom shook his head. 'I can't, mate. I just can't.'

'I can't come and see you. Mum will think I'm on your side.'

'There's no sides, son.'

He would have felt better if Hal had turned and ran there and then. That would have meant he was just angry, or overcome for now, something that would have passed in a day or two. But he didn't turn. He didn't run. His nod said yes there were sides as he continued backing away, his eyes never leaving Tom's face, until he reached the gate.

'Hal, where are you?' Hannah's voice floated out through the open front door. 'Hal? Come on now, time for bed.'

'I'm coming.'

Tom lifted a hand in farewell. Hal mimicked the action, though hesitantly, then turned away.

'Come on, Blue Dog,' Tom said tiredly. 'You heard what Hannah said. Time for bed.'

You Ought to Be in Pictures

The guesthouse was old and in need of a coat of paint, but it had grown old gracefully. To Allie, accustomed to the tightly packed houses of the inner city, it was a mansion. A mansion surrounded by lush green plants with exotic flowers. At least, they looked exotic to her. She'd recognised some of them as hibiscus, but those were in colours she'd never seen before. One stunted shrub bloomed irregularly in the Australia Street garden, and a few of her neighbours grew them in pots, but they bore small red flowers while these blooms were giants, with each bush bearing a different colour. Orange. Peach. Pink. Red. Absolutely beautiful.

Beneath and surrounding the hibiscus were impatiens in shades of deep purple through to pale pink, while a mix of bright and dark reds edged the pathway to the front door. A hedging of pink and white Sasanqua camellias lined the near side of a driveway. It sloped down beside the house and disappeared around a corner. On the far side, between the driveway and a paling fence, a narrow garden displayed gardenias interspersed with bracken fern. Two small squares of lawn would have put the patchy green of the Australia Street lawn to shame.

Some people might have thought the brightness and mix of colours garish, but to Allie it was magical. That, combined with the strong perfume of so many gardenias, made her feel light-headed. Forcing herself to look away from the dazzle, she stared up at the house.

The bay windows on both floors were curtain-free, though they faced north so she supposed they had blinds to pull down during late afternoon. She pictured love seats behind them, with dainty antique furniture and carpets in every room. Janet had said there were twelve bedrooms, six bathrooms, a dining room large enough to seat fifty people, and a large lounge room filled with comfortable chairs where people sat and drank coffee and liqueur while they chatted to each other or read. There was a kitchen, of course, but no one was allowed inside it except the cook – beg your pardon, The Chef – and his helpers. The Chef was a man. Everyone Allie knew who cooked was female. A helper called a kitchen hand did the washing up, and there were others The Chef could order about to do all the work. Janet had said he was more like a meal planner than a cook. He told the others what to do and made sure they did it the way he said. He only cooked on special occasions or for special people, like the boss lady's fiftieth birthday. Allie thought the helpers and the dish-washer would be women. Though come to think of it, Colin washed the dishes most nights at Grandma's house, and he sometimes cooked. He liked to cook, Hannah reported hearing him say, and added that she'd love to have a man around the house who didn't mind doing the cooking.

Okay, Allie, stop putting it off, she told herself. She had come to ask for a job. Not that she fancied cleaning up other people's messes, but because she could get food and board here as part of her salary, which meant being able to save all her pay, except for buying clothes of course, and maybe going to see a movie now and then. She loved movies, loved pretending to be an actress, though only when she was alone in her bedroom – something left over from her primary school days. All her girlfriends were the same. But while most of them left school, went to work and dreamed of meeting a movie star like Clark Gable who would sweep them off their feet, she wanted to make it on her own. She was never going to be another Vivien Leigh, but she could be a lawyer to the movie stars. Or a doctor, though she was a bit queasy when it came to blood. Failing those two, meaning if she couldn't afford all the necessary years at university, she'd like to teach. That was her dream and she was never going to let it go. She was never going to be like her mother and work like a slave for hardly any pay.

Anyway, if she had to be a housemaid/waitress for a year or two, she would rather work with Janet than be with strangers. And she loved the sound of the uniforms. She hadn't seen them yet, but black and white, and maroon in particular, all looked good on her. The owner of the place would see that straight away. She must know about clothes and colours or she wouldn't have picked such smart uniforms. No doubt she'd see that Allie had dress sense too. Everyone admired this pink dress with its Chinese collar, dropped waist and full skirt, and how many times had someone said it looked as though it had been made especially for her? Allie chose it, but Mum had paid it off on lay-by, a late birthday present.

Remembering that made her feel uncomfortable. Mum was struggling to pay the bills. She should have told her to keep the money instead of wasting it on a dress. But once she saw it, she couldn't resist. And everybody should have a birthday present, shouldn't they? There was that blue dress, but it was rolled in a bundle in the back of her wardrobe. She hadn't been able to bear looking at it after what happened to Mr Lenahan. And knowing it was second-hand and not new like Dad promised hadn't helped. Besides, Janet was right and it was much too young-looking for a sixteen-year-old. A young woman now, with periods, and hair on her private parts. And having to shave under her arms and the lower half of her legs. That was the worst part. Something else Janet had been right about.

Yes, she definitely looked her best, though she did feel queer about leaving home and being amongst people she didn't know. She'd thrown up over the side of the ferry on her way to Cremorne Point. She tried to convince herself it was seasickness, but she'd been aboard the ferry to Manly going round the heads many times, often with stormy weather making the ferry pitch and roll, yet she'd never been sick then. Nerves were her problem. She didn't know how to go about getting a job. Did she just bowl up to the boss lady and ask straight out, no mucking around, or should she ask for a time to come back?

Now she thought about it, she remembered Janet saying something about an interview. Oh God, she should have talked to Janet about this. She'd meant to, but her sister hadn't been home for ages. Seemed she was always working or going out with her friends: probably other housemaid/waitresses. There were lots of guesthouses and private hotels on this side of the harbour.

I should have phoned, she told herself, but I didn't. The sensible thing to do now is go home, phone from the corner shop and make an appointment. But I can't remember the boss lady's name. I'm not sure if Janet ever mentioned it. Can't call her Mrs Boss, can I?

'Stupid!' she berated herself.

'Not meaning me of course,' a male voice said from behind her.

A car had pulled up at the kerb while she was daydreaming. A beautiful car, black and shiny. One she couldn't help staring at until she saw the man driving it and couldn't take her eyes off him. Early twenties maybe. White-blond hair, tanned and freckle-free skin, and the bluest of eyes. That same deep blue like her dad. Their colour matched his shirt and she wondered if that was on purpose. Thinking about movie stars, he could easily be one, she thought, and blushed when he stared back at her, his smile showing white, even teeth.

'No, I . . . I was talking about me,' she stammered, feeling her face and neck staining redder, if that were possible.

'Why are you stupid?' he asked.

'You're on the wrong side of the road,' she pointed out to avoid answering his question.

He nodded, a quick nod with his chin held up and the smile growing wider. It looked untrustworthy to her, the smile and the admiration in his eyes. Wolfish somehow. She was too dazzled by it to care.

'And that makes me liable for a fine if I'm caught,' he said. 'I know it, so I guess I'm the stupid one. But you drew me like a magnet. Are you going to stay here?' He nodded towards the mansion posing as a guesthouse. 'I can recommend it. Good food. Nice rooms.'

'No. I . . .' She paused, not wanting to tell him she hoped to find a job. He was rich, she could tell that by the car even if he hadn't more or less said he lived here. Janet had told her that ordinary workers wouldn't be able to afford one of these rooms. 'I think that's a nice car,' she finished.

He did the nodding smiling thing again before saying, 'Thirty-eight Oldsmobile. Ten years on her, though you wouldn't know it to look at her, would you? She's beautiful to drive. Would you care to come for a spin?'

She wanted to say yes. She wanted that more than anything. Instead she said, 'I've never been in a car,' then wished she could disappear in a puff of smoke.

'You mean you've never been in an Oldsmobile?'

Too late now. She wasn't going to lie. 'No, I've never been in a car.'

'Never?'

Was he laughing at her? Who did he think he was?

'None of my kin can afford a car,' she said. 'But we're quite happy to walk or catch a tram. It's better for your health.' Let him put that in his pipe and smoke it! Tilting her chin up and matching his wide smile but leaving out the admiration, she opened the gate and strode down the path to the front door.

I can't just go barging in, she thought, and glanced back. He was still there, watching her. Opening the door, she barged in anyway and closed it behind her. Her mouth dropped open as she looked around.

The furniture was disappointing, being large and chunky and plain, much like the furniture in her home, but the carpet made her want to take off her shoes. Instead of blinds, the bay windows had velvet curtains tied back with golden cords. White roses surrounded by circles were carved into the high ceiling, evenly spaced, with sprays of pale pink roses along the cornice, and she could see three chandeliers in the hallway, a larger one in this entrance hall. Entrance room. It was too large to be called anything else.

If the whole place is like this, it would be heaven to live here and almost as good to be working here, she thought while walking slowly down the hall, studying a row of paintings. City street scenes entitled London and Paris hung on the palest of pink walls.

'Allie, what d'you think you're doing?' Janet hissed, seeming to come out of nowhere, and before Allie could answer, grabbed her arm and rushed her along a hallway and down a flight of stairs.

'Wait,' Allie said, digging in her heels to stop the rush. 'Where are you taking me?'

'To my room. Ya have to go out to get into it. Why are ya here? Is there something wrong at home? And don't ya know better than to go breezing in the front door?'

They'd gone along another hallway and into a garden that was just as colourful and lush as the one out front.

'I wanted to see if I could get a job. That maroon high-waister really looks good. Stop pulling at me.'

'You get me the bloody sack and I'll thump ya,' Janet said through gritted teeth. 'There's no jobs vacant so ya can't work here. You're too young anyway. Ya gotter be eighteen.'

'You weren't eighteen when you started here.'

'I put me age up and she didn't ask for proof.'

'Then why can't I do that?'

'Because ya don't look any older than sixteen. Now go home. Stop!' she shouted when Allie turned back towards the door. 'Not that way. Along the path.' She pointed. 'Don't talk to anyone. And why would ya want to foller me into this job anyway?'

'We're going to move to Grandma's place because Mum's new job doesn't pay as much as the taxi and we can't afford to stay in the old house,' Allie blurted out. Pausing long enough to draw in a breath, she added, 'Getting a top pass in my Intermediate Certificate helped me get that bursary for two years but I know Grandma will be at me to leave right away. I want to get a job so I can defer the bursary and save up to go back but I don't want to be by myself in a strange place.'

'Poor little Allie wants to stay at school forever.' Janet's tone matched her sneering expression. 'My heart bleeds for ya.'

Allie felt as if she'd been smacked in the face. 'I despise you, Janet,' she said.

'That's exactly how I feel about you. The little golden girl who thinks she's so smart it makes her better than everybody else. I'm glad Grandma's stopping Mum from giving ya your own way like she's always done. It's about time ya pulled yer weight.'

'You left home at just the right time, didn't you?' Allie snapped.

'Better than staying there and bludging, like you do,' Janet snapped back.

'God, you're a bitch.'

'I know. I like meself that way. Hang on.' Janet grabbed her arm when she turned towards the pathway to the front. 'Have ya seen anything of Dad? Has he been around?'

Allie hesitated. She wanted to walk away, but she was desperate to talk about her father. Her mother always cut her off if she mentioned his name. Hal grew sad.

'No,' she finally said. 'He hasn't been near us except when he's delivering the bread.'

'Are ya going round to the bakery to see him?'

Allie gave a quick shake of her head.

'Why not?'

'He left us, Janet. That's why not.'

'I don't know if he really left *us*,' Janet said slowly, as if she was just now making that conclusion. 'He just left Mum. When ya think about it, it was the best thing for both of them,' she grimaced. 'Though he could've waited a bit before moving in with Mrs Lenahan. Still, I don't know that we should be taking sides. Ya should go see him, Allie.'

'What about you?'

'I don't want to. Not for a while. I'm too pee'd off with him and he knows that. He knows he got me goat even before he left. But you always thought he was a little tin god.'

'He's never come to see me since he left, and I think he deliberately avoids me.'

Janet shrugged. 'He most likely thinks you're still pee'd off with him too. He's never been all that great at facing up to anything, has he?'

'He fought in the war, Janet.'

'Ha! He was in bloody Darwin. Bludging.' Janet said dismissively.

'What do you know about it?' Allie snapped.

'They haven't handed out medals to anyone who sat out the war in Darwin, have they?'

'Well, he was a boxer once. You have to be brave to do that.'

'Ya don't have to have brains to get yer head punched around a square of canvas, while people with enough sense not to do the same thing sits and cheers.'

'How can you talk about him that way?'

Janet grinned. 'Got you going, didn't it? Now ya might go see him and you'd both be happy.'

'*You're* still angry with him.'

'Yeah, well. It gets to ya, doesn't it? Him walking out like that. But he's not the first dad to leave home and he won't be the last. With Mum it was both her mum and her dad. That's a heck of a lot worse. I mean, if your own mum and dad don't like ya enough to stick around, who will?'

'I guess. At least ours are still around even if they're not together.'

Janet nodded. 'So we'll take turns missing him and hating him, but we'll get over it sooner or later. That's what Grandma said the other day and she'd be right.'

'About getting me a job here . . . ,' Allie began.

'Jeez, that was a quick turnaround. I thought ya wanted to talk about Dad.'

'I have to think.'

'Good luck then, but as for working here, forget it. To tell the truth, Allie, you're one of the reasons why I left home. I got sick of fighting with ya. We were getting as bad as Mum and Dad.'

'So now we can be more like friends?' Allie asked, liking that idea.

'Ya can forget that. And I don't wanna talk about it. You'll get the next ferry if ya hurry.'

Allie swallowed back a rush of tears and strode away. She should have known. It had always been like this. She'd have to find another guesthouse. She'd go home and put on some of her mum's make-up, maybe borrow a more adult-looking dress from one of the cousins, then she'd go from place to place until someone took her on. If Janet could do it, so could she.

'Is there a problem?'

It was the blond movie star again, leaning against his car and smoking a cigarette. Surely he wasn't waiting for her? Of course not, he couldn't have known she'd be back so soon.

'I'm in a hurry to catch the next ferry. I . . . ar . . . I'd forgotten I have an appointment,' she said, slowing to an amble.

'I'll drive you to the wharf.'

She shook her head. Her mum would kill her if she got into a car with a strange man. But she couldn't say that. Not to him.

'It's just down the road. And I don't know you,' she said.

'Jonathan Lawson. Johnny to my friends.' He grinned. 'No relation to the poet. He's a Henry and a writer and I'm a lawyer. At least, I will be when I'm finished uni.'

'A lawyer? That's wonderful. I thought you must have been in movies.'

That sounded gushy, even to her. Gushy and childish. She wanted to curl up and die.

'I wish. Would be nice though, and thanks for thinking it.'

He sounded as if he meant that.

'Actually, I was thinking the same about you.' He extended a hand. 'I'm very pleased to meet you, Miss . . .?

She caught in her breath. 'Gordon. Allie Gordon.' She'd meant to just touch his hand, but he slid his up to her wrist and closed his fingers.

'Is it true you've never been in a car?' he asked, and when she nodded, said, 'Then let me drive you to the ferry. You'll love it. Especially this car.'

He was a lawyer. The next safest thing to police. She had to be safe with a lawyer, didn't she?

'Allie? Can I speak to you for a moment please?'

Janet stood at the side gate, glaring at her.

'And she is?' Johnny Lawson asked, letting go of Allie's arm.

'My sister. And thanks for the offer.' Allie strolled around to the passenger side, trying to sound casual and unconcerned, and opened the door, saying, 'I'd love a ride in your Oldsmobile,' as she climbed inside.

'I promise to take her straight to the ferry,' he said, jumping into the driver's seat when Janet strode towards the car.

'You're not taking her anywhere,' Janet said grimly. 'I wouldn't trust ya as far as I could kick ya, Johnny Lawson. I know too much about ya.'

He looked up at her as he started the car. 'Not been spying, have you Janet? I could have you sacked for that.'

'Please yourself.' She raised her voice 'Get out of that car, Allie.'

Allie folded her arms and stared through the windscreen. Johnny Lawson grinned at Janet and gave a casual salute as he drove off.

'Now where is it we're going?' he asked.

'The ferry,' Allie reminded him.

'Tell me where you live and I'll drive you home.'

A picture flashed of Grandma and Hannah watching her drive up in this beautiful black car with a strange man who looked as though he'd just stepped out of a movie. Grandma would say she was out of her league and accuse her of all kinds of things. She shuddered at the thought of what her mother would say to Johnny Lawson.

'The ferry will do,' she said firmly.

Minutes later, he slowed the car to a stop beside the entrance to the wharf. 'It's because we've just met, right?'

She nodded. That was as good an excuse as any.

'Will you give me your phone number so I can call you?'

'I don't have a phone.'

'Of course you don't.'

She thought for a moment he was having a shot at her but he seemed lost in thought.

'Okay,' he said, taking a pencil and a white card out of a small case beside him. Scribbling down a few digits, he held the card out to her. 'I'll give you my number and you must promise to phone me.'

She took the card without looking at it and climbed out of the car. 'Thanks for the lift.'

'I can't believe you're walking away like this,' he said, and sounded as though he meant it. Allie couldn't be sure if his frown was caused by disappointment or a wounded ego. Did he think she'd faint at his feet? What would her mother say right now?

'You'll get over it,' she told him.

'Sit here and talk to me until the ferry arrives,' he said. 'I'd like to see you again.'

'Why?' she asked.

'You are very beautiful you know.'

That was a bit of nonsense, but he sounded so sincere, so sort of . . . Young. He might be nearly a lawyer and rich, but he wasn't full of himself. The tone of his voice, the look on his face reminded her of Charlie Lenahan.

Glancing up, she saw Janet striding towards them. The head forward, elbows out sideways, fists pumping told her that a tirade of abuse was about to embarrass them all.

'I'll phone you,' she promised. 'Next Friday at five. Okay?'

'Better than okay. I'll talk to you then.'

A broad smile, a wave, a rev of the engine and he was gone. A few seconds later, Janet arrived, red-faced and out of breath.

'You're here,' she gasped. 'He did bring ya.'

'Why would you think he wouldn't?' Allie asked airily.

'I was all set to call the police if ya weren't here.'

'Oh come on, Janet,' Allie said scornfully.

'I'm not kidding, Allie. He's got a lousy reputation. Girls write letters to him, phone him up all the time and he won't answer them. Les told me that. Les Renfrew lives at the guesthouse. Him and Johnny Lawson are sort of friends. That's his car Johnny's driving. He's always borrowing it and lairing around.'

'A fine friend that Les would be, talking about his mate like that.'

'They've known each other since they were kids, Les said, and their parents are friends so they have to be mates. Anyway, I don't have to explain all this to you. Just stay away from him. He's what Les calls a womaniser. He gets girls into bed, then he dumps them.'

'He won't be doing that to me.'

'Not when he finds out your age, he won't,' Janet said grimly. 'I'll tell him yer only sixteen and still going to school.'

'I won't be going to school, will I? I told you, Grandma's going to make me leave.'

'Because we're working class, Allie. Too different from the likes of Johnny Lawson. You start going out with him and ya heading for a fall. It'll just mean heartache for ya.'

'Boy, you really are jealous, aren't you?' Allie snapped.

'Jealous be buggered,' Janet said angrily. 'Yer still just a kid, Allie, and if anything happens to you with him, Mum will blame me.'

'Nothing will happen because I'm not going to see him again. I didn't tell him where I live.'

'Just as well,' Janet said, then turned and strode away.

She has no right to try and run my life, Allie thought as she watched her sister disappear around a corner. I'm a woman now. I can look after myself. Though she's probably right. Me going out with Johnny Lawson would be stupid. He probably thinks I'm easy because my family's poor. Rich people don't mix with working class. And we don't mix with them.

'That's what I think of you, Mr rich bloke Johnny Lawson,' she muttered, screwing up his card and tossing it into the water.

The Bargain Broken

'I hope I'm not too early,' Claude Macy said as Hannah opened the door to him. 'When you offered to show me around, you didn't specify a time.'

'No, it's fine. Please come in.'

Hannah gestured towards the hall, turning her face in that direction so he wouldn't see how much his presence flustered her. She'd been looking forward to meeting him again, wondering if her first impression would change after she'd got to know him. But Hal was out playing with friends and Allie had wandered off somewhere. It wasn't the impropriety of being alone in the house with a male stranger that bothered her. It was a tingling sensation, a heightened awareness of him and her and the empty house.

He hesitated. 'Are you sure? I could go and come back.'

She realised that he'd sensed something was amiss.

'No, it's just . . . The house isn't great. I mean, it isn't in a mess or anything like that. It's just . . .' She stopped and drew in a deep, calming breath. 'I'm twittering like an idiot. I feel like a schoolgirl getting a class inspection.'

He laughed aloud and she could see that he was laughing with her.

'It looks fine from here,' he said. 'The walls and ceilings look freshly painted.'

'Mill white on the ceilings, kalsomine walls,' she told him. 'It's much cheaper than paint, and it does the job of freshening and brightening, as you can see. But it's a horror to get off if you intend to use paint next time.' She led the way down the hall and into the kitchen. 'If you're clever enough, you can get it off by dampening with a wet rag, then taking off strips with a scraper, but usually only the professionals are good at that. Otherwise it's buckets of water and rubbing down with chaff bags.'

'Sounds like hard work,' he commented.

'Oh, it is. I've done it myself.'

Why am I raving on like this, she thought.

'Actually, the house looks excellent on the inside.' He made a production of looking around, studying the walls, the ceiling, the furniture. 'This kitchen dresser is beautiful work. Especially the leadlight on the doors.'

'Tom's grandfather,' Hannah said. 'He was very talented at making furniture. Would you like to have a look around outside?' There was no way she'd take him into the bedrooms. 'The outside of the house and all the yard needs a lot of work,' she added apologetically.

He nodded. 'Thank you,' and followed her outside.

When Old Harry Gordon moved into Australia Street, he'd divided his yard into four. He built a fence halfway across the width of the block, another cutting the back half vertically into two. The front of the block held the house on one side, the patchy lawn and what used to be flower gardens on the other. The back part held the quarter that was once a vegetable garden. It now grew nothing but weeds and a tangle of overgrown kikuyu grass. A fowl pen containing a ramshackle henhouse, more weeds, and a large tree occupied the last quarter.

'It's a bit of a mess,' Hannah admitted.

'This might sound stupid to you, but I'm happy with it,' he said. 'I spend much of my time in a suit and tie, imprisoned in an office, and I hate that. Here I'll be able to put on shorts and boots and get stuck in. And because there's nothing to keep, I can start from scratch. I'll build a great vegetable patch there.' He waved to the area that had once held vegetables. 'Flowers there. Roses. Carnations. Dahlias. Flowers that are great to look at either in a vase or on the plant. I'll have a ball.'

She glanced around, remembering what this yard looked like when Grandfather Harry was alive, and knew exactly what Claude meant.

'It was beautiful once,' she said.

He grimaced. 'I'm babbling on about what I want to do and forgetting this is your home, and of course you don't want to leave it.'

'Of course we don't,' Allie said as she joined them. 'I called out from the back door,' she added. 'Guess you didn't hear me.'

'Mr Macy, this is my daughter Allie.'

He held out a hand. 'I'm very pleased to meet you, Allie.'

She touched his hand then drew back.

'But you're not pleased to meet me, are you? This is the house you were born in. Clara Paterson told me that. You must hate the thought of leaving, and I'm feeling very guilty about it.'

'Then don't,' Hannah said. 'It's entirely our fault for not keeping Grandfather Harry's part of the bargain.' She glanced at Allie, speaking more for her sake than for Claude Macy's. 'I believe the agreement was that Gordons could live in this house for five shillings a week for as long as they took care of it, inside and out. That hasn't been done since Grandpa died, so it's only right we should leave.'

He smiled relief. 'Luckily, there's no shortage of rentals in this area of the city. Not a lot, but enough to choose from.'

Hannah had no intention of informing him that she couldn't afford the rent anywhere else. 'I've noticed. But if you've seen enough, would you care for a cup of tea?'

'Love one,' he said enthusiastically. 'Could I just have a look at the fowl yard first? I think this fence needs rebuilding. And that large tree in there, is that a plum tree?'

'It is, but I'd rather you didn't go in. Our rooster is very territorial.'

'He attacks anything that moves in there,' Allie stated, joining in the conversation after covertly studying Claude. 'Anything that moves anywhere, for that matter. He's pretty savage. Better than any watchdog.'

Claude laughed, obviously thinking she was exaggerating. 'Right. I've been warned.' They meandered towards the house. 'Tell me, Allie. Are you going to be all right, you and your mother and Hal?'

Hannah stopped and turned to face him. He glanced at her, but kept his attention on Allie. 'What do you think?' he added.

Allie shrugged. 'You should ask Mum.'

'Pride would make her say yes even if that weren't true.'

Hannah kept quiet, pleased by the fact that he hadn't asked the question behind her back.

'You didn't mention my dad,' Allie said.

'Mrs Paterson told me there was just you, your brother and mother here, so I assumed your father wasn't.'

'You probably heard all the gossip,' Allie said sullenly.

He nodded unsmilingly. 'Well, yes, but I didn't want to say anything that would upset you.'

'I was born here. Having to leave upsets me,' Allie said. 'You're not worried about that.'

'Enough, Allie!' Hannah said curtly.

'He doesn't need to take our house,' Allie said fiercely. 'He's got money. He could buy a house anywhere.'

Claude cut in before Hannah could answer. 'Please, let me explain.' He smiled, that smile she liked so much that lit his whole face. 'Perhaps over the cup of tea?'

'Of course.' She gestured towards the back door and followed him in, crowding Allie in front of her so she couldn't get away, and while she made the tea, Allie and Claude sat at opposite ends of the table.

'You're right, Allie,' he said, 'I don't need to take your house. But as I was telling your mother, I work in an office wearing a suit all day, and I hate it. I like working with my hands. Painting. Building. Landscaping. Gardening. When my grandfather was alive, I did those things with him. We renovated five houses altogether. He made a lot of money from them.' There was a repeat of that smile. 'It's been a while since I've had a chance to do that again, so when my accountant told me about this house, I jumped at the chance to practise what I learned from my grandad.'

'But we live here,' Allie put in.

'Yes, and I'm afraid I was selfish enough not to consider that. I thought, well, I thought you could move somewhere else and I could move in here and . . .'

'You're really going to live here?' Hannah asked, thinking she should probably warn him that the locals, the males anyway, would give him a hard time. All the families in this part of the city were manual workers. They might not take kindly to a moneyed man moving in to a house they considered as being Old Harry Gordon's. She'd have to make sure the word was passed around that he hadn't ordered her out, that she'd left of her own accord. Before she could tell him this, he continued his explanation.

'My business has people who can run it successfully without me. Probably better than me, for I don't really have the heart for it. So I plan to buy old houses and do what I love doing. But so saying,' he turned to Allie again, 'now I know what this house means to you, I won't ask you to leave.'

'But leave we will,' Hannah said firmly. 'The bargain is broken and the house desperately needs repairs, to the plumbing and electric wiring among other things.' Hesitating, she added, 'The rent must go up accordingly and much as I hate to admit it, we can't afford it.'

'I don't have to . . .' he began.

She cut him off. 'We're not desperately poor, you understand. There's no real poverty in this neighbourhood; we all manage to get along. Nobody goes hungry or without a roof over their heads. But like everyone else here, we need to watch our pennies. We're moving in with my grandmother and that helps us all. We'll be comfortable enough. She lives in this street, in the corner house, so we won't be moving far. We'll be happy there, won't we, Allie?'

Allie knew what was expected of her. 'Yes, I guess we will.'

'So now all that's settled, we'll drop the subject, drink our tea and talk of cabbages and kings.'

Allie stared at her as though she'd suddenly gone mad. 'Why would we want to talk about that?'

'*Alice in Wonderland*,' Claude said.

Hannah smiled. 'You've read it.'

'One of my favourites,' he assured her.

'Mine too,' Allie said quickly. 'I just didn't connect it for a moment.'

'What sort of books do you like to read?' he asked, and for the next hour they drank two pots of tea and talked of books, moving on to films and actors and the Old Vic tour by Vivien Leigh and Sir Laurence Olivier, then the upcoming London Olympics. They found they had identical taste in books, all being fond of crime fiction and historical nonfiction. They talked of cabbages – or gardening anyway – and Helen Keller's visit to Australia, of kings when Allie showed Claude the medallion a friend had given her. It was in celebration of the king and queen's silver anniversary. And of relatives of course, Allie naming her large extended family who lived in the area. Tom was mentioned, but only briefly, and Claude confessed that most of his kin lived in England, including his wife and son. Hannah could only surmise that he and his wife were separated. She managed to hide the fact that she was glad. Selfishly so, for even if he no longer cared for an estranged wife, he had to be missing his son.

It was Allie who commented, 'He must miss you. Your son, I mean. I know I miss my dad and he's only a few streets away.'

Claude's face darkened momentarily. Hannah could easily sense his pain.

'Yes,' he said, and immediately switched to another subject. 'I'm wondering if I can ask a favour of you?'

'Ask away,' Hannah said.

'I'm itching to start work on that yard. Would it put you out if I began digging over the vegetable patch within the next few days?'

'That would start everybody yakking,' Allie pointed out.

'Yes, of course. I didn't think.' He frowned. 'Stupid, but true. Not you, Allie,' he hastened to add. 'I mean the gossip.'

'I guess it would be all right if me or Hal was here,' she conceded.

'I couldn't care less about the gossip,' Hannah stated. 'There's no reason why you shouldn't start on the garden.'

'I could drop off the gear anyway,' he said, and she hoped he meant that as an excuse to see her again.

They walked him to the gate when he took his leave not long after three o'clock. Allie shook his hand with much more warmth than the earlier handshake. Hannah smiled relief, knowing he'd won her over from an initial dislike. That would make seeing him again easier for them all.

Bird

Nobody could remember Bird as a chick, nor was there ever an explanation as to when and how the rooster had arrived at number 19. Logic told Hannah that he had to be fourth generation. 'But if that was so,' Tom had told her, 'Bird went from an egg to fully grown in a few hours.' Which was nonsense, of course. Just as the idea that Bird was immortal had to be nonsense. Tom always denied it if she accused him, but she had a sneaking suspicion that he had a mate somewhere that bred these fowls. She had long ago decided that when Bird grew old and close to death, Tom took the rooster to his mate and brought a younger one back.

'Why would I do that?' he'd said.

'Because the girls and Hal think it's magic and you like to keep them believing,' Hannah answered.

Tom just laughed and turned away.

But whatever the truth of Bird, she avoided going through the gate into his pen whenever possible. Today she had no choice.

Forcing herself to breathe slowly and steadily, she opened the fowl-pen gate as quietly as the broken hinge would allow. Gripping the crossbar, she pushed up, stepped forward, then lowered the bottom end again, just managing to restrain a grunt at the effort. The wooden slats had sprung loose many times as she dived out, then slammed the gate behind her, and Tom's way of mending it had been to nail on more slats in a haphazard fashion, making the whole thing ten times heavier than it should have been – and so the broken top hinge. Tom hadn't inherited the handyman talent from Grandfather Harry, and he'd never learned. 'I never had to,' he'd said more than once. 'Pop did it all, and if I tried to watch, he said I got in his road.'

Leaving the gate ajar for a quick getaway, Hannah squatted on her heels and peered up into the branches of the plum tree. It was a large tree, and though it had lost most of its leaves, there was still enough foliage to hide the rooster, especially when he wanted to hide, which he did whenever someone entered his domain. Then he would attack, seemingly out of nowhere. Hannah had been caught often enough to be wary. Bird had striped the skin on her head and arms on more occasions than she cared to count. He seemed to sense when anyone was coming to collect eggs or grab one of the hens. Crouching in a fork in the plum tree or on the henhouse roof, he'd fly down, wings partly outspread, feet extended like an eagle, spurs ready to strike. She'd never been able to catch him to clip his wings and besides, clipping wasn't really needed to keep him from flying away. He would never leave his harem.

Now she wondered what would happen when he didn't have a harem to guard. With a bit of luck he'd go looking for another fowl yard. Other than that, she'd have to leave him behind and hope Claude Macy would feed him. Hal wouldn't let her chop off Bird's head, which she'd relish doing given half a chance, even though the killing, plucking and gutting was a job she hated.

Usually, when she needed eggs or a hen, she'd send Hal to get them. Hal was the one person unafraid of Bird, the one person who could collect eggs or entice a hen to follow him through the gate without being attacked. It had been that way since he first came to live in Australia Street, seven years ago now.

Seven years, when it seemed as though he'd been with her forever. Yet how could she forget the way he looked on the day Grandma Ade thrust him into her arms, saying, 'He's Lily's son.'

As children, Lily Gatley had been Hannah's best friend until she discovered Lily's true nature. Thought of her with a child made Hannah shudder.

'She's gone off somewhere and left him on his own. The welfare people will put him in the state home if we don't take care of him,' Grandma continued. 'He's in a bad way, and if you don't want him, I'll find someone who does.'

You did not allow kin to go into homes for the unwanted. You especially couldn't shrug away this kin, this little boy with the large soulful eyes, even though he was the image of his hellish mother except for colouring. Lily had dark red hair, very pale skin, and eyes the shade of old amber. Hal was fair, freckled and blue-eyed. One look at him, seeing the tentative smile, the expression that couldn't make up its mind between pleading and wary, had won Hannah's heart. She did want him, but not for a few months, or even a year or two. She liked the idea of having a brother for Janet and Allie, and Hal looked as though he could easily be related to them, or to Janet anyway. He had the Gordon colouring, though he was short and thin, like Lily and Colin. Lily's father and Colin's mother were siblings. Both named Gatley. Colin's parents had never married.

'You know I'd love to take him, but I remember Aunt Joyce's devastation when her son-in-law claimed her grandson after he'd lived with her for all those years. You get too fond, then you have to give them up,' Hannah had said. She'd seen it happen more than once. Was it worth the heartache?

'This little boy's health and safety is worth a damn sight more than a few of your tears,' Grandma snapped.

She hedged. 'When will Lily come back for him?'

'She wouldn't dare,' Grandma said, thrusting him into Hannah's arms, then walking away, literally leaving Hannah holding the baby; a frail, undernourished little boy, his pale skin evidence of his body rarely being exposed to sunlight. He had urine scald from his waist to his knees – which proved that Lily had kept him in nappies rather than be bothered toilet-training him. He also had sores around his mouth, and the saddest eyes. There were times when she still wondered what those eyes had seen. There were times when that haunted look came back and she wondered what or who had scarred his mind as well as his body, for when he finally allowed her to bathe him – a week later and only if Grandma was present – she saw the bruises. She knew for certain then that Lily wouldn't dare come back for him. She didn't know why Grandma had refused to talk about it. But for what Lily had done to this boy, or allowed to be done to him by not watching over him, the kin would find a way to make her sorry. Lily would know that.

The strangest thing, the best thing was that Allie and Janet had gained his trust within a few days. For Hannah it had taken more than a week.

For Tom much longer, probably because he was away at war during the first few years of Hal being with them. Then, when he did arrive, he was rarely home during the daylight hours. When he was present, the harsh words flew thick and fast. Hal would retreat to the far corner beneath his bed, or against the wall under the kitchen table until Tom either went to his own bed, slamming the door behind him as a warning for Hannah to sleep on the sofa, or he went out.

Knowing she was partly to blame for those arguments, she grimaced and slid her thoughts away from Tom by concentrating on the rooster. She couldn't see him anywhere, but his brown and grubby white mottled colouring made him a master of camouflage. He could be there in the tree, waiting for her to look away. Or inside the henhouse, aiming to attack her legs if she entered.

She remembered her fear in Hal's third month with the family when she realised he'd somehow managed to open the fowl-pen gate, or climb over it, and go inside. Picturing all kinds of horrific injuries from gashed legs to gouged eyes, she had raced to his rescue and found, to her undying amazement, Hal sitting in a fork of the plum tree with his arm around a strangely docile Bird. That is, docile until Hannah entered the pen. The rooster wouldn't let her anywhere near Hal and she had to fetch Grandma to lift Hal off the branch and bring him out. Even Bird knew better than to defy Grandma. 'Give me trouble and we'll have you for dinner,' she'd warned, and it seemed for all the world that Bird knew exactly what she said, and knew she meant it.

'He likes me,' was Hal's answer when Hannah asked how he'd managed to subdue the rooster. For that matter, it was still his only statement in regards to the bird. Allie said Bird recognised the fact that Hal needed protection, like the hens. Janet said the rooster just couldn't be bothered with so small a target. Like Hannah, she was afraid of him. Allie was just wary. Tom and Bird ignored each other.

'The bird and the factory wall. My pet hates,' Hannah stated. 'Where are you, you little mongrel?'

'He's behind you,' Hal told her.

Hannah swung around. Sure enough, there was Bird, almost half as big as Hal, cradled in his arms.

'He was going to get you from the fence,' Hal said, pointing with a nod of his head to the part of the high fence separating the fowl yard from what used to be the vegetable garden.

Hannah looked up and shuddered. The rooster must have been perched above the gate as she entered. He'd have come down on top of her from behind.

'I'm going to take his head off one of these days,' she said fiercely.

'He won't let you catch him.'

Hal spoke with confidence, and Hannah knew it was true.

'I need to get those last three hens,' she told him, not adding that the family would have to live on bread and dripping for the next few days if she didn't. She was flat broke until payday. That was Friday. This was Wednesday. Claude Macy hadn't pressed her, so she'd been putting off leaving for months, but if she didn't move to Grandma's house soon, Allie, Hal and herself would be living on bread and beans. Janet ate at the boarding house where she lived and worked, and Tom was obviously being well fed by Madge Lenahan. Hannah always looked the other way when he drove the bakery cart down Australia Street, but rumour had it that he was putting on weight. The mongrel.

'Bird won't have nobody if we eat the last three chooks,' Hal said.

'He'll have you,' Hannah pointed out – rather slyly, but what else could she say?

'Is Bird coming with us to Grandma's?' Hal asked.

'Of course,' Hannah lied, not wanting to tell him that Grandma Ade would never allow this rooster to cohabit with her spoilt-rotten fowls. They were being grown for her healing soup and had to live a life of ease and comfort to be a genuine ingredient. And, she supposed, smiling to herself, they must have to be virgins. Grandma had never owned a rooster, saying they were more trouble than they were worth, Bird being the proof of that. She bought her chickens at the market or was given them as payment for her herbal remedies. How she could pat, pet and spoil her fowls, then turn them into soup was beyond anyone's ken. Of course she, Hannah, intended to stew these hens, but she never petted them. She cleaned the fowlhouse every day and raked the yard once a week, but Hal fed the birds and kept their water bowls filled. He collected the eggs and made sure the nests were clean and dry, yet he never objected when one had to be killed.

Could a city-born and bred nine-year-old understand that chickens were raised for food and not to be pets? She looked thoughtfully at Hal. This nine-year-old certainly did. And he didn't shy away from seeing it done. Was that because he had seen much worse? One day she would find Lily and ask. But then, it might be better not to know.

'I'm going to cook these last three hens,' she told Hal. 'It's either that or we go hungry. You understand?'

Hal nodded.

'You know what that means, so do you want to go inside while I do it?'

He shook his head. 'Grandma said what's to be done must be done.'

Hannah blinked. 'And you understand that?'

'Grandma said things just happen. That's the way life is and you best get used to it or you'll be miserable all the time.'

'What a wise Grandma, and a wise kid who knows it.' The voice came from behind the gate. 'Though I can't help wondering what this kid's life has been when Grandma had to tell him that. And him understanding it is even more of a worry.'

Hannah grinned as Colin stepped forward and dropped a hand on Hal's shoulder. She guessed what would happen, and it did. Bird let out a high-pitched squawk, a sound that she always thought of as his war cry, hauled himself out of Hal's restraining arms and flew at Colin, who instinctively swatted out. Bird hit the ground with a thud but bounced up onto scrawny legs and flew at Colin again. Another swat. Bird hit the dirt and bounced up again.

'Leave my bird alone!' Hal demanded and charged, head-butting Colin in the lower stomach as the rooster's spur ripped a tear down his suit jacket.

'Bloody hell!' Colin yelled as he put his right hand on Hal's forehead to stop him from charging again – the boy was aiming for his groin this time – and fended off the bird with his left. Bird feinted left, dropped onto Colin's feet and came up between his legs, beak open, ready to strike. Desperate now, Colin grabbed the rooster by the neck and threw it into the henhouse. Amid a flurry of wings and frightened squawks from the hens, Bird raced out, on the attack again.

'Jesus wept!' The yell sounded more like a hen-matching squawk as Colin raced up the yard, Bird in close pursuit, dived into the house and slammed the door behind him.

Hannah fell sideways, laughing hard enough to bring tears.

Falling

When Allie left home at five-thirty, a storm had been threatening for the past hour. The ever-thickening clouds brought the dark in early and night had arrived with a vengeance. The narrow streets where houses crowded the front fences were gloomy and strangely silent. The customary sounds of children calling, babies crying, dogs barking and radios blaring were missing. Even the usual smells were absent. Blinds drawn to block out the expected lightning restricted any light that might have shone out through the windows, and to Allie there seemed to be more shadows than there should have been. She had a feeling of someone behind her – footsteps that stopped when she turned, like in a movie she'd seen last week. Of course there was nobody. Of course she was imagining things. The memory of the movie, the dark and a quiet street can do funny things to a person's imagination.

She kept to the middle of the road, only moving to one side when a car appeared, which didn't happen too often. At this time of the evening, most people in her part of the city would be at home eating their lamb chops and three vegetables.

Anxious to leave the sense of isolation behind, she jogged most of the way to the tram stop, so it wasn't surprising she hadn't seen Charlie Lenahan. She hadn't noticed him get off the tram, but he was just a few people behind her in the queue when she bought her ferry token. He could have been following her all the way from the Lenahan house. She had to pass it on her way to the tram stop.

Halting at the top of the gangplank, she was all set to tell him off the moment he came aboard. Luckily, the wash from another ferry caused the one she was on to lurch. Grabbing the railing to save herself from a fall gave her time to see that he was with a girl she didn't know, his hand on her back to steady her.

Something inside Allie lurched harder than the one caused by the ferry. Her throat felt strangely swollen, and she had to rub her eyes to hold back tears. Yet she made her expression show she didn't care as he looked straight at her while sliding his arm around the girl.

If you could call her a girl, Allie thought. She looks to be in her twenties. Too old for him. Just because he's left school and is working a year before he goes to teachers' college doesn't mean he's an adult already.

Lifting her chin and giving him what she hoped was a withering look, she walked away, pulling the band off her head and shaking her hair loose. Not because the girl had mouse-brown straight hair while Allie's was a lustrous dark-chocolate and curly. At least, that's what she told herself. It was because the skin on her head felt hot and clammy. It had to be turning red right down past her neck, though she felt suddenly cold.

She didn't need this. It was bad enough Mum sending her to see why Janet was staying away. Janet hardly came home any more, and when she did, she'd be there for less than an hour before yelling goodbye as she raced out the door. Yet there was no need for this visit. Allie could have told her mother that the reason was Grandma's nosiness. Grandma Ade always asked a hundred questions. Anyone could see that Janet didn't want to answer them. She couldn't lie. Grandma could pick a lie a mile away. So when the questions started, Janet fled.

'Find out why,' Mum said.

'It's got to be because she's going out with someone she knows Grandma wouldn't approve of. Maybe somebody who's married,' Allie had answered, then quickly added, 'Just joking, Mum. I know Janet wouldn't do that.'

She didn't know any such thing. Janet was single-minded and stubborn. If she set her cap for a bloke, nothing would stop her, not even a wife and a dozen kids.

Allie knew she was being not only nasty but unfair, thinking of Janet in such an unpleasant way, but right now her mind was filled with unpleasantness. She knew Janet would pick a fight within minutes of their meeting. She always did. And now this. This woman with Charlie. Him putting his arm around her in that possessive way when she was old enough to be his mother. Almost anyway.

The strength of her feelings shocked Allie. Charlie being with someone else shouldn't upset her, yet she felt as if she'd been hit. She should have been over him when his family stole her father.

Be fair, Allie, she thought. You know it wasn't Charlie's fault.

She'd been angry with him all this time for being disloyal, for deceiving her. She'd blamed him to stop herself from blaming her father. He was the deserter.

She wondered if it were possible for a heart to dissolve down into a stomach. That's how she felt right now. As though she was dissolving from the upside down. She should apologise to Charlie. But if she did, she'd cry. He was watching her now with that hangdog look he'd been wearing since his father fell and died. Since her father fell in love with his family. At least, that's what it seemed like to her. Why would her dad leave his own family if he didn't think Charlie's family was better? All those boys. That's what had won him. Couldn't have been Mrs Lenahan because she wasn't a patch on Hannah Gordon, not in looks or personality. And didn't Charlie realise that the misery he felt when he lost his dad, that's how she felt now? Her anger rose. Apologise be blowed. She should tell him just what she thought of him and his brothers. Him and his mother. But she couldn't talk to him now. Not while he was with that woman.

Keeping half a boat-length between her and them, she walked in circles until the ferry chugged into Cremorne Point wharf. The moment they lowered the gangplank, she hurried off, breaking into a jog when her feet touched solid ground, not stopping until she reached the guesthouse where Janet worked. By then her anger had regressed to anxiety again at the thought of seeing Janet. Nine times out of ten, her sister made her feel inferior. Well, stupid and naïve anyway. And when Allie started asking questions as to why she hadn't been home for a while, Janet was bound to tell her off for poking her nose in where it wasn't wanted, even though she was just acting on instructions from their mother.

Come to think of it, why couldn't Mum have come herself?

She was tempted to turn around and go straight back home. But now she was here, what would be the sense of that? Yet she knew better than to go to the front door. Down the path, around the back to her room, that's where Janet would be.

Although two lights shone down on the gardens, one at the front and one at the side, the colours were muted. Which couldn't be said for the gardenias. Even with only a few on each shrub, their perfume was strong enough to take her breath away. Striding past them, she turned the corner of the house. A single light at the back shone down onto the black Oldsmobile parked at the end of the curving driveway. Allie couldn't resist walking towards it, admiring it. She was right beside it, looking in through the windscreen when a head popped up. Though she had only met him that once, and then only for fifteen minutes, she immediately recognised Johnny Lawson. He must have been bending down, fiddling with something on the floor as she approached. Now he was staring straight at her and she could tell by his expression that recognition was mutual.

'You broke your promise,' he said.

'That was ages ago.'

'I didn't forget you.'

'I didn't either. I mean, I didn't promise.'

'As good as.'

'I lost the phone number.'

It was a lie and they both knew it.

'It's all right,' he said. 'I understand. There was something about me you didn't like.'

'What are you doing?' she asked to change the subject. 'This isn't your car, is it?'

'It is now. I bought it off my mate, Les. I'm cleaning out his mess and looking for a gold pen. Les's grandparents gave it to him when he graduated from uni.'

'You've graduated?' Allie asked, not able to keep the envy out of her voice.

'Not me. Not till next year.' His smile was disarming. 'I hope you can make it to uni. I'm sure you'll go well. Your sister told me you're pretty smart.'

'Janet said that?'

'Yes, she does talk to me now.' He smiled. 'I asked about you and she said you were hoping to continue on. What do you want to study?'

She took a deep breath. 'Law.'

'Good on you. I'll be able to help. Lend you books, give you hints about studying. Maybe even help you study. That's if you let me get to know you. And you should. With the same career, we'll be bumping into each other all the time.'

He was serious. He thought she could do it. She wanted to hug him.

'Want to take the weight off your feet?' He pushed open the passenger side door. 'Maybe you can help me find that blasted pen. I promised Les I wouldn't stop looking til I found it. He's sure it's in here somewhere.'

Tempted, Allie moved closer, then stopped. 'I'm supposed to be seeing Janet.'

'I saw her go out a while ago. She wasn't on at dinner tonight. Swapped her afternoon off I think. Come on, sit and talk a while.'

Her brain seemed to be stuttering, for without consciously making a decision to move, she was in the car beside him, shoulder to shoulder, the door shut. Her body felt hot though the windows were down, the night cool.

'It's a . . . ar . . . it's a lovely car,' she said huskily. 'Where do you think that pen would be?'

Staying as close to the door as possible, she leant down and scrabbled on the floor. He followed her lead. Their hands touched. She felt as though a bolt of lightning had shot out from his fingers. Her brain must have stuttered again. Before she realised what was happening, she was sitting back and he was leaning forward and over her, kissing her. She turned her face away, trying to catch her breath.

'You're so beautiful,' he said hoarsely. 'We were meant to be together, you know that, don't you. That's why you're here.'

One hand cupped her cheek, the other her breast. She had the weirdest sensation. Falling. Dissolving. She wanted to crawl into his skin. She wanted him to crawl into hers. The warning sounded in her brain when his hand moved from her breast to her inner thigh. This must be what happened to her mother. This is how Hannah got pregnant.

Sliding across the seat, Allie shoved him away with one hand while the other fumbled at the door handle. Finding it, she pushed down and half slid, half fell out of the car.

'You don't have to run,' he said as she backed away. 'I wouldn't have forced anything on you. I wouldn't have done that.' Sliding over to the passenger seat where he could look up into her face, he added, 'I'm in the phone book, Allie. I'll be waiting for your call.'

She turned and ran. Not from him. From who she didn't want to be. Though even then she knew she'd phone him before the week was over.

'Mr Macy. This is a surprise,' Hannah said as she opened the door.

Of course it wasn't a surprise. She'd been standing on the veranda when she saw him leave Clara Paterson's house and head in the direction of number 19. Backing up, she'd stood inside the front door, hoping he would knock and silently berating herself for acting so juvenile. Yet the sight of him made her feel like a teenager again. The unsteady heartbeat, the flush, the anticipation high. She hadn't felt this way since marrying Tom and she liked the feeling.

'I hope you don't mind,' he said, extending a hand. 'I was in the neighbourhood so thought I'd drop by and say hello.'

She touched it briefly. 'No, of course not. I'm glad you did. Please come in. You remember Hal, don't you?'

'Sure I do.' He gravely shook the small hand held out to him. 'The young man with the big voice and protective nature. How are you, Hal?'

'I'm very well, thank you.'

'I'm glad to hear that.'

They stood stiffly in the hall, the adults looking down at Hal to avoid looking at each other, Hal shifting his gaze from his mother to Claude, his expression somewhere between puzzled and wary. 'Did I get it wrong?' he asked Hannah.

Claude's laugh was neither strained nor false. 'No, Hal, you got it just right,' he hastened to add, smiling from the boy to Hannah. 'It's me and your mother who got it wrong.' He grimaced. 'I have to admit I feel rather foolish. No, that's the wrong word. I feel rather adolescent.'

'I was just thinking the same thing,' Hannah said, relaxing her shoulders. 'About me I mean.'

'Don't you like him, Mum?'

Obviously reading Hannah's embarrassment, Claude answered for her. 'I think perhaps it's the opposite, Hal.' He looked into Hannah's face. 'I believe it's called mutual attraction. At least, I hope so.'

'Everyone's entitled to their beliefs,' Hannah said haughtily, then smiled when he winced and stepped back. 'Sorry, I couldn't resist.'

He nodded. 'Serves me right for being so forward.'

Hal's smile mirrored his relief. 'Would you care for a cup of tea?' he asked, again shifting his gaze from one to the other.

'What a well-mannered young man.' Claude's face showed no sign of amusement when Hal's grin wavered. 'I certainly would care for a cup of tea. But not unless you permit me to help. I believe that's the polite thing to do when you visit someone.' He flicked a glance at Hannah. 'And everyone's entitled to their beliefs.'

'Touché,' she murmured.

Hal's grin almost split his face. 'You can do the kettle then.'

'Thank you.'

'But it's heavy,' Hal warned.

Claude nodded. 'Yes, I know.'

'You overheard that the first time you were here?' Hannah asked.

'And my memory is excellent. I hope you don't mind?'

'I'm not sure.'

'About me accepting the cup of tea,' he said, taking Hal's out-stretched hand. 'It's too late to be pardoned for the other.'

'You're very welcome.'

Claude pretended to resist as Hal dragged him towards the kitchen. 'This is a great kid you have here.'

She nodded. 'I know it.'

'Mum? Are you there, Mum?'

Hannah tried not to let her annoyance show as Janet appeared in the kitchen doorway. Not that she didn't want to see her eldest daughter. She just wished Janet had chosen another time to drop in.

'Janet? I didn't expect you. Allie is on her way to your place to find out why we hadn't seen you for so long.'

Janet smiled politely at Claude. 'Sorry, I had no way of letting you know. You'll have to get a telephone. How do you do?' She held out a hand. 'I'm Janet. The eldest.'

Hannah swallowed back a sigh of relief. A few months ago, Janet would have asked Claude outright who he was, why he was here almost alone with her mother, and probably added something even more embarrassing. Apparently working in a swank guesthouse had taught her the manners she, Hannah, had never been able to instil. Janet was too much like her father, in nature as well as looks.

'Pleased to meet you, Janet. Claude Macy's the name.'

'Right. The owner.'

'We're making a cup of tea,' Hal said importantly.

'Then I'm just in time. Lucky me.' Janet's wink as she half-turned away from Claude and looked at her mother could only be called wicked. 'Lucky you.'

'Mr Macy's gunner help me,' Hal said, pulling at his hand again.

'Claude. Please call me Claude. With your mother's permission? I'm sure we'll get to know each other well enough to make that okay.'

'Hmmm,' Hannah said, not able to hold back a smile when Janet raised her eyebrows and licked her lips behind Claude's back.

Janet sat on the chair that was known as her chair, even though she'd been gone for months. 'Do you visit often?' she asked Claude as he manoeuvred the heavy kettle, following Hal's pointed instructions.

'No, this is my third visit, and I'm hoping it's not my last.'

'I'm sure it won't be,' Janet answered. 'But you're not intending to kick Mum out sometime soon, I hope.'

'Of course not. Tell me, Janet. What do you do?'

The conversation stayed with small talk from then on, polite but relaxed. Hal had obviously taken a shine to Claude, who just as obviously responded in kind. When the teapot had been emptied, and Hal's toy soldiers had been examined and applauded, Claude took his leave, offering to drop Janet off at the quay. His car was parked in front of Mrs Paterson's house. Hannah could see that Janet was tempted to refuse, wanting to stay and hear more about Claude and what Hannah thought of him. But, 'This'll keep, I want to hear it all,' she'd muttered in an aside, and accepted the invitation. Hannah and Hal stood on the veranda, watching, until the car rounded the corner and disappeared from sight.

Somebody's Out There

Walking home from the tram stop, Allie had that feeling of being followed again. This time she knew it wasn't Charlie Lenahan. She might have missed him on the ferry. It was more crowded than usual and she had tucked herself away in a corner, not wanting to meet him face to face. He surely would have read Johnny Lawson on hers. What he had done. The kissing. Touching her breast. How he had made her feel. Her face flamed at the memory.

But Charlie hadn't been on the almost empty tram. She would have seen him. So why this feeling of being followed? She quickened her pace, then stopped suddenly. There. Definitely two footfalls after hers. Two strange footfalls, as though the owner had a limp. It couldn't be Charlie. She looked around. The streets were deserted. Should she knock on the door of the nearest house? But what would she say? I'm sorry for disturbing you but there's someone out there? That didn't make sense when there was no one in sight. Nothing in sight really. Except for pools of light under the street lights, and cracks around drawn blinds, the street was ink black.

A cat ran across her path. She stifled a scream by chewing on a knuckle. Tears of fear prickled her eyes. Her skin felt icy, her legs leaden as though her blood had ceased to flow. Terror quickened the beat of her heart when the mournful howl of a dog sounded from somewhere close by. She remembered Grandma saying that a dog howling late on a dark night meant death was nearby. Leaping forward suddenly, she sprinted around the corner into Australia Street but skidded to a stop when she reached the wall. There were just two street lights, and between them, large pools of darkness. Anybody could be hiding in there. Yet whoever was following her had to be behind her. But maybe that was her imagination. Maybe the real danger lay ahead.

'Is anyone there?' she called hoarsely, and immediately wished she hadn't. If somebody was there, somebody up to no good, he wouldn't be likely to answer but he'd know she was running scared.

'Stupid,' she told herself, and clenched both hands in an effort to still the trembling. Should she scream or run or both? Stretching her shoulders back, she took a deep breath.

'Is that you, Allie?' a male voice called from behind her.

She swung around. It was a man, short and stocky and favouring his right leg. His wooden right leg. Her breath escaped in a whispered, 'Oh God.'

'Mr Peters, it's you,' she said thankfully. Her voice caught as she battled to hold back tears for the third time that night, though for an entirely different reason. This time it was relief.

'Sorry if I scared you,' he said as he limped towards her. 'I should have called out sooner. I saw you get off the tram but I was a fair way back.' His voice sounded slurred, as though he'd been drinking.

A drunk somebody I know is a lot better than a stranger any day, she thought as he reached her, even though she had never liked Fred Peters. He was a dour man, full of himself and God, always preaching. He'd become grumpier and even more judgemental since Maisie's disappearance. But if there was someone else out there, he'd surely cause them to back off. At this particular moment, she felt like giving him the biggest hug he'd ever had. Which she might have done if he hadn't twisted his face into that nasty, accusing look, as if he knew she'd been thinking about Johnny Lawson and the way he made her feel.

'You shouldn't be out at this time of night, not on your own. It's dangerous,' he said harshly.

She tried to step back. The wall stopped her. He wasn't tall but he was a big man. Broad. She couldn't see around him. All she could see was him, his face creased in a scowl, his eyes narrowed to slits. She felt a flutter of that fear again.

'I went to see my sister. You know, Janet. Maisie's best friend? Mum sent me.'

'She shouldn't let you go out on your own at night.' He grabbed her arm. Shook it. 'Anything could happen. You could disappear forever.'

'Leave me alone!' she cried out.

He winced, as though she had hit him. Holding up both hands, palms vertical as if meaning to ward her off, he stepped back. Allie quickly moved around him, feeling rather foolish when he winced again. She had known Fred Peters all her life. He had always been morose, keeping mostly to himself and never speaking unless someone spoke to him. She remembered Grandma Ade saying he'd once been an easy-going man, popular with everyone in the neighbourhood though a bit on the shy side. Losing half his leg and two brothers in France during the war had taken away his sense of humour and his ability to make friends. Losing Maisie had been the final straw. Some people said he was close to being mad. Yet as Allie looked in his face now, seeing that scowl turn to consternation, she felt a rush of pity.

'It's all right, Mr Peters. I guess I'm a bit jumpy. The dark and the quietness and everything.'

He nodded, and stepped further back. Until then, he had blocked out the figure standing at the school corner.

'Is that you, Dad?' Allie called.

Of course it wasn't her father. Whoever stood up there was short and slight. She had just wanted it to be her dad because she still felt nervous. Mr Peters had that strange, scowly look on his face again.

'A girl. What's she doing out so late all by herself?' he said, using that same harsh tone.

Allie ignored the question. 'Hello there, are you all right?' she called.

Whoever it was turned away when a voice answered, 'Allie, is that you?'

Her mother appeared under the first light down Australia Street. Allie glanced at her, then back towards the corner. The girl had disappeared.

'Yes, Mum. It's me.'

'Come on then, I'm waiting.'

'Go on ahead, Allie,' Mr Peters said. 'I'm in no hurry. Just taking the air before bedtime.'

Allie watched as he walked away towards the corner, as quickly as his pronounced limp would allow. Swinging around, she ran down the street.

'I thought I heard you call out to your dad,' Hannah said as Allie reached her.

'There was somebody standing at the corner, a girl I think, though for a second I thought it was him. Probably because I've seen him hanging around Australia Street a couple of times at night, usually across from our house. Checking on us I suppose.'

'Or checking on his precious wall,' Hannah muttered sourly.

Even what could be seen as a slur on her father couldn't dull Allie's gratitude at Hannah being there. Linking arms, she said, 'Janet wasn't home.'

Hannah gave her a surprised, pleased look and hugged her arm closer. 'She arrived not long after you left. Your trams must have passed each other. I guessed you'd be on the nine o'clock tram coming home and thought I'd walk up to meet you. Sorry you had the trip for nothing, love.'

Oh, it wasn't for nothing, Allie thought, glad the darkness hid the rush of blood to her face as she again thought of Johnny Lawson.

Prettied Up

Tom sat up on the bunk and looked at the clock. Five-thirty.

'Why can't a bloke sleep in any more?' he asked Blue Dog, who was curled up on the next bunk. 'Gorn,' he added, 'If yer gunner ignore me, ya can take yerself outside and sleep in yer kennel like yer supposed to.'

Blue Dog didn't move.

'Gorn, I said. Hop it.'

An eye opened, studied him for less than a second, then closed again.

'All right, but you'll get it if Madge catches ya.' Tom moved sideways on the bunk to look through a crack in the plastic strips covering the door opening. Dark was hanging around, but a full moon and a sky full of stars boasted that the day would be a good one.

Bob had built this veranda onto the back of the house not long after young Bobby was born. He'd boarded it halfway up, covering the upper half with screen wire. Along with the plastic strips, that kept out the mozzies and flies. Apart from four bunks – the boys liked to sleep out here on hot nights – and the bedside table, the only furniture was a small but sturdy table and five chairs. There was no covering on the floor, and if you played around, wrestling one of the boys on it, you ended up with a bum full of splinters, and muscles giving you heck the next day. Tom had found that out during the second week of his stay here. Unlike Hal, who wasn't fond of rough-housing, Larry and young Bobby liked to mock battle. Sometimes with wooden swords, though Tom had banned them when he got whacked over the head one day. By accident, Larry said, but Tom had to wonder at that. Larry was the last of the three boys to take a shine to him. Now they got along like a house on fire, him and all of Bob's boys. But going back to the mock battles, wrestling was the favourite. Boxing gloves second. They didn't pull punches and some of those punches hurt, but how could a bloke worry about that?

Especially a bloke like me, he thought, who never had brothers or sisters, no dad to muck around with, not even a mum. The grandparents were past the mucking around stage by the time I reached it. Well, that isn't quite true. Pop was too busy with his gardens and his chooks, Grandma with her housework, cooking and bottling fruit. They never had much time for horsing around, or the inclination for it. How many times did I hear, 'Not now, Tom, go find a mate to play with.'

He had Hal, but Hal was a quiet kind of kid. He didn't mind playing handball against the wall, and he'd get out in Australia Street with the kids for cricket, but he preferred painting and drawing and suchlike to physical games. Grandma Ade was giving him lessons on that ancient piano of hers, and Hannah had often said she'd get him painting lessons one day when she could afford it.

But then, that would've been one of her snide ways of having a go at me. If she cottons on to this Macy feller like she seems to be doing, maybe he'll pay for Hal to fool around with paints.

He rubbed his head, noting with satisfaction that his hair was still as thick as ever. Not like that Macy bloke who's been hanging around Australia Street, making out he's there to visit old Clara Paterson. Anybody could see he'd go bald young. Thin hair. Deep widow's peak. Yair, he'll be bald by the time he's fifty. Hannah mightn't think him so special then. He's been visiting her for months now. She should realise that everybody will be gossiping about it. She shoulda shown him the door the second time he turned up, sniffing around her like a randy dog. He's kicking her out of the house she's been living in for over eighteen years, and she welcomes him with open arms. With that special smile of hers anyhow. I seen it with me own eyes. Just passing by, out for a walk, and I seen it.

Not that I've got a right to complain. I'm the one who left. Walked out on a lousy marriage that was nothing but yelling and snide remarks. Let's see, today's the fifteenth. August 15, just past six months since I moved into the bakery. Jesus but the time goes like a bloody train when a man's flat out working. But if I ever find out that she's having it off with that bloke, well, that'll be the end of me holding back from hopping into Madge's bed. And that's getting harder every night. She let me know by just about every way she could without actually saying it out loud that she'd be more than willing. Isn't fair to a bloke, that. I explained to her, nice like so she wouldn't think I wasn't interested, I explained that I'd sleep on the veranda so there'd be no talk, so the boys wouldn't get their noses out of joint. I don't want them to think I'm trying to take Bob's place in more ways than just looking after them, and I want to be able to look Hannah in the face and tell her I'm not cheating on her. Never have and never would, not till I'm sure we won't ever get back together.

Not unless I find out she's fooling around with that Macy feller. I'll be really pissed off if I'm playing it straight while she isn't.

Here I am, five-thirty on a Sunday, me one day off working in the bakery, the morning colder than a bullfrog's bum, and I'm wide awake, can't get back to sleep, freezing like a bloody fool all alone when I could be snuggled up in there with Madge.

And me thinking about that, look what's happened here. Old Willie's standing up straighter than a soldier saluting. Needs a good work-out, that's his problem. Gotter stop thinking about Madge's bed. Gotter stop thinking about Madge that way. She reads it on me face and I'm a goner. Oh Christ, that's her now.

Grabbing the blanket, he pulled it across his lap as Madge pushed open the back screen door with her shoulder. She spotted Blue Dog right away.

'Dog! Get!' she ordered, and Blue Dog hit the floor running. Leaping at the plastic strips, he almost strangled himself in his hurry to be out of there. A yelp, a thud as he hit the pathway, and he was gone.

Tom stared at her. He'd never seen this side of her before. She'd really put the wind up Blue Dog. Maybe she wasn't the marshmallow he thought she was.

'I heard you awake,' she said, smiling at him, 'so I made you some breakfast.' Placing a tray on a stool beside his bunk, she stood back, surveying it with pride. 'Bacon and eggs just how you like them, toast with vegemite, orange juice and a cuppa tea. Strong and sweet.'

'You're a bloody beauty, Madge,' he said, noting that she'd put on her best dressing-gown, the pink frilly one, and that she'd combed the sleep out of her curly hair, put on some lipstick, and coated her eyelashes with that black gunk she liked so much. Must do because she used a lot of it. Every day. But then, she liked to dress herself up, did Madge.

'What?' she asked. 'Why are you looking at me like that?'

'Not looking in any particular way,' he answered. 'Leastways, I don't think I was. Maybe I was wondering why you'd prettied yerself up so early.'

'You must know the answer to that, Tom.'

He paused, thinking she was probably fishing for a compliment. He couldn't think of one right off so he said, 'Wouldn't have a clue.'

'It's because of Hannah.' Her chin went up. 'I know I shouldn't, it's wrong of me, but I'm doing my best to compete with her. She's a natural beauty while I have to use make-up and nice clothes to make you notice me.' She corrected herself. 'Hoping you'll notice me.' She looked down at his lap. 'And I can see that you have at last.'

Tom thought about saying it was because he hadn't been to the dunny yet, but she'd know the lie. She would've heard him flush the toilet earlier on if she'd been awake long enough to cook breakfast. And it wouldn't sound the best anyway, him talking about dunnies to her. You're not supposed to mention things like that to women. He might have done with Hannah, but they were married. If I think about Hannah, that'll stop me from grabbing Madge and tossing her on her back.

Old Willie had wilted under Madge's probing eyes, but stood to attention again at that thought.

She moved closer but hung on to her elbows, hugging herself. Her chin was still up in the air as she said, 'I have to know, Tom. Will you be going back to Hannah or are you staying on?'

'I won't be going back, Madge,' he said without stopping to think about it. 'It's over, me and Hannah. It was over a long time ago and I reckon we both knew it. We just didn't say it.'

'And are you staying here?'

'I'm happy here.'

'I need to know if you're staying. If you're not, I'll stop being so forward.'

'And if I am?' he couldn't help asking.

'Then I can't see the sense of you sleeping out here alone and me in there alone. You know my meaning without me spelling it out.

I've been giving enough hints and I think you know it. You're not that slow, Tom.'

'What about the boys?'

'Their dad's been gone six months now and they think the world of you. I'm sure they'll be happy if you and I get together.'

He thought about reminding her that they couldn't get married, not while he was still married to Hannah, but she knew that. Instead, he said, 'I mean what about the boys right now?'

'It's Sunday and early, they always stay in bed until after eight.'

It was time to listen to Old Willie.

Reaching out, Tom, grabbed her hand and pulled her onto the bunk.

'What about your breakfast?' she asked, breathless already and he'd hardly touched her.

'Bugger the breakfast.' He almost ripped the frilly pink gown as he pulled the buttons out of their holes. That's when he discovered that she was naked underneath.

Long Pants

'Hal, where are you?' Janet burst through the back door and almost danced into the kitchen. 'Where is he, Mum? I've got a present for him.'

'What?'

'You'll see. Where is he? Not under the table again.' She bent down and looked. Shook her head.

Hannah smiled. 'He doesn't go under there any more.'

'No more shouting, eh? He's not out somewhere, is he? Please don't tell me he's at Grandma's. If I go there Great-Aunt Florrie will say I'm working too hard and losing weight and insist I eat something. I'll never get away because Grandma Ade will want to know every move I've made since the last time I saw her.'

'Great-Aunt Florrie's way of showing her love is to press food on you. You know that. And Grandma's just interested, Janet. You've always been one of her favourites.'

'I know, but she'll dose me because I haven't turned up for herb day this month, then she'll sit me down and grill me. Till I'm well done.'

'Yes, she will.' Hannah smiled. 'Hal's probably out back with Bird.'

'No I'm not. I'm here,' Hal said from the back door. 'Janet!' He threw himself at her, flinging his arms around her waist.

'Missed me, eh?' She picked him up, arms around his waist, hugged him hard. 'I missed you too. Lots.' She kissed him. 'I sure do miss these cuddles.'

'And I miss Dad,' he said into her neck.

'I know ya do. That's why I'm here. Just to see you. God, you're getting big.' She slid him onto his feet. 'And I brought ya a present.'

'What do you say?' Hannah asked as he took a brown paper parcel out of Janet's bag when she opened it for him.

'Thank you very much, Janet.'

'My, aren't we Mr Polite. Go on, open it.'

Taking his time, savouring the moment, he slowly pulled away the wrapping while Hannah moved closer and Janet almost danced with impatience.

'Long pants!' he cried out, his eyes shining.

'Now you're officially grown up,' Janet told him. 'Go try them on.'

He rushed away into the bathroom, throwing the door shut behind him.

'Oh God, he is growing up,' Janet groaned. 'He's shutting the door so we can't see him without his duds on.'

'Janet, you really are a doll.' Hannah grabbed her in an impulsive hug. 'You knew I couldn't afford them and he's been wanting them for so long. The other boys are starting to tease him.'

'How is he, Mum? I mean really. How is he without me and Dad?'

'He misses you both terribly, but he never says anything. You know what he's like.'

'Do you think he misses his real family? You know, his real mum?'

'I wouldn't think so. You must remember what he was like when Grandma brought him here.'

Janet thought back. 'Yeah. I remember. That Lily Gatley needs shooting.'

'Who's Lily Gatley?' Hal asked from the bathroom doorway.

'Oh wow! Don't ya look fantastic!' Janet exclaimed.

'I'll take them up tonight and you can wear them to school tomorrow,' Hannah said. 'You look so grown up, Hal.'

'Mum, you've got tears,' Janet said.

'I guess I don't want him to grow up too quick.'

'Who's Lily Gatley?' Hal asked again, frowning.

'You know the name, don't you?' Hannah asked.

Hal nodded.

'Lily is your mother.'

He shook his head. 'You're my mum.'

'That's right,' Janet said. 'Lily's yer mother and this is yer mum. Our mum.'

Hannah knelt on the floor in front of him. He had the scared, anxious look she'd been noticing for months now. He'd had it when he first joined the Gordon family, but it had gradually faded after a year and she'd thought it was gone forever. Now here it was again. Thinking back, it started a few weeks before that terrible birthday when Bob died.

'Do you remember Lily at all, Hal?' she asked.

He shook his head, then nodded. 'She's got red hair. Really red. And curly. She sleeps a lot.' He stared towards the bedroom. 'She was angry lots of the time, but not with me. With them. With him. The one with the black hair and the big nose. He didn't like me.'

'You still remember all that, do you, Hal? Or has something happened to bring it back into your mind?"

'The man with the big nose is in the dreams.'

'And Lily, your mother, do you dream about her?'

'She screams. But not at me. She doesn't look at me. The lady with the grey hair gives me my dinner. Sometimes. I think. I don't know if that's dreams too.'

'It was a bad time, eh?' Janet asked softly.

He looked up at her. 'Only the dreams. But she's coming back for me one day, Lily my mother. She told me.'

A cold shiver ran down Hannah's back. 'In the dreams?'

'I saw her.'

'Where?'

'Outside the school.'

The shiver deepened to cold fear. 'When? When was this, Hal?'

'A long time ago. Before Mr Lenahan fell off old Jessie.'

'Not since then?'

He shook his head. 'But she'll be back.'

'Did she say so?'

He shook his head again. 'I just know. Will I have to go away with her?'

'No.' Hannah said definitely. 'You will not. You're my Hal.'

'Ours.' Janet said, planting a smacking kiss on his forehead.

'But you won't be here.' His eyes filled. 'Dad won't be here. He's got those other boys now. Charlie and Larry and Bobby.'

'Hal, listen to me.' Hannah turned him towards her. 'No matter what, I'll always be your mum, and Tom will always be your dad whether he's here or around at the bakery. Do you understand that? He loves you very much.'

'Like we all do. Me and Allie and Mum and Dad,' Janet said. 'Just because me and Dad are not right here in this house doesn't change that, does it, Mum?'

'Never ever!'

'We're all a family, us and Grandma and Great-Aunt Florrie,' Hal said, seemingly satisfied.

'We are. And all the rest too. All the cousins and aunts and uncles.' Hannah's smile showed her relief. 'And now we're going to have a cup of tea. What's more, you are going to make it, Hal, now that you're practically grown up. And because this is such a special day, we'll use the best crockery.'

'I'll do the kettle,' Janet said.

Grinning broadly and with an obvious swagger, he headed for the dresser where Hannah kept the good china tea set.

House Mates

'I don't know what the fuss is all about.' Grandma Ade said as she opened out an old blanket over the kitchen table. 'You can store your furniture in Clara Paterson's house, then move in here on Sunday.'

Hannah picked up the scissors. 'Mrs Paterson?'

Handing a piece of chalk to Allie, then pointing to threadbare parts of the blanket, Grandma nodded curtly. 'Yes, that's what I said. You can have the second bedroom, the one next to Colin's. Share the double bed with Alma.'

Allie stopped marking and looked up. 'Share?' she echoed.

'I'm speaking to your mother, if you don't mind!' Grandma stated. 'I want those squares cut all the same size, and not so roughly if you please, Hannah. Leave a piece large enough to fit the ironing board. And you'll need to bring Hal's bed with you. It'll slot in under the window.'

'I'm to share with Hal too?' Allie rolled her eyes. 'I won't have any privacy.'

Pushing the remnants aside, Grandma gathered up the squares as Hannah continued cutting. On the nights when she and Great-Aunt Florrie were listening to plays on the wireless, the squares would be stitched together to make a whole blanket, or kneeling pads and kettle holders.

'So,' she said irritably, laying out another blanket, this one equally worn. 'The miss wants privacy. All right then. You can bring your own bed from the house and put it in the herb shed.'

'I'm not sleeping out there!'

Hannah noted with a sigh of relief that Allie had been tempted to slam the chalk down, but refrained at the last moment. 'Of course you're not. You'd have to move out again next week. There wouldn't be enough room once I've been to Chinatown to fill the list Grandma's just given me,' she said with mock seriousness, trying to lighten the conversation. 'Do you want me to start on that camphorated oil, Grandma?'

'Don't baby her, Hannah,' Grandma ordered. 'You've spoilt her for too long now, and though she looks like you and that foreign man your mother married, she is her father's daughter thinking of nobody but herself. And I've already powdered the gum camphor. It's in that pint bottle.' She pointed to the dresser. 'Just fill it from that jug of olive oil and put it away, then you can continue cutting the blanket.'

'It's not true!' A warning frown from Hannah made Allie lower her voice. 'I mean, I am Dad's daughter but I'm not spoilt. It's just that I'm too old to be sleeping in the same room as a boy.'

'To get back to what we were talking about before you so rudely interrupted me, Alma, I need more carron oil. You can get the ingredients together while your mother and I finish these blankets. And I suppose you'd like me to turf out Colin so you can have the third bedroom, would you?'

Hannah knew Allie didn't have a prayer of getting what she wanted. She also knew what was coming next, but was powerless to stop it.

'The walled-in back veranda is empty,' Allie began.

'What about your mother sleeping in the same room as Hal.' Grandma raised her eyebrows. 'Isn't she too old?'

'That's different. That's . . .'

'That's not you, eh? Go away, girl, before I lose my temper and put your bed out in the yard.'

Allie opened her mouth, then closed it again. She would have known through experience that arguing with Grandma Ade was useless. Worse than useless, because Grandma never forgot and sooner or later she'd make Allie pay for back-answering. If she said one more word, the bed would end up in the yard and she'd be made to sleep there for a week. Grandma would bring her into the hallway if it rained, but the moment the rain stopped, she'd be out again. Hannah remembered that from her own childhood.

Holding back a sigh of relief when Allie pressed her lips tightly shut, she avoided her daughter's beseeching look by turning aside from her.

Allie pushed the chalk across the table. Pushed, not threw, but still earned a glare from Grandma.

'I'll get the lime out of the herb shed.'

'Just a minute, miss,' Grandma said when Allie walked towards the door. 'First you can tell me if you remember the recipe.'

'Add half an ounce of slaked lime to a quart of water. Shake it, then leave it until morning. Strain off the clear liquid and mix it with an equal amount of linseed oil.' Allie lifted her chin. 'Correct?'

'Close enough,' Grandma conceded unwillingly. 'But I don't believe you'll ever be good enough to follow in my footsteps.'

Hannah cut in before Allie had a chance to answer. 'I'm not sure Mrs Paterson will want to store my furniture.'

'Of course she will,' Grandma said, motioning for Allie to leave.

Allie did so willingly, and Hannah knew she'd stay away until Grandma shouted for her.

'That girl really riles me at times.' Grandma heaved an irritable sigh. 'She's bone lazy.'

'That's not true,' Hannah protested. 'Allie has schoolwork, she does twice her share of the housework now Janet's gone, as well as studying and working at the fruit shop weekends and afternoons. You'd hardly call that lazy, Grandma.'

'I asked her two days ago to pound those comfrey roots and they're still not done.'

'She can't do everything!'

'Tell that to Jean. That ulcer on her leg is taking its time to heal and she needs that comfrey.'

'Then I'll do it. Or Hal or Colin.'

Grandma gave a one shoulder shrug, signifying an end to that conversation. 'About Clara Paterson,' she said. 'I shouldn't have to explain when I tell you what's what, but I will this once because I know living with Tom Gordon has made you quarrelsome. And it's made you forget your manners. You don't argue with your elders. Not that the constant state of war between you and him is any excuse for you living in separate houses. You had your trial before marriage. Hence Janet. But once you make your bed, you lie in it.'

Pausing halfway through cutting a square, Hannah straightened and looked into her grandmother's face. 'You're the one who never liked him, who said I should never have had anything to do with him in the first place.'

Grandma's stare was just as straight. 'But you ignored my advice, didn't you?'

'I'm not the one who left, Grandma.'

'I'm aware of that, though I believe you should take your share of the blame. No doubt your constant nagging and your refusal to ever bend his way drove him out. Your attitude must have made him feel useless. Which of course he was and always has been until now. At least he's doing that poor widow Lenahan and her family some good.'

Hannah slammed the scissors onto the table. 'Well I certainly hope so,' she said curtly. 'I'm sure that's just what Madge Lenahan planned the moment he walked in the door after Bob's accident.'

'That's what you think, is it?' Grandma asked, waving at her to continue cutting.

Hannah made no attempt to curb her rising temper. 'Any other woman would have pulled up her socks and got on with her life, but not Madge Lenahan. She had to have someone to fall back on, and the first idiot she clapped eyes on happened to be my husband.'

'I see,' Grandma said as she picked up the scissors and began cutting. 'Leaving you heartbroken I suppose?' she asked without looking up.

'No, I wasn't heartbroken, but I was angry. Angry and humiliated. I put up with a lot from Tom after the war. His drinking, not working. Most of the time I kept him. I fed him, bought his clothes, put up with his drunken behaviour. And look what I got for it.' Hannah kept her voice low, though anger was plain in her tone, her narrowed eyes and clenched fists.

'And tell me, dear, do you think you're the only woman whose husband came back from that war a changed man?' Grandma asked, still not looking up. 'Did he beat you like Gus Markham beat Doreen? Did he sit in a corner and stare at the wall for hours on end like Jean's husband, Dally? Or perhaps he has screaming nightmares, like Colin.'

'Grandma, Colin was a prisoner of war. Other men saw untold horrors across the other side of the world. Tom never left Australia, for heaven's sake!'

'Darwin was bombed, Hannah.' Grandma looked up at last. 'For a whole year the Japanese dropped bombs on that place. Haven't you seen pictures of the devastation? Has Tom ever told you exactly what he saw, what he went through?'

Hannah refused to be diverted. 'He told me nothing, but he did use and abuse me. Constantly. Accusing me of things that didn't happen. I stayed loyal while he was away, you know that, and I stayed with him when he returned even when I wanted to run. Let me finish.' She held up a hand when Grandma opened her mouth to speak. 'I'll be the first one to admit that I don't miss him, I don't want him back. But what gets to me, what really hurts is that he works like a slave at that bakery, besides keeping up a vegetable garden and doing jobs around the house. He's even stopped drinking.' Her face twisted. 'So why couldn't he have done that for me?' she cried out. 'Why couldn't he do all that for his own kids?'

Hannah wanted to say more, to spill out all the things that were twisting her insides, to have Grandma salve her hurts the way the carron oil would salve a burn. But Allie could walk in at any moment. Knowing her daughter's blind devotion to Tom, she couldn't face her with Tom's inability to love them, to take care of them the way he should. She bit down on her lip, holding in the words, knowing if she spoke them, she would cry.

It was Grandma who stopped her from breaking down by saying, 'It was still your mistake in the first place, not choosing wisely, so don't blame others for your own bad choices.'

Hannah stared at her, stunned that she could be so insensitive. Grandma didn't seem to notice.

'Now, back to what I wanted to tell you,' she said, gathering the last of the blanket squares. 'Clara Paterson hasn't got any furniture to speak of. She sold it off a piece at a time in order to feed herself, so I'd say she'll be glad to fill her rooms again. A word of warning though. Clara will be selling off your goods too the moment she starts to feel the pinch. You know yourself how hard it is to pay rent and bills and keep food on the table, and nobody's going to go hungry when there's something in the house to sell. Here.'

Straightening her back, she handed Hannah a handkerchief out of her apron pocket. Hannah took it, wiped her eyes and blew her nose as Grandma turned away and placed the blanket squares on a chair behind her. Hannah recognised that as her grandmother's way of allowing her, Hannah, to get her emotions under control. She also knew the change of subject was for the same reason.

'So if you want to hang on to what you've got, you'll find a place quick smart,' Grandma continued. 'And as for you, missy.' She looked up as Allie entered the room. 'You know full well I keep that veranda room free. Nobody stays in it for more than a week. So if you want it for a week, that's fine by me. But then you'll leave this house for good. Maybe your father will make room for you if his woman allows it. If that doesn't suit and you don't want to sleep in with your mother and Hal, there's the herb shed, or we can put the settee in the hallway. I'll hear no more from either of you. Now off you go to see Clara Paterson.'

Adding a sniff as a full stop – her way of ending the conversation – she walked away into the backyard. Yet before she did, Hannah saw the tears in her eyes.

'I don't know why the old dragon has to keep the veranda room empty,' Allie muttered as she followed her mother out onto the footpath. 'And I don't know how she can ignore the way we feel about anything.'

'She doesn't, Allie. Not really.' Hannah put an arm around Allie's shoulders. 'I was getting a bit too emotional back there and I think you might have too if she hadn't cut it off.'

'So?'

'So there's a time and place, and it's never while Grandma's nearby,' Hannah told her. 'She's terrific with people in trouble, unless they're people she loves. Then she's afraid she'll break down and show how soft she really is.'

'Why? I don't understand.'

'I don't understand it either. That's just her. And about that veranda room. It's kept for emergencies, you must have seen that by now. It's for women and kids who've been abused. Somewhere to stay until Grandma finds them a safe place. Just be glad she's taking us in or we might have been sleeping in the park. I'm broke, and I still owe rent on the old house.'

Her face drooped into lines of sadness as they passed number 19, though she'd forced herself to look the other way. It was just too much of a struggle to stay on. Determined not to take advantage of a growing friendship, she had been voluntarily paying the same rent as other houses along the street. They weren't poor enough to starve, but with Allie and Hal still in school, paying for anything except the bare necessities was just too hard and she was tired of the struggle. It wouldn't be easy living with Grandma again, but they'd cope.

And who knows what the future will bring, she thought.

'I could win the lottery any day,' she said. 'At least, I could if I bought a ticket.'

Allie had stopped to rest a hand on the gate of number 19. 'Dad will have a fit when he finds out you've left. He's lived here since he was a baby.'

Hannah shook her head. 'I don't believe you, Allie. Who is it that left?'

'He'd have come back.'

'And you think I'd have him back after him living with Madge Lenahan all this time without a by-your-leave or even a see-you-later? I thought I'd made the answer to that pretty clear.'

'You only married him because you were pregnant with Janet. I heard him say that to you. You never loved him, did you?'

'He wore it out,' Hannah said wearily.

'You shouldn't leave the furniture with Mrs Paterson anyway. What if she starts selling it? Dad says it belonged to Grandpa and Grandma Gordon, so it's really his.'

'I'll pretend I didn't hear that. Come on, hurry up. We'll see Mrs Paterson, then we'll have to try and find some helpers to move the furniture.'

'We could ask Dad.'

Hannah knocked on Mrs Paterson's door. 'And a cow could jump over the moon.'

Allie's expression was close to being sly as she gave her mother a sideways look. 'I suppose he'll be too busy helping Mrs Lenahan in the way he's never helped you.'

'Yes, I suppose he will. And the word is us, not you. He's never helped us,' Hannah answered, emphasising the 'us' and wondering why Allie was being so provocative. It's not my fault we have to move, she thought. Why does she always take her father's side? Am I such a rotten mother?

'Hannah and Allie! This is a surprise.' Clara Paterson smiled, though she looked wary as she stepped onto the porch, half-closing the door behind her.

'Hello, Mrs Paterson, I hope you're well,' Hannah said, wondering how to broach the subject of storing her furniture without turning it into a plea, which would make a refusal difficult. She didn't want that, though she couldn't help doubting Grandma's report on the emptiness of this house. Mrs Paterson had always seemed well off. A private-school accent, Tom always said when they wondered about the elderly lady's origins. It seemed she had no family.

'Thank you, I am very well. Is there some way I can help you?'

'Well, yes. I'm here to ask a favour.'

Clara's folded arms, the way she stood squarely in the doorway as though to block entry, made Hannah wonder if she should mutter some sort of an excuse and leave. She'd been surprised by the fact that she hadn't been asked in and offered a cup of tea. That was the usual procedure when neighbours called on each other. Yet despite all the years they had lived close to each other, she'd never been inside this house. For that matter, she couldn't think of anyone who had. Mrs Paterson often minded children around the neighbourhood, but never in her own home.

Allie slumped sideways, giving her mother a seemingly accidental nudge. 'It's about our furniture,' she prompted.

'I have to move out of number 19 and Grandma's allowing me to stay with her until I find somewhere else,' Hannah blurted out. 'The trouble is,' she added, slowing her speech, 'Grandma's house is bursting at the seams and I don't want to sell or give my furniture away. I was wondering if you'd have room . . .'

'What makes you think I have a need for your furniture?'

It was obvious by Mrs Paterson's attitude that Hannah had said the wrong thing, though she couldn't think what.

'I didn't mean to infer you had a need of it. It's just that I can't afford to store it. I'm already behind in my rent and there's other bills.' Hannah turned to leave. 'But you don't want to hear my problems. I'm sorry I disturbed you.'

'Wait, Hannah. Please.' Clara Paterson opened her door, then stood back, ushering Hannah and Allie inside with a wave of her hand. 'Pride goeth before a fall, or so my mother used to say. I'd be foolish to refuse you when we could both benefit. If people have guessed the sparseness of my house, it's hardly worth the effort of trying to conceal it. Look for yourself.' She pointed into the front room, which was the main bedroom in the other terrace houses and they had all been built to the same plan. This room was bare except for curtains – a pretty, rose-patterned cotton-backed with a thick grey material. One of those rough old blankets like those the Salvation Army gave away was Hannah's guess. No doubt the aim was to block out prying eyes, she thought as she followed Allie and Clara Paterson down the hallway.

The next room contained a single bed and an antique cheval mirror standing beside a matching chair. Three cotton floral print dresses, all copies of the one Mrs Paterson wore except for the colour, hung on crochet-covered wooden hangers hooked onto the picture rail, while underwear and cardigans were neatly stacked in two banana crates sanded to a smooth finish and painted brown. Another banana crate, this one upended onto its side, held a brush, a hand mirror and an ornately carved jewellery box that looked very old.

Moving on, they entered a lounge/dining room that held another antique chair, and a handmade table identical to the one on Hannah's back veranda. The kitchen, which opened onto steps going into the small backyard, held a cabinet with stained glass doors, a wood-fire copper in one corner, a gas stove holding two small pots in the other. A coin-fed gas meter was fixed to the wall beside a bare window that looked out onto next door's backyard. As in all the other rooms and the hallway, worn autumn-patterned linoleum covered the floor. The walls were painted the palest shade of blue. There were no photographs, no sign of anyone else ever being in Clara Paterson's life. The only ornaments were a few painted jars, obviously used as vases though empty now, and an Australian landscape in oils hanging in the dining room opposite the window. Hannah just managed to hold back a gasp of surprise when she saw the signature.

'It's beautiful. Fantastic,' she murmured.

'You recognise it?' Clara asked.

'I wander around the galleries whenever I get the chance,' Hannah confessed. 'And I'm lucky enough to have a friend who works at the state gallery so I get in for free.'

'This was left to me by my grandmother. One of my few treasures I'm determined to keep, though its only value is sentimental,' Clara said, her expression showing she knew Hannah had some knowledge of its true worth and pleading for her to understand.

Hannah nodded to show that she did. When you lived in a terrace house that could be broken into with a hefty shove of the front door, it would be the height of foolishness to broadcast the fact that you owned an expensive work of art.

The bathroom, which held a chip heater and an old but clean claw-footed bath, was at the bottom of the steps from the kitchen, the toilet at the far end of the yard next to a gate that opened onto a lane. The small cobbled yard held a dozen pots holding vegetable plants: silver beet, carrots, potatoes and beans. And there, the last two along looked like those foreign vegetables Maria liked to grow. Aubergine and capsicum she called them. Grandma named them eggplant and sweet pepper.

'This is great,' Hannah said as they re-entered the house. 'I won't have to split up my stuff all over the neighbourhood. I'd been thinking I would have to ask each of my kin to mind a piece of furniture for me. You're a lifesaver, Mrs Paterson.'

'Thank you, dear, you are very tactful. And please call me Clara. I see now that your grandmother has told you I have no furniture of my own. And I thought I was being discreet as I sold each piece. There's little that passes her by.' She smiled. 'It will be nice to have furniture again, and I promise you I will not sell any of it.'

'Of course you won't. Our main problem is getting it from my place to here.' Without anyone seeing us, she could have added but did not, knowing Clara would understand.

'Claude Macy will help. You, him, Allie and myself should be able to manage. And perhaps Janet?'

'Claude Macy?' Hannah asked.

'I knew his grandparents and parents, having lived near them many years ago. His mother was my school friend. Unfortunately, we lost touch after my marriage. Claude rediscovered me after his father passed away and I renewed that friendship.'

'She comes here?'

'No, dear. She is wheelchair bound. I visit her. But Claude . . .' She paused. 'Claude is very persistent. I couldn't keep him out of my home without being extremely rude so he knows of its sparseness. He offered to gift me with furniture he said his mother no longer needs, but I have no doubt he intended purchasing it. He is a kind and generous man. Of course I couldn't allow him to spend his money on me.'

'And do you know his wife?' Hannah asked, trying her best to sound casual. Claude Macy had been to her home twice more since that third visit. The first to look around the yard again and take a few measurements. The second, after he'd unloaded various garden tools, they sat at Grandfather Harry's table, drank tea and again chatted for a short while, talking about anything and everything except family ties. He had stayed an extra half hour alone with Hal on the weedy lawn, discussing school while acting out a battle with the lead soldiers. Hannah had started to hope that the attraction between Claude and herself would lead to something more.

The smile in Clara Paterson's eyes was a contradiction to the solemn tone of her voice as she answered, 'I have never met her, though I did know her family. It was a great shock to them, and to Claude, when she wouldn't return from England. Perhaps that's the reason why Claude decided he wanted to move into number 19 while he worked on the renovations. A break away from the marital home. But I'm gossiping now, aren't I?' Gesturing towards the lounge/dining room, she added, 'Would you care for a cup of tea? There are no biscuits I'm afraid, but I could make you toast spread with some of my plum jam. The plums are from your Aunt Jean's tree.'

'I'd love to say yes, but I've too much to do. I really have to go,' was Hannah's way of avoiding using any of what had to be a small and precious stock of tea and bread. Besides, she wanted to think about the fact that Claude Macy was a free man. Well, as good as. Separated anyway. Not that you're actually a free woman, Hannah, she told herself. At least, not yet.

As she followed Allie back up the hallway, a voice called from outside, 'Is anybody home?'

'Goodness gracious, who could that be?' Clara exclaimed as she hurried past them.

'Sounds like Colin,' Hannah said.

'G'day, Mrs Paterson. Allie. Hannah,' Colin said cheerfully. He stood at the doorway ahead of six men of various ages and sizes waiting by the steps. 'Grandma told me to round up a few of me mates to help with some moving. I'm the overseer. Mrs Paterson, you work out where ya want things put while that mob do the work. Best ya go open up your front door, Hannah.'

Hannah glanced down the street. Claude was standing beside Hal at the gate of number 19. She felt a thrill of pleasure.

'I think you should move anything of any possible value out of harm's way before we start,' Hannah said to Clara, nodding back towards the painting. 'The kitchen things will be first,' she added, moving past Colin onto the porch.

'I'm not sure . . .' Clara began.

'Too late to worry, Mrs P,' Colin said in the same cheerful way. 'We all know the stuff's going from there to here so ya might as well let us get on with it.'

Clara smiled wryly. 'You always were a cheeky blighter, Colin Gatley.'

'Can't help meself,' he agreed.

'It's very good of you to give up your Sunday morning for Hannah and me,' she called to the waiting men.

'Yes, thanks for that,' Hannah said. She didn't offer payment for she knew they'd refuse and have their feelings hurt into the bargain.

'That's okay,' a tall man, known of course as Shorty, said as he sauntered up the steps. 'Can't say no to a mate, specially when that mate's Hollywood here,' he added, giving Colin a friendly pat on the back that almost sent him head first into the wall.

'Go easy, mate. Don't know your own strength, do ya?' Colin grinned at Hannah. 'That's the reason I picked him. A long skinny piece of pelican poo, but strong enough to hold a bull out to pee. And I knew the rest of them would be bored, the pub being shut on a Sunday, so we're doing them a favour by giving them something to do.'

His grin widened at the chorus of objections and insults. 'That's all right, don't thank me too much,' he told his mates. 'Now we best get to it. You too, Allie. You can do ya bit. And don't go looking at me like that. Not now we're gunner be housemates.'

Allie shot a glare at him, stalked past, head in the air. Her stride faltered when she noticed Charlie and Larry Lenahan standing behind the group of men.

'And you can just go home,' she told them. 'We don't need your help.'

'That's enough!' Hannah called. 'I'm sorry, Charlie, Larry. You don't need to be rude, Allie.' But she couldn't help a twinge of satisfaction when the boys turned, heads bent, and walked away.

'They should send Dad home to us,' Allie said loudly enough for them to hear, then stalked off in the opposite direction.

'Grandma's right. You've spoilt her rotten,' Colin told Hannah. 'But I have to admit she's smart. Picking a fight and walking off gets her out of helping with the moving.'

'Like hell it does,' Hannah said. 'Allie, you wait right there,' she called, and strode after her, calling back, 'Bloody stirrer,' at Colin's shout of laughter.

'I got that impression of him too,' Claude Macy said as she reached him and Hal.

Allie had ruffled Hal's hair and given Claude a smile that looked more like a grimace before going inside.

'I'm sorry, I didn't know you were coming today,' Hannah told him.

He placed a hand over his heart. 'I hope you're not too annoyed. I thought I had made an impression.'

'You have,' Hannah said smilingly. 'But I didn't realise you intended coming back today.'

She could feel a reaching out between them and knew that had they been alone, he might have made that reaching out physical.

Aware of Colin just behind her, she added, 'You looked so out of place in my yard. Your yard.' She smiled. 'In this street for that matter.'

'He still does.' Colin said. 'Sorry, mate, you'll have to come back later. We're moving the furniture up into Mrs Paterson's place today. You'll be able to have this one on Monday.'

'I'll help,' Claude volunteered.

'What, in them clothes?'

'Should I go home and get a suit?'

Colin grinned. 'I'm not doing the lifting and carrying, mate. I'm the overseer. And I got nothing else to wear anyway.'

'G'day,' Claude said as the rest of the men joined them. 'Can you blokes do with another pair of hands?'

Shorty clapped him on the back. 'Long as ya know Hollywood there will work ya like a dog. He seen ya eyeing orf Tom's missus.'

Hannah ignored that. 'Hal, you know you have a job to do too, remember?'

'I remember,' Hal said, and ran towards the back of the house.

As she hurried inside, Hannah noticed that Claude hadn't staggered with the friendly back-slap in the way Colin had done, though knowing Colin, that might have been exaggerated. She watched from a front window for the next few minutes, wondering what would happen. The men, all Colin's friends from the Golden Barley, were obviously ribbing Claude. She wondered how much he could take. Would he lose his temper and walk off? But he must be giving as good as he got. They were all laughing now.

'They're strange animals, men,' she said aloud.

'Talking about animals, what are you gunner do about that bloody bird?' Colin asked from the doorway. 'You know Grandma won't have a bar of him.'

'I don't know what to do. I can't catch him to give him away and anyway, Hal would never forgive me if I killed Bird.'

Claude joined Colin. 'You're worried about Hal's pet rooster?'

'Bird's not exactly a pet,' Hannah said slowly, hating herself for what she was about to do but knowing she must. Hal would be devastated if something happened to Bird.

'He's a rooster,' Colin explained to Claude. 'A big bloke.' Darting a look at Hannah, he added, 'He'll be around here somewhere, waiting to introduce himself. You can bet ya bottom dollar on that.'

Hannah shook her head. 'Hal's keeping Bird in the pen while we shift the furniture.' She turned to Claude. 'Grandma Ade won't let him mix with her hens. I don't know what to do about him.'

'Maybe you'd like to keep him here, eh, mate?' Colin suggested. 'He's a great stud, that rooster. A real strutter. You'll have a yard full of chooks in no time. They'll be leaving their home in chook pens all over the country to come here once they know he's staying.'

'I have to tell you that he does tend to get a bit cranky,' Hannah confessed. 'He takes dislikes, you see. He can't stand Colin.'

'I'm sure the bird and I will be great mates.' Claude slapped Colin's shoulder. 'No offence intended. Mate.'

'No offence taken, mate,' Colin said, shoving Claude's shoulder and putting a little more effort in it than necessary.

Talk about strutting roosters, Hannah thought, smiling to herself as Claude made a show of staggering before they walked away, still fencing with words. She began shoving packed boxes into the hallway.

Stark Staring Mad

Allie shot up in bed when the first scream echoed through the house. It was followed by another, deep and throat-tearingly harsh. The third, a whimpering cry, ended in a loud, 'No. No! Please, God, don't.' Then a screaming, 'Not him. Not him.'

'Sweet Jesus,' Hannah whispered, and moments later grunted and doubled over as Hal dived onto the bed, head first into her stomach. Sliding off her, he burrowed down into the blankets, stopping beside her feet, shaking uncontrollably.

'What was it, Mum?' Allie gasped.

'Oh God. God. I don't know. Somebody's been hurt.'

'Shush,' Allie hissed when someone tapped on their door. Her face, whiter than the sheet beneath her, glowed in the semi light caused by a full moon shining through the blindless window.

I should do something. I should get up, Hannah told herself. Her body felt numb. Her muscles refused to respond. Hal began to cry.

Allie jumped out of bed and grabbed her shoes, holding one in each hand, ready to hit out with the heels. 'Who is it? Who is it?' She cleared her throat but couldn't remove the tremble. 'I've got a knife.'

'It's all right, dear. It's just me.' The door opened a crack and Great-Aunt Florrie's face appeared in the opening, outlined by the hall light behind her. 'Remember your first night here? Remember how your grandma told you about Colin's nightmares? I'm afraid he's having one now. Everything's all right. Don't be afraid. He won't hurt you.'

Allie slumped onto the side of the bed and knuckled her eyes.

Grandma pushed into the room. 'Get back into bed, girl, before you catch your death. Where's Hal?'

'He's here,' Hannah said huskily. 'Under the covers down the bottom of the bed.'

Grandma's face softened. 'Poor child. I tried to warn you, but there's no way you'd understand until you heard it yourself. It's the war you see. The prison camp. He's back there. He dreams of it. Go on, off to bed, Florrie. You're shivering cold.'

'Is Colin all right?' Hannah asked.

Grandma sighed. 'He will be. At least, he'll never be all right again, but he's awake now so you'll hear no more from him. There's nothing anyone can do but leave him be. Back to sleep, all of you. I'll see you in the morning.'

Backing out, she closed the door gently behind her. Hannah listened to her footsteps fading down the hallway before saying, 'Come on, Allie, get into bed before you catch your death. Hal? Can you hear me, love. Come up here with me. Don't be scared. There's nothing to hurt us. It was Colin having a bad dream.'

Reaching down, she slipped a hand under his armpit and helped him to slide up beside her. He was still shaking.

'You have bad dreams sometimes, don't you? Oh darling, don't scrunch your face up like that. If you want to cry, then cry. It's all right to cry when you've had a bad scare. Look at Allie, she's crying.'

'That mongrel! He's stark staring mad scaring us like that,' Allie said suddenly. 'He wakes everybody up carrying on like a little kid because he's had a bad dream, then we're to let him nod off back to sleep while we're wide awake. Who does he think he is!'

Jumping to her feet, she strode out of the room.

'Wait, Allie.' Hannah sat up. 'Stay here, darling.' Planting a kiss on Hal's forehead and pulling the blankets up to his chin, she hurried after Allie, calling, 'Wait!' again as Allie opened the door to Colin's room. Light blazed out into the now dark hallway as Allie disappeared inside.

'Mum?' Hal was beside her, grabbing her hand.

She looked down at him, looked back towards Colin's door.

'Mum?' Hal said again. 'Will he hurt Allie?'

His eyes were wide open and dark with fear. Hannah felt her body going numb again.

'Of course he won't. It's our Colin,' she managed to say and, forcing herself to move, she lifted him up, hugged him close and staggered into Colin's room.

At first she thought it was empty. Then she saw Allie down on her stomach, staring under the bed.

'It's all right, Colin. It's me. It's Allie,' she said in a choked voice.

He moaned, a long, drawn-out sound that engendered the same reaction as fingernails dragging across tin.

Hal's arms tightened around Hannah's neck as she tried to put him down. Kissing him on the cheek, she knelt slowly, placing his feet on the ground, then lowered herself down to her stomach, bringing Hal down with her when he refused to let go. He lay down beside her, his eyes fixed on Colin.

'I was going to yell at him but I couldn't find him, then I heard him and looked under here and, oh Mum. Look at him,' Allie said tearfully. 'It must have been the worst dream ever.'

Colin lay curled in a foetal ball, his face turned towards them, his eyes wide and staring. His breathing came in short, shallow gasps.

'Not just a dream, Allie,' Hannah said softly. 'A memory. He lived this nightmare. He's living it over and over again.'

'Why doesn't he ever talk about when he was in that war camp? He never does,' Allie whispered.

'I can't answer that, love. I guess some things are just too horrifying to talk about.' For a moment, Hannah's mind flashed back to Tom and the way she'd get upset because he would never talk about his experiences in Darwin. 'Perhaps talking about it brings back the memories even clearer,' she added softly.

'What can we do, Mum?'

'Try to help him in any way possible.'

Allie nodded. 'Colin? It's me, it's Allie,' she called and crawled slowly towards him, crooning softly in the way Hannah remembered her doing when Hal first came to live with them. He, too, always dived under his bed whenever one of his bad dreams came to haunt him. He pulled away from her now and began to crawl forward. As his face drew level with hers, she saw that the fear had gone. His expression now was that haunting sadness he wore at times, usually when her and Tom were fighting. She hadn't seen it since Tom left.

Allie reached Colin and fitted herself to his back, the way she did with Hal after one of his nightmares, and slid her chin over his head, humming now, soft strains of a lullaby Hannah used to sing to her.

Hal curved himself around the other side of Colin, his stomach around Colin's bent knees, his head nestling under his cousin's chin as it lifted to allow him in. Tears oozed down Hannah's cheeks while she watched Colin's eyes blink a few times then close, the tautness of his body slowly relax. Moving in, she curled around Hal.

Staring at Colin's face in repose, she couldn't help thinking again of how he'd aged. The prison camp had changed the slight but well-muscled and good-looking young man into a shadow of what he had been. His face and neck resembled a map with lines heading in all directions. His skin was now more yellow than tanned, his eyes sunken. Though he still seemed extroverted and endlessly cheerful, she knew it was often forced, or fuelled by alcohol. She had caught him off guard at times and seen his pain. Her pity had grown over the past few months, though she would never insult him by allowing him to see it.

Ten minutes later, her body stiff from lying on the hard floor, she wriggled out from under the bed and switched off the light. The blind hadn't been drawn, and the moon, dipping down to the west now, lit the room with an ethereal glow. Hannah moved to the window and stared up. Last night's full moon was on the wane and she couldn't help comparing that with Colin's life. As she remembered the slowing of his ragged breathing when Allie and Hal comforted him, something besides pity overwhelmed her. The sure knowledge that his life would be short made her feel as if something in her chest had started to bleed. The feeling stayed with her as memory replayed the years Colin had been her dearest friend.

The moon had sunk even further when she finally woke Allie and Hal and guided them, both half asleep, to their room. Colin hadn't moved.

Schooling

'I don't know what you mean,' Allie said. But she did, and she had a fair idea what Grandma would say next. Fingers crossed she'd got it wrong.

'I asked why you quit your job at the fruit shop,' Grandma Ade snapped. 'It's not a difficult question. Do you have another job lined up?'

'But I worked right through the holidays. And I didn't quit. Now I'm back at school, I've just changed to working afternoons and Saturdays.'

'It's about time you stopped being lazy, Alma. About time you got yourself a full-time job.'

Allie squeezed her eyes shut, then opened them again. She knew it. She just knew it.

'What about school?'

'You have gained the Intermediate Certificate you wanted so much, then continued for another year. That year is now almost over and where has it got you? What good that extra year will do you or anybody else is beyond my knowing. So why would you want to stay at school another year? To carry on for this Leaving Certificate is a load of nonsense. That's just an excuse to laze about. You don't need one of those to work in a shop or a factory. What sort of work can it possibly get you?'

'If I go to university —'

Grandma cut her off. 'That is not possible.'

'What did Mum say? Is this coming from her? Did she say I had to leave?'

'You think you're too smart to leave, so you should be smart enough to know that workers like our family don't go on through school. There's no point.' Grandma Ade held up a hand. 'I've heard you talk about a bursary or some such nonsense, but that only pays for books and suchlike. It doesn't put money into the household. We can't afford your ambitions, my girl.'

'You spend money on other people. On strangers,' Allie said. 'Mrs Markham has been staying in the veranda room all week and we hardly know her. She's not kin or anything. Looks to me as if she's hiding from someone the way she never leaves that room. She even eats in there.'

'Doreen Markham had been hurt, you saw that for yourself. But I don't have to explain myself or the use of my rooms to you. I know you're disappointed but there's no help to it.' Giving an impatient sigh, she added, 'I remember having this same conversation with your mother twenty years ago. I'll tell you what I told her. It's a waste of good money. You'll get to seventeen and you'll marry, just like she did. You'll have children that you'll be needing to stay at home for, like her, and there goes years of schooling and us struggling to keep you, right down the drain.'

Allie swung around as Hannah began to enter the room then backed out again. 'Mum. Tell her,' she called. 'Tell her I don't have to leave school at the end of the year.'

'Oh Allie. My wage barely covers food and clothes for the three of us. If it wasn't for Grandma letting us stay here . . .'

'I hate you!' Allie screamed, and ran – along Australia Street, around to the other side of the biscuit factory, up another street. She stopped running when she reached the bakery gate.

Tucking away the memory of good times and good friends here before Mr Lenahan died, Allie concentrated on remembering that this was the where and why her father had left his rightful family.

'It's Saturday so he'll be —' She choked on the word 'home'. 'He'll be here now he doesn't go to the pub any more.'

Marching up the front steps, she banged on the door. Charlie Lenahan opened it. 'I want to speak to my father,' she said coldly.

'Do you want to come in?' he asked, stepping back to allow her entry.

She folded her arms. 'No. I want to speak to my dad and not to anyone else in this place.'

'I'll get him,' Charlie said angrily, and threw the door shut in her face.

Minutes, and words too muffled for Allie to understand, passed before Tom opened the door. 'Come on in, Allie.'

'I don't want to come in.' Allie spoke loudly in an effort to hold back tears. 'I want to know if you're going to help me stay at school.'

'It's not up to me,' Tom began.

'Yes it is. It is up to you. Grandma says I have to leave.'

'What does your mum say?'

'She reckons she can't afford for me to stay. So you have to help. You have to pay.'

Tom shook his head. 'I'm sorry, Allie. I told you before. There's no money for schooling.'

'There's money for Charlie to go to teachers' college.'

'That's not my money. Not ours.'

'Then whose is it, Dad? You've been working here, baking, delivering. I heard you've made a garden and you've even painted the house.' Her voice became more impassioned. 'You never did any of those things for us, and you don't do it for nothing, do you? You're not the husband here. You're not the father. Can't you put some of your pay aside for me to go to school?'

'I don't get any pay, Allie. I'm making up for us being the cause of taking away Madge's husband. Their father.'

Allie didn't allow him to say more. Turning on her heel, she strode away.

Respect by the Truckload

Tom watched her out of sight. Her bowed head, slumped shoulders, the feet that usually dance-walked dragging along the concrete, all made him feel lower than low. A useless drunk, Hannah always called him, and Allie was the one who fought with her for saying it. You could bet she wouldn't stick up for him now. He was her dad. He was supposed to help. He knew that. She knew it.

The thirst rose up in him. His body and brain cried out for a drink. He wanted the taste of it in his mouth. The cold wet slide of it down his throat. The slow fogging of his brain, the knowledge that he was all right, it was the rest of the world that had turned to shite. He wanted a drink a hell of a lot more than he wanted to go out back and weed that bloody vegetable garden. A man should have a drink when he felt like it. He worked hard enough, didn't he? Madge kept money in that cupboard drawer, the one in the lounge room near the hall doorway. He'd seen it there. Enough to get good and drunk like he wanted. Like he deserved.

He turned towards the door, towards that cupboard drawer, when he felt the hand on his back. He knew without looking that it belonged to young Charlie. He must have gone out the back door and around to the front, probably hoping to catch Allie before she left.

'Everything okay, Tom?' Charlie asked.

Those few faded old notes and handful of coins were drawing him like a magnet, but he didn't want Charlie following him inside. 'Yeah, sure, mate. It's just Allie being Allie, wanting the world and everything in it,' Tom answered, trying to dismiss the younger man without sounding too dismissive.

'Wish I could give it to her,' Charlie said.

'Yair, mate, so do I.'

'But we can't and that's all there is to it.'

Tom nodded. He knew how Charlie felt about Allie. Couldn't help knowing. It was written all over his face when he looked at her. 'Yair, mate,' he said, his mind racing, trying to think of a way to get rid of him.

'Look, Tom, why don't you take a break? Read this paper maybe.' Charlie held out a folded newspaper. 'I'll do the weeding.'

Tom turned slowly, not taking the proffered newspaper, still seeing that money in his mind's eye. 'Why don't you sit yerself down and read it,' he said, still wondering how he could get rid of the lad without being too rude. 'You been working as hard as me. You're a good lad, Charlie.'

But he's not a lad any more, he thought. He's a man now, going on for eighteen and working at the brick yards besides helping out in the bakery.

'And you're a good bloke, Tom. I reckon you saved this place.'

'I don't know about that.'

'I do. And as for Mum.' Charlie shook his head. 'Well, you know.'

'I do, mate. I do.'

'I'll go start the weeding. Larry'll help.'

Charlie smiled, a rather nervous smile in Tom's reckoning, and backed down the steps. Something on his mind, Tom thought, and he don't know how to spit it out. Maybe it's the same thing been worrying me. Now's the time while the other two boys are round the back and Madge is cooking something up in the kitchen.

'Hang on a bit, Charlie. I need to talk to yer,' he said.

But how do I say it? Still and all, it needs to be said else I'll be getting round here with me head hanging down, scared to look any of the them in the eye. It don't seem to worry Madge, but secrets always feel like swords hanging over me head.

Charlie had stopped and turned. He walked back up the steps to the last one and stood quietly, patiently waiting.

'It's about me and yer mum.'

'Don't have to say it, Tom. I'm not blind and deaf you know.'

Tom leant back against the door frame. He hoped the movement looked casual, while in reality he needing propping up.

'Larry know?' he asked.

Charlie nodded.

'He not blind nor deaf neither, eh?'

It was a bad attempt at joviality, he knew that the moment he said it. Trouble was, he didn't know what else to say, especially when the lad was just standing there, feet apart, solid like a rock, not letting on how he felt. The porch was barely big enough to hold them both, and Tom started to feel nervous. Charlie looked a lot bigger up this close.

Has he come up so we don't have to talk loud in case his mum hears, or is he about to take a swing at me? Don't think I could hit him back. Not Charlie.

'I s'pose yer think I'm letting yer down, you and yer brothers.'

Charlie hesitated for a long moment. Long enough for Tom to think he was going to agree with that, but 'We'd been expecting it,' he said. 'I talked to Larry a while back. Matter of fact, he brought the subject up.'

Tom glanced down the hallway, making sure Madge wasn't there somewhere, listening in. She didn't seem to mind the boys knowing. Leastways, she never tried to hide it like he did. But one thing she would mind was him offering to give her up.

'It's only happened a couple of times,' he said, pushing himself away from the doorframe. 'But I'm telling ya now, if it's worrying you and Larry, then I'll make sure it stops.'

'People are already talking so there wouldn't be much point in that, not if it's what you and Mum want. Not if you love her?' Charlie said quietly, and the last sentence was definitely a question.

'Course I do,' Tom said stoutly. 'I wouldn't do anything to hurt yer mum, not for quids. Not you or yer brothers neither.' He paused for a moment before asking, 'Does young Bobby know?' adding, 'Aw, shit,' when Charlie nodded.

'What happens with you and Mum is your business, yours and hers. It's not up to us to approve or not,' Charlie said in the same even voice. 'Like I said to Larry, we'll be leaving home one day. Me next year, him not too long after. Bobby might hang on a while, but one of these days he'll leave too, get married, have kids of his own. It does hurt us a bit, seeing Dad gone and you and her together, but in the long run, we're happy if she's happy. It makes us feel better to know she won't be alone when we're making our own lives.'

He wasn't usually much of a talker, Charlie, and Tom was glad he'd been able to say all he needed to say without getting heated about it. Which maybe meant he'd been planning to bring up the subject himself.

'I 'preciate that, Charlie, and I 'preciate you saying it. We'll keep on being mates then, eh? Me and youse boys?'

Charlie ignored the outstretched hand to say, 'One thing, though. Are you going to stay on here? I mean, are you aiming to stay with Mum?'

What he means is, am I going to leave her like I did Hannah. Guess my record ain't the best up till now.

'That's my aim,' Tom said, keeping his hand out there ready to shake, even though he'd never thought it through, this business of staying with Madge till kingdom come.

When Charlie took his hand and shook it, his grasp firm without being too hard, Tom felt close to tears. He could see by the red flushing Charlie's face, by the hand shaking slightly before it gripped his, that the lad's part in this conversation, and him managing to keep his voice and eyes level, was a much greater effort than it appeared. He had no doubt that Charlie was also close to tears as he handed over the newspaper along with a clap on the back before ambling off, picking up the gardening trowel on his way, saying, 'I'll get on with that weeding then.'

This is the kind of support I've been getting since the day I arrived at the Lenahan back door, Tom thought.

'We're so lucky to have you here,' Madge had told him.

He was still waiting for her to grieve. He'd supposed it would come later, yet to his mind, it never had. It seemed to him that she cried at the funeral because people expected it. Confusion had turned to anger at Bob for dying and leaving her in such a pickle.

Yeah, Madge needed him. Her and the boys. They'd been stricken by their dad's death and were worse than useless as far as the work planning went. It was a crime to see how thankful they were when he took over the worrying. They did everything he told them to do, them and their mum. Never back-chatted. Never made him feel like he was a pain in the bum. Worse than useless, that's what Hannah and Janet thought of him. And Allie broke his heart the way she doted on him. Her love was so thick and strong it smothered him. He was always scared she'd find him out. Not any more. He'd fixed that by not living up to what she wanted him to be. Who ever does?

Madge never let a day go past without saying she didn't know what she'd do without him. The boys didn't say it, but they acted it. Respect by the truckload, that's what he got from Charlie, Larry and young Bobby. That's what he was going to keep on getting, even though they'd found out about him and their mum.

They knew there was more important things in life than bloody schooling.

He'd leave young Charlie to do the weeding and he'd go clean out the bakehouse. That would give him Sunday to take it easy. No pubs open on a Sunday so he wouldn't be tempted. Funny thing though, he didn't feel as though he wanted a drink now.

Affinity

It had felt strange, knocking on the door that had been her front door for eighteen years.

'I was passing by and saw your light, thought I'd ask again if there was any way I could help. I feel guilty that Tom let the place go and now you have so much to do,' Hannah had said, knowing she was talking too fast but unable to help herself. Now here she was, sitting at a table with him, sipping brandy that was a lot more mellow than her. Not that she knew much about brandy, but this one felt so fine sliding down her throat that it had to be one of the best. An occasional beer on a hot day was more her scene, though she didn't mind a glass of wine with tea. Not tea. Dinner was the correct term, she'd learned that much while driving taxis. Not breakfast, dinner and tea. Breakfast, lunch and dinner was the proper way. But why was she bothering her head about that right now?

Oh God, she felt as nervous as a teen on her first date, alone after dinner in this house with Claude. Not that it was a date. Nor did she think for one minute that he'd take advantage. Her problem was the realisation that she wished he would. Why else had she come here? She knew he'd refuse her offer of help with the house. She'd offered twice before.

They talked about neighbours, Australia Street, the biscuit factory. He teased her about her obvious antipathy to the wall, saying she made it sound as though it had the ability to think.

'Much like that darn bird. I should have warned you,' she said, laughing at his wry smile. Claude had learned to be wary of Bird just a few days after moving into number 19.

The conversation had been friendly and relaxed until she asked about his child. Instead of answering, he stood, offering to make coffee, and walked away to the sink. No doubt he thought she was looking for gossip. What could she say to reassure him? Perhaps waiting for him to bring up a new subject would be the way to go.

After glancing at him, stiff and straight as he stood by the kettle, she stared around at the kitchen that had once been hers. All that remained of the old kitchen was the marble sink. He'd built new cupboards, installed the latest and most expensive gas stove, a refrigerator, modern appliances, and a beautiful rosewood table with matching chairs. The floor was covered in a pale grey carpet and she could see thicker, lusher carpet in the hallway and leading into the bedrooms. It showed what money could do to a house.

It could ruin it, that's what it could do, she thought, trying not to let the thought show when he turned towards her. Avoiding his eyes, she continued to look around. It seemed to her that despite the gloss of new paint and new additions, the kitchen appeared gloomy, as though it was mourning the loss of old friends. He had destroyed the character of the old house, the feeling of being surrounded by the friendly ghosts of people who had lived here over the past sixty years. Who had loved here.

'What do you think?' he asked.

'You've done wonders,' she said hesitantly, not wanting to insult him by admitting she didn't care for it.

But then, she thought, he has also banished the bad times, the cutting words and hard expressions. She couldn't imagine raised voices and thrown crockery in this house now. Nor could she envision loving touches and laughter. It had become a book of blank pages waiting for new people to fill it.

'I've stuffed it up, haven't I?' he said, looking around the kitchen. 'It's all too new for an old house.'

Grimacing, she nodded. 'It does feel too . . .' She searched for the right word, one that wouldn't sound too disapproving. 'Too cold. Perhaps it's that particular blue you have on the walls.'

'I should have just spruced it up a bit. I should have bought antique furniture.'

Hannah nodded again.

'I think I tried to turn it into my mother's house over on the North Shore,' he confessed. 'She has impeccable taste. But the inside doesn't match the outside here. Or the street. Or the neighbourhood for that matter.'

'I'm sorry if I spoke out of turn. Asking about your family, I mean,' she said.

Placing cups and saucers on the table, he stepped back and looked into her eyes. 'I was rude, wasn't I? I didn't mean to be. It's just a very painful subject for me.'

'I understand.'

'We went to London for a holiday and my wife refused to come back,' he said, the simplicity of his words, the level tone of his voice a direct contrast to the hurt in his eyes. 'Sarah doesn't care for Australia. The social life is far better over there. More sophisticated. The opera. Theatre.' He paused before adding, 'I hated it.'

'Didn't you talk about it before you were married?' Hannah couldn't resist asking.

Claude seemed to consider his answer. 'I guess she took it for granted we'd live there. That's where we met. At university.' After pausing for another moment, he added, 'And I guess I took it for granted she'd have realised I wouldn't live anywhere but Sydney. We tried to compromise by spending half our year here, half over there, but that didn't work. So we've gone our separate ways and we're both happy about that. Or I should say we've adapted to it. Getting on with our lives. I stopped missing her about a year ago.'

Hannah decided against asking about his child again, but he must have read the thought.

'My son is a year older than Allie. Victor is his name. He lives with his mother. She won't let him come here. I think she's frightened I'll keep him.'

'But you wouldn't.'

'If he consented to stay? My oath I would.' He smiled when she laughed. 'Not that there's a chance of that. He's happy in London with his school, his family and friends. When they're not in the city, he and Sarah stay at her parents' house in the country. Victor loves it there.'

Hearing the note of sadness, Hannah tried to lighten his mood. 'So he's a country boy at heart. From everything I've heard about it, England has beautiful countryside. Perhaps that's why he'd rather live there than in Sydney.'

The kettle called to him with a shrill whistle and he moved back to the stove. 'My grandfather left me a small beef cattle property just south of Mudgee, but Vic has never taken to that,' he said, as he poured boiling water into the teapot. 'It's hot there in summer, and often dry. Nothing like the soft green hills of old England.'

She frowned. 'You own businesses in the city and a property out west? I can't help wondering why you're slumming it here in Australia Street.'

He looked searchingly at her. 'That sounds like something Colin would say. And said the way he'd say it.' He placed the pot on the table and remained standing. 'I came here originally because I like working with my hands and I knew I'd enjoy renovating this house. I moved in because it's easier that way, but I stay because I like being here. I like the friendliness of the people. I like the neighbourhood.'

'I didn't mean to sound disparaging —,' she began.

He cut her off. 'My grandfather, then my father worked hard for what we own. Me, not quite so hard. I have a hell of a lot more than I'll ever need but I can't force myself to regret that.'

'Why should you?' Hannah asked, her voice softly apologetic. 'I'm sorry. It's difficult to be casual about money when you've never had any and the future shows no likelihood of you ever getting any. Enough to live on without worrying about it anyway. And it's a sore point with me at the moment. Allie wants to continue on through school, then university, and I can't see that happening for her.'

He sat down at last. 'It's a shame for a bright girl like her to miss out on higher education because of the cost.'

'And hundreds, perhaps even thousands like her who come from the working class.' Hannah's tone became grimmer. 'Ask some of them about the unfairness of a system where only the children of the rich can afford a decent education.'

'There are bursaries and scholarships,' he began.

She cut him off. 'I know.'

But you don't, she could have said but refrained. This man would know nothing about dreams crashing because of a lack of funds, because the bright girls and boys had to go out and earn not only their own living but contribute to the family budget as well. Their first priority wasn't education, it was food on the table, rent, electricity, gas. Feeling her resentment rising, she bit down on her lip. It was hardly Claude Macy's fault that people like Allie had to leave school early. People like . . .

That's when she realised it was actually her own experience of leaving when she desperately wanted to continue that was stirring her. She thought she'd put that behind her long ago.

'How did we get onto this topic anyway?' she asked, forcing a smile.

'We were talking about Allie's ambitions. She certainly is a bright young woman. And like her mother, very attractive.'

Hannah's smile was natural this time. 'Thank you. There is much more pleasant and interesting things to talk about than schooling.'

He nodded. 'We could talk about us.'

'Us?'

Standing, he took her hand and pulled her to her feet. The thought flashed through her mind that this very moment was her one chance of backing away from something bound to happen if she didn't stop it. Another second and it would be too late.

They were both almost naked by the time they reached his bed.

'Wait. Wait,' she said, but she was pulling him onto the bed, pulling him on top of her as she said it.

He kissed her hard, fiercely, and her response was just as ferocious as she kissed him back, then arched up to him, biting down on his shoulder as he wrapped his arms around her, lifting himself to a sitting position, her in his lap, her legs around his back as they continued to kiss, not wanting to separate, as he swung her around onto her back again. There was no waiting, no soft slow foreplay; just passion and heat that was more like a contest than lovemaking. Short and explosive, and they both lay panting for breath when it was over.

As her breathing grew easier, her uncertainty returned and she searched for something to say. Something witty perhaps. No, that would sound as though she'd done this a dozen times before. She could assure him that she hadn't, but why would he care? This was just a one night thing, wasn't it? That thought made her feel uncomfortable. The safest thing was to say nothing until he did.

Perhaps she should get dressed. Or should she wait for him to move first? Was there a protocol? Tom had been her only lover. She wasn't sure what she was supposed to do or say with Claude. He was lying so still now. She couldn't hear his breathing. Perhaps he'd had a heart attack. Her own heart was still thumping. She had to bite a knuckle to stifle a giggle. He'd think her an idiot.

'Christ!' he said suddenly, and leapt out of bed.

She sat bolt upright. He was dancing on the spot. Jigging up and down. Like Irish dancing, she thought, looking down at her feet so she wouldn't burst out laughing. This was embarrassing. Now he was slapping himself.

When she glanced up, he'd moved back from the bed and had become a vague shadow in the darkness. They hadn't paused to switch on a light. But there should be one beside the bed. Everyone had a lamp beside their bed. Reaching out, her hand felt the shape of a bedside table, fumbled outwards until she felt the lamp, fumbled upwards and switched it on.

He turned slowly, head up, searching for something, listening intently. His body was sweat-slicked, his hair sticking out at all angles. He had two long scratches down his back. His penis swung sideways then back as he turned suddenly. She heard a high pitched whine. A mosquito.

This time she couldn't help it. Laughter bubbled up and out in a gush of mirth.

Claude stared down at her, at first in amazement, then chagrin.

'Bloody things. Mosquitos. I'm allergic to them,' he explained. 'Come out in hives if one of the mongrels suckers into me.'

She snorted laughter again.

'I've blown it, haven't I?' he said.

More laughter. She was almost crying.

He nodded. 'Bad choice of words. Not very romantic. I've been lying there, trying to think of something poetic to say. Now I'm running around stark naked chasing a bloody mosquito.'

With your thing swinging in the breeze, she wanted to say but managed to hold back. Which was more than she could do with another snort of laughter.

'I know. I know,' he said miserably.

He looked so dejected she held out her arms to him.

This time, the foreplay was long, slow and loving. As was their coupling. When they were finally satiated, she knew that despite their very different backgrounds, their affinity was more than sex for the sake of it. Whether it was the beginning of love was another matter.

One of These Days

Except on the odd late afternoons when someone required Grandma's herbal assistance, she and Great-Aunt Florrie shared the cooking duties. They rarely disagreed on a meal plan or ingredients, and both liked to eat later than most of the local families. Usually around seven. This evening they made a huge pot of vegetable soup thickened with lentils, enough for three nights, accompanied by Grandma's freshly baked bread. Dessert – usually only served every second day but on the menu this night because Janet had arrived – was home-bottled peaches and a thick egg custard. Great-Aunt Florrie had just finished preparing a tray for the guest who had been staying out of sight all week. She was about to take it to the veranda room when an ear-shattering thumping on the front door resounded through the house.

'Somebody needs to mind their manners,' Janet said as she put down a handful of knives and spoons and strode towards the hall.

'Wait.' Grandma held up a hand. 'Anyone who bangs that loud is up to no good. I think I know who it is. Keep him there for a few moments.'

'I'll answer the door. You finish setting the table,' Hannah told her eldest daughter as Grandma hurried towards the veranda room.

'Come on, open up,' a male voice called. 'Come on, Doreen, I know you're in there.'

'Keep your shirt on,' Hannah called, pulling the door open.

Facing her was a large, untidily dressed man. Not tall, but thickset, with beefy neck and arms and a belligerent attitude. His face, what she could see of it through black stubble, was even redder than his bleary eyes. His overlong black hair, devoid of its usual coating of Californian Poppy hair oil, looked as though it hadn't been washed or combed for a week. His clothes looked as if he'd been sleeping in them for longer than that.

A quiver of fear ran through her. This man was famous for his aggression, the way he could snap into an outburst of violence at the slightest provocation, especially when he'd been drinking. Which, judging by the smell of his breath, he'd been doing for most of the afternoon.

Keeping her tone as casual as possible, she said, 'Oh, it's you, Gus Markham. What do you mean by carrying on like this, scaring people half out of their wits?'

'Where's Doreen? I know she's here.'

Stepping back from the anger emanating from his expression and stance, she snapped, 'She certainly is not. And I'll thank you not to go yelling at me like that.'

'Yer lying,' he snarled.

Shoving her aside, he strode down the hall, throwing doors open and peering into each room as he went.

'Get out!' Allie yelled at him when he poked his head around her bedroom door. He just managed to avoid being caught as she kicked the door shut in his face.

In the kitchen, Hal sat tightly curled in a ball under the table while Grandma began ladling out bowls of soup and Janet set out the cutlery. Great-Aunt Florrie kept her head down as she sliced the hot bread. The smells were delicious enough to stop Gus Markham in his tracks. Nostrils flaring, he stared at the pot, wiping his mouth with the back of a hand before snapping out, 'Where's the veranda room? I know she's here.'

'That way,' Hannah said, pointing the direction. She knew they had nothing to worry about. The house had two back doors. One in the kitchen, the other in the veranda room. By now Doreen Markham would be hiding in the herb shed, or she would have gone through the lane gates into next door. Hannah had seen this routine before. As Gus Markham searched under the bed and in the wardrobe before stumbling through the back door, she turned to Grandma.

'Are you going to let him get away with acting like that? Scaring Hal and Allie. And me for that matter.'

'Right. I'll throw him out,' Grandma said, clenching her fists and stiffening her arms to display muscles that were almost non existent.

'I'll help ya,' Janet stated. 'I reckon between the lot of us we could send him on his way.'

'What do you say, Hal?' Grandma called, glancing meaningfully towards the table. 'Will I chuck him out or give him a dish of soup?'

'Soup please,' Hal called back.

Taking a deep breath, Hannah sunk into a chair. 'Good idea, Grandma,' she said, waving at Janet to sit beside her. 'The poor man's probably hungry, that's why he's so angry.'

'You can't argue with a man who's been drinking. They just get stubborn and rough. They don't know what they're doing half the time,' Great-Aunt Florrie said softly. 'He'll calm down when he doesn't find her.'

Grandma nodded. 'He'll go away after he's had a look, and there's nothing we can do anyway. He's too big, even for all of us put together, and by the time one of us went for help, he'd be gone.'

'I heard all that,' Gus Markham said from behind Hannah. 'Doreen's here somewhere, isn't she?'

'You can see she's not.' Grandma retorted. 'But go search the whole house if you don't believe me.'

'She left the two girls with me mum, then she took off. They said she was coming here.'

Grandma placed her hands on her hips. 'You listen to me, Gus Markham. Doreen is not here, and if you've hurt those girls to force them into telling you where their mother is, I promise you'll pay for it. I'll get the cops onto you, I swear I will.'

'What are ya talking about? As if I'd hurt me girls,' he blustered.

Grandma stared into his face. 'You bash your wife, don't you? I saw the bruises.' She curled a lip. 'A cowardly wife basher, that's what you are. And don't start going on about what happened to you in the war. It won't wash with me. That was over three years ago.'

'Who d'you think you're talking to,' he snarled.

Great-Aunt Florrie moved to stand beside Grandma. 'She's talking to you, Gus. Now be a good man and go home.'

Janet and Hannah jumped up and moved in front of Grandma and Great-Aunt Florrie as Gus stumbled towards them, his hands clenched.

'Hold it right there, mate.' Colin stood in the doorway, a cricket bat resting casually over one shoulder. 'That's me gran you're having a go at.

Can't let ya do that, mate. Doreen's not here, you've seen that for yerself. Now it's time for ya to go.'

Gus's voice was low and menacing as he answered, 'You thinking of clobbering me with that bat, eh Colin?'

'What, me? No, mate, no way. We're mates, ain't we? Wouldn't clobber a mate.' Colin grinned. 'Thought we might round up a few bodies and have a game out in the street. I won't be bowling as good as me usual self though. Had a couple of home brews at Shorty's after the pub and it's going straight through me. Been travelling to and fro to his dunny while he wets hisself laughing. I'm all right now though, I reckon. Long as I stay in running distance of a dunny that is.'

'I could offer ya mine but it hasn't been cleaned for a week,' Gus said darkly, glaring at Grandma Ade.

Allie appeared behind Colin. Both hands were curled around a thick crystal vase. 'Then why don't you clean it?' she snarled.

'Quiet now,' Great-Aunt Florrie said softly, smiling at her. 'The men are talking.'

Colin grinned. 'See, mate? I got these women trained. Come on, let's go. Maybe I can get me grandma to send ya round some of that soup later.'

'What about Doreen?' Gus said uncertainly, looking around the kitchen as though he expected to see her tucked away in a corner.

'Ah, forget Doreen. We'll worry about her tomorrer. I'll help ya look for her then, how's that? She couldn't be too far away.'

Grandma and Great-Aunt Florrie had gone back to getting the meal on the table. Allie obeyed a hand gesture from her great-aunt and sat at the table, hands folded over the vase in her lap. Pretending to ignore Gus but staying between him and Grandma, Janet and Hannah watched the soup bowls being filled.

'She's not here, is she, Colin?' Gus sounded confused. 'I thought she was here. The girls said she was.'

'Well, maybe they thought she was, but they were wrong.'

Gus looked at Grandma. 'I still reckon you been helping her.' His tone was quieter now. 'When's she coming back?'

'I can't answer that, Gus. Soon maybe,' Grandma said, not looking at him as she lifted a spoonful of soup and allowed it to slowly fall back into the pot.

The old girl's tormenting him with the smell, Hannah thought. You can bet your life he hasn't eaten properly since Doreen left.

'Come on out of there, Hal. Dinner's ready,' she said as Gus followed Colin up the hallway.

'Think it's too dark for cricket,' she heard Gus say.

'Think you're right, mate,' Colin said. 'Oh well, I'll do me daily exercise and walk ya home.'

'Not much point going there with Doreen gone, no one to cook me tea and the girls with me mum.' Gus's tone grew rough again. 'That old girl's got something to do with Doreen going. I'll bet me life on it. Everybody knows how she pokes her nose into things that don't have nothing to do with her. One of these days someone will make her pay. And if I find out she's hiding my Doreen, that someone will be me.'

Colin's answer became fainter as they walked onto Australia Street. 'Steady on there, cobber. Come on, I'll cook yer bloody tea if that's all what's bothering ya.'

'He's a mongrel, barging in here like that. Why is Colin being so nice?' Janet muttered.

'Like Florrie says, you can't reason with a drunk,' Grandma pointed out. 'And we were darn lucky Colin showed up when he did. I think Gus Markham was ready to turn nasty.'

'We should call the police,' Allie said.

'Coppers,' Grandma snorted. 'They wouldn't do nothing. They've been letting him get away with bashing Doreen for years. It's a domestic, none of our business they say, and they look the other way. But one of these days women will change that, you wait and see if they don't. The pollies will pass a law and the wife bashers will get what's coming to them. Now sit yourself down and eat some of this soup before it gets cold. Come on out of there, Hal.'

He crawled out slowly, staring towards the door, his face white, his eyes rounded with fear.

'Oh, darling,' Hannah cried out, kneeling on the floor and pulling him up into a hug. 'Everything's all right. See? He's gone. Colin took him away. Mr Markham can be a nasty man at times but he won't hurt you. We wouldn't let him. Colin wouldn't let him.'

'But she might take me away,' Hal said into her neck, his voice trembling even more than his body.

'She? Who do you mean?'

'Her. Lily my mother.'

'Where did that come from?' Grandma asked. 'Why are you worrying about that now?' She frowned at Hannah. 'Have you been saying things to him about Lily?'

'Of course not,' Hannah protested. 'Though he did say a while ago that he thought he'd seen her outside the school.'

Grandma's frown grew heavier. 'Why wasn't I told?'

'There's been no sign of her. I thought Hal was mistaken.' She pulled back from Hal to look him in the face. 'Have you seen Lily again?' He shook his head. 'Then what is it, Hal?'

'I did see her. I did. And that man was with her.'

'Mr Markham?'

Hal nodded.

Hannah knew then that the bad times that began with a full moon on Friday the thirteenth hadn't gone away yet. Something more would happen. She just didn't know when.

That Thing He Did

Allie chewed at her thumbnail. Not exactly biting it. Sucking at it. Like a baby. She stopped and pushed both hands into the pockets of her skirt. She'd promised herself not to chew her nails any more. A filthy habit, Grandma Ade always said. But she was nervous. And a bit scared.

She was sitting by the window at a milk bar, waiting for Johnny Lawson. This was the third time she'd gone out with him since that night he'd kissed her. Well, not exactly gone out. Those other times she'd met him at the quay and they'd walked around for a while. They talked about the law and university. At least, he talked while she listened, and they laughed a lot. After walking around for a while, they'd had a milkshake, then she'd gone home, refusing to allow him to take her there. Though the last time they'd met, he did drive her to the tram stop where she normally got off. She'd told him about the trouble it would cause if her mum saw her in his car and he said he understood, yet he was always trying to talk her into going to the King's Head pub, even after she explained that her mother and grandma would have pink fits if they smelled alcohol on her breath.

Tonight would be different. Not the alcohol. She wouldn't touch that no matter what. She'd seen too much of what it could do. But she'd promised to go for a drive. That's why she felt more than a little scared. Not of him. Of herself. Would she be able to stop him if he wanted to do more than kiss? Every time she thought about that last time she felt as though her body was beginning to melt from the you know where and up.

God, you're such a child, she told herself. Why don't you just run? Okay, why don't I? Oh God, he's here.

'Hi, Allie. Great to see you,' he said as he grabbed her by the wrist and pulled her to her feet. 'Come on, we have to go. I've parked where I shouldn't and I don't want to get fined.'

'Why don't we go to the movies?' she asked as they reached the car.

He stopped, his fingers resting on the handle. 'Do you have any money?'

She shook her head.

'Neither do I. Spent the last of my allowance on books this morning and the parents won't send more until next week. We'll go to the movies then. Promise.' He opened the door for her. 'Come on, we won't go far. I don't have much petrol.'

She was glad of that. But still she hesitated.

'What is it?' he asked.

'Nothing. I'm just . . . It's nothing.' She climbed into the car, adding 'Where are we going?' when he slid behind the wheel.

He started the engine, then leant back. 'You choose.'

For some reason, that made her feel better. And for some reason, judging by his smile, he knew it would.

Where did you go in a car when you weren't going somewhere in particular?

'I have no idea.'

She'd meant to think it but said it aloud.

'What about we drive to Watsons Bay, then I'll take you to the tram stop the long way round?'

She nodded and smiled. 'Sounds good to me.'

What seemed like a few minutes later, though it had to be longer, he pulled up at the edge of Gap Park.

'This place gives me the creeps,' she said, hearing the sound of waves thundering against rocks. 'This is where sad people come to kill themselves.'

'Afraid of ghosts?' he laughed.

'Not afraid of them exactly. I just don't want to disturb them.'

He looked curiously at her. 'You don't really believe they exist?'

Hesitating a moment, afraid he'd laugh at her, she shrugged. 'I don't not believe.'

He did laugh. 'I'd forgotten how young you are.'

'It's got nothing to do with age,' she said huffily. 'It's to do with beliefs.'

'You're not a Christian then?'

'Of course I am!'

'Not if you believe in ghosts.'

That made sense, she knew it made sense.

'But . . .' She frowned. 'Now you're confusing me. I've never seen anything wrong in believing in other things besides Jesus.'

'You'll make a great lawyer,' he stated, and leaned over and kissed her, long and lingeringly. Once, twice, pulling back to look into her face between kisses, three times.

His hand enclosed her breast, not moving, but hot. She had that falling feeling again. More like drowning, and his lips were all that could give her life-breath. She couldn't stop him. Didn't want to. His tongue was hot in her mouth. His hand slid down her waist, across her hip, her lower stomach, down, between her legs, rubbing now, his thumb rubbing, stronger. She felt an explosion throughout her body then a sweet . . .

'Stop. Stop it!' She pulled away, fumbling with the door handle.

'Allie, don't be stupid. You can't get out here. All right. All right!' Putting both hands in the air, he slid back away from her.

'You can't.' She was close to crying but determined not to. 'I can't.' But what was that thing he had done to her? And he knew he'd done it. She could tell by his expression.

'But you want to,' he said confidently, starting the engine again. 'And you will one day soon, Allie. I can wait.'

She didn't answer. She was still trying to breathe properly. Still concentrating on not throwing herself at him, kissing him. Wanting to feel that thing again, that thing he'd done.

'Do you want me to take you all the way home?'

She nodded. Shook her head.

'Okay, the tram stop it is.'

She was walking towards Australia Street when she realised she'd got out of the car without saying another word.

Saturday Afternoon

Tom stood at the bakery gate, his face pointed towards the sun, enjoying the heat of it on his skin. Saturday was his favourite afternoon. He didn't deliver house to house on Saturdays or Sundays. Though he didn't really mind the delivering. In fact he enjoyed talking to people who stood at their gates for that very purpose. But he got weary at times. It was good to have a break come weekends. He still got up early on a Saturday to fill the shop orders, and he often took leftover loaves to the bloke who had that piggery out Hawkesbury way; but after all that was done, he had the day to himself. The booze bogeyman still came after him at times, haunting him with the memory of how a cold beer felt sliding down his throat. So far he'd managed to chase it way. The only thing he couldn't manage to chase away was how much he missed his kids.

Of course if he was back in Australia Street, Janet wouldn't be home now she was working on the other side of the city. But Allie would be there. Difficult as she was, he missed her like blazes. And Hal. He was still waiting for Hal to visit the bakery. That's why he was standing here at the gate now. Hal would come one day, he had no doubt of that. Madge's youngest, young Bobby, was in Hal's class at school, played with Hal out of class times. He reckoned Hal never asked after him but he wouldn't, would he? There was that silly business about sides. But you could bet your life Hal would pop up one day soon. He'd come running round that corner down there. Hal ran everywhere. He could be quieter than a mouse at times, but when he wasn't, he acted as though he'd swallowed a bag of jumping beans. Just like his mum. Yeah, like her in a lot of ways except for that spiteful streak she had. Look in Hal's eyes and you could see Lily. Poor, mean little Lily Gatley with a chip bigger than her shoulder.

Tom swung his thoughts away from Lily Gatley by picturing Allie.

'Bloody sides. I'll just have to get up me nerve and go talk to Hannah about it,' he said aloud.

'You talking to me?' Charlie asked from behind him at the door.

'No, mate. Meself.'

Charlie joined him at the gate. 'Won't get an argument that way.'

'Don't put any money on that,' Tom said sourly. 'I'm forever fighting with meself.'

'About being here?'

'About going to see Allie and Hal. I'm a bit of a squib, Charlie. Hate the thought of facing up to Hannah. Should have done it months ago.'

'Think she'll be mad at you?'

'Bound to be.' Tom sighed loudly. 'Not because I'm gone though, she'd more'n likely be pleased about that. I suppose you heard about me and her fighting all the time, eh?'

'To tell you the truth, Tom, anyone walking past your house heard you and Mrs Gordon going at it hammer and tongs.'

'Yeah.' Tom sighed again.

'I guess you miss them a lot.'

'Miss who?' Tom asked, trying out a grin that couldn't look right because it didn't feel right.

Charlie just looked at him.

'Yeah, Charlie, I miss 'em. Real bad at times. I fit in pretty well here I reckon, but you ain't my Allie.'

'Nowhere near as pretty,' Charlie agreed.

'That's for bloody sure.' Tom draped an arm around his shoulders to show he meant no insult. 'But yer not bad for a bloke.'

'But there ain't no going back,' Tom stated after a long silence. 'If yer mum kicks me out, I reckon I'll head bush.'

'She won't do that.' Charlie snorted laughter. 'And I can't picture you out bush, Tom. No offence, but you're city through and through.'

'Yair, Pitt Street bloody farmer, that'd be me. They reckon the real bush blokes can't stand 'em. But that's all right. I don't have much time for bushies. Ones I've met are slower than a wet weekend. Though I have to admit I've only met 'em at the pub when they've had a skinful.'

Still grinning, Charlie glanced up the street. 'Here comes Janet,' he said. 'She always stops and talks.'

Tom stared, then turned away. 'She'll bail me up and have a go because I haven't been to see her mum.'

'You'll have to face them sooner or later.'

'I know that, mate, but the later the better far as I'm concerned,' Tom answered as he ushered Charlie through the door. 'Told you I was a bit of a squib, and to tell yer the truth, I don't want me Saturday arvo ruined by a rowing match with Janet. She always gets the best of me. I want a peaceful life. No rowing and fighting, nobody expecting more of me than I've got to give.'

'Janet was good with me at first, her and Hal. But I bumped into her last week and she looked right through me as if I didn't exist.' He paused, obviously thinking it over. 'No, I think maybe she was hoping I hadn't seen her.'

Tom shook his head. 'Why would she be hiding from you?'

'She was going into a pub so maybe she didn't want me telling you that.' Charlie looked uncomfortable. 'And now I've blabbed it.'

Tom rubbed his chin. 'I can't imagine Janet going into a pub. Can't imagine her drinking. She's always been bad as her mum where grog's concerned.' Turning on his heel, he hurried back outside. 'I should have a word to her about that. People see her and they'll be calling her names. Plus she's too young.' He watched Janet turn the corner. 'Bugger it, I've missed her.'

Charlie joined him at the gate again. 'I shouldn't have said anything. She'll say I should mind my own business.'

'That's exactly what she'll say to me.' Tom shrugged. 'And she'd be right. Janet's smart enough to take care of herself. She's not likely to get herself into any trouble.'

'You hope,' Charlie said quietly.

'I hope,' Tom agreed.

The Deal

'Here comes Janet,' Allie said from the front porch and was almost knocked over in the rush.

Laughing, Hannah and Grandma Ade jostled each other up the hallway, Hannah crying out a protest as the very slim Great-Aunt Florrie slid past them both and was first to the gate.

'It's been so long since we've seen you. We were beginning to worry,' she said, placing her hands on either side of Janet's face. 'Dear girl,' she added, and brushed her lips against Janet's forehead.

'You leave it too long between visits,' Hannah said, but without real reproof, and linked arms. Grandma Ade copied Great-Aunt Florrie's greeting before calling, 'Put the kettle on, Allie.'

'If I get this reception every time I come home I'll be here more often,' Janet said, then smiled hugely, obviously loving the fuss. 'And I brought some of Mrs Best's swank coffee. She pays a fortune for it. I'll have that instead of tea.'

'No you won't,' Allie said. 'We don't have a coffee maker thingo.'

That huge grin again, then, 'Yes we do,' as Janet pulled a small manual coffee grinder and a four-cup pot out of her carry bag.

'I'm not sure if I'd like it,' Great-Aunt Florrie said. 'The only coffee I've had is the coffee-chicory in the bottle that Colin buys and I don't care much for the taste of that.'

'Give me a cup of good English breakfast tea any time,' Grandma said as she led the way inside. Turning, she added, 'But of course I'll try your brew, Janet dear.'

'Anyone would think she'd been away for a year,' Allie muttered.

'It seems longer,' Hannah said and, clasping Janet's arm, pulled her to a stop as they entered the hallway. 'What's keeping you away from us? Do I sense a romance?'

Janet made a show of rolling her eyes as she gave what was supposed to be a casual shrug. 'Maybe.'

Grandma swung around. 'I hope you're not going to tell us you're going out with a man who lives in that place for rich people. He'd be after something you shouldn't be giving him.'

'Now Grandma, how can you possibly say that? You haven't met him,' Hannah protested.

'No, I haven't.' Grandma stared into Janet's face. 'And is there a reason for that?'

'Oh Grandma, what big eyes you have,' Janet said, laughing. 'I was having youse on. There's nobody. We're short of staff and I've been working overtime.' Leaning forward, she planted a kiss on Grandma's cheek.

'You knew that would stop the questions,' Allie said when Grandma 'tsk tsked' and hurried away into the kitchen. 'But she'll be on the attack again as soon as you've had your swanky coffee.'

Janet ignored her, saying, 'I can't stay long, Mum. Gotter work tonight. Where's Hal?' Spotting a movement just inside his bedroom doorway, she added, 'I've got a present for him, but if he isn't here right now I'll have to take it back with me.'

Hal jumped into the hall. 'Here! I'm here! I was gunner jump out and scare you.'

Janet grabbed him in a hug and, after receiving a hug back, whispered, 'Have a look inside my bag. The one down there on the footpath.'

Hal dug out a box-shaped parcel and ripped away the covering. His eyes widened. 'Cars,' he said in a hushed voice. 'Six cars. Six of them. Six. They've got all their wheels and everything. Look, they've all got a man inside. And look. Look!' His voice rose. 'It's a sort of tablecloth thing, but stiffer. Felt. It's felt. And it's got roads and trees painted on it. And here's a box of houses and things! Bridges and signs and trees.'

'What do you say to the new Santa?' Hannah asked.

Hal looked up into Janet's face. His mouth opened and closed but no words came out. Janet was almost in tears.

Hannah gave her a one-arm hug. 'They're great, Jan.'

'One of the guests left them behind. A family with two boys from England. Mrs Best telephoned them when she knew they'd be back in London and the man said to give them to someone who'd appreciate them enough not to go off and leave them behind. Of course I claimed them for Hal. Go on, sweetie.' She kissed his forehead. 'Go play with them while I show everyone how to make swanky coffee.'

'I'm never gunner leave them behind,' Hal vowed. 'Only when I go to school. I'll keep them under my bed so they won't get lost. See, Allie. Aren't they great?'

'They are,' Allie agreed, smiling as he lifted the case and half-carried, half-dragged it up the steps and along the hall into his room. Of course she was happy for him, but sorry it wasn't her who could give him such things.

If they'd let me go to uni, I'll buy him a hundred cars when I'm a lawyer, though I suppose that's never going to happen, she thought as she walked past the others and into the yard.

Colin had been leaning against the side fence, smoking. He flicked the cigarette into the lane when he saw Allie. 'Look at that long face,' he said, lowering himself onto a bench. 'Quit ya bloody sulking and sit yourself down here with me.'

'What do you want?' Allie's tone bordered on belligerence, though her sloped shoulders signalled the opposite as she sagged onto the four-seater bench.

'Well I don't want you snapping me head off. That's what I don't want,' Colin said.

She looked sideways at him. Wonder of wonders, he wasn't wearing his coat or tie, and his shirt was unbuttoned halfway down. Even though he wore a singlet, he looked almost naked.

'I've been sunbaking, and I hope ya not looking at me hairy chest,' he added, clasping his shirt together.

'What hairs? What chest?' Allie mumbled.

'Ar, you wanner joke, do ya?'

'Who's joking?' she couldn't help saying.

It had become a rite between them, this jousting with insults, ever since that first night she joined him under the bed. She still did sometimes, but Hal usually went to him now when Colin had one of his dreams. Mum and Grandma hadn't liked that idea at first, but in the end, it turned out to be the best thing. Hal would quieten him by rubbing his forehead and singing that old lullaby learned from Hannah. Colin's dreams were fewer now. And here he was, not wearing a suit.

'So, you wanner toss insults around. And I was thinking how miserable ya looked,' he said.

'I am miserable,' she told him irritably, then sniffed loudly to hold back a sudden rush of tears.

She thought he would say something soothing. Maybe pat her back or something like that. Instead he just sat there, staring across the cobbled yard. He made her so mad at times. He never did what anyone expected him to do. She was at the point of turning on him, yelling at him to nick off and leave her alone, when he nudged her shoulder with his.

'Stop whingeing,' he ordered, 'or I'm not gunner tell ya about how me and ya mum got it worked out how ya can stay at school and get ya Leaving Certificate.'

Allie stared at him.

'Oh, all right. Stop twisting me arm. I had a talk with Mrs Trilby at the Corner Shop. She says ya can work there every afternoon after school and all day Saturday. It won't pay a fortune, but she'll cough up more than the fruit shop does. That should be enough for ya school things the bursary don't cover. And she'll give ya stuff that's about to go off and broken biscuits and such.'

Allie continued to stare, too overwhelmed to say anything.

'Well?' Colin asked into her silence. 'Didn't think you'd need time to think about it. And what's the reason for the red face? Is it all right by you or not?'

She nodded, still not able to find words.

'First time I've seen you speechless. I suppose yer thinking about all that work. School, house and shop. Guess we'll see how much ya really want it. Anyway, Hannah will make sure yer properly dressed and I'll sling in some of me pension money to Grandma so she won't starve ya.'

'Why would you do that for me?' Allie asked quietly. It was more than her dad would do.

'I'm not doing it for you, am I? Doing it for meself. I've been drinking too much and that'll put a stop to it. Always wanted to be a weekend drinker. Another goal reached, hey? And I wanner do ya a deal.'

'What sort of a deal?' She would have promised him anything.

'Well, it's like this. Me old man died young and I had to get jobs to help out me mum with me five sisters. They're all married now. Not me mum though.'

'Where is she?'

'First off she went to live in the country with me sister, then her and Lily's mum set up house together when Lily's dad buggered off. Me sisters are all gone from the city. They all married country blokes, farmers they met while they was working on the farms in war time.'

'What sort of work did you do when you were a kid?' Allie asked curiously. Colin hardly ever talked about his childhood.

'Selling papers off the trams, running milk off the milko's van and selling lollies and ice-cream at picture shows. Didn't give me much time for schooling. I left young and worked at the biscuit factory till I went bush. Didn't need an education to do any of that. I can read all right, but I'm not much chop at writing. Never had to do much of it, ya see?'

Allie nodded, not surprised. More than a few of her older relatives were semiliterate. Some, like Colin, could read well enough, but needed help if they had to write a letter. They'd get someone else to do it then sign their names. If asked, they'd say the same as Colin. Never had to do much of it.

'But we're supposed to be talking about you, not me,' Colin said, nudging her shoulder again. 'Deal or not?'

'It certainly is a deal,' she said hastily. 'Thanks, Colin.' She bowed her head. 'Though it should be Dad, not you.'

'Because he's responsible for ya, hey?'

When she nodded, he added, 'And for how long does that go on? I mean to say, in most working-class families like us, the young uns go out to work when they turn fourteen. You're a couple of years past that. And if Tom's still responsible while ya go to university, you'll be past the age of voting by the time ya finished. Bit much, ain't it?'

She refused to argue. 'It means a lot to me, going on through school.'

'I sort of worked that out, but don't thank me. It was ya mum's idea. She wants ya to get a good job so ya can take care of her in her old age now your dad's not gunner do it.'

'Yeah, I could imagine Mum not taking care of herself. She did that even when Dad was around. Took care of him too. Of all of us.'

Colin nodded. 'Maybe not for much longer. She's getting pretty friendly with that Macy bloke and he's got money. Money makes a difference. If the bloke you're with has money, ya don't have to take care of yourself, do ya? Same thing the other way round. That's why I never got meself married. I'm waiting for someone rich.'

Allie stared at him. 'I don't believe you. Not Mum and Mr Macy. They're too different.'

'Yeah.' Colin nodded solemnly. 'He's a bloke while she's a sheila.'

'But he's rich. His family's rich and always has been from everything I've heard. He's got a couple of houses. A car yard and who knows what else? They couldn't mix with each other's friends and relatives, could they? His would think Mum's were not good enough, and hers wouldn't want anything to do with the toffee-nosed set. It would never work out.'

'Is that what you really think?' Colin asked. 'Or are yer hoping yer mum and dad will get back together?'

Allie pulled a face. She'd come to realise there was little chance of that ever happening. But surely there was even less chance her mum and Mr Macy would get together. They were poles apart. Like her and Johnny.

Yet we've been seeing each other for months now, she thought. So it is possible, isn't it? At first he'd kept his promise. He'd waited. They'd gone to the movies twice. Just walked a couple of times. But last week he'd taken her to Gap Park again. It had taken all her willpower to deny him.

Was that happening with her mother and Claude Macy?

Ghosts

Hannah rolled over and reluctantly opened her eyes. It was time. She had to get up and go.

'Not yet,' Claude said.

'Did I wake you?' she asked, knowing that she hadn't. He'd been watching her pretending to sleep.

This was the eighth time she'd shared his bed and not once had she been able to doze off, even for a few minutes. It didn't feel right, being intimate with a man you weren't married to. Maybe that's why they didn't fit together. Before sex, the grabbing and pulling at each other's clothes, the tangling of arms and legs, the urgency of their need allowed no doubts or regrets. Much like being sixteen again, though she did at glorious times experience the slow, fluid lovemaking, guiding her mind into that non-thought area of bliss. Yet when she tried to snuggle into him after sex, their juts and hollows didn't match as they had with her and Tom. Perhaps because she and Claude were new to each other.

'I wasn't asleep,' Claude said. 'What are you thinking?'

Banishing Tom's ghost by sliding her hand along Claude's inner thigh, she said, 'You realise that if we're found out, I'll be called horrible names for the rest of my life.'

'That's right, a respectable married woman doesn't sleep with a man other than her husband.'

His smile looked more like a sneer and she didn't like the undertone of amusement. She pulled away from him.

'Especially if that man is a rich blow-in slumming for a few months while he plays around renovating his house.' She kept her voice level.

'Is that a general opinion or just yours?' When she rolled onto her side and didn't answer, he added, 'If you really thought that of me, you wouldn't be here. Does it bother you, your neighbours thinking it?'

She shrugged. 'I stopped being bothered by other people's opinions when I married Tom. If I hadn't been so worried about what people might think, I would have had Janet without the benefit of clergy. I wouldn't have married Tom, and who knows what I might have done with my life? I could be someone entirely different from who I am now. Then again.' She heaved a sigh. 'So could Tom. He seems much happier than when he was with me. Perhaps Grandma was right when she said I'm trying to blame someone else for my own bad choices, though I hate the thought of Allie never being born and she's very much a part of Tom.' Rolling back, she propped herself up on an elbow and looked down at him. 'You know, it really galls me when men get a pat on the back for having sex outside of marriage while women get a stoning.'

He smiled again. 'Is that why you won't stay the night? Because your relatives will throw rocks at you?'

'Word rocks. Words and attitude. I lie to protect my precious reputation. Oh God, I've turned into a liar. Something I've always hated in anyone else. I hate it in myself.'

He curved a hand around her cheek. 'It's only a lie by omission. You don't actually walk up to people and lie.'

'I'm supposed to be dancing at the Trocadero right now. That's a lie.'

'But you don't lie for yourself, do you?'

'Allie believing I go out with you just for the dancing keeps the accusations away. It makes no difference to her that Tom's with Madge Lenahan. I'm supposed to sit and wait for him to come home.' Her tone became savage. 'And that will be the day hell freezes over.'

And yet I can't sleep in this room, she thought as she lay back on her elbows and stared up at the ceiling. Though I never give Tom a thought while Claude's making love to me. It's afterwards he seems to be standing somewhere nearby. She could smell him then. His body. His shaving cream. The beer and cigarettes. His toothpaste – that green paste in a tin he liked so much and no one else in the family would use. His smell had become so much a part of this room, she sometimes thought it was her smell.

The harder she tried to block out Tom's presence, the more solid his shape grew in her mind. Perhaps because he'd slept with her in this room for eighteen years. Their bed had found a new home with Clara Paterson, but this was the same room. When she stood, she would look out at the wall and remember the way he used to smile at it as though it was a pet, like a dog or a cat. As though it were alive.

'What are you thinking?' Claude asked again, reaching across to smooth her frown with the pads of his fingers.

His voice and his touch, his callous-free hand gliding down her cheek, her neck, across her shoulder and onto her breast banished Tom's presence, as always.

'I'm just trying to will myself to get up and go,' she sighed.

'If we were married you wouldn't have to go.'

She held back another sigh. They'd had this conversation before. 'I'm already married,' she pointed out. 'And so are you.'

'I'm sure Sarah wouldn't fight a divorce. Would Tom?'

No, Tom wouldn't fight a divorce. But if she divorced him, she'd have to marry Claude or leave town. The kin would find out about her relationship with him sooner or later. Did she want to marry Claude? It would solve a problem for Allie, who would see her dream come true. He would pay for Allie's schooling, for university. They could move away from here, from the kin, from that wall. But when she'd freed herself from Tom, would she want to be Wife again, with all that entailed? Be Mother. Granddaughter. Anyone but herself. Did she want to live off somebody else? But then, who or what did she want to be, could she be? She was thirty-six, uneducated and broke. Without any qualifications or skills except the ability to mix herbs. She was now almost as good as Grandma at deciding which particular herbs a customer needed.

Throwing back the covers, she swung her legs over the edge of the bed. When he rolled across to lay beside her, she stood and groped around on the floor for her clothes. Knowing he watched, he always watched, she turned her back to him and began to dress.

Tom never watched me dress, she thought. Not because he didn't want to. Because he knew I didn't like it. You'd think Claude would know by now.

'Switch on the light,' he suggested when she banged her hand on the bedside table and swore when reaching for her panties.

She gave a quick shake of her head. 'Not until you get new blinds.' He'd thrown the old ones out and when the light was on, anyone outside could easily see through the lacy curtains.

'Your grandmother must know about us,' he said. 'I've heard she knows everything.'

'Shows what *you* know.' Shoving her rolled up stockings into her purse, she stepped into her shoes, edging closer to the window away from him when he held out a staying hand. 'And it isn't because of Grandma. I just don't care for the idea of anybody walking past looking in and seeing me getting dressed. I really do have to leave,' she said, moving closer to the window when a movement outside caught her attention.

He sat up on the edge of the bed and followed her stare. 'You seem to have an obsession with that wall. It is just a wall, Hannah.'

Sometimes she couldn't help thinking it was alive. Sometimes, especially on a windy night, she could see it moving in and out; breathing. Sometimes, when she left here to go to what was now her home, she had the distinct impression that it frowned down on her, threatening her, ready to destroy itself by falling if it had no other way of crushing her into submission. It would kill somebody one day. It only had to find a way, of that she felt sure. She had once confessed this to Tom.

A wall can't think, he'd said, and laughed. But this one could.

And sometimes, like now, she thought she'd seen Tom standing in front of it, watching over it. For a moment she could swear he was at the edge of a pool of light thrown by the street lamp a short way down from the house. She blinked and he was gone. Or had he stepped aside and back into the deep shadow of the wall? The first time she thought she'd seen him, she marched out there, ready to lecture him for spying on her. He wasn't there. Of course he wasn't there. He was with Madge Lenahan.

About to turn away, she again saw a movement out of the corners of her eyes. She swung back and stared. There, just on the outer edge of the light. Someone was definitely there. Someone short and slightly built. No doubt she'd thought it was Tom at first because he'd been on her mind.

'What about tomorrow?' Claude asked. 'Can I see you tomorrow afternoon?'

Surprised by the question – Claude never suggested a time for their next meeting – she glanced at him. When she looked back through the window, the figure had disappeared. Leaning forward, pressing her nose against the window pane, she stared intently into the darkness surrounding the circle of light.

Nothing. I'm imagining things. A guilty conscience, she thought.

'Sunday is herb day,' she told Claude. 'Most of the kin turn up for their weekly dosage and I always help. I'll be there for most of the day.'

She spoke without looking at him. Her mind was still on Tom, remembering their courting days when he did stand in the street outside her bedroom window. Hoping to catch a glimpse of her before he went to sleep, he'd say.

'Herb day.' Claude said loudly, showing he'd realised she wasn't paying attention. 'I've heard about that. And about your grandmother. She's quite a somebody, isn't she?'

He had surprised her again. 'How do you mean? She's just Grandma.'

'But look what she's done with her life. I've only been here a short while, but I already know that the whole suburb regards her as a true healer. Seems she's the one who keeps them healthy in body and in mind. And she does a lot of work with abused women and children. People around here think the world of her. Quite an achievement for someone widowed young and having a small tribe of kids and no education, wouldn't you say?'

'I've never thought about it like that. You're right of course, but how do you know so much about her?'

'Clara. She regards your grandmother as a saint in clay shoes.' He grinned. 'Her words, not mine. Do you know that some people believe she's a witch?'

Hannah smiled. 'Of course she is, and I'm her apprentice.'

He frowned a question.

'There's nothing Grandma doesn't know about herbs, about which combination can cure, can help people get well or stop them from getting sick in the first place. She can diagnose most illnesses. It's been in the family for generations, this knowledge, this ability, passed down from mother to daughter. Though you do have to have natural potential to start with, or so Grandma says. She will choose a successor for their ability. My mother began to learn, then she ran off and Grandma passed the knowledge on to me.'

He laughed. 'So you're going to be a witch too?'

'Not if I can help it, and it's nothing to do with witchcraft. Like I said, it's knowing which combination of herbs will help. The practice has been around for thousands of years. Midwifery. Natural medicine. Knowledge passed down through centuries added to what some people call a sixth sense.'

'If you take over from her, you'll have to stay in Australia Street forever.'

Hannah shook her head. 'I want to travel if ever I get the chance.'

'Then why are you helping now?'

'Because I owe her.' She shrugged. 'Because she asks me to.'

'Your grandmother is getting on in age, isn't she?' Claude asked. 'What will the people around here do if for some reason she can't continue? Won't you have to take over then?'

'I'll find someone else,' Hannah said hesitantly.

'Allie?' Claude asked.

'Allie likes learning about the herbs, but she has all kinds of plans for her future and none of them will keep her here.' Fully dressed now, Hannah inspected herself in the mirror and began combing her hair. 'One of my cousins maybe,' she said thoughtfully. 'Colin would be my choice. He learns fast and he's fascinated by it, but I don't think he'd convince Grandma. She says it has to be a woman. Probably because it always has been.'

'Do you think it would be all right by Mrs Ade if I came tomorrow? I'd like to know more.'

'Sundays are definitely kin only. She'd kick you out. Maybe you can visit another time, get a tonic or something. I'll ask her.'

'Your kin. It's like a tribal thing,' he said teasingly.

She turned to him. 'We are a tribe.'

'I like that idea. I don't have an extended family, not here anyway. They're all in England.' Taking hold of her shoulders, he pulled her close and kissed her neck. 'When we're married, will I become a part of yours?'

Spinning away from him, she murmured, 'I must go. I'll see you later.'

'When later?' he called as she opened the front door.

She pretended not to hear.

Hurrying along Australia Street, she stayed on the footpath opposite the wall and kept her eyes averted. At times like this she felt the wall watching her. At the gate to Grandma's house, she finally glanced across the street. Seeing the corner, knowing the wall didn't go on forever made her feel better.

The hairs on the back of her neck fluttered. For a fraction of a second she saw Tom looking back at her and the wall extending past the corner, never-ending. A blink restored the corner but did not delete Tom. He took a step towards her. She walked forward, prepared to meet him halfway. As she stepped onto the street, he disappeared. Squatting close to the gutter's edge, she put her face into her hands and concentrated on not crying.

'Come on.'

Hannah didn't need to look up when two hands rested on her shoulders. She knew the voice.

'Come inside now. You'll catch your death out here in the cold.'

'I thought I saw . . . I thought . . . Maybe it was a ghost.'

The hands tugged. 'Shh. Quietly. You don't want to wake Allie.'

'I didn't go to the Trocadero, Grandma.'

'Shush!' It was a command. 'Don't tell me anything that will stop you from looking me in the face over breakfast.'

'I don't have to, do I?' Taking the proffered handkerchief, Hannah blew her nose, then climbed wearily to her feet. 'You already know.'

'I know about ghosts,' Grandma said. 'Colin's ghosts visited him again tonight.'

'He's been looking so much better. Putting on weight. Not drinking so much.' Hannah placed a restraining hand on Grandma's arm as they reached the door. 'You've been curing his body, Grandma, haven't you got something to cure his madness?'

'Not curing his body, Hannah. Easing his pain is all I can do. His body has taken too much of a beating. But as for him being mad, Colin's the sanest person you'll ever meet. He's just fighting his ghosts, and nobody can cure them. He has to learn to live with them.'

'He's been so good,' Hannah mourned. 'It's been a while since he had an episode. Maybe he should see one of those psychiatrists. The army would pay, wouldn't they?'

'Head doctors.' Grandma snorted derision. 'Colin's ghosts have nothing to do with the head, and he can't get rid of them by talking about them to someone else. He needs to talk to them, to reach some kind of agreement.'

'I don't understand what you mean by ghosts. Real ghosts?'

'They're all real and we all have them. Some belong to us, some are left behind when someone close to us dies. Those can be the worst because it's too late to right the wrong done to them. Or the wrong they did to someone else. People try to chase them off with doctors. They pull blankets over their heads with pills, but it doesn't work. Sooner or later the ghost drags the blanket off.'

'Ghosts or guilt? Or regrets. Maybe fear or bad memories . . .'

Grandma interrupted. 'All the same thing. They all haunt. Ghosts.'

'Who are your ghosts?' Hannah asked as they entered the kitchen.

'People you never knew.'

'Grandfather?'

Grandma smiled. A wistful, soft smile that took years off her age and softened the harsh lines on her face. A smile Hannah had never seen before.

'Lord no. He wouldn't be game to come back and haunt me.' The smile faded, though the last of it remained in her eyes. 'Now off you go, you'll need sleep to get you ready for tomorrow. And you'll have the room to yourself. Hal's under Colin's bed with him and Allie's in his bed.'

'Was it bad?'

'It's always bad.'

'Has he been taking those sleeping pills the doctor gave him?'

'I picked up a new bottle just last week so I suppose he has.'

'You don't approve, do you?'

'Chemicals!' Grandma snorted. 'He's better off being awake.'

'You're probably right.' Hesitating for a moment, Hannah added, 'You usually are. You were right all those years ago when you told me not to marry Tom. You said we weren't suited.'

'Why are you talking about this now?'

'He's haunting me, Grandma. I keep seeing him out there in the street.'

'He can't haunt, he isn't dead. Though he has gone to another life. That's the thing bothering you, Hannah. He's chosen someone else and your ego doesn't like that. Besides, you still have a fondness for him as he does for you. It's good to hang on to that for the sake of Hal and the girls, but you'll both need to get over the habit of each other before you can be happy with someone else.' She smiled, taking away the sting.

'But I'm not sure I want a someone else,' Hannah said slowly. 'I mean, not permanently. Not a husband. That's just being bogged down again.'

'Not if it's where you want to be and who you want to be with.'

'You never remarried after Grandfather died,' Hannah pointed out.

'Now where would I have found a good man willing to take on a woman with six daughters? Especially a woman like me with a mind of her own.'

Hannah stared at her, not sure how to answer that. Grandma would know if a lie was told just to please her and the truth would hurt her feelings.

Grandma smiled and nodded. 'Go to bed, Hannah, and sleep well.'

Hannah leaned forward and kissed her cheek. Something she had never done before. Grandma didn't give her time to wonder why.

'You know I don't approve of soppiness, Hannah. It weakens the will. Goodnight.'

At least she didn't push me away, Hannah thought before crawling into bed.

Capabilities

Sleep was impossible. Hannah's mind was filled with the figure she'd seen, or thought she had seen, through Claude's window. She now remembered seeing that same figure at the far end of Australia Street on the night Allie had gone to visit Janet at the guesthouse. Thinking about that night now, there was no doubt in her mind that whoever it was had been watching either Fred Peters or Allie. But who or why? Could it have been Maisie missing her parents, wanting to come back home but not having the courage to face her father? No, Maisie was a tall girl. But why would anyone want to follow Allie? Or Fred, for that matter.

Hannah's thoughts turned circles. She didn't know why that slight figure preyed on her mind, she just knew there was something familiar about it and that familiarity made her feel uncomfortable. It worried her. Yet she couldn't think of a reason why it should. Determined to put it behind her, she got up and heated a glass of milk, added a spoonful of honey and sipped it while concentrating on reading herself to sleep.

The book had dropped out of her hands and she was on the point of dozing off when it hit her. That figure, that slight shape reminded her of Lily Gatley.

Had she come back for Hal? Impossible. As Grandma had said, she wouldn't dare show her face again. Grandma was so sure of that, had even hinted at the police being involved if she did. Yet Hal said he'd seen her outside the school. But that was months ago and he hadn't seen her since. No one had. Perhaps she'd just wanted to take a look at Hal before moving on. Surely that would be it. Knowing Lily as she did, Hannah felt sure a child would only get in her way.

Lying back in the bed, she recalled the day Lily turned from best friend to enemy. It had begun on Lily's twelfth birthday. She'd taken the day off school – everyone did on their birthday – but had waited at the gate, perched on a blue and silver bicycle.

'Seeing as you give me half your lunch every day, I'll let you have a ride when we get to the next corner,' Lily had told her, and pedalled off.

Hannah saw her heading for the black and white kitten. Colin had rescued it, the only one still alive out of a box of five abandoned at Newtown railway station. It spent most of the day sunning itself on the footpath outside his house. Lily knew that, but she seemed to be riding straight for it.

'Watch out, Lily! The kitten!' Hannah cried out, but Lily kept riding fast and hard.

The kitten saw her coming and scrambled out of the way just in time. The front wheel of the bike missed the little thing by a hair's breadth; but still, Hannah could imagine the bulging eyes, the tongue hanging out, the trail of blood from the corner of its mouth. Just one week ago, Great-Aunt Florrie's cat had been trampled by the milkman's horse. Hannah had seen it happen. It was still giving her nightmares. Lily knew that.

'You could have hit it!' Hannah screamed.

Lily pedalled back and stared at her with a strange, gloating expression. 'It's a feral. It knows to get out of the way,' she said, unconcerned when Hannah began to cry.

'You could have hit it,' Hannah said again, crying harder. Not for this kitten, but for the cat last week.

'I would have done it a favour if it hadn't got out of the way. Colin only brought it home to get in good with you because you were carrying on like a baby over my grandma's stupid cat,' Lily said.

Her eyes were shining and her teeth were parted in a strange smile, as though she was happy the cat was dead and Hannah was crying.

'You tried to run over that kitten,' Hannah accused her.

'You'd believe that but you wouldn't believe what I told you about my dad,' Lily shot back.

'Because your mum told Grandma that you're a liar,' Hannah said harshly, wanting to hurt, wanting to get back at her.

'So?' Lily said – sort of casual, as though she didn't care what Hannah thought. Turning the bike, ready to ride away, she saw Bob Lenahan and

Tom running towards them. Jumping onto the footpath, she practically threw the bike at Hannah, saying, 'Here, you can ride now.'

Before Hannah had time to say she didn't want to ride, Bob reached them and snatched it away. 'That's my bike,' he said angrily, glaring at Lily.

Looking up at Bob, eyes wide, lips trembling, Lily said in that husky, coaxing way she had, 'I tried to tell Hannah not to take it.'

Hannah's mouth dropped open. She was too shocked to deny it.

'Don't lie, Lily,' Tom said. 'I saw you.'

'You're just saying that because you want to do sex things to her, don't you, Tom Gordon? You and Colin both.'

Hannah couldn't believe she'd heard right. What would Lily know about sex things? No more than Hannah, and she knew nothing.

'You're a thief and a liar,' Tom said, looking at Lily in the same contemptuous way Lily had looked at Hannah. 'Come on, Bob. Hannah. Let's go.'

Hannah hesitated. She was already doubting what she'd seen and heard. Lily couldn't be like that

'Well, what are you waiting for?' Lily asked. 'Don't look at me all cow-eyed, Hannah. I know what you do with boys to make them like you.'

'I don't do anything,' Hannah said, even more bewildered. 'Why are you being so hateful?'

'Because I hate you,' Lily said, 'and one day I'm going to make you wish you'd never been born.'

Until that day, Hannah had loved Lily like the sister she'd never had. They never spoke to each other again except to say things that cut and stabbed. Then Lily's mother took her to the country, to Dubbo. Lily returned to the city occasionally to visit aunts and cousins, but she never stayed long. When she finally came back on her own, she stayed well away from the kin. Hannah hadn't seen her, or heard anything about her until Grandma brought Hal to the house in Australia Street. She had hoped she'd never see or hear from Lily again, but she'd learned that once Lily turned against someone, she hated them with a passion beyond reason, and would do anything within her power to make them miserable. She would have known that when she disappeared, Grandma would rescue Hal from being put in a home. She'd have guessed Grandma would take him to Hannah. Could Lily be following a plan she'd worked out years ago? Hannah shuddered at the possibility. She knew Lily Gatley was capable of anything.

Herb Day

Grandma Ade's backyard was average-sized for this part of the inner city, covering about the same area as the floor space of the house, and cobbled with brick seconds wheeled there a barrow-load at a time by fathers and sons who worked at the brick yards. The surface was uneven now, worn in patches from years of hanging out and bringing in washing, kids playing, the kin waiting for their Sunday herbs. And women pacing out their problems while waiting for a private word with Grandma.

A three-tiered stand holding pots of herbs and vegetables ran the length of one side fence, a solid wooden bench lined the other, joined to the side wall of the toilet. Great Grandfather Ade had erected a corrugated iron shed about three-quarters the size of a one-car garage, panelled it with old packing cases and built tiered rows of shelves for Grandma's tins, pots and jars of fresh and dried herbs, and a small ice chest. Next was the fowl pen standing between the shed and the laneway gate.

Tom stood at that gate for ten minutes before finally getting up the courage to enter the yard. Grandma was seated on her usual herb Sunday seat. Her tone held no clue to how she felt as she glanced at Bobby, who clung even more tightly to his hand, and asked, 'What can I do for you, Tom?'

'It's the young feller here. He's got that cough again.'

'I know what it is.' She raised her voice. 'Hannah, I need you out here.' She smiled at Tom's dismayed expression. 'It's about time you fronted up. She won't bite.'

'She won't bite *you*,' he said, and turned to face Hannah, who stopped when she saw him. 'It's young Bobby. He's sick,' he said hastily and squared his shoulders, waiting for the tongue lashing.

'The asthma again?' Hannah asked after a pause that lasted no more than a few seconds.

Tom nodded. 'It was bad last night.'

'Poor kid.' Her concern sounded genuine. 'It's that rotten westerly. It brings all the pollen in. I'll make up his medicine and the inhalant if you want to wait.'

He felt the warmth of relief spread through him like a hot bath on a cold day. 'Thanks, Hannah. That ud be good.'

He could see that her smile was forced as she looked from him to Bobby, then turned back to the house. Minutes later, Janet strolled out.

'So it is you. Jingos, Dad, ya got more hide than an elephant, bringing him here. Haven't you ever heard of a chemist?'

'Chemicals!' Grandma Ade snorted. 'Madge knows that my medicine will stop his cough and you should know, missy, that nobody gets turned away from this house. Especially not kids.'

Janet frowned. 'You can't take his side against Mum's.'

'There's that bloody sides again,' Tom said. 'You taking sides, are yer? Me and Madge on one side, yer mum and that Macy bloke who took over me house on the other.'

'I can't believe you said that,' Hannah stated flatly from behind Janet.

'Fight, you buggers, I can't stand peace and quiet,' Grandma said loudly.

All eyes turned to her.

'About time this nonsense come to an end, don't you think?' she asked. 'You've gone your separate ways and that's that. No sense in hurting the kids because of it – not your three, not Bob Lenahan's three. You can be civil to each other, for their sake if not your own. Give me that medicine, Hannah, and go inside and think it over. Tom, you get yourself back to the bakery and do the same. And you, Janet, I want a word with you. Seems to me you been doing your best to avoid me every time you come here. I want to know what you're up to.'

Janet glanced at her watch. 'I want to catch the early ferry, Grandma. Got to clean up me room today or I'll lose me job.'

'A watch, eh? Since when did you have money to waste on such things? Or was it a present, eh?'

It was Tom's turn to stare. 'He must be mighty keen to be giving ya things like that.'

'Keen or with more money than he knows what to do with,' Grandma put in.

'Janet, is there something you're not telling us?' Hannah asked.

'Yeah,' Janet said abruptly. 'I'll tell ya something. Grandma is sicking youse onto me so you'll forget to fight with each other. I'm out of here.'

She stalked away, through the back door, stopping long enough to pick up her purse, then out the front, breaking into a run before anyone had time to stop her.

'Nicely done,' Grandma said sourly. 'She's up to something and I'm not going to rest until I find out what.'

'You'll just drive her away,' Tom stated. He knew his eldest well enough to know that.

'He's right, Grandma,' Hannah said, surprising him again by agreeing with something he said. 'She'll tell us what's going on in her own good time. Here's the medicine, Tom.' She thrust it into his hand. 'Madge knows what to do. Now I've got herbs to mix. The kin will be arriving any minute.'

As Tom watched her walk inside, Grandma said softly, 'Not thinking about changing your mind, are you Tom?'

It was never really made up, he thought. But it's out of me hands now.

'How much do I owe you?' he asked.

'You can work it off with bread. Saves me worrying about that bill for a few weeks.'

'Thanks.' He nodded. 'I'll be on me way then.'

'You could go in and see Hal and Allie.'

'That'd be pushing me luck with Hannah. I'll be round to see them another day.'

Swinging Bobby up onto his shoulders, he took off at a fast walk, through the gate and up the street, pretending not to hear when Allie called his name. He'd had enough for one day. Heart to hearts or swapping recriminations had never been his idea of a good time.

Allie dropped onto the backyard bench and stared out across the yard, not really seeing it. Along with Hal, she'd been grinding and measuring herbs since Grandma roused her out of bed at seven-thirty. After twenty minutes off for breakfast, they mixed the herbs to Grandma's exact recipe written out for each of the kin, carefully wrapped the mixture in a note explaining how and when it had to be taken, then tied it all together with a length of string. All this had to be done under the watchful eye of Hannah, who seemed to know as much about the herbs as Grandma, yet always deferred to her when it came to diagnosing. And while Hannah sympathised and cajoled the kin, Grandma commanded with, 'Take it or leave it, but if you're gunner leave it, don't come back next week whining to me about being sick.'

Unlike Hal, who looked forward all week to Sunday mornings and the gathering of the clan, Allie thought the whole thing was boring and repetitive, though the need for concentration warded off her problems to be pondered sometime later. Hopefully, much later. Next year would be good. But once the work was done, her mind was free to worry about the future. She had fared even better than expected in the bursary exam that would help her go to university, despite the long hours working for Mrs Trilby at the Corner Shop, serving, stacking, cleaning and delivering. Then there was the housework Grandma made her do as well as school and homework. Besides all that, worrying about Dad and the Lenahans and Mum and Claude Macy kept her awake at night. Studying had been close to impossible. She hadn't seen Johnny Lawson for weeks.

The headmaster at her school had suggested that she work for a year or two and save for university. Although she hated the idea of waiting, that seemed to be the only answer. Mum would help. So would Colin. She'd pay them back when she became a lawyer. That's what she wanted, though she hadn't told anyone except Colin and Johnny. The others would laugh and say she was too big for her boots. Grandma would. Maybe Mum wouldn't.

'You never know where you are with Mum,' she muttered.

'Shhh,' Colin hissed.

She'd vaguely noticed him sit at the end of the bench five minutes ago, but being lost in thought at the time, she hadn't spoken. He'd seemingly been just as thoughtful.

'It's that bloody bird,' he added in a harsh undertone.

Allie glanced down the yard at Bird squatting by the side of the herb shed. Probably after the hens but hiding from Grandma.

'If he sees me I'm gone. I'm too far from the back door,' Colin whispered.

Allie couldn't help it. She snorted laughter.

'Now you've done it. He heard you,' Colin groaned.

Bird stood. Wagged his shoulders and pushed his head forward in a challenge. Pawed the ground in the way she imagined a bull would do. Not that she'd ever seen a bull.

'Bloody hell,' Colin moaned. 'Hal!' he shouted when Bird strutted forward, wings outspread, for all the world as if he was saying, 'Come on, I'll have ya.' The boys at school said things like that when they were spoiling for a fight.

Thinking for a moment that Colin would grab her and push her in front of him, Allie slid along the bench out of his reach, far enough back that she could see both him and Bird. She wanted to watch the fun. She knew she was safe. Bird had picked his mark. Allie was sure he could smell fear and knew how to take advantage. Grandma had said on more than a few occasions that it would do to remember that the rooster was just a bird. Nastier than most, but a bird nonetheless. Hannah maintained that he was a devil in disguise. One thing for sure, he had Colin bluffed.

Moving slowly, Colin lifted a chair and held it up, legs facing outwards. 'Come any closer and I'll brain ya,' he warned.

'As if he can understand what you're saying,' Allie said.

Bird made a noise in his throat. She could have sworn she heard a growl. Was Bird really a bird or something more sinister, like Mum said?

'Oh Christ, he's coming at me,' Colin moaned.

'He won't hurt you,' Hal said, walking towards the bird, shooing at him with the backs of his hands.

Bird hesitated for a moment, then stalked out through the gate into the lane. Colin heaved a sigh of relief.

'You're such a squib,' Allie told him.

'I didn't notice you jumping up to chase the mongrel away. I tell ya now, that bird will be the death of someone one day.'

'He does that sort of thing at me too, but he's never actually attacked me.' She frowned. 'Though he does take a dislike to some people for no particular reason. Hal says Bird totally ignores Mr Macy. I guess he knows that's where he gets his food.'

'How could he know things like that, or take dislikes? He's a bloody rooster. A birdbrain. A chook.'

Allie shrugged. 'Hal thinks he's something more.'

'Then maybe Hal knows why the blasted thing hates me. The mongrel's taken to following me around. Watching me. Look at this.' Pushing up his shirt sleeve, Colin showed her a gouge along his forearm. 'I'm walking past your old home up the road and that mangy bird come at me out of nowhere. Chased me up the bloody street. Only turned back when he got to the corner. Lucky for me, he's one chicken who won't cross the road.'

When Allie snorted laughter again, he shot her a disgusted look and walked away.

Minutes later, her thoughts had again turned to her future. The trouble was there were too many questions and not enough answers. She was relieved when Hal interrupted her daydreaming, glad to be distracted from the circle of her thoughts.

'Screwing your face up like that gives you more lines than Grandma,' he said, bending forward to peer up into her face. 'What are you worrying about?'

'How do you know I'm worrying?' Allie asked, pulling him onto the bench.

'You scrunch up your face and your eyes go like the bottom of Grandma's ginger-beer bottles when you're worrying.'

'Ginger-beer bottles?' Allie laughed. 'You mean glassy.'

He nodded. 'Ginger-beer glassy. 'Cos your eyes are brown like those bottles.'

'I'm worrying about what to do next year. I won't be able to go to university so I want to get a job where I can earn lots of money. I don't know where that would be.'

'Colin would know.'

'He doesn't know everything, Hal.'

'Most things but.'

Allie glanced at Colin, who was now standing near the herb shed talking to Hannah. Teasing her, judging by the look on her face, Allie thought. He's such a torment.

'He doesn't know how not to be scared of Bird,' she told Hal.

'Nobody does except me and Grandma. She's not scared of anything, is she, Allie?'

'She's a tough old bird too,' Allie said, chuckling when Hal gave her a horrified look.

She knew she was safe. Grandma was too busy doling out herbs and telling the kin how to live their lives to listen in to Allie's conversations. Which she does whenever she can, Allie thought.

'But she helps a lot of people,' Hal said as though he'd read Allie's mind. 'I wish I could be a herb person when I get old enough.'

'Maybe you can.'

Hal shook his head. 'Grandma says you have to be a girl.'

'But you're only ten and you're really good at it already. I heard Mum say so. She says you have a feel for it.'

Hal beamed. 'Maybe Mum can get Grandma to teach me.'

'Or maybe Mum can teach you herself,' Allie said. 'She can teach you about herbs and you teach her how to handle Bird. He had another go at her a couple of days ago. Look, he's come back,' she said, nodding towards Bird perched on the fowl-pen roof, peering down at Grandma's prized hens. 'Better chase him home before he gets amongst those hens. Grandma will have his head off in two seconds flat if that happens, and Mum wouldn't need much of an excuse either.'

Hal jumped up, walked casually across the yard watching Grandma out of the corners of his eyes, then slid out through the laneway gate, clucking to Bird. The rooster gave one more covetous look at the hens and flew down to him. Allie smiled at Hal's look of trepidation turning to relief when he waved to her from the gateway before heading in the direction of number 19, Bird at his heels.

Claude Macy had said that when he'd finished cleaning up the yard and rebuilding the fowl pen, he'd buy another harem and clip Bird's wings to keep him at home. Colin, Allie and Hannah had laughed at that, begging Claude to let them know when he planned to do the clipping so they could watch.

Allie frowned, remembering how easily Claude laughed at himself. It's hard not to like him, she thought. But I can't. Wouldn't be right. But then, what would Dad care? He's got the Lenahans.

To take her mind off her father and the Lenahan family, she watched Grandma handing out doses of herbs along with curt instructions on diets.

'Sitting there like the Queen of Sheba on her throne,' Allie muttered, lifting her hand to her mouth to make sure Grandma didn't read her lips. It was one thing to poke fun at her, another to be caught doing it. Especially today. You didn't do anything to upset Grandma on Sundays, not unless you wanted a clip across the ear in front of cousins who wouldn't let you hear the end of it for the rest of the week. You couldn't make Grandma realise you were too old now to be clipped across the ear.

Thirty-seven kin had arrived in various stages, from age newborn to over seventy. At ten o'clock, most of them had taken their potion of herbs, though some of the little kids had yet to be persuaded. Especially the ones taking castor or cod-liver oil. Each of them was given a half orange to take away the vile taste, but Allie knew from experience all that did was make oranges taste like oil forever more. Yet she had to admit that her kin, and others in the suburb who visited Grandma regularly, were probably the healthiest people in the inner city. Except for major illnesses of course. Even Grandma admitted they needed doctors for that. If she wasn't sure of a diagnosis, or thought she couldn't help, she'd send the visitor to old Doc Howe.

While other kids at school suffered bouts of colds, flu, allergies and whatever else was going around, Allie had never been sick, not even with the usual childhood illnesses like measles, mumps and chicken pox. Whether that was good luck or Grandma's ability to build up her immune system, she couldn't be certain. But hearing the praise first-hand and seeing the results of Grandma's powers, as she did now she helped with the grinding, mixing and dosing, respect had turned to something close to awe. Usually, that is. But not today. Today Grandma had been nagging at her. Nothing she did was good enough, and once the old girl had even slapped her for not moving quickly enough. Downright degrading that was. How would she like someone to slap her in front of all their kin?

As though she'd wished for it, the tall man Allie knew as Shorty stormed through the gate. He headed straight for Grandma, pushing aside anyone who got in his way, and raised his hand as if he meant to strike. Grandma stared up at him, unflinching. Nobody moved or spoke.

'What have I done to deserve such disrespect?' she finally asked into the silence.

Shorty's hand fell to his side. He looked defeated, as if the mere action of entering this yard without being invited had taken all the courage he had.

'You gave her something, didn't you?' he asked tiredly.

'Gave who what?' Grandma snapped.

'Me wife. Lorraine. I know she come here on Friday night.'

Grandma darted a glare at Colin.

'Not me,' he protested. 'I never told him.'

'It don't matter who,' Shorty said. 'Somebody. And you gave her something to kill our baby because she reckoned we got enough now. *You* reckoned we did.'

'Lorraine isn't pregnant. She was bloated. Sick in the stomach, and I gave her something to ease it. She needs to see a doctor, Shorty.' Grandma's voice softened. 'There's something growing inside her all right, but it's not a baby. She needs to get it taken out but she's too scared and she doesn't want to leave her kids while it's done. I told her I'd find someone to mind the kids if she can find the courage to go before it's too late.'

'You don't know what you're talking about,' he blustered.

Grandma's tone stayed soft as she said, 'You need to give her that courage, Shorty.'

'There's nothing wrong with her that you didn't cause,' he answered. 'You just leave my family alone, d'you hear?'

'I'll leave them alone when you get Lorraine to a hospital.'

'You can't tell me what to do. You're no kin of mine,' Shorty snarled.

'Okay, mate. That's enough,' Colin said, resting a hand on Shorty's shoulder. 'All this shouting and arguing is getting the kids upset.'

'She can't tell me and mine what to do,' Shorty said stubbornly.

'I'm with you there. You know how to look after your wife and kids.

You know what's right and what's wrong. And I'm sorry to hear about Lorraine being sick.' Colin slowly moved him towards the gate. 'Anything I can do to help out?'

'She's home spewing her guts out,' Shorty said in a choked voice. 'What am I supposed to do? I don't know what to do. The kids are mucking up on me and I'm buggered if they'll do anything I tell them.'

'Well, we'll fix that.' Colin turned back to the watching women. 'Any volunteers to help out Shorty and his missus?'

'I'll come,' Great-Aunt Florrie offered. 'What about you, Mavis?' she asked one of her nieces.

Allie watched Shorty disappear through the gateway with the two women, quickly followed by a third. She smiled, knowing Shorty would get all the help he needed, and wondered if that was his intention from the start.

'And what's so funny, eh missy?' Grandma snapped.

'Nothing. I was just . . .'

Grandma didn't allow her to finish. 'You can wipe that smile off your face, that's what you can just do. Then you can tend to the tea-making in five minutes time and sit quietly and behave yourself in the meanwhile.'

'Cranky old biddy,' Allie muttered when Grandma gave her a final glare and turned aside.

'She hears you, you're dead.' Colin dropped into the chair beside her.

'Wish you wouldn't sneak up on me like that,' Allie complained.

'I won't help ya make the tea if you're gunner be snappy.'

'What kind of a word is snappy? Nothing I've shown you in my books.'

'Yeah, yeah, pick pick pick.'

'Who's picking on who?' Hannah sank into the chair on the other side of Allie. 'Or should that be whom?'

Trying to think of a smart reply, Allie happened to glance towards the laneway gate. Three people had entered, two men and a woman, all around Hannah's age. They stopped just inside. The woman's head turned in a slow half circle as if she were looking for someone. She seemed nervous. The men looked uncomfortable. Allie didn't recognise any of them. About to ask Hannah and Colin, she noticed Hal halfway between her and the newcomers. He was edging sideways towards the back door, up on his toes as though his bare feet might be loud on the cobbles. The whiteness of his face, the wide, staring eyes made her stomach turn over.

'Mum, look at Hal.' She thought she'd spoken aloud but the words were barely a whisper. Sliding a hand across to Colin sitting on the other side of her, she grabbed his arm. 'Look at Hal,' she said again.

As Colin turned to look, Hal staggered a little, recovered his balance and raced inside, throwing the door shut behind him.

Hannah spoke at the same time. 'I don't know those people who just came in. I don't believe they belong . . . Oh God, that's Lily!'

'Get her out of here,' Colin hissed, and chased after Hal with Allie close on his heels.

Lily

Hannah stared at Lily as though she were looking at a ghost. Which she was, of course. A ghost of her past. Memories peppered her, hitting her mind with force and exploding into moving pictures. Their days as best friends. Laughter. Tears. Playing on footpaths, hiding in toilets, whispering instructions to their invented games, as quiet as mice, afraid of Hannah's mother and Lily's father. Hugging each other because no one else would. Then after what happened with the kitten, Hannah had been the victim of countless cruel jokes, countless vicious rumours until Lily's mother took her away to the country. She'd come back occasionally, but had kept her distance. Yet even now, twenty-four years later, Hannah could hear those words: *'Because I hate you and one day I'm going to make you wish you'd never been born.'*

Was today that day? Was she here to take Hal? That thought hit Hannah like a shove from a giant hand. Leaping to her feet, she raced across the yard.

'Why are you here?' she demanded angrily as she stood squarely in front of Lily, blocking her way. 'You're not welcome, not after what you did to Hal.'

Picking at a jagged thumbnail, Lily bowed her head as she answered, 'Gramma took Hal away for no reason. I didn't do nothing.'

'Then you allowed it to be done,' Hannah said coldly. 'I saw the results. And the humble act won't work with me. I know you too well.'

'Ya don't know me. We ain't seen each other in years.' Lily turned her head until her lips were close to Hannah's ear. 'Ya got no notion of what I can do if I put me mind to it,' she whispered. Lifting her head, she added aloud, 'I come to see me own gramma and me son. Ain't nothing wrong with that is there? I got a right.'

'Great-Aunt Florrie isn't here at the moment and Hal doesn't want to see you. You should leave. You and your friends.' Nodding sideways, Hannah indicated Lily's two male companions: one a stranger, the other Gus Markham who had threatened Grandma as he looked for his wife. He stayed near the gate as though ready for a quick retreat.

Lily half-turned and glared at them, giving Hannah time to study her. She was still the same Lily in appearance. Pretty in a waif-like way; thinner than ever. Her loosely curled dark red hair hung well past her shoulders and looked in need of a wash and brush. The amber-coloured eyes that seemed too large for her heart-shaped face were bloodshot, and the dark smudging beneath them highlighted the pallor of her skin. As ever, there was a childlike quality about her that made people feel protective – until they got to know her. Lily had always been fiercely independent.

'I got a right to see me son,' she repeated defiantly, cringing as though Hannah was about to hit her as she looked towards her companions again.

Grandma Ade got to her feet as fast as her varicose veins would allow and hobbled across the yard to stand beside Hannah. 'What did I tell you about coming here, eh Lily?' she demanded.

Lily stepped back, pulling her shoulders inwards as she whined, 'That was years ago, Grandma Ade. I've sobered up and I want to see Hal. I'm ready to look after 'im now. I promise.'

'He doesn't want you. Ask anyone here.' Hannah gestured to the group of kin who were standing in a half circle to one side. All were quiet, watching and listening intently. 'Hal's happy where he is.'

Lily looked towards the group. They stared back at her, their expressions showing nothing of their thoughts. Her voice was a plea as she said, 'Youse ask her if she knows that my boy don't like school. He don't play with the other kids. He just sits in a corner all by hisself. He's waiting for me, his real true mum, to come and get him, that's what it is.'

'Don't be stupid, Lily.' Grandma Ade clicked her tongue, showing her annoyance. 'In case you don't remember them, these are all kin here. They know about you. They know what a happy boy Hal is and how he's got more mates than he knows what to do with. You tell me now, do you know he's good with music, and with painting and suchlike? What do you know about him, eh?'

Lily's voice was close to a shriek as she cried out, 'Because you stole him away when he was nothing but a baby, that's why I don't know them things about him.'

'And you don't care,' Hannah put in. 'You never did.'

'Says you.' Lily curled her upper lip. All semblance of the cringing, humble woman disappeared. 'You and Tom couldn't make a boy of yer own so ya took mine. Grown pretty fond of my Hal, haven't ya? Thought ya would. I know he's living with you. I knew all along that the old girl would take 'im to you.' Her expressive eyes, so much like Hal's except for colour, gleamed with malice. 'Well thanks for minding 'im, but I'll 'ave 'im back now. Ya can send me a bill for what I owe.'

'So it was you I've seen hanging around Australia Street at night,' Hannah said. 'You've been spying on me.'

Lily smiled suddenly, the knowing, spiteful smile peculiar to her. Hannah remembered that it always presaged something hurtful.

'I know ya playing up with that rich bloke who took ya house. Hoping to get it back through him, eh lovie? What does that make you, eh? A fitter person than me to be looking after me son?'

'Anybody's a fitter person than you,' Hannah snapped.

'So it might be better if 'e was with Tom.' Lily looked towards the kin again. 'Tom's a fitter person, ain't he? Come to think of it, Hal always did look a bit like Tom.'

'Nice try, Lily, but it won't wash.' Hannah tried to make her own smile just as malevolent. 'I know any one of a dozen men who could have been the father, but Tom isn't one of them.'

Lily continued speaking to the group as though Hannah wasn't there. 'Maybe I was keeping 'im company while she was running round the place driving taxis. Youse know me. I've never been too fussy. Me nor Bob's widow. You know, that blow-in raised out back of the black stump what youse all felt sorry for. Think I don't remember, hey?' She glared at Grandma. 'How youse all took to her, being nice and inviting her into ya houses, you and me own gramma while youse was turning ya backs on me, ya own kin.'

'I don't know how you can think that,' Hannah began.

'Everything I ever wanted, you took away from me. You, Hannah miss popular,' Lily shouted, and her vehemence forced Hannah to take a step backwards. 'Now ya got me son. But I won't let ya keep 'im. I'd rather see 'im dead.'

Hannah's anger grew. 'You just wanted everything *I* had. Every thing and every one.'

'That's enough been said,' Grandma ordered. 'We're not gunner stand here pulling hair all day. You're still drinking, Lily. One look at you tells me that. And even if you wasn't, you couldn't have Hal back. It's not because he don't like you, and he don't. It's because he's scared stiff of you, and that has to be for a good reason. Now you get yourself out of here and away, a long way away, or I'll turn you in to the coppers for what you did.'

Lily lifted her shoulders, trying to appear as belligerent as her voice, but the sideways droop of her head made her look even more childlike. Hannah had no doubt that was to keep her male friends onside. Up until now, they'd stayed by the gate looking uncomfortable. Whether that was because of the words being spoken or the prospect of coming up against a dozen women, she couldn't tell. When Lily half-turned towards them, directing the women's attention their way, they seemed to shrink within themselves.

'The old girl's got no proof I did nothing,' she said, keeping her voice low, then added stridently, 'I went out for a packet of smokes, just gone ten minutes, and while I was gone she sneaked into me house and stole me boy.' She took a step towards the two men. 'She stole 'im away so as to give 'im to this tart who couldn't have a boy of her own. I told ya that and ya promised to get 'im back for me. He's in there.' She pointed to the house. 'There's nobody here to stop ya.'

'You ought to be ashamed of yourself, Gus Markham, coming here to make trouble,' Grandma stated. 'That's no way to get Doreen to come back. And you with the grey hair, who might you be and why haven't you got more sense?'

'We want no trouble, missus,' the stranger stated. 'But we reckon if you got her kid, you should give him back.'

'Oh yes, that's what you reckon, is it? And I reckon if you think she's got a right to take that lad, you give your reasons to the coppers. Colin's gone to get them and they should be here any minute now. And if you don't know Colin then you should. He's Lily's cousin and that bloke you're with is supposed to be his mate.'

'You never said nothing about coppers,' the grey-headed man told Lily. 'Come on, mate. I can't afford no trouble with them.' He gestured toward the gate with a nod of his head. Gus Markham followed him out without uttering a word.

'Just as I thought.' Grandma nodded. 'Any mates of yours, Lily, won't want nothing to do with coppers.'

'You listen to me, y'old bitch,' Lily snarled. 'I seen a lawyer. The one who took me kid was you, and ya had no right. Yer not Welfare. He's mine and I got the papers to prove it. If I took it to court, the judge would give 'im back to me and you might land in jail. The lawyer said so.'

When Hannah began a protest, Grandma held out a hand to her, palm up, then said in a reasonable tone, 'So why do you want him, eh Lily? Men coming round don't want a kid hanging about.' She raised her eyebrows. 'Or do they? Is that why you want him? You promised him to someone? You selling him, eh Lily?'

Lily's eyes narrowed. 'You're a bloody-minded old woman, ya know that, Gramma Ade? What I want with Hal's me own business. Ya might as well give 'im up now as later. The lawyer says I just got to get a paper ordering you to turn 'im over and that's what you gotter do or the cops will come and get 'im for me. You go and get my Gramma Florrie and she'll tell ya to 'and 'im over.'

Hannah's anger began to fade under a wash of fear. Could Lily take Hal? She *was* his biological mother. And what did Grandma mean by sell him? Sell him to who, and for what? She felt sickened as one reason edged its way into her thoughts.

'Fair enough, Lily.' Grandma nodded. 'We'll go to court and the judge can decide who's got rights when I show them me little Kodak Box Brownie and the photographs I took at your house that day. Then two of your cousins I took with me as witnesses will tell what they saw. The state of the place. The state of Hal. That dead bloke not much more than a boy still. I already showed them to Florrie and she don't want nothing more to do with you neither.'

Lily's fists closed and Hannah thought she'd lash out at Grandma. Stepping between them, she again faced Lily down.

'Go, Lily, before we throw you out.' Hannah nodded at the group behind her. By their expressions, they were all ready to take part in the throwing.

Lily glanced over at the gate. She was on her own. Her friends had disappeared. When she looked back at the group of women, three took a couple of paces towards her. One of those, the Jean known as Fat-Auntie Jean, was more solid flesh than fat. In size she would have made two of the diminutive Lily.

'Gorn, Lily, nick orf now. You said yer piece,' she stated.

Lily turned to Hannah. 'I'm going, but I'll be back. You just won't know when.'

Hannah felt herself go cold as Lily swung around and stumbled away.

Fat-Auntie Jean gave a theatrical shudder. 'That's one girl shoulda been drowned at birth.'

'I think I can handle her,' Grandma said. 'Now no more excuses, Jean. You drink that mix down, it'll help with the pain. And I don't want you taking any more of them powders. Poisonous they are, and if you keep taking them, you'll do in your kidneys and liver. That's what's been giving you the headaches and the bellyaches in the first place. I'll give you some of my dry mix to take with you. Fix yourself a dose morning, noon and night and I want you back here next Sunday.' She turned to Hannah. 'You go and check on Hal.'

'Will Lily be back, Grandma?' Hannah asked quietly.

'No doubt about that. Lily's got three things keeps her going. The drink, money and nastiness. If she wants Hal, she wants him for one of those reasons. All three more'n likely. But she's got to get past us first.' Placing a hand on Hannah's arm, she walked her towards the back door and out of earshot of the other women. 'She couldn't have told that lawyer the truth or he wouldn't have said she had a hope of getting Hal back. And no, I don't wanner talk about it out here. You go ask Colin, he knows. I told him about it the other day when he had word that Lily was back in Sydney. Their mums are still together out at Dubbo and he got a note to say Lily was looking for trouble.'

'Colin knew she was back? Then why didn't he tell me? Why didn't you?'

'We didn't think she'd have the hide to show her face around here. You go ask Colin and tell him I said it's all right for you to know.'

Legal Rights

Hannah strode into the house and found Colin and Allie sitting on Hal's bed, their backs to the wall with Hal wedged between them. Kneeling on the floor in front of them, she placed her hands on Hal's knees then slid them down and began rubbing his feet and ankles. This had never failed to relax him – that and gently stroking his eyebrows – but this time his muscles stayed tense. He switched his stare from the doorway to her face. His eyes asked the question.

'Yes, darling, she's gone.'

'She'll come back,' he said, and there was no gainsaying the conviction in his tone. 'She'll take me away.'

'That won't happen,' Hannah stated, and the promise in her tone put hope into his telling eyes as he continued to stare at her.

'Listen to me, Hal,' Colin said, shifting so he faced the boy. 'Look at me, mate. That's right, look in me eyes and know I'm telling the God's honour truth when I tell you that Lily won't get nowhere near ya. That's my promise and I swear it on the souls of all them mates of mine who died at the camp. You remember I told ya about them, about how brave they were?'

Hal nodded slowly.

'Then I want ya to be brave like them and know I mean what I say.'

'She won't come by herself,' Hal said.

'She'll need an army to get past us, past Hannah and Allie and Tom and me and Grandma. Past all your kin, the uncles and aunts and cousins. They'll all be looking out for ya, Hal. Ain't that right, Allie?'

'Course it is.' Allie nodded solemnly when Hal turned to look at her. She grinned and winked at him, then added, 'But there ain't no such word as ain't.'

A smile flickered on Hal's face. His muscles had relaxed and his wriggling toes were an instruction for Hannah to keep rubbing.

'So we're all right then?' she asked him.

'We're all right,' Hal said.

'Good. Now there's some ladies outside waiting for their cup of tea. Allie can read you a story while Colin helps me.'

Hal nodded, satisfied, and pointed to a book on the bedside table. '*Boys' Adventures* please, Allie.'

Colin tossed the book to her and she began to read as Hannah and Colin left.

'I want to know about Lily,' Hannah said the moment they were out of earshot. 'What happened that day Grandma took Hal?' When Colin stared into her face as though he was deciding what and how much to say, she added, 'Grandma said you'd tell me. If Lily is being truthful about Grandma just walking in and taking Hal, then Lily would probably be within her legal rights to have him back.'

He nodded. 'I'd say that's the reason why Grandma never talked about it. The least said, the least known the better. But she never thought Lily would come back for him.'

'Well she has, and I want to know what I'll be fighting.'

'I don't need to explain Lily to you, do I?' he asked while taking cups and saucers out of the dresser and placing them on the table. 'You and her were pretty close as kids. I never did find out why ya turned yer back on her so sudden. She reckoned it was because you were jealous, but I never believed that.'

Hannah placed the kettle on the burner and lit the gas. 'Let's just say Lily let me see the real person,' she said while putting Anzac biscuits onto plates. 'I was glad when her mum took her off to the countryside because . . . Well, you know what Lily is like. She has this way of getting around you, even when you've realised her true nature. I don't know why she delights in hurting people. I don't know what she did to Hal, but I can imagine by his fear of her that it was something terrible.'

'Could have been a lot of somethings over his short life with her,' Colin said thoughtfully. 'Mostly neglect though. I reckon that when he thinks of her, he remembers being alone. Alone and hungry, with strangers – men who gave him a hard time – and he connects them with Lily. I've noticed how he hates being by himself.'

Hannah nodded. 'Even now he has to have someone he knows nearby where he can see them.'

'Yeah, Lily would go off on a bender and leave him for a day, maybe two or three. When she came home wasted he'd be crying, hungry, wet and cold and she'd do her block with him. I'm not saying she hurt him too bad, but she couldn't have felt much for him. Seems she left him with some pretty suspect types. People who scared him, or worse.'

'How do you know all this?'

'I been told by people who know she's me cousin. And you gotter remember she is that, Hannah. Me first cousin.' Dumping a stack of plates on the table harder than necessary, he looked into her face. 'She didn't have much of a life herself when she was a kid. You know that.'

'Neither did you or I.' Hannah's voice was level. 'But we didn't do the things she's done.'

'We had each other,' Colin pointed out. 'She had nobody, and what was done to her was a lot worse than what we put up with.'

'You're taking her side?'

'Bugger sides. What does taking sides mean? I'm just telling ya a truth.'

Hannah was silent as she began to arrange the crockery. 'What happened to make Grandma step in?' she finally said.

Colin nodded as though they'd reached an agreement. He leaned against the dresser, watching her. 'One of the kin had a friend living next to Lily in a terrace at Paddington,' he said in a voice most people would use to read a grocery list. 'The friend was about to bring in the cops because she'd heard Hal crying for a couple of days and she hadn't seen hide nor hair of Lily in all that time. It was nothing for her to go off and leave Hal alone, but this time was longer than usual. The friend told our cousin about it and she told Grandma, and you know what Grandma's like with kin.'

Hannah nodded. 'With any child.'

'She went to the house, couldn't get an answer when she knocked and shouted, though she could hear Hal crying, so she broke down the door. Her and Fat-Auntie Jean. They found a filthy house and little

Hal wandering around the kitchen trying to find something to eat. And there was a bloke in the bedroom looking as if he'd been dead for two or three days.'

'Oh God!' Hannah's expression was somewhere between shock and disbelief. 'Grandma said something about that. I thought it was just something to frighten Lily. Was he really dead?'

'Stone cold,' Colin said in the same matter-of-fact way. 'Though I'm supposing he was still alive when Lily went out, probably on a bender with one of her blokes. I'd say he was meant to be looking after Hal. Not even Lily would leave her kid alone with a dead bloke who wasn't much more than a kid himself. Anyway, a day or two later, newspapers got hold of the story. They said he'd died of a heart attack caused by alcohol poisoning. Drank himself to death. Probably not used to it. At least, not the amount he was putting away if he was keeping up with our Lil.'

Hannah flopped onto a chair, placing her elbows on the table, fingers across her mouth, and watched Colin intently as he pulled out a chair opposite and sat. Leaning back as though totally exhausted, he looked towards the ceiling as he continued.

'Grandma didn't call the police straight off. If she'd called them before she had a chance to get Hal out of the way, the welfare people would've taken him. Christ only knows where he would have ended up. She wasn't about to take a chance on that so she took him out of there, handed him to you, then called the cops.' He looked at her before adding, 'And knowing Grandma and her second chances, she probably hoped Lily would change, or she'd decided that a spell in prison would only make her worse. Besides, Lily's kin.'

Hannah nodded understanding. 'And like you, she's Great-Aunt Florrie's grand-child, which would make Grandma all the more determined to protect her if she could. What happened then?'

'Cops didn't find her. House was rented in someone else's name and none of the neighbours knew hers. Well, they didn't admit to knowing it. It was a tough area.' He stood. 'The coroner decided the young bloke had drunk himself to death and whoever he was with, persons unknown because it seems there was about four of them, had cleared out and left him. Coppers let it drop when the verdict came out as accidental death.'

'But they might reopen it if someone gives them Lily,' Hannah said thoughtfully. 'Maybe that's how we can get her to leave Hal alone.'

'Threaten it maybe, but not do it,' Colin said as he poured boiling water into a battered old tin teapot. 'We can't tell them the whole story. Welfare might decide to take Hal and give him to strangers. Maybe put him in a home.'

'Why would they do that when I'm more than willing to be his mother?'

'We're talking about the government,' Colin said dryly, 'You wanner take the chance on them doing the sensible thing?'

Hannah thought it over for less than a minute. 'Not likely.'

'Right then, how many for tea?'

She stood and walked towards the door. 'I can't think about cups of tea right now.'

'Where are ya going? I'll come with ya.'

'I'm going to see Tom. He's part of this.'

Colin nodded slowly. 'Fair enough, but what do ya expect him to do?'

'Maybe he could find Lily. Go and see her, talk to her. She might listen to him.'

'Lily doesn't listen to anyone.'

'She used to be keen on him. That's one of the reasons why she hates me. I have to go, Colin. I have to do something and talking to Tom is the only thing I can think of right now. Or Claude. Claude might be able to help.'

'Yeah, one of them's bound to be able to save Hal.'

Colin's face had shut down. Hannah knew she'd hurt his feelings but she hadn't time to worry about that now. No doubt a good part of Lily's determination to take Hal was to hurt her. Lily had carried a grudge for all these years and now had a chance at what she thought was the perfect revenge. Tom might know how to get around her.

Getting Sick of It

Tom heard the brass knocker thumping against the front door. It was loud enough for the people halfway up the street to hear, but he chose to ignore it. After that rather harrowing visit to Grandma Ade's house, he'd cleaned out the bakery and was now enjoying a cold drink. Not a beer. He'd never be able to stop at one beer. It was cordial only for him now. Some sort of muck that stained his piss a queer pinkish colour, not like the healthy dark amber of beer. This red stuff was probably loaded with sugar, and Grandma Ade reckoned too much sugar was bad for your health, but at least he didn't suffer the headaches and gut sickness any more, and he hadn't had a fight, hadn't had his lights punched out since he'd given up the grog. Hadn't had much fun either. He missed his mates at the pub, the blokes and the women. He missed the grog highs, missed the mateship. Come to think of it, he even missed the Friday night sing-along at Grandma Ade's place.

Friday nights the kin around his and Hannah's age would turn up and Grandma would bang out songs on her old piano. She'd never had lessons, but sing a tune a couple of times and Grandma could pick it up. She used to play piano at the silent movies. Saturday nights was the old folks' night. He'd usually had too much to drink to turn up then, but Hannah and the kids would make cups of tea and be general dogsbodies to the old folks. Saturday afternoons, the blokes went to the pub to talk about sport, women and the war, and give their weekly donations to the starting price bookies. Not too many blokes won on the gees or the dogs regular like, though he didn't do too bad for himself. The older women played cards at Grandma's while the younger ones took their kids to one of the parks or the beach. Bondi and Cronulla were the favourites.

Yair, funny thing him missing all that so much when he never gave it a second thought while he was with Hannah. Guess you can't miss something while you've still got it. Madge's relatives lived in the country, and since he'd given up drinking, the nights and weekends had got a bit boring. He supposed the same went for her. She didn't get to go to a sing-along or hang out at a park with Hannah's kin any more. That was his fault. Madge and Hannah used to be mates, like him and Bob. Not any more though. Funny, but him being here instead of back in Australia Street didn't affect the kids. Except for Allie carrying on like she did, the kids hung out together like always. Played cricket in Australia Street like they'd been doing for years, and Hal knocked about with young Bobby at school. Sensible people, kids.

The doorknocker banged again, but he'd be buggered if he'd get up. Charlie had taken the younger boys for a swim at Cronulla, and Madge's nose would be buried in a book while she lay back in the old rocking chair she inherited when her dad died. Four years ago now, and she reckoned she still missed him. Matter of fact, she talked more about her dad than she did about Bob.

Thinking about that, he hoped she didn't believe talking about Bob would worry him. She shouldn't think it. Him and the boys talked about Bob all the time. They liked to hear about the days when their old man and Tom were tearaway youngsters, playing footie, going to the beach on Sundays to talk to the girls. Didn't drink hardly at all in those days, neither of them. He told them about the time he and Bob got locked in the biscuit factory on a four-day long weekend. Easter, it was. They sneaked in just before knock-off time to steal some biscuits, saw the foreman prowling and hid in one of the crappers. Sneaked into the office when the foreman turned back and the office staff had gone. Too clever by half. Got locked in and weren't game to yell for help. Thought they might have gone to gaol for being there. Or worse, got their heads kicked in by coppers who'd have been rightly pissed off at having their Easter interrupted. So him and Bob nearly got their bums frozen off that long weekend. It turned out to be cold one. They lived on biscuits. Kept them from starving, those biscuits. He hadn't eaten any kind of biscuit since.

He and Bob laughed about it afterwards. Wasn't funny at the time though. The boys laughed too when he told them. Madge didn't look too impressed. 'Not the kind of thing to boast about, is it, Tom?' she said.

He was getting a bit sick of the way she parked herself on her backside, a cup of tea or a smoke in one hand and a book in the other, and wouldn't move until he practically yanked her onto her feet. She was getting spoilt, that was the trouble. He was doing too much. Cleaning the bakehouse, doing the gardening, the deliveries. She'd even got him onto washing dishes when the kids weren't around. Definitely not a man's job. Housework was women's work. Next thing you know, she'd be expecting him to cook the meals. He did just about everything else. He had discovered the answer to, 'Oh Tom, I don't know what I'd do without you.' She'd have to get off her bum and do a bit for herself, that's what she'd have to do.

'Can you get that bloody door?' he yelled when it sounded as though someone was putting their boot to it.

Cocking his head to one side, he listened intently. Silence in the gap between attacks on the door told him that Madge had no intention of moving. Heaving a sigh at the unfairness of life, he pushed himself out of his chair, strode up the hallway and threw the door open.

'My, my,' Lily said from the top step, 'you really are pissed off with life, aren't ya? Getting sick of that silly bitch ya hooked up with, eh?' Her smile was straight malevolence. 'Seems to me she's conned ya into keeping the bakery afloat while she swans about the neighbourhood playing Lady Muck. And denying to anybody who'll listen the fact that you're doing her.'

When he stared at her without answering, struck dumb by the fact that she'd turned up after all this time, she took another step onto the porch and added, 'You know, sticking it into her.'

'Yer still as foul-mouthed as ever,' was all he could think of to say.

'It's funny how people accuse me of that while I'm just saying it like it is,' she said, staring him up and down with that 'Want to do it?' look he knew so well.

'What d'ya want, Lily?'

'Aren't you gunner ask me in?'

'What d'ya want, Lily?' he asked again, stepping onto the porch and pulling the door shut behind him. She knew he wasn't going to ask her in. He could tell that by the silly smirk. 'I haven't got all day,' he added, crowding in on her, almost pushing her down a few steps.

She held her ground. 'I want Hal, that's what I want.'

He tried again, another pace forward, taking a deep breath in and pushing his chest out. 'Ya gotter be joking.'

This time she did back down a step. Being a head shorter than him, she had no choice if she wanted to look him in the eye. Which she obviously did. 'I mean it, Tom. He's my kid and I want 'im back.'

'No harm in wanting.' But he couldn't help asking, 'Why, anyway?'

'Don't matter why.'

'Ya got two hopes, Lily.' He turned towards the door. 'Buckley's and none.'

She poked him in the waist. 'Don't you turn your back on me, ya mongrel, or I'll tell Hannah about you and me.'

He swung around. 'There's never been a you and me and there never will be,' he snarled. 'Hannah knows that.'

'We went out a few times. Did it a few times too, both of us too pissed to know better. Remember that, Tom?'

She climbed a couple of steps again, looking up at him, her nose almost on his chin. He looked into the redness of her hair. That colour had always excited him, and she knew it. He tried to look down into her eyes and could feel his own eyes starting to cross. Laughter bubbled up inside him at the ridiculousness of the situation. He had a hunch that she knew that too.

'You and Hannah fighting and ya get back at her with me even though she don't know about it. Woulda dropped ya like a hot brick if she did. You must remember that, Tommy, eh?' she said softly, taking a step backwards so he could look into her face, see those almost yellow eyes going all smoky amber like they did when she had the hots for a bloke.

'Back off, Lily,' he said evenly, hoping his voice and expression didn't show that he couldn't help wanting her. That was the thing about Lily. Skinny and undersized, pale and haggard-looking like she was right now, she knew how to get into a bloke's wanting.

'Memory coming back, eh?' she asked in that husky voice she had. Sounded kinda sexy, though it was probably from too many smokes.

'It's not gunner work, Lily, so yer can just nick off,' he said harshly.

'Yeah, I can see by the look on yer face that it is. But all those lovey dovey words were bullshit, weren't they, Tommy? Yeah, just your way of getting into me pants. Now maybe ya should start counting back from when Hal was born and ya might get a shock. Or have ya already done that?' When he stared at her without answering, she added, 'If ya don't help me get Hal back, I'll tell the world he's yours.'

'Tell the world what you bloody well like, Lily. Nobody's gunner believe yer. Everyone knows what a crazy bitch you are, and everyone knows I can't stand a bar of yer,' he said, stepping forward again to crowd her down to the bottom step. 'Never could, yer know. Anything yer think I said or did is just your boozy imagination. I got no wish to ride the town bike.'

'You listen to me, Tom Gordon.' She grabbed his arm and he couldn't help feeling surprise at the strength in that bony hand. 'Ya have to help me. For old times if for no other reason. We went everywhere together when we was kids. We was mates. Don't that count for nothing?' Her tone became more compelling. 'I'm no angel, I know that, but what chance did I ever have? You know what my dad did to me. I told ya all those years ago.'

He shook her off. 'I didn't believe it then, and I don't believe it now,' he said roughly. 'Yer old man was a drunk and a layabout, much like I was for a lot of years, but he wasn't a bloody deviate, no more than me.'

'No, you just two-timed yer wife while you was living off her.'

'Piss off, Lily.' He raised a hand, the back of it aimed at her face. 'On yer bike now while I can still stop meself.'

'Hal's my son, not hers,' she cried out, and her expression added to the plea. 'He's all I've got in the world. If he's with me, I'll change. I'll give up the grog and be a good mother to him, I swear I will.'

His hand dropped to his side. 'How come yer got this sudden change of heart?' When she looked away, obviously trying to think of an answer he'd believe, he added, 'Don't give me that crap, Lily. How would having Hal around make yer any different?'

'It just will, that's all,' she said sullenly.

Tom's stomach lurched as he stared into her face. 'What yer really want is to have a go at Hannah. Ya know she thinks the world of that boy.'

'Let her go have a boy of her own.'

'Jesus, Lily, I can't work you out. Hal would just be a nuisance to ya.'

'Right back when we was little, she took everything from me. All the kids liked her better than me. You, Bob, even Colin and he was me own cousin. Youse all ran after her and treated me like shit.'

First her hands, then her arms and shoulders began to shake with the force of her passion. Her voice grew louder, harsher.

'Her dad never did to her the things my dad did to me, and when I tried to tell her, she looked at me as if I was lying through me teeth. I hated her guts from that day on and now I'm supposed to hand over me boy because she can't have one of her own. No, not by a long shot, Tom. I'm telling ya now, I'll see 'im dead first. I told that to her and now I'm telling you.'

Tom stepped back, shocked by her ferocity. 'Yer a sick woman, ya know that? You've always been sick.'

'Sick because of what people like her did to me,' Lily cried out. 'Pretending she didn't know. Her and me mum. Gramma too. She wouldn't listen neither. They thought it was my fault, but it wasn't. It wasn't, I'm telling ya.'

He shook his head. 'Yer lying through yer teeth again. Maybe Hannah wouldn't listen because she didn't have it in her to believe men did that kind of thing. But Grandma Ade would've heard ya out.'

'Not her. Not Gramma Ade. My gramma.'

'Yer talking about Great-Aunt Florrie? Nah.' He shook his head. 'That's crap. No better woman than her. It's a pity her only granddaughter is someone like you. A bad seed, Grandma Ade used to call ya, and I reckon she had it right.' Tom's voice was as harsh as hers. 'There's no way in this world I'll let yer take Hal. He's a good kid. He doesn't deserve you.'

Her eyes narrowed. 'And you're so good, aren't ya?' she sneered. 'I've seen ya hanging around Australia Street at night, watching Hannah going up to the old house, having it off with that rich bloke while you're standing around outside. Picturing it, eh Tom? Is that what ya do? How sick is that? Or are ya still nuts about her and like to torture yourself?'

Grabbing her upper arm, he dug his fingers into the muscle until she cried out.

'What I do or don't do is none of your business, Lily. None of my family is any of your business, and that includes Hal. He's mine now, mine and Hannah's. You stay away from them, d'ya hear me? You stay away from Hal. I catch ya trying to grab him and *you're* dead.'

Moving his hand up to her shoulder, he pushed hard, meaning to shove her through the gate. She grabbed the railing to stop herself from falling flat on her back, and lifted up her face to him. The expression in her eyes changed from shock to soul-wrenching agony as he added, 'I mean it. I'll kill ya.'

'Keep yer bloody hands to yerself, Tom.'

He swung around when the voice came from out of nowhere. Colin was approaching fast, glaring at him.

'Since when did you start knocking wimmin around?' Colin asked.

Lily stared at him for a second or two, then slowly thudded down the last step and onto the footpath. Sliding her arms around him, she lay her head on his shoulder and burst into tears.

Tom didn't know what to say. He didn't want to provoke Colin, poor sick bugger that he was, but he wasn't going to have Lily putting it over both of them neither. He didn't for one moment believe that look in her eyes. She'd always been a good actor.

'She's after Hal,' he finally said. 'Just to have a go at Hannah.'

'What's going on, Lily?' Colin asked into her hair. They were much the same height.

'He's my boy,' she cried out. 'I know I didn't look out for 'im when 'e was little but that's changed now. I've been doing me best to straighten out. Hal could help me do that, I know 'e could.'

'And what if he doesn't?' Tom asked harshly. 'He gets neglected again. Left alone for days with nothing to eat in the house and Christ knows what kind of blokes. That what ya want for yer boy?'

'I'll look after him. I swear I will.' Her voice sounded desperate, but Tom couldn't help remembering what she'd said just minutes ago about Hannah. Who could trust someone like Lily? Nobody, that's who.

'Like it or lump it, Hal's staying where he is,' he said. 'He can't be responsible for you trying to dry out. Ya had yer chance and ya stuffed it up. Ya nearly killed him, Lily. You stay away.'

So saying, he walked inside and partly closed the door, leaving it open just a crack so he could hear.

'I need a chance,' Lily wailed.

'Stop yer howling and look at me,' Colin commanded.

'Ya gotta help me, Col. You're me cousin. You owe me above Hannah. What's she ever done for you but spit in ya eye?'

'Never mind about Hannah. We're talking about you. Yer still drinking, Lily, I can smell it on ya. Ya can't be a mum to Hal and still be a drinker. The two don't go together. I remember that much from me own kid days.'

'I'll stop. I promise.'

'Tell ya what. You stop, then we'll talk some more.'

Tom heard no more as they walked away.

What You Need and What You Get

Leaving the house at a half run, Hannah headed up Australia Street. When Claude called out to her through his front window, she pretended not to hear. She had reached the end of the street when he caught up with her.

'Hannah, wait.' He took hold of her arm. 'You look terrible. Something dreadful has happened.'

She was about to deny it when the tears came. Leaning her head onto his chest, she sobbed. He stroked her hair, not saying a word until her crying had subsided to occasional quick intakes of air. When she quietened at last, he whispered, 'I don't know what it is, but I know I can help. Come home with me.' He began to lead her back, his arm and his concern enclosing her.

'I have to see Tom,' she said, but made no attempt to break away. It felt so good, letting Claude take over. The realisation that she had grown weary of doing everything for herself came as a shock. She'd never realised that independence could be so lonely.

'Tell me,' he said when she hesitated at his gate.

Glancing towards Grandma's house, she saw Allie walk onto the footpath. She couldn't face her questions right now. She didn't want to soothe Allie, to calm her. And what could she say anyway? Lily had moved away long before Allie was born and none of the kin ever talked about her. Allie wouldn't know anything about her, and telling the true story of Lily Gatley would take hours, days. She'd have to contradict herself a hundred times over while trying to explain Lily to anyone who hadn't experienced her. Who hadn't loved her when she was the sweet Lily, the best friend an unloved child could have. Who hadn't hated her when she was the reverse of those things.

Not looking back, Hannah entered the house, pulling Claude with her, and closed the door behind them, talking as she went. When she'd finished telling him about Lily, and how and why Grandma Ade had given Hal over to the Gordon family, he poured her another shot of brandy. She'd already downed two.

'And what do you think Tom can do?' he asked.

'I don't know, but he loves Hal as much as I do.'

'What you need is a lawyer, Hannah. The best this country has.' He held up a hand. 'I know you can't afford it, but I can. There's no strings attached. I'm not doing it for you. It's for Hal. I've grown very fond of him. Who could help it? He's a kid in a million. We can't let that woman get her hands on him.'

Hannah nodded. She had to stop Lily, but she listened with growing impatience while Claude told her how justice would save Hal, how his lawyers would wear Lily down, would break her until she told the truth. That was the trouble with a man who had gone to private school, on to university, then on to owning enough businesses to be able to do things like renovating houses while his hired help ran those businesses. Whatever Claude had wished for throughout his life, his family's money had provided. He didn't know about fighting tooth and nail for what you wanted, about going without. He didn't know you could yearn for something with every fibre of your being and never obtain it. Claude had never mixed with ordinary people until he came to Australia Street. He was an idealist who believed that people got what they deserved, good or bad. What goes around comes around, he'd say. Hannah knew better. Hannah knew you got what you fought for or you went without.

'Leave it to me,' he said. 'It's Sunday afternoon so I can't do anything right away, but I'll make an appointment with the best lawyer I can find and we'll sort this out.'

After all she had told him, he still didn't understand that something must be done as soon as possible, that Lily wouldn't wait around for the niceties, wouldn't wait around for lawyers to poke their noses into what was essentially family business.

Claude touched her arm, showing that he had realised her attention had wandered. 'Bring Hal here. Let him stay with me for a while. I promise I'll watch over him every minute. With Colin's help, of course. Are you listening to me, Hannah? If that's not enough, I'll hire a bodyguard for Hal. Two if you think it's necessary.'

'A bodyguard?' she echoed. 'That's ridiculous. Hal's just an ordinary kid, not some sort of celebrity.'

'I know that, Hannah,' he said gently, 'and I know the idea of it is foreign to you. But what better way to keep him safe?'

She stared at him without answering. He was right, the idea of a bodyguard was alien to her. It seemed completely over the top. Something out of a movie.

Something out of Claude's world, which isn't mine, she thought. It's up to me. The trouble is, I don't know what to do. But Tom might.

A half hour and another brandy later, she stood at the Lenahan gate staring at the front door. The idea of Madge opening it if she knocked made her balk. Madge would invite her in and there was no way she would enter that house. That would be the same as forgiving the woman. She might be desperately afraid of losing Hal, but she wasn't about to humble herself.

'Tom!' she called, and louder, 'Tom, come out here. I need to see you.'

The door flew open and Madge rushed down the steps. 'I saw you walking up the footpath,' she said. 'Please, Hannah, please come inside. I want to talk to you. To explain.'

'Explain what?' Hannah's voice dripped ice. 'About you and my husband? I'm not interested in that. I'm not here to whisk him away. I just need to speak to him for a few minutes.'

'We could still be friends,' Madge pleaded, though her expression showed she knew the impossibility of that. 'You don't understand,' she added in a whisper. 'You'll never understand.'

'Of course I do. You needed someone to take care of your family because you didn't have a clue how to do it yourself, and Tom was available. Of course I do think it's strange you saw that when I didn't. I can't help wondering how friendly you were before Bob died. But good luck to you anyway.'

Madge looked shocked. 'Of course there was nothing between us when Bob was alive! But I don't know what we would have done without him afterwards. He saved us, Hannah.'

'How lovely for you. How nice that you've taught him how to care for someone besides himself,' Hannah said, and would have either walked away or punched that bloody smarmy face in front of her if Tom hadn't appeared at that moment.

'Hannah! What's happened?'

'What makes you think something's happened?' she snapped. 'Maybe I just wanted to see if you're still alive, seeing as you've completely ignored your own family in favour of this.' She waved a hand, indicating the house.

He stepped in front of Madge as if to protect her. 'It's about Hal, isn't it?'

Hannah's hands clenched. 'You know about Lily?'

'She was here.'

'Of course she was.' She curled a lip at Madge. 'It seems they're forming a line.'

'I need to talk to you, Hannah.'

'What you need and what you get are two different things, Tom. I thought I should tell you that Lily wants to take Hal, but it seems you already know that and you didn't see the need to come to me.'

'She was here just twenty minutes ago.'

'I'm sure Tom could do something,' Madge said. 'He could help you, I know.'

'I don't need his help,' Hannah said, and walked away, head up, shoulders straight. She could feel them watching her.

'Come inside, Madge,' she heard Tom say, and though she didn't turn, she visualised his arm around Madge's waist as he guided her inside. Her hands remained clenched though tears slid down her face as she rounded the corner.

Good Enough for Them

Allie stood at the gate staring up Australia Street for ten minutes or more, trying to decide the meaning of what she had seen. Finally, no matter how hard she tried to deny it, she was forced to concede that her mother was having an affair with Claude Macy. The knowledge didn't come as a complete shock. She'd realised weeks ago that there was more to her mother and Claude than she'd thought possible so soon after her father left. But it was plain in the way they had looked at each other, the way they touched. The way they walked, his arm around her, their bodies close. No matter how far back she searched her memory, Allie couldn't recall a time her mum and dad walked like that.

She didn't like the idea, but she knew she'd have to live with it. I don't want anyone interfering in my life, she thought, so I can't very well interfere in Mum's. He's a nice enough man. I suppose I'll get used to it after a while. I just hope she's happy with him like Dad seems to be with Mrs Lenahan.

A lump formed in her throat as she realised that her family would never be the same again.

Lily's trying to straighten herself out and she believes Hal can help her do it. That sounds fair enough, Allie thought. Mum raves on about Lily being no good but she would say that, wouldn't she? She wants to keep Hal. Of course I remember what he was like when he came to our house. I was just a kid myself yet I could see what he'd been through. But that was a while ago when Lily was drinking all the time and Hal had to be looked after. It's different now. He doesn't have to be nappy-changed or hand-fed. That's what a judge will see. We'll lose Hal for sure. And Janet's gone. She'll never come back, nor will Dad. Doesn't matter that he's doing it too. He'll never take Mum back, not when he finds out she's been having sex with Claude Macy. He probably knows that already. Everybody's probably known for ages. Everyone except me.

All right then. What was good enough for Hannah and Tom Gordon was good enough for their daughter. Her world as she knew it was falling apart so she'd make a new life for herself with Johnny Lawson. He loved her. He'd said so a dozen times. They'd get married and she'd work while he finished school and became a lawyer, then it would be her turn.

First things first. She'd prove her love for him and she'd do it tonight. They hadn't made arrangements to meet, but he'd be at the guesthouse. He was adamant about Sunday night being his study night and nothing could alter that, but she felt sure he'd change his mind when he knew what she had in store for him on this particular Sunday night. She could phone him from one of the public telephones at the quay and ask him to pick her up there.

She'd say she was going to see Janet, then Grandma would give her money for the tram fare – which happened without the usual directions and complaints. Allie took that as a good omen. Having finally made the decision to commit herself to Johnny Lawson, she felt light-headed. Getting out of cleaning up after the kin, by telling her mother that she needed to study, she spent the rest of the day in her room so no one would guess. It had to be written all over her. Every time she thought about what was about to happen, her face flamed. Her eyes grew heavy. Her body alternated between flushing hot with expectation and shivering cold with apprehension. She remembered what Grandma and Hannah had told her about sex, about the risk of becoming pregnant, of sexual diseases. They'd skimmed over that last one so she didn't know much, but Johnny wouldn't have any diseases, would he? Though Janet said he had the reputation of being a womaniser. No, of course he wouldn't, and being a womaniser meant he should know how to protect her from falling pregnant. Yet thinking about those things made her feel queasy. Sex didn't sound like such a good idea after all. Or did it? Only one way to find out.

Now, what to wear? It had to be something Johnny hadn't seen before. Something to make her appear older, sexier. She looked despairingly through her wardrobe. The only piece of clothing looking reasonably new was the blue dress. She'd kept it because Dad had given it to her, because she didn't have the heart to pass it on to one of her cousins as was the usual habit amongst her kin. She'd hardly worn it, but it made her look closer to twelve than eighteen. A dress that hadn't been worn to death didn't exist in her wardrobe. Yet her and her mum were pretty much the same size now. Turning to Hannah's side of the wardrobe, she pulled out the few skirts, blouses and dresses, and draped them across the bed.

Hannah was no richer than her as far as clothes were concerned, but a mid length burnt-orange skirt with a black kick pleat at one side looked right. A black short-sleeve blouse, black high-heeled, open-toed shoes and a black handbag. Perfect. She wouldn't bother with stockings. Be too awkward taking them off.

She giggled nervously at that thought.

A touch of make-up. Not too much. She didn't want to look cheap. Would he think that of her? Of course not. He loved her.

Calling out that she'd have tea with Janet, she covered up with an old coat, left it on the veranda on her way out, grabbed the handbag and shoes from where she'd hidden them earlier, and took off at a run.

Her plan for Johnny to meet her at the quay stalled when a snooty female voice answered the phone.

'Mr Lawson is not available at the moment,' the voice informed her.

'By not available, do you mean not at home?' Allie asked, wanting to but forbearing to add, or is it just that you can't be bothered getting him.

The voice became even snootier. 'I mean he is not in his room.' Then, grudgingly, 'I suppose I could take a message. Who shall I say called?'

Allie was about to say girlfriend then changed her mind. 'His fiancée, Alma Gordon.'

'Fiancée?' From snooty to disparaging. 'I hardly think so. He happens to be outside in his car and . . .'

'Thank you.' Allie cut her off by hanging up. That was the one thing she liked about telephones – the sense of satisfaction obtained by banging down the receiver on snooty people. And she should have known Johnny would be in his car. He often parked it under the light and sat in it to study. The only way to peace and quiet, he'd told her.

A half hour and a tram and ferry ride later, she stopped to breathe in the heady perfume of the gardenia border while trying to calm her racing pulse. What should she say or do? She could get into the car with him and let nature take its course. He would kiss her, want her, then they'd go to his room and make love. He shared a room with his friend Les, but he'd said that Les always stayed at a girlfriend's house on weekends. But what if he wanted to do it in the car? That was too crowded, too public, too . . . Too sordid. She would talk to him through the window, suggest going to the privacy of his room. He'd then know why she was here, but that was all right.

Her mind still turning circles, her body still alternating between hot and cold, she hurried over to the car before her courage failed. The driver's side window was down. His voice was husky but clear. She heard every word.

'We love each other so it's all right, honey. We're both adults and we don't have to bother about what other people might say.'

But he wasn't saying it to her.

Shock was a physical blow, sending her staggering back, both hands to her mouth. She would have fallen if she hadn't thumped into the light post. Her chest tightened until she had to fight for each breath.

It had to be someone else in there. Johnny wouldn't do this to her. He loved her, he'd said so a dozen times. But it was his voice, softly persuasive, saying those words she'd so often heard before. Before, each one had stirred her, made her want him until she was almost crying with the need. Now they were knives.

'We can't go inside,' he said. 'Someone will see us together and you'd lose your job.' His voice grew more impelling. 'It's all right here. Like last week. It was good then, wasn't it?'

Silence. They had to be kissing.

The light overhead dimmed. The world around her grew dark. For a moment she thought she'd pass out. Then she realised she was holding her breath. Letting it out slowly, easily, her surrounds became normal. The best thing to do, the least mortifying, was to back off, turn around and go home. But she had to be sure it was really him. Walking forward unsteadily, praying she'd heard wrong and that it was someone else inside Johnny's car, she bent from the waist as though bowing to the occupants and looked through the window. They were in the back seat. She couldn't see the girl's face, but she could see enough to know that Johnny's mouth was on hers. His hand cupped her breast.

Allie drew in a sharp breath. He lifted his head, turned, looked straight at her. A frown, but no sign of consternation, of shame, even regret. His expression was a shrug. She felt as if he'd punched her in the stomach. Another punch followed when she recognised his partner – the long blonde hair loosened from its pins, the lipstick-smeared mouth, the half-closed eyes, the face slack from wanting.

Still bent, she backed away. By the time Janet called out to her, Allie had turned the corner of the house.

Like last week. It was good then, he'd said.

Allie felt the punch again. She cried out with the pain of it.

Janet. He was making love to Janet.

The mongrel. The bitch.

Her anger was short-lived. It had turned to a heavy-stomach, sweat-faced humiliation by the time she reached the wharf. How could she have been so naïve? Had they been laughing at her all this time, all this time she imagined herself in control, handling the situation, telling herself she was chaste and honourable while all the time, let's face it, she was just terrified of falling pregnant, of being found out, of what other people would think. Now she felt as though the whole world knew she'd come here for sex. Would she have thought about getting married within the next ten years if she hadn't been looking for someone to help pay her way through university? That made her a whore, didn't it? Selling herself for money. Even if you get married, if you do it for money that made you a whore.

There weren't many people on the ferry, but the ones who were there seemed to turn aside as she passed, staring after her, whispering among themselves. She didn't stop to think how or why or the impossibility of it, but she felt sure they knew. Avoiding eye contact, she hurried through to the other side of the ferry and leaned against the rail, staring down at the black, oily-looking water. Within minutes, the surge and flow of it had mesmerised her. She swayed with the rhythm, staring down, shuffling closer to the rail to watch the barely perceptible slap of waves against the ferry's side. She looked up but couldn't see the moon. It was hidden by cloud. She could see the glow of it, but not the actual moon. A bad omen, Grandma would say. A sign of deception.

Think about your grandmother and the moon and anything else so you won't keep seeing his face, their faces, his hand on her breast, hearing his words, 'It was good last week, wasn't it?'

She wanted to cry, to scream, to howl like a dog. She couldn't bear this pain. Moving closer to the rail she bent over it, feeling it push into her stomach, harder as she leaned further forward. Just a little further and she could slide over. She raised up onto her toes. There was no fear, just a terrible sadness. Her pulse slowed. It would be so easy.

'It looks great, doesn't it?'

She didn't need to look. She knew his voice.

'The ferry's lights reflected on the water,' he added. 'They seem to wave to you. Funny idea that, isn't it? The lights waving to you. But be careful. If you bend too far, you might fall.'

Her heels settled onto the floor. 'Go away, Charlie,' she mumbled.

'I saw you the other night. I wanted to introduce you to my cousin Rita but you wouldn't stand still long enough. Rita's staying with friends over at Cremorne. Down from the country looking for work. She's sure to find a job okay, don't you reckon? Plenty around.'

She straightened, but didn't look at him. 'Just go away.'

He moved closer. Their shoulders touched and he nudged her away from the railing. 'Not while you've got that look on your face. I'll leave you alone if you go inside. Come on, Allie. Nothing's that bad.'

To her complete and utter mortification, she burst into tears.

'I wasn't going to. I would have changed my mind, I know I would have. I'd never be that desperate. I couldn't,' she sobbed. 'Go away and leave me alone, Charlie Lenahan. I hate you.'

Placing an arm around her waist, he pulled her close. Her resistance lasted for less than a second. Nestling her face into the hollow under his chin, she breathed in the clean smell of him: soap, perspiration, and a hint of baking bread. Her sobs eased to an occasional sigh as he said, 'Shut up, Allie. Just shut up,' into her hair.

Ten minutes later, her tears still wet on Charlie's shirt, she ambled off the ferry holding his hand. Though she still felt eyes following her, she kept her head high. His fingers tightened when a middle-aged woman whispered to them, 'Everyone loves a lover,' as she walked past. Charlie grinned as he looked at Allie and caught her staring up at him.

'You going to tell me about it?' he asked as they waited for the tram. When she frowned, he added, 'About back there on the ferry.'

Allie thought about it for less than a second. 'It was nothing. Just silly. Mum and Dad and now there's trouble with Hal,' she said.

She might be stupid and a bit naïve, but she knew enough to understand that some things were best kept to yourself.

The Only One

Hannah glanced around the table, then lowered her eyes. The tension was almost palpable. Hal was crying again. He'd been bursting into tears at the drop of a hat since he woke. That was unusual for Hal, it had to be a hangover from yesterday. Colin, still edgy from another one of his nightmares, no doubt also caused by Lily, wouldn't talk to anyone. He wore suit trousers and a lightly starched shirt, probably because he hadn't anything else. As far as she knew, he had no casual clothes. This morning he hadn't bothered to shave or comb his hair, and that was unheard of for Colin. Beside him, Great-Aunt Florrie sat with her head down, eating as though it was her last meal on earth, and Grandma hadn't touched her breakfast. Allie looked more mutinous than usual. She'd woken in a happy mood and even hummed as she dressed for school. That hadn't lasted long. Mainly because Grandma snapped at her every time she moved or spoke.

'You're going to have to make a decision about your daughter,' Grandma said, as though continuing a conversation despite the fact that no one had uttered a word except for the usual good mornings, and even they hadn't been much more than a chorus of grunts. Not counting Great-Aunt Florrie, who couldn't be unpleasant if she tried.

'I hope by now Alma has made up her mind she won't be going to university. There's no money for it, bursary or not. No sense her staying on at Trilby's shop either. It doesn't pay enough. She'll get more by working in the city. Buckingham's looking for girls. They have a fashion parade every Friday, and though I shouldn't say so when she values herself too highly now, she could make extra by modelling. We could do with the money, little enough though it may be.'

'I'm here, Grandma. Right across the table from you. You don't have to talk about me as if I'm somewhere else,' Allie grumbled. 'And it's not Mum's decision to make. If I'm old enough to work, I'm old enough to choose where that will be.'

'I've found that talking to you is like talking to the chooks. I get no sense at all.'

'Can we discuss this later?' Hannah asked. 'I'll be late for work.'

'I'd like to get things settled. We're short of money and if I can't rely on Allie paying her own way, I'll need to start charging the kin a fee for consultation besides the one for the potions.'

'Now, Grandma, you know you'd never do that,' Colin said.

'Never say never,' she snapped. 'I'll do what I have to do. And what you have to do is take Hal to school this morning and pick him up this afternoon, so you'd best stay out of the pub.'

Hannah stared at her. 'You think that's necessary?'

'I wouldn't have said it if I didn't.'

'Maybe I should . . .' Hannah paused. She was going to say she should pick him up herself, but she couldn't say it in front of Colin. He'd think she didn't trust him. 'But I can't afford time off work.'

Colin didn't look at her as he said, 'I can look after him, Hannah.'

'No sense in getting your nose out of joint,' Grandma told him. 'That woman's got friends and they're bigger than you. You get Fat-Auntie Jean or one of her boys to go with you.'

Hannah's look pleaded. 'That might be best, Colin. Lily had two men with her yesterday.'

He glanced at Hal, who was staring back at him, wide-eyed.

'Yeah, sure. I'll ask Big Les. He's off on compo this week with a crook knee. And don't worry, Hal.' He screwed his face in an exaggerated wink. 'Everything's gunner be fine, you'll see.'

Hal sat back in his chair, obviously satisfied.

Allie stood. 'I'd better get going or Mrs Trilby will be wondering where I am. I said I'd stack the fruit this morning.' She looked at Grandma. 'I'll finish early and go in to Buckingham's. If they can use me, I'll put my notice in with Mr Trilby. But I'm telling you now, I'll defer my bursary, not quit it. I'm going to save up and —'

'That will take forever. Just make up your mind to the fact that you're a worker, not a rich woman's child,' Grandma said dismissively.

'I know what I am, Grandma. And I know what you are but I'm not allowed to say it,' Allie replied, then stalked out while Grandma was still sitting with her mouth open. Hannah followed her so Grandma wouldn't see her grin. Colin didn't bother to cover his snort of laughter.

'I'm glad you think that girl's backchat is funny,' Grandma snapped.

Colin grinned. 'She didn't backchat,' he pointed out. 'She managed not to, even though you asked for it. You've been on her back since I don't know when.'

'She's got ideas above her station.'

'Oh yeah, and what and where's that? Your idea of who she should be because that's what you are and what ya forced Hannah into? Don't take your guilt out on the kid, Grandma.'

Hannah had been about to re-enter the kitchen to make a sandwich for her lunch, but she stopped just out of their sight, waiting to hear Grandma's answer. It was as she expected.

'You're saying I should have allowed Hannah to continue on at school? You're blaming me? She was pregnant. She had to do right by Janet and give her a legitimate father.'

'She would never have settled on Tom Gordon if she knew she could go to uni. She wouldn't have got pregnant.'

'So you're blaming me for Hannah's bad choices, are you?'

Hannah heard a chair scrape and guessed that Great-Aunt Florrie had stood, ready to leave. Great-Aunt Florrie could never bear arguments and escaped them whenever she could. She liked a peaceful life, so Hannah could hardly believe she was hearing correctly when her great-aunt spoke.

'Hannah never had a choice,' she said quietly. 'She didn't choose to be left behind by her mother, then her father. She wasn't given any choices when she fell pregnant. No one told her about the joys and pitfalls of raising the child alone, or about adoption or even a termination. And she liked the fact that Tom chose her when all her friends were trying to win him. Hannah was flattered, as any girl would be. And there's nothing wrong with Tom. He was a wild young man, but honest and good-hearted. Yet he and Hannah were never suited to each other. We all know that. Hannah knows it now.'

Great-Aunt Florrie was the one who calmed everybody else, who never spoke out of turn.

'And I'm sorry, Emily,' she continued, 'but I agree with Colin. You're making Allie's life a misery because you've always regretted not letting Hannah continue her education. You and I both know we could have worked something out. But you want her to take over from you with the herbs one day, and you knew back then she'd never have done that if she had a choice. Now you're determined to stop Allie. That's only because if she makes a success of her life away from here, you'll know Hannah could have done the same. She'll know it too, and you don't want that. You're afraid of losing her. But you must one day. She won't take on the herbs. She'll break away sooner or later and go to find the life she should have had. She just needs to find a key.'

'Hannah has the feeling in her bones about what people need. She's good at it, and she knows the herbs better than anyone,' Grandma said firmly.

'That well may be,' Great-Aunt Florrie agreed, 'but she should be able to choose.'

'Shouldn't we all?' Grandma's voice had grown softer. 'I didn't choose to be a widow with six kids but I got on with it. I didn't want to scrub floors and do other people's washing and ironing but I did what I had to do to raise my kids right, just like hundreds and thousands of other women now their men are war dead. We get on with it. That's what we do. Now someone has to take over helping the women around here, take over making sick people well and well people look after themselves better. Someone has to take all that over and do it soon. I'm not getting any younger, Florrie. I'm not getting any fitter neither. Gets harder and harder to get out of bed come mornings. I've always counted on Hannah being the one to carry on, to put other people's needs above her own. Now you tell me she can't do that. At least, she doesn't want to. Who else is there then?' Grandma Ade asked, and her voice now held a tremor.

'Colin or Hal, or maybe both could do the herbs,' Great-Aunt Florrie stated. 'They have the knack too, and they're quick learners. They'd do well together and I know Hal wants it. Isn't that right, Hal?'

Though Hannah couldn't see Hal from where she stood, she felt sure he would have nodded.

'I'm not sure about Colin,' Great-Aunt Florrie continued. 'About him wanting it. But I know he'd be good.'

'Maybe I would, but I'm not well enough to make the learning worthwhile,' Colin said quietly. 'Hal would be the one. That would give him a future. He's not extra smart at school and could be he's not got the build to take on hard yakka.'

'You're being ridiculous, both of you,' Grandma said, though her tone had lost its snap. 'It has to be Hannah. Without her, who'll help our kin and the other women around here?'

'Guess they'll have to learn to help themselves. Like we all do in the end,' Colin said brusquely. 'Come on, Hal mate. Let's get you ready for school.'

Great-Aunt Florrie is right, Hannah thought. What I want, what I've always wanted, is the freedom to choose what to do with my life.

She walked away before they saw her tears.

People Have Sex

For the next few days, Allie see-sawed between loss, anger and a sensation of scarring inside. She thanked the heavens daily that she hadn't given in to Johnny Lawson's persuasions as Janet obviously had, yet remembering how close she had come, how much she had wanted it, she still felt as if she'd lost her virginity. To her mind, nothing would be new to her except the final act of sex. She believed she'd experienced everything else.

Any thought of Johnny Lawson would bring the blood rushing to her face. Not from humiliation any more, but from anger. Memory of that moment he'd turned from Janet to look at her served to cause disgust. Disgust and dislike. How could she have ever thought she loved him? How could she have ever thought he held a candle to Charlie Lenahan? Yet all that was as nothing when compared to the knowledge of Janet's treachery. How could her sister treat her that way? How long had she and that rotten man been laughing behind her back?

Determined to be better than Janet could ever be, to top the class at school, to be a rich, famous and prosperous lawyer while her sister cleaned up other people's mess, she grimly concentrated on school work, bringing out her books every night and studying until Grandma ordered her to turn off the light and stop wasting electricity. She might have to leave school soon and go out to work, but meanwhile she'd be top of the class and make sure her teachers would do their best to help her get what she so desperately wanted.

She knew her mother had sensed something was wrong, but she asked no questions. Probably believes I'm upset about her and Mr Macy, Allie thought. Yet when compared to Johnny Lawson, Claude Macy was impeccable. He had eyes for no other female but her mother, who was working overtime at the shirt factory and came home most nights late for tea, too tired to do more than eat, spend a little time with Hal and Allie, then fall into bed.

Deciding to ask about Claude Macy, and put her mum's mind at rest by telling her she had no objection, Allie had gone into their bedroom one night when she thought Hannah was getting ready for bed, first giving Hal paper and pencils to ensure they wouldn't be disturbed. She even considered bringing up the subject of Johnny Lawson. Not to cause trouble for Janet, but to ask why some men were inclined to cheating and lies. Not all men. Not Charlie or Colin. And Claude Macy perhaps. Best not to mention Dad. Allie still hadn't made up her mind about him. Yet when she opened the door, her mother was lying across the bed, half undressed and sound asleep. Allie pulled her legs straight and covered her with a blanket and went back to studying Shakespeare.

No opportunity for a private talk presented itself for the rest of the week, and Allie's feelings were still a bubbling mix when Janet arrived for one of her now rare visits. Grandma and Great-Aunt Florrie were knitting cot blanket squares while listening to 'Beyond the Creaking Door', their favourite Friday-night program on the wireless. Colin was reading to Hal in his room, Allie writing an essay at the kitchen table, when Hannah arrived arm in arm with Janet, who had met her at the factory door.

'I still don't know what the fuss is all about,' Janet told her mother as they entered the kitchen, obviously carrying on a conversation started while on their way here. 'You're talking about Lily Gatley. Wringing wet she'd only weigh half as much as you. She'd fall over if ya blew on her.'

'It's not Lily by herself, though you shouldn't underestimate her,' Hannah told her eldest daughter. 'She's a lot tougher and stronger than she looks, and she has men friends who would do anything for her.'

Janet's upturned lip showed her disgust. 'Oh come on, Mum. She made all these threats last Sunday and ya haven't seen or heard from her since. A week's gone by. She probably got on the booze and she's forgotten all about it by now. If she was really interested in Hal, she'd have been back for him years ago.'

'That's what worries me,' Hannah said grimly. 'She has something dreadful in mind, I'm sure.'

'She's just trying to straighten herself out,' Janet said dismissively.

'What do you know? You weren't here. You're never here. You haven't seen what she's like,' Allie snapped.

'That's no way to talk to your sister,' Grandma said curtly. 'You keep a civil tongue in your head, missy, or go away.'

'I'm gone,' Allie retorted, and stalked out of the kitchen, hesitating in the hallway, in no mood to join Colin and Hal.

'What's going on between you two?' she heard Hannah ask.

'It's not me,' Janet said. 'It's her. We've never been best friends.'

'But she's only seen you a couple of times in the past few months. You must know why she's being so quarrelsome.'

A pause in the conversation – or more than likely a whispered exchange, Allie thought – was followed by Janet saying, 'I'll ask her if that'll make ya happy.'

'You know damn well what it is,' Allie said when she stalked out into the backyard with Janet hard on her heels.

'Well, I'm guessing it's to do with ya seeing me with Johnny Lawson, but I can't see how that affects you.' Janet paused to close the back door behind them. 'And don't be yelling unless ya want the whole street to know our business.'

'I remember you telling me to be careful of him. He's a womaniser and you can't trust him.' Allie mimicked Janet's tone, but kept her low.

Janet shrugged. 'Neither ya can.'

'You've been sleeping with him,' Allie stated.

Janet grinned. 'We're not doing all that much sleeping.'

'How charming,' Allie snapped.

'Oh come on, Allie, grow up. People have sex. That's the way it is. And anyway, it's my problem. My life. I can handle it.'

'Without a second thought of me.'

Janet looked mystified. 'What's it got to do with you?'

Allie stared at her. 'He hasn't told you, has he?'

'Told me what?'

'I've been going out with him for months. We usually meet at the quay, have coffee, then we go parking at the Botanic Gardens or Gap Park.'

It was Janet's turn to stare. 'You're lying!'

'He's the liar. I heard some of those things he said to you. He's said exactly the same things to me. About being in love, about being meant for each other. About being grown up enough to know what we want.'

Janet continued to stare, shaking her head in denial of everything Allie was saying.

'Or was that last bit just for me?' Allie asked. 'You've already given him what he wants.'

'I don't believe a word of it.' Janet turned towards the door.

'You mean you don't want to believe it. But why do you think I was so upset? He's told me a hundred times that I'm the only one.'

Janet's blue eyes darkened to the colour of the ocean on a stormy day as she swung around. 'Ya lying bitch!' she spat out, covering the space between them in a couple of strides. Her hand was raised, ready to strike, and when Allie didn't flinch but lifted her head and looked defiantly back at her, she lashed out with enough force to knock her sister onto the ground. Allie grabbed hold of a bench and pulled herself onto it, gasping with the shock of the attack and clutching her cheek where an angry red mark grew darker with every passing moment.

'Lying bitch!' Janet spat out again, and Allie came up swinging.

Janet, who was easily the bigger of the two, caught Allie's fist, grabbed her forearm and twisted, throwing her across the bench, and raised her hand again. Allie kicked out, catching her in the stomach. Air gusted out of Janet's lungs and she bent double, then slowly hunched down onto the brick cobbles. Dropping forward onto her hands and knees, she began to dry-retch, her body convulsing with the strength of each heave.

'Oh God, God. I'm sorry,' Allie whispered harshly. 'Janet, I'm sorry. Are you all right? I'll get Grandma.'

'No. No,' Janet gasped, shoving Allie's arm away. 'Get away from me.' She sucked at the air in small wheezing breaths, hiccuping, 'ShutupAllie, shutupAllie,' when Allie squatted back on her haunches and continued apologising.

Minutes passed and her breathing gradually became easier, though she was in obvious pain as she rocked back and forth, clutching her stomach.

'What? What?' Allie cried out, in tears now.

'Cramps,' Janet wheezed.

'I'll get Grandma,' Allie said again.

'Don't ya dare!'

'Mum.'

'No!'

'What can I do?'

'Just shut up for two minutes, can't ya?'

Putting a hand over her mouth as if to stop the flow of words, Allie watched as Janet's breathing slowly became normal.

'Are you all right?' she finally said, but cautiously, expecting to be told to shut up again.

'Think so,' Janet sighed, not trying to hide the catch in her throat that threatened to turn into tears at the slightest provocation.

'I really am sorry. I just didn't want you to hit me again.'

'I shouldn't have done that. Look at ya cheek. I hope it don't turn into a bruise or Grandma and Mum will want to know why. We can't tell them about Johnny.'

'I'll say I fell over.'

Janet nodded wearily. Clinging to the side of the bench, she pulled herself up and onto its edge. The action was slow and unsteady, as though she had aged fifty years within minutes.

'It still hurts, doesn't it?' Allie asked. 'I think I'd better get Grandma. You scared me. I kicked really hard.'

'I don't need Grandma. I just need ya to tell me you were lying.'

'I would be lying then. I really have been going out with Johnny.'

Janet dashed away an ooze of tears with the back of her hand. 'I guess I expected something like this. I've always known what he's like. But it never entered my head that it would be you.'

'Everything I said was true,' Allie stated earnestly.

'That explains the look on yer face the other night. I wondered why ya was so horrified when ya saw me with him. Seems like he's been stringing both of us along. Oh Christ, Allie. You're still a babe in the woods, but I should've known better. I kidded myself that with him and me it was different.'

'Maybe it is.'

'Nah, he conned us. Me more than you, but that's your good sense in not going to bed with him.'

Allie wondered if she should tell Janet her reason for going to the guesthouse that night. She decided against it. It was nice, talking honestly with her sister like this, but she didn't fool herself that it would last. No doubt they'd argue again in the not too distant future and if she told Janet the truth, she'd have it thrown up in her face in the nastiest possible way.

'He won't make a fool of me a second time. I've got no intention of ever seeing him again,' she said firmly.

Janet looked away without answering.

'Don't tell me you will,' Allie said incredulously.

'I love him.'

'You have to be joking!'

'Things are not just black or white, Allie.'

'This is.'

'No it's not. There's things you don't know.'

'Like what?'

Janet hesitated before saying, 'Just things.'

'Keep them to yourself then.'

'I will.'

'You can be such a bitch, Janet.'

'You should talk.'

'Oh, what's the use.'

'Where are ya going?'

'In to do the dishes. I don't suppose you want to help.'

'Ya not going to say anything to Grandma or Mum?'

'Say what? That I'm an idiot but you're downright stupid?'

'Go on, nick off then.'

Allie did.

Look at Me

Hannah breathed a sigh of relief as she climbed into bed. The day had been a frantic one. A particularly nasty influenza strain had been going around the neighbourhood, resulting in absenteeism at the shirt factory. The manager had arrived to give those who had turned up a lecture on loyalty. 'For the factory to keep running and obtain more orders to keep you in work, you must put the fulfilment of current orders on time ahead of your own wellbeing and work the overtime,' had been his instructions in a nutshell. A brief union meeting followed his speech and to Hannah's surprise, most of the workers agreed. She would have told him where to go with his orders and his loyalty. Where was that loyalty when record profits were made last year and the workers asked for a rise in pay? They'd been turned down of course, but she was outnumbered five to one on a vote to work an extra two hours every day for another month. Four hours this day to get a special order finished on time. Her 'I don't agree so can I leave at the usual time?' had been treated with scorn, and a warning of being blackballed if she didn't go along with the majority.

'We want the overtime. We need the money,' that majority said.

'So do I, but there's a principle involved,' she argued.

Money versus principle turned out to be no contest.

Arriving home after nine o'clock tired, hungry and irritable, she was met by Grandma Ade in a matching mood, though while Hannah wanted to list her grievances, perhaps even needed to list them, Grandma was nowhere near as forthcoming. When Hannah asked, all she got was a tirade on the pressures of having to cope with 'smart-mouthed youngsters and dirty-livered grand-daughters.'

'Tea was over hours ago. The washing-up's done and if you want something to eat you'll have to get it yourself. I'm tired. There might be some soup if you're lucky. Don't cut into that fresh loaf and don't leave a mess. Hal and Allie are in bed asleep and that's where and what I intend to be in the next ten minutes. I don't want to hear any more complaints from you,' were her final breath-free instructions.

Hannah gave up trying to be civil and flounced off to bed hungry, sweaty, and nursing a pounding headache. So she was less than impressed when she was woken ten minutes after finally falling asleep by smashing glass and what sounded like someone attacking the wall with a hammer. When she rushed out into the hall, Great-Aunt Florrie poked her head around her door.

'Lily?' Hannah gasped.

'No, love, it's Colin,' her great-aunt whispered. 'It's best to leave him be when he's like this. He'll get over it if you just leave him be.'

Adding a sympathetic smile and a shrug, she pulled back and closed the door.

'In a pig's eye I'll leave him be. It's all right for him. He doesn't have to get up early and go to work. It's about time he learned to think of someone besides himself,' Hannah muttered angrily. 'You two stay in bed and go back to sleep. Don't you dare get up,' she ordered angrily when Hal and Allie stared at her.

Not stopping to knock, she threw open his door.

'What the hell do you think you're doing,' faded halfway through the sentence when she looked around his room. Clothes, blankets, sheets, newspapers, magazines and shoes had been thrown in all directions. The bed was upended, the wardrobe pushed over, his cheval glass fragmented. Clad only in underpants, Colin was trying to tear his bedspread in half. His skin had turned a shade of purplish-red and the veins in his face, arms and chest stood out like ropes.

'Get out!' he hissed at her, his tone as vicious as his glare.

'What are you —'

'Get out!'

'You're not having a nightmare. You are a bloody nightmare. Look at you. Look at this mess.'

Throwing the bedspread aside, he strode over to her, lowered his shoulder and slammed it into hers, hurling her backwards against the door frame. 'Get out or I'll bloody well throw ya out head first.'

Closing her hand into a fist, she lashed out with a roundhouse right, missing the side of his head by a hair's breadth as he ducked just in time.

'Bastard,' she hissed, and launched the other fist.

He ducked again, stepped back and stared at her.

'Jesus, Hannah.'

'Don't you hit me. Don't you dare even try,' she said, and ran at him, shoving him backwards across the room. He hit the wall, bounced forward, then threw himself sideways when she lashed out again. Her fist hit the wall as he slid downwards.

'Mu-um? Mum!' Hal called out from the next room.

'Go to sleep!' Hannah yelled.

'It's all right, Hal,' Colin called. 'It's just ya mum and me playing silly buggers against the wall.'

'Can you do it quietly?' Allie shouted.

'Ahhh, Christ. Christ,' Hannah groaned, nursing her damaged hand and dancing around the room in small hopping pain steps.

'Serves ya right, attacking a man in his own bedroom.'

'Look what you've done. It's broken,' she moaned.

'The wall's a bloody sight tougher than you, and if ya didn't know that, ya have to be off yer bloody trolley.'

'I didn't mean to hit the bloody wall,' she snarled.

'No, ya meant to bust into my room where yer not wanted or needed and attack me when I'm minding me own business.'

'Look what you've done.' She pointed with the damaged hand. 'Ow, ow. That hurt.'

'My room. Nothing to do with you.' He stood. 'Show me.'

'Stay away, you mongrel.'

'Go wake Grandma then. It might be broken.'

'As if she'd be asleep with the racket you've been making. As if anyone would be asleep! They're all in bed awake, thanks to your noise, and taking care not to upset you. Well, bugger that for a joke. It's about time someone told you off for being so bloody selfish! And I can't afford to have a broken hand. I need to work. They'll think I did it on purpose to have sick days because I didn't agree with the vote.'

'You had a vote on whether or not to break your hand?'

'Don't be stupid.' His eyes showed a hint of a smile. 'It's not funny, Colin.'

'Sure it is. Show me.'

'What do you know about broken bones?'

'I've seen enough of them.'

'Ow, ow.' But she allowed him to take her hand. He stroked it gently, pushing down a little on each bone.

'Not broken,' was his verdict, 'but it'll swell and be sore. Grandma will have something to take the swelling down and make the nasty hurt that was all naughty Colin's fault go away.'

'Very funny. You're a real card, Colin.'

'I know, and I ought to be dealt with. And you've got a pussy punch or ya hand really would be broken.'

She glanced around the room again. 'You've done this before, and not in your sleep either, haven't you? But when Grandma or somebody comes in you make out you're in a nightmare. You're a fraud, that's what you are.'

'What, I'm going to tell 'em I go off me brain every so often?'

'This has to be frustration with a capital f.'

'Haven't you ever wanted to smash and break and yell?'

She didn't hesitate. 'Yes, but I don't.'

'Right. Always in control, aren't ya, Hannah,' he said, his voice heavy with sarcasm.

She ignored that. 'Look what you've done to the mirror. That's not Grandfather's cheval glass is it? The one that used to be in Grandma's room?'

'And still is. This one came from Auntie Jean's Treasure Chest.'

'But why, Colin? Why smash it like that?'

'Because I looked into it. Jesus, Hannah. Look at me. Look.' He opened his arms wide. 'This is what that bloody war did to me. Skin and bone, and yellow skin at that. Liver and kidneys shot and now me ticker's acting up. All me teeth fell out. Hair's gone grey. Look at me. I'll never have kids. Never get married. I'll never have sex unless I pay for it. Who the hell would have someone who looks like this? And wipe that pity off ya face or I'll wipe it off for ya.'

'It isn't pity, Colin. It's disbelief. Okay, you're probably right about not having kids, but I don't understand why you think you'll never find anyone to love you. If you think that, you don't know yourself. You don't know women.'

His eyes were like knives, slicing through her camouflage of assurance. 'Oh yeah. What about you, Hannah,' he said softly. 'Would you marry someone like me?'

'If I loved you.'

'But you don't, do ya? And maybe that's my fault. Maybe I should've offered "try before you buy" all those years ago. That night your father dumped ya here with Grandma, I reckon I could've had ya then if I'd been game enough to try.'

'I was a mess,' she began.

'I should've taken advantage, then maybe ya wouldn't have ended up with good-looking Tom Gordon who all the girls were fainting over. Maybe he's still the one ya want. Or is it Mr Claude bloody Macy with the looks and the body and the bags of money? But I was first, Hannah. First to look anyway. Remember that? About seven we were. I'll show ya mine if you show me yours. Remember that?'

She looked down, looked away from him, around the room, taking in the chaos, seeing him wreaking it in her mind's eye, feeling his frustration.

'I'm sorry,' was all she could think of to say.

'Sorry I feel the way I do or sorry you don't?'

'I didn't realise.'

'Are ya blind?'

'I must be or I wouldn't have come here to live where you live.'

'I've been in love with you since I was five,' he said matter-of-factly. His tone changed to almost vicious as he added, 'And I know, don't say it, ya love me like a brother. I don't want to hear it. Just piss off and leave me alone.'

Knowing that was all she could do, she stepped back, avoiding looking into his eyes, and walked out.

Allie was standing at the doorway to their room.

'Will Colin be all right?' she asked.

'How much did you hear?'

'Most of it. But I knew, Mum. I mean, I thought it. It's in the way he looks at you when he thinks nobody sees.'

'We'll have to move out of here.'

Allie nodded. 'Yeah. Come on, let's go to bed.'

Hannah straightened the bed covers, then climbed in and moved close to Allie. They cuddled up like lost children.

Sisters

Allie hadn't needed persuading when her mother said, 'Janet didn't look at all well the other night. I'd be grateful if you'd check on her, please, Allie. I'd go myself but I have to work overtime again this afternoon.'

'I'll go straight after school, before work,' Allie promised, glad of the chance to see if Janet had recovered from that kick in the stomach. She'd still been pale when she'd left for the guesthouse that night. Five evenings ago and they hadn't heard from her since.

Now, walking up from the Cremorne wharf, Allie's footsteps lagged. Johnny might be there, and the prospect of facing him was daunting. Should she tell him exactly what she thought of him, or should she look right through him as if he didn't exist? She really hated him. At least, she really wanted to hate him. But whenever she allowed her thoughts to wander to the way he'd kissed her, the way he'd touched her, she felt as though she was melting inside. How stupid was that! And she'd caught the ferry directly from school as she'd promised her mother. Johnny had never seen her in her school uniform. She looked so young in it. Well, she was young! Too young to know how she could hate someone yet not want him to see her looking anything but her best. It didn't make sense.

She wouldn't be able to ignore him. What she would do was recall the way she'd felt when she saw him and Janet in the car that night.

Steeling herself as she reached the guesthouse, she squared her shoulders and marched around the house to the back garden. His car wasn't there.

'Coward,' she called herself as a gust of air left her lungs in a huge sigh of relief.

'Janet, are you there?' No answer. She knocked again, harder this time. Still no answer. Allie pictured her sister inside the guesthouse, inside Johnny's room. But she didn't work afternoons. After serving lunch, she had time off until the guests had to be welcomed to the dining room and served from five-thirty. Maybe she'd gone into Cremorne for a few hours. Mrs Best, the owner, would know.

About to go looking for the office where the owner would most likely be, Allie heard a moan. It sounded stifled, but it was definitely a moan. A picture flashed of Janet doubled over, gasping for breath.

'Janet, are you in there? Are you all right?'

No answer again. She tried the handle. The door wasn't locked. Carefully and quietly, aware of the fact that Janet had a roommate and she, Allie, was trespassing, she pushed the door open just enough to slide her head inside and look around.

The room was small. Poky. The walls a washed-out beige. The only furniture was two plain wardrobes, a just as plain dressing table, two high-back chairs, and two beds – their covers a washed-out blue.

She barely had time to register the room and its contents when she heard the moan again, saw the lump in the bed nearest to her.

'Janet?'

'Help me.'

It was barely a whisper, but unmistakeable. Allie covered the distance in a couple of strides and pulled the cover down. Janet lay curled in a tight ball, holding her stomach. Her pillow was wet with tears. The sheet beneath her was soaked in blood.

'Oh Christ, Janet. Oh Janet. What's happened? Somebody stabbed you!'

'No. No.' The moan again, this time long, drawn out. The embodiment of pain. Janet's eyelids fluttered open, then closed again as her body arched back, then curled in again. 'My baby.'

Allie stared down, stunned.

'Ambulance,' Janet cried out.

Whirling around, Allie raced through the door, around the house and in the front door.

'Telephone! Where?' she demanded of a man and woman about to exit the doorway. They stared at her.

'Where's the bloody telephone!' Allie shrieked.

The man pointed. Allie ran again, skidded to a stop just long enough to open a door before running inside. A woman sat behind a desk. She looked up, wide-eyed, as Allie crashed into a chair.

'Ambulance,' Allie panted.

'I beg your —'

'I need an ambulance. My sister. Janet. She's dying.'

The woman stood. 'Janet Gordon? I'll just —'

'No you bloody won't! You'll take my word for it. Phone the ambulance.' Allie swallowed back a rush of tears. 'Please. I think she's lost her baby.'

'Baby?'

'Please. Please.'

The woman nodded as she lifted the receiver and started to dial. 'Go tend to her.'

Allie turned and ran, lurching against the front door jamb as she tried to skid around it, whacking her head on the corner but not stopping. When she reached the room again, Janet was sitting up in bed, still clinging to her stomach.

'Oh Allie, oh Allie,' she wailed.

'It's all right, Jan. The ambulance is on its way. It won't be long. Be here soon.'

'Shh. Shh,' Janet gasped. 'Don't talk, Allie. Don't carry on. Just hold onto me.'

Allie sat on the bed next to her, placed her arm around her, crying with her. They sat like that, Janet doubled over, Allie clinging to her, until the ambulance arrived.

The ambulance officer, a short, sturdy man in his mid-fifties, took one look and knew.

'Can you walk?' he asked Janet.

She shook her head. Nodded. 'I'm not sure.'

'Never mind,' he said, and beckoned to his partner, who wheeled in a stretcher.

'What about you, miss?' he asked Allie.

'Me?'

'Your head. It's cut.'

Allie put a hand up, rubbed her forehead, then looked at her fingers. Blood, but not a lot. 'I bumped it, I think,' she said. 'I'm all right.'

He turned away from her to help Janet climb onto the litter.

'I'm going with you,' Allie said.

'Sorry, miss. Not enough room. We've got another one in the ambulance.' He looked at Janet and sniffed. 'That other one's about to have her baby at any minute.'

'Why are you looking at my sister like that? It's not her fault,' Allie stated angrily.

'No time to argue, love. She'll be at Crown Street Women's Hospital if you want to find your way there.'

Allie watched them slide Janet into the ambulance, watched it take off up the street, siren wailing. The woman she assumed was Mrs Best, the owner, walked to the gate.

'Don't you ever barge into my house like that again,' she said in an icy voice. 'And tell your sister not to bother coming back. We do not want her kind here.'

'It was your kind got her that way,' Allie snarled, then raced for the wharf.

She missed the ferry by minutes and had to wait an hour for the next one, pacing up and down the wharf, crying, trying not to cry, not caring when people stared at her. If only she had money she could chase the ambulance in a taxi. But she didn't have money. Just enough to get home. Enough to get to the hospital anyway. Would that ferry never come! Twice she began to leave, thinking she'd run all the way, and knew that was stupid. Couldn't be done. A whole hour! Where was Johnny bloody Lawson and his rotten car when he was needed! Maybe he was back by now.

She ran back to the guesthouse. No car. Ran back to the wharf, in a sudden panic that she'd missed the next ferry and would have to wait another hour.

Maybe she should call a taxi, ask the driver to take her to the hospital, then run away without paying.

'Yeah, sure,' she said aloud, 'and end up in gaol. A fat lot of good that would do Janet.'

A young couple standing nearby looked uneasily at her and moved away. She couldn't have cared less. When the ferry finally arrived she was the first on it, the first to leave at the other end. Then she had to wait for a tram.

'Hurry hurry hurry,' she repeated over and over, ignoring a few grins from passers-by, a few glares, a few worried looks.

'Can I help, lovie?' one elderly woman asked.

'I wish, I wish. Thanks but no,' Allie said.

Over two hours from the time she'd last seen Janet, she jumped out of the tram while it was still moving, ignoring the conductor's call of, 'Hey, watch out, girlie, that's a good way to get yourself killed.'

And that would just serve me right, she thought, again mopping at the slide of tears that had been oozing down her cheeks since she left the guesthouse. She was determined not to cry. Her sister would say she was putting it on just to gain forgiveness. But how could Janet forgive her when she'd never be able to forgive herself? It was her fault. She knew it was her fault. She had killed. Or caused a death, which was much the same thing.

Breathing in a deep gust of air, she held it, holding back the sobs, the guilt, the sudden urge to throw herself in front of a passing car. She hadn't meant to hurt Janet or her baby, but she'd done it just the same. How could her sister ever forgive her? And what if she died like the baby? That didn't bear thinking about.

The hospital at last. Charging up the steps two at a time, she raced down the hall, almost knocking over a nurse on the way.

'Sorry. Sorry,' she gasped. 'Janet Gordon. Where is she?'

'It's not visiting hours, love.'

'Oh please, please.'

The nurse, a young woman not much older than Janet, grimaced and nodded. 'Okay, the one at the end of the hall that way. But just a few minutes, okay?'

Allie ran again.

Pausing at the doorway of the room Janet was sharing with seven other women, she called out, 'Sorry. Sorry,' to the still-watching nurse before tiptoeing across the floor.

'Bit late for the hush walk now, lovie,' a woman in the bed under a window said, adding a chuckle to show the words were meant more as a joke than a criticism. Allie was too busy staring down at Janet's face to pay attention.

Freckles that had always looked barely there now stood out like mud-flicked spots. Janet's cheeks were hollowed, her lips almost white. Without their usual coating of mascara, her lashes were pale yellow spikes resting on the dark half circles beneath her eyes. She looked to have aged ten years in a few days. Allie wished now that she'd taken time to telephone Claude's house and leave a message for her mother. Though Janet wouldn't have thanked her for that.

'Janet,' she whispered, 'it's me, Allie.'

'It's not visiting hours. Where've you been?' Janet asked without opening her eyes.

'This is my fault, isn't it?'

'You seen the doctor? What did they tell ya?' Again with her eyes closed.

Allie choked back a sob. 'I didn't think. I didn't see anyone.'

Janet opened her eyes at last. 'That's all right.'

'It's my fault, I know. That kick in the stomach. How can you forgive me? How could I expect you to?'

'For God's sake, Allie, stop rattling on. Not everything's about you. Did ya come here to get me to clear ya of all blame? If that's all ya want, then I do, so now ya can go.' The words ended in a sigh.

Allie knelt beside the bed and tried to take her sister's hand. Janet avoided that by sliding her hand under the blanket.

'I came to see if you're all right and you're not.'

'No I'm not, Allie, and I'm not in the mood to make you feel better.'

'Don't be a bitch, Janet. Not now.'

'All right, when?'

Allie hiccupped. Half laugh, half choked-back sob. But that was better. More like Janet. Star bright and always ready to fight was their father's description of her. That's what Allie wanted now. Of course she had come to make sure her sister was on the road to recovery, but she also wanted to take her share of the blame. Even though she hadn't known about the baby then. So when you think about it, it really wasn't all her fault.

'I wouldn't have kicked out like that if I'd known,' she said. 'You should have said something. It was you who started it. You should have told me.'

'You're the last person I'd tell. What happened at the guesthouse? Was it you who phoned the ambulance?'

Allie shook her head. 'Mrs Best. She said for you not to come back.'

'Wow, that's a relief. No job now either.'

'This isn't the time to make jokes, Janet. She said she doesn't want your kind there.'

'Thanks for telling me that, Allie. Not that I give a damn about what she thinks or says. She'd have guessed who the father is and half the people there have the hots for Johnny. Her too probably. But you'd know all about that.'

Allie could feel her temper rising. She used guilt to turn it down. Janet had every right to be as nasty as she wished. Allie was perfectly willing to take anything Janet wanted to dish out if it made her sister feel better.

'It was my fault, wasn't it?' she mumbled.

Janet stared at her for what seemed like minutes before saying curtly, 'I went to Mrs Bowrie.'

Allie pulled back as if she'd been slapped. 'Mrs Bowrie from Clegg Street? She . . . She does that for money. And people says bad things about her, that she doesn't really know what she's doing.'

'Opposite to Grandma who does it for pity,' Janet said sourly. 'Well I didn't want her pity and I didn't want to listen to her lectures on self control for the rest of me life like she gives to Mum. I suppose next thing you'll be saying I should have told her anyway.'

'Of course you should. She'd have helped you. This wouldn't have happened.' Allie waved a hand, indicating the ward, the hospital, the other women. 'She'd have taken care of you. Though she believes it's the last resort. She would have wanted you to keep the baby.'

'Yeah, like Mum kept me and married Dad. Look how good that turned out,' Janet said bitterly, and for the first time Allie realised that their parents' break-up had hurt Janet as much as it had her.

I'm so bloody selfish, she thought. 'I never think about other people, do I?' she murmured.

Janet heaved a sigh. 'Don't go whining to me about your problems and bringing what happened to me onto you,' she said, waving her hand as if flicking away a fly. 'Go home, Allie. Right now I've got more important things to think about than you feeling sorry for yourself.' Frowning, she muttered. 'Me own stupidity for a start.'

'But you must have loved Johnny.'

'Of course I loved him.' Janet's voice caught. She turned her face into the pillow. 'I'll always love him.'

'If you love him so much, why did you want to get rid of his baby?'

'Oh, I suppose you wouldn't have,' Janet said fiercely. 'Even though ya knew he'd never marry ya. Even though ya knew he never loved ya and he's just an arsehole anyway. For God's sake, Allie. Look what he did. Stringing us both along. Saying he loved us both. Hoodwinking us both. Next thing he would have been playing us off against each other. That's the kind of mongrel he is.'

'Did you tell him?' Allie whispered.

'Of course I didn't. What would be the point of that?'

'Oh Jan, I'm so sorry.'

'Don't you dare feel sorry for me. Save it for yerself.'

'I never slept with him.'

'Of course not. You'd never do such a thing, would ya? No sex out of marriage for our darling little Allie.'

'Why are you talking like that? Why do you hate me so much?'

'I don't hate ya. I just don't like ya. You always think you're better than me.'

'I always knew we were nothing alike, but I never though I was better, Jan. Poles apart, but not better. There's a lot of difference.' When Janet stared at her without answering, Allie added, 'God, everything's such a rotten mess.' She forced a smile. 'I guess you really hate him now even if you do still love him.'

'I couldn't hate anybody as much as I hate meself,' Janet stated, trying to sound blasé but failing miserably. 'I've never believed in it. Abortion. A terrible word. It's a terrible thing. But what else could I do? Raise a baby on me own?' She began to cry. 'I was so angry with him for the things he said that I didn't want any part of him any more. But that's not a real reason. There was no real reason.'

'Shh, it's all right, Jan. I mean, it will be. Don't cry like that. You'll make yourself sick.'

'I want my baby back, Allie. I want my baby.'

'Shh now. Shh.' Allie climbed into the bed and put her arms around Janet, holding her tight enough for it to hurt. Janet shifted a little, seemed about to pull away, then hugged back. They lay like that until their tears subsided. They might have stayed longer if the nurse Allie had almost knocked over hadn't arrived.

'What's going on here?' she demanded.

'We're sisters,' Allie said, sliding her leg across Janet and holding her even tighter.

'That doesn't give you the right to smother her,' the nurse said. 'Best get out of there before Matron comes. It's not visiting hours until tomorrow and she's due any minute. She'll go berserk if she sees you.'

'Okay. Thanks,' Allie said, reluctantly starting to gently extricate herself from Janet's clinging arms. 'Just give us a minute, will you?'

'Five, no more,' the nurse warned, and smiled. 'You'll hear her coming anyway. She sounds like a platoon of soldiers. I'll make you both a cup of tea and tell her you fainted so I let you stay until you felt better.'

'Thanks,' Allie said again.

The nurse nodded. 'I've got a sister too. I wish we were as close as you two.'

The Busiest Day

Shrugging her shoulders to ease the ache in her neck, Allie leaned her elbows on the counter and stared out through the Corner Shop window. With most shops shut over the weekend, Friday was always the busiest day, but at last the steady flow of customers had slowed to an occasional lone shopper. The rush would start again when children arrived home from school and mothers who had no time to shop, or couldn't be bothered, sent their offspring on the rounds: butcher, greengrocer, grocer, and messages to friends and kin. Now the T-intersection outside the store had been empty of cars for the past ten minutes. The only sign of life was a skinny brown mongrel up on its hind legs, searching a school garbage bin for the castaway sandwich crusts it always held, and her father leaning against the fence just around the corner.

He'd been there every afternoon for the past two weeks. Not waiting for her as she'd hoped when she first saw him. She worked until six and he arrived at quarter past three, which was fifteen minutes before the bell rang to signify the end of the school day. She didn't need more than a second thought to realise he was keeping an eye on Hal. No doubt he stayed out of sight so Colin wouldn't feel as if he couldn't be trusted to arrive on time, though he wasn't here yet.

Colin was supposed to be at the school gate waiting for Hal before the bell rang. Where the heck was he? Grandma would hit the roof if she knew he'd arrived late. Maybe something was wrong. Despite her father being so close, Allie began to feel uneasy. Something was about to happen. The shop, the street, the school all seemed uncannily quiet: no sound, no movement, not the hint of a breeze. Like the calm before a storm.

Silence turned to bedlam in the blink of an eye as the bell rang and the classrooms disgorged their charges for the day. Allie breathed a sigh of relief as children from kindergarten to sixth class poured across the schoolyard into Australia Street, shouting farewells or insults depending on the gender of the shouters. The girls tended to be more subtle than the boys, their expressions and the strength of their waves from a vigorous two-armed crossover to a casual hand flip saying it all without the need for speech. Allie felt a little envious as she watched the push and shove of the boys as they raced for the gate, the parry and thrust of the girls as they sought attention or tried to disappear into the background. The shy girls and boys dragged their feet and peered enviously at the popular kids from under lowered brows. The cocky ones called out and clowned around, oblivious of anything except themselves, their mates, and the end of another school week.

These kids are at their best age, though they don't know it, she thought. Not a care in the world. Except for Hal. He's still freaking out about his real mum, Lily. She's pretty, beautiful really, but in a strange way. That Sunday morning in Grandma's backyard I didn't get a good look at her before I chased after Hal, but what I saw reminded me of an old black and white vampire movie. Hair redder than fire, and dark eyes. They looked black. White skin. Frail and pale. She looked sort of . . . innocent. No, fragile is a better word. As if she'd break into bits if you touched her too hard. But there was something just under her surface. I can't think how to explain it, but whatever it was, it scared the heck out of me. Anyway, there's been nothing from her for nearly two weeks. But talking about Hal, where is he? And where's Colin? Colin and Big Les are supposed to be keeping guard till Hal gets back to Grandma's.

There's Hal coming through the gate now. Poor kid, he looks worried.

Not worried, scared.

Scared of that car?

A black sedan pulled up, blocking Allie's view of Hal as he stepped back inside the school gate. She felt another quiver of foreboding. Cars never pulled up outside the school at this time of the day. All the kids at the Australia Street school were locals. They walked. Even the parents who owned a car wouldn't have thought their sons or daughters needed to be driven home. So who was this? And why did Hal look so afraid?

Throwing back the counter flap, she rushed outside. Most of the kids had dispersed, gone within minutes, so she had a clearer view. A couple of Hal's particular mates were pushing at him as though urging him to move. His body seemed as frozen as his expression of open-mouthed fear. Gus Markham was the driver of the car. Allie remembered that time he'd barged into Grandma's house looking for his wife. He was a horrible man. Yet he was a mate of Colin's. A drinking partner at least. He couldn't be too bad if Colin drank with him. So why was Hal so afraid?

She understood when she saw Lily get out of the back seat, leaving the door open, and walk towards Hal. Not in a hurry. Brashly confident. Not looking around so she wouldn't have seen Colin running towards the car from the direction of Grandma's house with Big Les rumbling along behind him. And there, her dad taking the corner in a skidding run.

'Leave him alone!' Allie screamed, partly to let Hal know she was there, partly to divert Lily's attention and give her dad and Colin time to reach him. What it did was spur Lily on. In a hurry now, she grabbed Hal's arm and dragged him across the narrow footpath. He didn't fight, didn't even look at her. The droop of his body showed resignation.

Tom reached them as Lily shoved Hal into the back seat and dived in after him. 'Get us out of here,' she screeched at Gus Markham.

'Stop her!' Allie shouted, and grabbed the door handle on the opposite side to Lily, trying to yank it open. It was locked. 'Hal, open the door,' she called. He lay along the seat where his mother had thrown him, not moving.

By then Colin had reached the car. He stood directly in front of it, hands on the bonnet, eyes wide and fixed as though his glare could stop Gus Markham from running over him. Returning the glare, Gus revved the engine as a warning. Allie felt the rumble through to her bones.

'No!' she cried, clinging to the door handle with both hands and staring down at it as though she could stop the car by sheer strength of will.

Her father reached the car, leaned in and grabbed Lily's dress, dragging her onto the footpath, making no attempt to stay her forward movement as she fell towards the gutter and banged her head on the mudguard. Gus revved the engine again, but left the gear in neutral.

'Help me, Gus!' Lily screamed.

He looked from Colin to Tom, then folded his arms. 'Gotter be bloody joking,' he stated.

Allie's breath caught in a sob that was part relief, part laughing acknowledgement of a chorus of gasps and nervous giggles from the twenty or more boys and girls who had stayed to watch. 'Ohh, he swore!' she heard one girl say in a tone of scandalised glee.

Reaching in, Tom caught hold of Hal's legs, pulled him across the seat, turned him, then lifted him up.

'Is he all right?' Allie asked as her dad straightened and Hal flopped over his shoulder, eyes closed.

'Are you all right, lad?' Tom whispered huskily.

Hal nodded, but did not open his eyes. His body went rigid when Lily began to shriek insults and curses. Some of the watching children nudged each other and made horrified faces, though their eyes sparkled. Others winced or turned away, suddenly afraid.

'Shut up, you foul-mouthed whore,' Tom said harshly.

To Allie's amazement, Lily fell silent, though her glare spoke volumes. Blood seeped from a cut on her forehead and she rubbed at it with the back of her hand, spreading the red gore across her face. That combined with mascara-caked eyelashes, strands of long red hair caught across the perspiration on her face and the overbright lipstick gave her a clownish, grotesque appearance. Nothing scary about her now, Allie thought as, head down, Lily climbed back into the car and pulled the door shut.

'All right, kids, show's over. Off you go now,' Tom called, shooing at them with one hand while pressing Hal tightly against his chest.

Most of the children took off at a run. Four boys scuffed at the bitumen with already battered shoes and backed away a few steps but seemed determined to stay. Allie recognised them as Hal's closest friends.

'He's all right now,' she assured him. 'My dad will take him home.'

They nodded, but still seemed reluctant to leave.

'Don't look at me like that, mate,' Gus Markham said as Colin moved around to the driver's side window. 'She asked me to drive her boyfriend's car here to pick up her kid. I didn't know it was gunner be like this. He's her kid, I thought everything would have been sorted.'

'Pig's bum, ya thought it had been sorted,' Colin snarled. 'Ya reckon we'd hand a kid over to her, you're as bad as she is. And I know ya haven't got a licence, never had one, so you drive one more inch and I'm dobbing ya in to the coppers.' Not waiting for an answer, he turned away. 'All right, you kids, fun's over,' he said. 'On yer bikes now.' When not one child moved, he shouted, 'Now, I told youse!'

The boys scattered, and Colin followed Tom and Hal down Australia Street to Grandma's house. Big Les met him halfway and turned back, neither saying a word.

'Wait up,' Allie called, her voice as shaky as her hands as she stepped away from the car. Glancing through the window, a jolt of fear made her stagger as Lily lifted her head. Her expression as she stared at Allie was sheer venom. She was defeated for now, but Allie knew this woman would never give up. This was just the start of it. Turning aside to hide her fear, Allie strode away.

'Drive the car,' she heard Lily shout.

As she walked the rest of the way, Allie occasionally glanced back to make sure the car wasn't roaring down the street towards her. It hadn't moved. Gus Markham was walking in the opposite direction. She reached the corner terrace house as Grandma began a scathing attack on Colin.

'You were supposed to be at the gate when school finished. Where were you, at the pub again I suppose,' she said, not waiting for an answer before continuing. 'I asked you to watch over him, just take him there and pick him up, but you couldn't even do that, could you? You're hopeless, Colin.'

His face whitened, but he didn't protest.

'It was me, Grandma,' Big Les mumbled. 'I was late. I got a dicky knee.'

'Colin didn't have to wait for you,' Grandma snapped. 'He should have been at the school when the bell rang. Too lazy to get off his back, that's his trouble.'

'No, Grandma,' Allie protested. 'Colin did get there and I think the bell was a few minutes early. And we hadn't heard anything from Lily since that Sunday two weeks back so nobody expected her to turn up now.'

'You stay out of this, missy,' Grandma ordered.

Still feeling the shock, Allie burst into tears.

'Stop that blasted caterwauling and go in to Hal. He's the one needs comfort. He's in there with your Auntie Florrie cuddling him. Not you, and not his precious blasted cousin here who he thinks is God's gift to kids,' Grandma ranted. 'He needs to know somebody close cares about him and isn't too tired or too coward—'

Tom cut her off, saying. 'Ya got it all wrong, Grandma. Why don't you cut out yer squawking for two minutes and I'll tell ya what happened.'

Grandma's face crimsoned. 'How dare you talk to me like that. And who invited you into my home, Tom Gordon? What's any of this got to do with you anyway? You left Hal when you left the rest of your family.'

'I never left me family. I'm just not with them any more.' His voice rose when Grandma tried to interrupt. 'Just listen up for two seconds, will yer? Colin was just one swish of a dog's tale too late to pick up Hal. Lily shoved him into the car and Colin here stood right in front of it. If anybody but Gus had been driving, they'd have gone straight over the top of him. It was him who saved Hal, nobody else.'

'That's exactly what happened,' Allie said huskily, wiping her eyes with the back of her wrist. 'But it was Dad too. He grabbed Hal out of the car.'

'Well. I don't know what the world's coming to,' was Grandma's idea of an apology.

Giving her a black look, Colin walked up the hallway and out, slamming the front door shut behind him.

'Come on, Grandma.' Tom took hold of her elbow. 'What we need is a cup of tea.'

'I thank you for your help, Tom Gordon, but I can make me own tea.'

'Course you can. And mine's black with one sugar.'

'I suppose I owe you that,' she conceded.

'You don't owe me nothing. He's my boy and I mean to look after him.'

'I shouldn't have gone on like that at Colin,' Grandma said fretfully. 'My tongue runs away with me at times.'

'You were frightened for Hal,' Tom said soothingly.

'Scared stiff,' she agreed. 'Who knows what that bitch would do if she got half a chance.'

Allie paused at the doorway to her room. She'd never heard Grandma Ade swear before. Not even a damn. Tom's snort of amusement showed that he'd never heard her swear either.

'I wouldn't put anything past Lily in the mood she's in,' he said. 'You'd better start locking yer doors at night.'

'Nobody locks their doors. Nobody's got anything worth stealing.'

'Ya got Hal living in this house and a ratbag drunk after him,' he reminded her. 'And maybe a ratbag drunk after you. Gus has really got it in for ya. That's most likely why he was driving the car for Lily. Ya need to watch yerself with him. Any excuse he gets he'll do ya harm.'

'I've never locked my house and I'm not about to let Lily or Gus Markham nudge me into doing it now,' Grandma said stubbornly.

Allie didn't hear her dad's reply as one of them closed the kitchen door. About to turn away, she looked down as a small hand slid into hers. She could tell by his expression that Hal had overheard.

Great-Aunt Florrie spoke from his bedroom door. 'It's just your dad being worried for you, Hal. Everything will be fine, you'll see.'

He looked up into Allie's face. His own was paler than it should have been. He looked frail and lost. Grunting loudly, she picked him up, then allowed him to slide back down.

'You're getting too big,' she said. 'Come on, hop up on your bed and I'll read you a story. But not one from Grimm's tales again, they're too grim.' Smiling down at him, she tightened her hand around his. 'Biggles would be good, wouldn't it?'

'Will Lily my mother try to get me again?' he asked.

'Mum and Dad and Grandma will sort it all out.'

Oh God, let that be true, she thought as he led the way to his bed.

'What if she does get me, Allie?' he asked as he crawled in on top of the covers. 'She won't keep me, will she?'

She had to ask. 'Would you hate that more than anything?'

He nodded. 'I don't like being all by myself.'

She took his hand. 'What do you remember about her, Hal?'

He thought before answering. 'Her going out and I'd be all by myself. Sometimes one of the bad men would be there and he'd yell at me.'

She didn't want to ask him about the bad men, knowing it would only bring them back into his nightmares.

'I want to be with you and Mum,' he said. 'And Grandma and Great-Aunt Florrie and Janet when she comes home and Dad when I see him. And the kin on Sundays and . . .'

Allie nodded. 'And that's how it will be, Hal. We're never going to let you be all by yourself again. Okay?'

His answer was to hand her the Biggles book.

The Only Solution

Hannah glanced up at the wall clock. Past ten o'clock. After a long family discussion, and many promises – including one from Hal that he would fight for all he was worth if Lily tried to grab him again – everyone else was finally asleep. Grandma and Great-Aunt Florrie had gone to bed over an hour ago. Hal soon after. Colin hadn't returned. Grandma said he was probably helping Shorty drink his latest batch of home brew.

Strangely enough, it was Allie who needed more comforting, more reassurance. Allie was certain Lily would keep trying until she got what she wanted. For that matter, so was Hannah, though she pretended otherwise. What worried her more than anything was a statement from Claude's lawyer. Claude had insisted on phoning him after Hannah revealed what had happened.

'Lily won't bring the police into it. There's too many questions she'd have to answer, and any one of them could see her in jail,' Hannah told the lawyer. 'She'll try to take him by stealth or by force.'

'If Miss Gatley succeeds in recovering her son, it would be almost impossible for you to get him back through the courts,' he'd said. 'There's no proof that she ever mistreated him, no proof that Miss Gatley or her son were in the house when those photos were taken. Your grandmother didn't include the boy in any of them. An act of pity, I'm sure, but still a mistake. And she did take him illegally. In fact, if this did go to court, there's a fair chance you could lose. If so, your grandmother would face charges. If you managed to prove that Miss Gatley is an unfit mother, it's unlikely the boy would be given back to you. It's more likely he'd be sent to a home.'

'Either way, Lily wins,' Hannah said. 'She wouldn't care if Hal was sent to a home. She just wants him away from me.'

'The only solution,' Claude told her, 'is to remove Hal from danger altogether. There must be somewhere he can go where Lily won't find him.'

Hannah had dismissed his idea, afraid Hal would see that as banishment. But now she was having second thoughts. She had to get him away from the threat of being kidnapped. And she couldn't be sure that if it came to the crunch, Great-Aunt Florrie wouldn't help Lily get Hal back. After all, her first loyalty surely belonged to her grand-daughter.

'Maybe the time has come to offer Lily a helping hand. Maybe we could all work together for Hal's sake,' Great-Aunt Florrie had said. 'She's worth taking a chance on. Everyone's worth that much.'

'You think I should turn Hal over to her?' Hannah asked, shocked that her great-aunt could even think such a thing. 'Then what would Hal's chances for a happy life be?'

'She'll end up in gaol for a long spell one of these days, you mark my words,' Grandma said. 'Then the welfare people would take Hal. No sense in that, and it wouldn't do Hal much good to put him through it. He thinks of Hannah as his mum.'

'But she's not, is she?' Great-Aunt Florrie pointed out. 'Maybe I could work with Lily and she'd let Hal live here. We could all keep an eye on him then. I am his great-grandmother after all.'

'I can't believe you said that.' Hannah turned her back and began to walk away.

'He'd be here, Hannah, with all of us, and Lily wouldn't feel so alone.'

Hannah swung around. 'She hasn't given him a second thought until now.'

'You don't know that, just as you don't know if your mother thinks of you. I'm sure she does. But it's too late for her. Please don't make it too late for Lily.'

'I'll fight her every inch of the way,' Hannah stated grimly.

'Are you fighting her for Hal's sake or for your own?'

'She only wants him to spite me,' Hannah shot back.

'She might think that's *your* problem,' Great-Aunt Florrie said softly. 'Perhaps she thinks you want him to spite her. There has always been a great deal of rivalry between you.'

'I don't want to give him up to her or anyone else. That's for no other reason than I love him and think of him as my own. But if Lily was even halfway decent I might agree to give it a try, us all looking after him I mean. Yet she's not, is she?' When her Great-Aunt didn't answer, Hannah added, 'I don't understand why you're on her side.'

'She doesn't have anyone, Hannah.'

'It seems she has you.'

'I'm not saying you should hand Hal over to her. He doesn't want to go, does he? He's afraid of her. And she doesn't have a ghost of a chance of getting him through the courts. I'm just saying we're her kin and we should be helping her like we would any other kin.'

'I'm with Florrie,' Grandma said abruptly, surprising everyone. 'We'll try to help Lily for her sake if for no other reason.'

'Help her do what?' Hannah demanded.

'Get her life straight. Give up the booze and running around. We could take her in, keep an eye on her.'

'Take her in? Here?' Hannah asked, aghast at the suggestion. 'The day that happens, I'll leave.'

After more discussion, a lot of it heated, they finally agreed on offering to find a decent place for Lily to live where they could keep an eye on her, and to help her beat her drinking addiction in any way they could. First thing would be to get in touch with her and invite her for tea and a talk. They'd go from there. But first they'd make sure Hal was safe.

Which is all the more reason to get him away before she tries taking him again, Hannah thought. Two months should do it. Three at the most. Lily would never stay off the booze and behave herself for that long. If a safe place can be found, maybe Allie or Janet could go with him.

She'd go herself if that was the only way. The trouble was, she had no money for travel, no money saved for rent and food. She'd have to borrow from Claude and she didn't want to do that. But what was more important – her pride, and freedom from being indebted to Claude, or Hal's life? She was certain he'd never survive being with Lily again. If it hadn't been for Grandma, he might not have survived the first time.

She glanced at the clock. Ten-fifteen. Claude wouldn't have gone to bed yet. It would be better not to put it off any longer.

I'll talk to him now, she thought. I'll get Hal to a safe place as quickly as I can.

The front door was locked. That shocked her. Grandma never locked her doors. The fact that she deemed it necessary meant she was truly afraid of Lily, and Hannah had never known Grandma Ade to be afraid of anything or anyone. She must believe that Lily and some of her friends could try sneaking into the house in the middle of the night. Yet the only toilet was outside, so the house residents wandered in and out at all hours of the day and night. The key to the back door had disappeared years ago. But then, Grandma's bedroom was the closest to that door and she was a light sleeper. She obviously believed she'd hear anyone coming in or out.

Right on cue, Grandma called, 'Who's wandering around out there?'

'It's me. I'm going to see Claude and talk to him about ways to make Hal safe,' Hannah answered, keeping her voice low as she poked her head around the door. 'I'll be back in a half hour,' she added, quickly averting her eyes and banging her shoulder against the door frame in her haste to retreat.

Once out, she stood and stared at the door, trying to absorb what she'd seen. The two women, both in nighties, were lying on top of the covers, their arms wrapped around each other, Great-Aunt Florrie with one leg under Grandma's legs, the other over, holding the bigger woman tight against her lean frame. At the moment Hannah had spoken, Great-Aunt Florrie, who was turned towards the door, had looked into her eyes.

Hannah had heard the rumours, there were always rumours, but she'd never believed them, had never been able to picture these two elderly women as anything other than dear friends. Now, seeing what she had just seen, she felt dazed. All these years, ever since Hannah could remember, Grandma had been strait-laced, even prudish. Daze turned to shock, then a feeling bordering on anger. Not because of the unbelievable fact that Grandma Ade and Great-Aunt Florrie were lovers, and probably had been for years. It was the long term lie that angered her, the way Grandma shrugged away any attempt to kiss or hug her as being a sign of weakness.

'Go through the front and leave the door unlocked so you can get back in,' Grandma called now, unaware that Hannah had been in her room. 'Big Les is parked around the corner keeping an eye on the back lane, and I'll be awake.'

Head bowed, Hannah turned away, was about to walk away when the door opened. Great-Aunt Florrie, her nightie covered by a blanket wrapped around her like a cloak, stepped into the hallway. Her eyes searched Hannah's face.

'Many thing are not what they seem, Hannah dear,' she said softly.

'I don't want to talk about it now. I have to concentrate on Hal's safety,' Hannah said, and backed away.

'Tomorrow,' Great-Aunt Florrie said before retreating to her room.

Hannah stared after her for a few moments, then poked her head around the door to the room she shared with Hal and Allie. They were asleep, Hal on his back, his coverings barely rumpled while Allie lay curled in a ball, a pillow over her head, the blankets wrapped around her like a cocoon. Sleeping in the same bed with Allie was a night-long fight for a share of the blankets. Remembering last night's battle for space and covering, Hannah couldn't help smiling. It had been one of the few times she'd managed to hold her own. But as she stared at Allie, the picture of Grandma and Great-Aunt Florrie flashed into her mind.

I must put it out of my head until I've made Hal safe, she thought.

Revolving Door

Allie heard the door open. Sure it was Hannah checking on her and Hal, she pretended to be asleep. The door closed. For a moment she wondered if she should have spoken, but what was there to say? Every thought, every suggestion concerning Lily and Hal had been pulled to pieces, rebuilt, then pulled apart again a dozen times. And she couldn't talk about Janet and Johnny Lawson. She'd promised not to. Yet she couldn't stop thinking about them. About him. The ache, the goose bumps came back even while she deliberately recalled Janet's haggard face, the way she had cried, the feeling of that first-time togetherness as they cuddled on the hospital bed. She didn't want to return to the hostility that had separated them for as long as she could remember.

Janet means more to me than him, and I think I'd rather be with Charlie, though he doesn't make me feel the way I feel about Johnny. Maybe that's because I haven't given him the chance. What would happen if we kissed and touched that way? But why am I thinking these things? There has to be something wrong with me. I'm as bad as Lily.

Not wanting to wake Hal, she pulled the blankets over her face to muffle the sound when she cried again. He'd heard her crying before and joined in, his sobs becoming deeper and louder until his whole body shook with the force of them. He had tried to smother his too, but she heard, couldn't help hearing, and climbed into bed with him, whispered soothing nonsense-words until he finally drifted into an exhausted sleep. Moving as quietly as she could, she pulled the covers up around his neck, then moved back to her own bed.

The door opened again. Bad as a revolving door, she thought, but kept her eyes closed. She knew if she started talking to her mother, she would end up telling her about Janet.

Moments later, she felt the bed move as someone sat beside her and pulled the blankets away from her face. A hand brushed hair back from her forehead. It was a gentle hand. A loving gesture. She took a deep breath, expecting to inhale a bouquet of lavender from the underwear drawer sachets, aloe vera and jonquil hand cream, and the particular brand of face powder that Great-Aunt Florrie wore. Instead she smelled rosemary, sage and old roses. And there was more than a hint of the bottle of stout Grandma drank every day. Two on Saturdays, none on a Sunday.

Grandma. It was Grandma whispering, 'Look at that teary face. Poor darling, I know I'm hard on you. I just don't want you to waste your life, and I know there's a beautiful one waiting for you. But you sleep now and don't worry, things will turn out for the best, you'll see.'

Allie's eyes filled again as she felt the scratch of dry lips pressed to her forehead. She watched as Grandma smoothed Hal's sheet and kissed him, then turned back at the door for one last look before gently closing it behind her.

'I've always thought she didn't like me,' she whispered, wiping her eyes on the pillow.

Turning her face into it, she rolled over onto her stomach. A while later, she had no idea how long, she heard the door again but drifted back to sleep without opening her eyes. Perhaps a life might have been saved had she called out.

The Darkest Night

As Hannah closed the gate behind her, she noticed that Australia Street was abnormally dark. A lot darker than it should be, she thought, and looked up, searching for the moon. A full moon would be good – big and round and beautiful, a symbol of romance and mystery to many people. Though not to her, not since the day of her thirty-sixth birthday when it combined with Friday the thirteenth and heralded a major change in her life. So much had happened since then, and hardly any of it for the better. Of course meeting Claude was a bonus, she reassured herself. But was it? She was beginning to find him very possessive and she did not want to be owned. And now Lily trying to take Hal. Could her life possibly get any worse?

It all started with the full moon on my birthday. But where is that full moon when I need it?

Most of the residents were in bed and asleep, so no lights shone out of the houses. Added to that, the street had just two lights and the one closest to Grandma's corner house was out. Had somebody broken the globe? Somebody who didn't want to be seen.

You're being silly, she chided herself. This business with Lily and with Grandma locking doors has spooked you. But was that a movement? There, across the street. She narrowed her eyes, trying to pierce the darkness.

'Is that you, Tom?'

No answer, but she felt sure he was there. He was still watching over Hal, but for reasons of his own, he didn't want her to know. Okay, if that's the way he wanted it.

'You can go home now,' she called. 'We're watching the front door and Big Les is keeping an eye on the laneway.'

Still no answer. Perhaps it was her imagination after all. Still, she was too edgy to walk up Australia Street in the dark. Grandma kept a torch on the refrigerator for night visits to the toilet. It was a small torch, its light narrow and weak, but it suited the purpose. She'd borrow that.

A minute later, she was back at the gate and shining the torch across the street. Its light barely reached the opposite gutter, but it showed enough for her to see that if anyone had been there, he or she was gone now.

Halfway along Australia Street, she heard footsteps behind her. An uneven sound. Someone with a limp. It had to be Fred Peters, but still her heartbeat quickened as she swung around and backed against a fence. Why was he wandering around at this time of night? This wasn't the first time she'd noticed him out late, and there was something about him that always made her feel uneasy. She remembered that Janet and Hal couldn't bear him.

'Who's there?' she called. 'Is that you, Fred?'

'Sorry. Didn't mean to scare yer, Hannah,' he answered as he appeared out of the gloom, the beam of light turning his face to a pasty copy of the hidden moon. She turned the torch aside when he put up a hand to shield his eyes.

'Why are you out so late?' she challenged.

'I was thinking the same thing about you. People are talking, Hannah. You spend a lot of time with Claude Macy. People notice things like that.'

'Where I spend my time and who I spend it with is nobody's business but my own,' she snapped. 'Good night, Fred.'

Not giving him time to answer, she walked away, switching off the torch and slipping it into her skirt pocket. She could feel his stare following her as she reached Claude's house. Should she try to avoid more gossip and keep walking? Like hell she would! Opening the gate, she banged it shut behind her and strode to the door. It opened as she reached the porch.

'Were you standing there waiting for me?' she asked angrily.

'Whoa!' Claude held up his hands in a staying motion. 'I was just going to bed and I heard the gate. How could I be waiting for you when I didn't know you'd be coming?'

'I thought you might be keeping tabs on me like everyone else seems to be.'

'Hey now, what brought this on?'

She grimaced. 'Sorry, Claude. I just bumped into Fred Peters. Seems like you and I are the topic of all the gossip around here.'

'You expected that, didn't you?' He led the way into the kitchen. 'Tea or something stronger?'

'Better make it tea. No, blow it, I'll have a brandy.'

'What is it, Hannah? This business with Lily and Hal? Clara Paterson told me everything that happened this afternoon.'

'That's what I mean,' Hannah said, feeling her anger rising again. 'Everybody knows my business.'

'You once told me that Clara makes it her business to know everybody's else's. She's good at worming information out of anyone, but as far as I know, she doesn't usually repeat it.' Pouring a generous slug of brandy, he handed it to her, then poured one for himself. 'And everyone likes to know what's going on around them,' he continued as she gulped a mouthful. 'Don't you? Listen to gossip I mean. People like to know about other people's dramas. When your own life's dull, it eases the boredom. And please don't drink my expensive brandy like that. Show a little respect.'

Knowing the joking reproof was intended to lighten her mood, she smiled at last. 'You're right of course.' Sinking into a chair, she sipped the brandy and made a show of licking her lips in appreciation.

Touching her face with his fingertips, he leant down and kissed the top of her head, then pulled a chair close to her and sat. 'Want to tell me about this afternoon?'

After another mouthful of brandy that was again more gulp than sip, she told him of the attempted kidnapping as Allie had told it to her.

'Then you were wrong about your husband,' he said when she'd finished. 'You thought he didn't care about any of you.'

'It seemed to me that he was totally wrapped up in his new family.' She managed to keep the bitterness out of her tone. 'Yet Allie tells me he's been at the school every afternoon this week. And he told Grandma he's been there of a morning as well, over by the toilet block where he can see the whole yard. He stays until the classes have gone in. And he's seen Hal's teacher, told her not to let anyone she doesn't know take Hal from class. I never thought to do that.'

The tone of his voice was an arm around her as he said, 'It's obvious he loves Hal and wants to protect him. As you do. As I do.'

Hannah stared into her empty glass. 'Lily claims that Hal is his son.'

Taking her hand, he held it between both of his. 'Do you believe her?'

'He's proved he's not the loyal type. God knows how many women he's been with.'

'Do you believe her?' Claude repeated.

'It's been haunting me, thinking it might be true. I love Hal as though he's my own flesh and blood, but I hate the thought of her and Tom together.' Pulling her hand free, she slid her fingers through her hair, dragging it back from her face. 'But of course it's one of her lies. Tom never liked her. Couldn't stand her even when we were kids.'

He leaned forward until his face was directly opposite hers. 'Are you still in love with him, Hannah?'

She shook her head. 'He spoiled that with his drinking, not working, the way he was. Perhaps I never was in love with him. I don't know any more.' She had avoided his eyes, but looked into them now. 'Perhaps I wanted him because all my girlfriends did. Then I got pregnant. I didn't know what else to do but marry him, though we were never suited. Grandma told me we wouldn't make each other happy and she was right. Not that she suggested any alternatives.'

'Why does it hurt so much that he might have had sex with Lily, or with Madge Lenahan?' he asked quietly.

'Hurt?' She frowned. 'I don't know. Maybe I do love him without being in love and hate the thought that he'd be unfaithful. There is a difference, isn't there? Loving and being in love. We were good together before we were married.' She paused again. 'Afterwards, too. Until he joined the army in fact. When I think about it, the war between him and me started when he came home from the other war.'

'And what about me?' He touched her face again. 'Do you love me? Are we in love?'

'I love going to bed with you. But that's not enough, is it?'

Standing, he held out a hand. 'It'll do for now.'

She stood. 'And later?'

'I believe you will love me once you've got Tom clear of your head. You were married to him for a long time. There's all sorts of loyalty issues. Family issues.' He moved close but did not touch her, though she could feel his body heat. 'Habit issues. You got used to being with him. Now you need to get used to being with me.'

She stepped back. 'How did we get on to this subject? You haven't told me what you think. About Hal, I mean. About what I should do.'

'I think you should take him away. I'll go with you. We could go to another state. Another country. A long holiday in France. Or Italy. You'd love Tuscany.'

'What about Allie and Janet?'

'Janet's made a life for herself away from you. Allie will follow soon enough. Especially if she goes to university, and I can make that possible, Hannah.'

'Grandma?'

'Is quite capable of taking care of herself.'

'I have to think about it.'

'Then think about it in bed. Afterwards,' he said huskily.

As they reached the bedroom, a noise from outside made her shiver. 'What's that?' she gasped. 'Is that Hal?'

'Hal's at home asleep,' he said soothingly. 'It was that blasted bird. The damn thing screams at every passing dog, cat or person.'

Hannah thought back to the sound. He was right. It was definitely Bird. She'd heard that harsh cry often enough. Smiling at the thought of some poor animal or person fleeing from that blood-icing call, she allowed Claude to pull her onto the bed.

Twenty minutes later, still haunted by that sound, she rolled out of bed, drew back the curtains and peered outside. All she could see was murk and the looming, deeper dark of the wall. Pressing the side of her face up against the window, she stared towards the school. There was someone coming down the street. A man. Fred Peters again? He'd reached the first light. It was Colin. A drunken Colin judging by the stagger.

I'd hate to be in your shoes when you get home to Grandma, she thought. I should go with you. Picking up her clothes off the floor, she dressed hastily. She knew Claude was awake, though he made no move to stop her as he usually did. The sex had been wild, and over in record time. Now she just wanted to go before he started a discussion on it. To her mind there was nothing wrong with an occasional bout of wild sex. Who wanted it to be the same every time? And who wanted to analyse it every time? Certainly not her. But Claude could never let things just be. Never let his emotions take control without dissecting his feelings later.

Skirting around the bed, she leant over and kissed his forehead. When he opened his mouth to speak, she placed a finger against his lips. 'Colin's out there and I think he's had too much to drink. I'd better see him home,' she said, and left, pulling the front door shut behind her. Most of the street was still dark but she took comfort from knowing that Claude was at the window watching her, and she still had the torch in her pocket. Taking it out, she switched it on and swung it in a half circle.

Remembering Bird's cry, she paused at the gate, wondering if the rooster was nearby, waiting to pounce. There was no sign of him, no movement, and no sign of Colin. Judging by the way he'd been staggering when she saw him near the school, he couldn't have reached home yet. She could make out something across the street, an indistinct shape against the wall. It appeared to be someone squatted on their haunches beside the gutter a few houses down.

Colin is there after all, she thought. He must have made it that far, then had to stop. Probably being sick.

'You know you shouldn't drink so much,' she said, walking forward and aiming the narrow beam of torchlight at his face.

His eyes were squinted, his mouth hung open in what appeared to Hannah as a silent scream. When he looked up, his eyes widened to a glare of horror. She followed his face with the light as he stood.

'What? What is it?' she asked, slowing her walk, afraid of what she could see in his eyes.

Throwing up an arm to protect himself from the beam of light, he turned towards Grandma's house and staggered away, almost falling twice before disappearing into the darkness.

After following his progress for a few seconds, Hannah aimed the torch towards what looked to be a bundle of clothes on the footpath. It outlined a slightly built woman, her dress hiked up around her knees, her face turned away from the wall. A pool of something wet on the footpath, oily and claret-coloured, and more of it matted in her hair reflected the light. It had to be blood. Hannah knelt beside her and looked down into a face that was almost unrecognisable in its expression of fear.

'Lily? Can you hear me?'

Her eyes were wide and staring and her body had the stillness of death. Leaning closer, Hannah placed her ear just above the brightly painted lips. There was no sign of even the faintest breath. Moving slowly, as though in a dream, Hannah lifted her head and turned until there was just a hand's breadth between their noses. Even with her face twisted in such a grotesque way, Lily's beauty was evident in the bone structure, the widely set eyes, the perfect nose.

Grabbing her arm, Hannah shook it roughly, as though trying to wake someone from a deep sleep. When they were children, Lily liked to jump out from a hiding place, then laugh at the screams of fright. Even though she'd done that to Hannah dozens of times, Hannah had always fallen for it, had never expected it. Lily had to be doing it now. Wanting to frighten her. Wanting her to realise that even though there was so much hurt between them, in their hearts they'd always be best friends. Who else was there? Neither had found another one.

Please, God, let Lily be doing that now.

Another shake brought no response. 'Wake up. Please wake up, Lily. I'm sorry for everything. Please look at me,' Hannah begged, even while knowing that wasn't about to happen.

Keeping the torchlight directed at Lily's face, she closed the staring eyes and then, in a continuous movement, drew her hand downwards, pulling skin and flesh into a more serene death mask. Memories flashed of a gentle time when two best friends played together, laughed together, teased each other, loved each other as only children with unhappy homes and no siblings could.

Not sure whether her tears were a mourning for Lily here and now or for a once special friendship, Hannah sat back on her heels and rocked forward and back, the movement ponderous and awkward as though the heaviness in her chest had suddenly doubled her weight. The torch moved with her and when she again noted the hiked up skirt, she pulled it down and smoothed it over legs that were little more than skin and bone. It was as she looked back at Lily's face, shining the torch towards her chin, that she noticed the rope of drying blood across her neck leading down to a pool on the pathway above her shoulder.

She had thought that Lily must have tripped against the wall, then fallen and struck her head on the gutter. Drunk probably, not able to see where she was going in the dark. Hannah hadn't seen the other wound, the hole in her throat as though a blade had been thrust forward and up. And she'd seen Colin bending over Lily just minutes ago. But he'd been defending Lily to everyone. He'd never hurt her. Someone had followed her here, or been here with her, and that someone had killed her.

Climbing unsteadily to her feet, Hannah switched off the torch, not able to bear the sight of Lily in death a moment longer. Looking around at the darkened street, the rising tier of wall that seemed to be leaning over her, bleak and menacing, she backed away, swung around suddenly and staggered towards the gate, screaming for Claude.

Running Away

The uniformed police arrived within minutes of Claude's phone call. Two detectives and an ambulance followed almost immediately. By then, half the occupants of Australia Street were lined up along the footpath or hanging over their gates calling out questions to each other. After giving a brief statement, ignoring the knowing smirks when she revealed she'd been on her way home from Claude's house when she discovered the body, Hannah was told she could leave and was asked to give a full statement at the police station the next day. Claude caught up with her before she'd reached the house next to his.

'Come inside with me,' he said.

She looked around at the watching eyes and shook her head.

'Then let me walk you home. I remember you telling me that you and Lily were once very close. You must be flattened by all of this.'

'I'm all right. I'm fine.'

'No you're not. You're as white as a sheet. Let me go with you.'

'I can get home by myself,' she snapped, then immediately softened her voice and added, 'Sorry, Claude. Those smart-mouth detectives got under my skin. I will be fine. Really. But I'd appreciate you not mentioning Colin until I've had a chance to talk to him.'

'Do you think he did it?'

'I'm sure he didn't. Colin couldn't hurt anyone, let alone do that.' She gestured towards Lily's body being carried to the ambulance. 'But I don't know why he ran when he saw me,' she added fretfully.

'I won't say anything about him being here. At least, not yet. But tomorrow the police will have to be told, Hannah. I can't lie to them.'

'I know.'

She strode away, keeping to the centre of Australia Street, then broke into a run when a neighbour called out to her. Her shoes were sling-backs, not made for running. She kicked them off at Grandma's gate and continued to run, head up, arms and legs pumping, her bare feet slapping on bitumen as she kept to the centre of the streets, turning blindly from one into another, concentrating on the running, trying to go faster and faster until a stitch in her side forced her to stop.

Doubled over, she concentrated on slowing her breathing. When the pain in her side gradually receded she became aware of the soreness of her feet. The days of going barefoot had vanished when she'd turned fourteen and found a job. Before that, her one pair of shoes were kept for school. Now her feet had been encased in shoes too long.

Idiot, she told herself, and looked around, dreading what she thought would be a long walk home. Yet she was at the bakery gate, just ten minutes from Grandma's house. She'd been running in circles. Accident, she wondered, or had her subconscious brought here?

She was tempted to bang on the door and call out to Tom. Had she seen him in Australia Street earlier or was that her imagination? Whichever it was, she'd have to wait to find out. She could hardly disturb the whole family in the middle of the night, and Tom would never admit to being in Australia Street at all hours anyway. But if he was there, why was he? Not to stand guard over Hal, not for all this time. From what Allie had said and from her own observations, he'd been a watcher since a few weeks after he moved in with the Lenahans. Was he sorry he'd left? Did he want to come back? Yet he'd know she'd been sleeping with Claude. He wouldn't forgive her for that.

Maybe he was just missing that blasted wall.

Hobbling now, she made her way back to Australia Street, putting the memory of Lily's death mask out of her mind by fixing her attention on the mystery of what had happened. Where would Lily have been during the hours between when she tried to grab Hal and when her body was found? Who would she have been with? Was that who had killed her? And why was she in Australia Street? Trying to grab Hal again? Or could she have been with Colin?

She remembered the way he'd almost destroyed his room on Sunday night. But that was a mirror, furniture and clothes. Not a person. Not an undernourished girl/woman who looked as if a puff of wind would knock her over. And when Hannah had first looked through Claude's window and seen Colin staggering along Australia Street, he had definitely been alone. He'd found Lily lying on the path. His expression of horror when Hannah shone the light on him proved that.

Lily had to have been murdered some time between when Hannah left Grandma's house and when Colin staggered along Australia Street.

Her heart lurched as she reached the gate. It was open. The front door was open. Yet Hal would never be in danger from Lily again. Hannah had to fight back tears as she slowly climbed the few steps to the porch. Here she paused, stopped by a rancid smell. A male cat was her first thought, but the smell was more powerful than that.

It would have to be half a dozen cats, she thought, gagging at the sickening odour. I'll clean it in the morning. Hopefully, it will be bearable by then.

Another shock waited for her as she glanced into the small front room where Grandma saw the people who came to her for help. Hal sat on the sofa staring back at her, his freckles standing out starkly in the pallor of his skin, his arm curved around Bird. The rooster fluffed out his feathers and gave a warning throat-rumble when she entered the room.

'Hal, why aren't you in bed? Why is Bird here?'

Her heart quickened its beat again when his stare slid across her and fixed on the doorway. Taking a deep, slow breath to calm herself, she added in a quieter tone, 'Grandma will have a fit, you being up so late.'

Bird opened out his wings and gave another throat-rumble as she moved closer.

'The bird has to go, Hal.'

'He's looking after me,' he answered without looking away from the door. 'Is Lily my mother coming to get me?'

'No, she is not,' Hannah said firmly, managing to stop grief from cracking her voice. She began to reach out to him but Bird warned her away.

'You're shaking like a leaf, Hal. Whatever is wrong?'

He looked at her at last. 'Colin's angry. He wouldn't talk to me.'

'How did Bird get in here?'

'The door was open. Why is Colin angry with me, Mum?'

Now she understood why Colin had run. Not from her. From Bird. In the dark, she hadn't seen the rooster, but he had obviously followed Colin home. Colin had retreated to his room and left the rooster out here. Bird must have given that horrible cry and woken Hal. She wouldn't have heard because she'd been trying to run away from the inescapable fact of Lily's murder.

'I'm sure Colin isn't angry with you, love,' she told him. 'He's probably angry with himself. I'll go and talk to him as soon as I put you to bed.'

'He said he feels sick and he's going to sleep now and I'm not allowed to go in.'

'Well he didn't tell me not to go in, so I will. But first you have to send Bird back to Claude's place, then hop into bed.'

'Are we gunner get into trouble, Bird and me?'

'Of course not. That's silly. But you have to send Bird home. Where is everyone? Where's Allie?'

'She cried for a long time, then she went to sleep. Why was she crying?'

Hannah paused before answering. She knew Hal wouldn't be put off with a lame excuse, but how do you explain emotional draining to a ten-year-old?

'Well, I think part of it was for Lily being at the school and Grandma being so nasty to Colin. But that was only part,' she hastened to add, not wanting Hal to feel in any way to blame for Allie's fragility. 'I think something happened when she went to see Janet. I think they might have had an argument, though she won't talk about it. But what about Grandma? Didn't she hear you out here?'

'I was creeping. Will we be in trouble, me and Bird?' he asked again.

'Definitely not,' Hannah said firmly. 'Now I want to hug you and put you to bed but Bird won't let me near you. Can you send him home to Claude's place?'

'Bird doesn't want to go out in the street. People go out there and he doesn't like people. They might hurt him,' Hal said.

'I think you have that the wrong way round,' Hannah said dryly. 'But that's okay, you can send him up the laneway.'

The bird looked as though he was about to attack at any moment. The low, back-of-the-throat noise he made sounded suspiciously like a growl, and with his feathers fluffed like that, his wings outspread, he looked twice as large as a normal rooster. Hannah backed off into the hall, watching his every move. Hal followed, one hand on the rooster's head, the red comb gripped between his second and middle fingers.

'Is that you, Hannah?' Grandma called.

Great, Hannah thought. Now you hear. Hal looked up at her, eyes wide. The bird seemed to shrink in size. The damn thing's terrified of Grandma, she thought, liking the idea that someone had him bluffed.

'Just keeping Hal company while he goes to the toilet,' she called back.

At the laneway gate, Hal gave Bird a final hug before sending him home. 'Can I sleep in your bed with you and Allie?' he asked as she took his hand and led him back inside.

She had already decided not to tell Hal or Grandma about Lily until the next day. It had been a long, bad day for him and he looked utterly exhausted. His eyelids matched the droop of his body.

'It isn't a very big bed so three will be too crowded, but I tell you what. You can sleep in my bed with Allie and I'll sleep in yours. Will that be okay?'

He nodded, satisfied, and after being kissed and tucked in, he was asleep within minutes. Hannah made sure he'd stay asleep by stroking his face for another five minutes. She needed to talk to Colin. She needed to know exactly what had happened between him and Lily, if anything. Lily must have been lying there, left for dead when Colin stumbled upon her. His hand had been under her head when the torch outlined them. He would have been checking to see if she was breathing. But why did he run? She had to know.

She'd stepped into the hall when Great-Aunt Florrie came out of the kitchen carrying a glass of water.

'I get thirsty through the night,' she explained. 'Could we talk now, Hannah? I'm worried about what you might be thinking. That expression when you walked into our room earlier has to be called accusing.'

'Please, not now, aunt. Something's happened.' And no, I don't want to tell you about it. I have to talk to Colin.'

'All right, Hannah, I won't push. Let me say just one thing for now. We're human, your grandmother and me, and all humans need the touch of others. We all need to be cuddled and held.'

Hannah slowly shook her head. 'In all the years I've known her, all the years I've lived in the same house, Grandma has never hugged me. I've never seen her hug anyone.'

'Nevertheless, that's what we do, Emily and me. And Hannah, that's all we do.'

Hannah nodded, not really comprehending as she watched her Great-Aunt walk away. Her mind was still with Lily. She waited until the door closed before entering Colin's room. He was lying on his back staring up at the ceiling.

'Don't knock or wait to be asked in,' he said she sat on the edge of the bed. 'You'd do your block if I walked in on you like that.'

'We need to talk.'

'Ya mean you need to talk. I'm gunner put a lock on me door come morning.' When she sat looking down on him without answering, he added, 'That bird's out there with Hal. Wonder the bloody thing didn't come barging in too.'

'Bird's gone and Hal's in bed asleep. What happened with Lily, Colin?'

'What do ya think happened,' he asked. The words were slurred.

'I don't know. That's why I'm asking you. I just know that Lily's dead, that she's been killed.'

'The coppers will blame me. I've been sounding off. Telling blokes what happened this afternoon. I've been saying I'll kill her if she comes near Hal again.'

'But you're the one who wanted to help her,' Hannah protested.

'Yeah. What I said at the pub was booze talk. Big-noting meself. Somebody'll tell the coppers.'

'Threats are not doing. I've threatened to kill her too. So has Tom.'

Colin looked at her at last. 'But you think it was me, don't ya?'

'No, I don't.'

'Then go to hell.'

His vehemence shocked her. 'You want me to think you did it?'

'You think I'm Colin who couldn't hurt a flea. Colin the wimp. But

I have killed people, Hannah. At the end of the war when everyone knew the Yanks were coming and the Japs started running off, I killed as many as I could catch.'

'War was different. Men had to kill then. The enemy, not someone like Lily.'

'Poor little twisted, corrupted bitch,' he said softly. 'She tried to tell people what her father was doing but nobody believed her because of who and what she was. Nobody stopped to think it might have been him made her that way.'

'So that was true?'

'Who's to know? It's what she told me. There had to be a reason why her mother took her away like that. I think that's why Grandma didn't send the cops after Lily over that business with the dead bloke in her house and the way she treated Hal. Just in case it was true.'

'If you believed her, why didn't you say something at the time?'

'I tried to tell Mum. She threatened to wash me mouth out with soap. I don't know why she didn't want to hear it. Unless she thought the telling would make it true and she didn't want to know. What do ya do about something like that? And I was nine at the time.'

'I didn't believe her either,' Hannah said wearily. 'I didn't believe something like that was possible. Mothers ignored you and fathers took care of you.'

'Yeah, like your father. He walked off and left ya. Or a bastard drunk like mine,' Colin said, but the once bitter tone he would have used when speaking about his father was missing.

I guess he's outgrown it, Hannah thought.

'What do you think happened to Lily?' she asked.

'It looked as if someone hit her with an iron bar,' Colin said. 'Or something like it. And she had a wound on her throat.'

Hannah shuddered as the image reappeared in her mind. 'Why did you run from me?'

'Not from you. From Lily. When I got back here I'd almost kidded myself that I hadn't seen her. Could've been the DTs. But I had the DTs once and saw little black crawly things. Not Lily.'

'Why would you think you were delirious?'

'I was pretty well boozed up. Been drinking for hours.'

'You're not drunk now.'

'Seeing Lily with her head stove in is enough to sober anyone.'

Hannah squeezed her eyes shut but she couldn't stop the ooze of tears, or the image from reappearing.

'I've seen death a hundred times. Seen it happen slow, seen it come from a bullet, a bayonet. Lots of blood and guts.' Colin said hoarsely, his voice growing more ragged. 'I seen it all before. But that was Lily. Jesus, Hannah. Our Lily. She went bad with the drink but she didn't deserve that.'

His pain was obvious. He would never have hurt her.

'Who would do such a thing?' Hannah cried out.

He didn't seem to hear. 'And Hal. Hal was out there. In the lounge. What could I say to the kid? I ran from him. He tried to talk to me and I told him to piss off and leave me alone. What sort of a mongrel is that?'

'I didn't tell him either,' Hannah confessed.

'That bloody bird was there.'

'I know. I know. I made Hal send him home. And I saw Fred Peters wandering around. He's a strange man, and he follows people. Women I mean. He's followed me. He's followed Allie.'

Colin swung his legs around, narrowly missing her, and sat up. She put out a hand to steady him when he swayed.

'Poor bloody Fred. Yeah he's strange. Been strange since Maisie disappeared. Now there's a real father for ya. He watched over her for all he was worth. Gave her all the love he had to give and what did he get for it?' Colin said. 'He told me once that he knows she's been murdered by some ratbag. She'd come home if she was able. And he's probably right. The cops think so. Maybe that same ratbag came back and found Lily wandering round in the dark.'

Hannah took deep breaths to hold back her tears. She knew if she started crying, she wouldn't be able to stop.

'But they'll blame me, Hannah. Once they know I was there, they'll blame me. They'll shove me in jail and I'll stay there if they can't find anyone else. I can't do it. I can't be in a little bloody cell. The dreams will come and I'll go nuts. I'd rather be dead.'

'Don't say that!'

'Who'll miss me?' His voice had lowered to a whisper. 'I'm no use to anyone.'

'Hal idolises you. Allie thinks the world of you. So do Grandma and Great-Aunt Florrie. Don't you know how loved you are?'

'And you?' Lifting his head, he looked her in the face this time. 'What about you?'

'I love you too. I always have, but I don't know if it's the sort of love you want. I remember being devastated when you went away without telling me you were going, without even saying goodbye. I know now it was because you thought I was in love with Tom. But I wasn't then. And it doesn't help to know I wasn't worth staying for, fighting for. And no, I'm not just saying this to make you feel good. You should know me well enough to know I wouldn't do that.'

'And what about if I fight for you now?' he asked huskily.

'It's too late.'

'Get into bed with me,' he said, a command more than an invitation.

'What?' She couldn't believe she'd heard right.

'Get into bed with me.'

She stood and half-turned to look down at him. 'We'll talk in the morning.'

His eyes hooded. 'Can't bear the thought of me touching you, eh?'

'I'm not even going to try answering that. You don't know me at all, do you?'

'I want to know it all.' His voice was slurred again.

'What are you saying? You want me to have sex with you?' Anger was winning. 'Now?'

'That would be good.'

'It isn't going to happen.'

The slur became more pronounced. 'I just want you close to me for a while.'

'You're lying.'

He turned his head away. 'Course I am.'

'If what you're doing is trying to push me away, you're succeeding.'

'Good.' Still not looking at her.

'I'm going to bed now, Colin.' She knew she sounded uncertain. Did he just want comforting? That made sense after what had happened.

'Yeah.' Dropping back on the bed, he closed his eyes. 'Goodnight.'
'I love you, Colin,' she said softly.
He draped his forearm over his eyes. 'But you love Mr Moneybags more.'
'Not more, just differently,' she said in the same soft voice. 'You're one of the best parts of my life and you always have been.'

She left, still not knowing what he wanted from her. Not realising that she had already given it.

Putting it Off

'Murdered!' Great-Aunt Florrie gasped when Hannah told her of Lily's death the next morning. 'The poor little soul. Now she'll never have the chance to redeem herself.'

'But of course it wasn't Colin's doing,' Grandma said firmly, frowning at Hannah as though expecting her to argue.

'I know that,' Hannah said. 'He's already told me that. I'm just telling you he found her before I did.'

Before any more could be said, there was a knock on the open front door and Tom called out, 'You there, Hannah?'

'Dad!' Hal yelled, and raced out of his bedroom and up the hall, throwing himself into Tom's outstretched arms.

'Hey there, matey. Ya nearly knocked me over.' Tom hugged him hard, then set his feet back on the floor. 'Where's yer mum, is she home?'

'Here.' Hannah stood at the kitchen doorway. 'We've just made a pot of tea if you're interested.'

'Am I what,' Tom said, and Hannah smiled at his surprised look.

'I just came . . .' He paused, looking down at Hal who was holding on to his hand. 'I heard about what happened. Does he know?'

Grandma had her arm around Great-Aunt Florrie's shoulders. 'The grapevine's working overtime,' she said. 'Quicker Hal's told, the better.'

'I haven't had a chance.' Hannah looked at Tom. 'I'm glad you're here.'

'Come on, Florrie.' Grandma turned her towards the door. 'They don't need us for this, and you can do your crying in private.'

Great-Aunt Florrie allowed herself to be led away and as Hannah watched her go, she saw the old lady's shoulders start to shake. Her own eyes filled with tears.

'What?' Hal asked, and the beginning of fear showed in his widened eyes. 'Is it about Lily my mother? She's not going to get me, is she?'

Tom sunk onto his knees to bring himself down to Hal's size and turned him so they were face to face. 'You know something, Hal. I can see by the look on yer face. What have ya heard, eh son?'

'She got hurt,' Hal answered hesitantly.

Tom held up a staying hand when Hannah began to speak. 'Only way to say it is to come right out with it,' he said, still with his eyes fixed on Hal. 'It's bad news, mate. Lily yer mum's gone for good. She died last night.'

Hal uttered a choked, gurgling sound and staggered against Tom, throwing both arms around his neck, clinging on as if his life depended on it.

'Did you have to tell him like that?' Hannah demanded.

'No good beating around the bush. How did I know he'd take it so hard,' Tom protested when the boy began to cry – harsh sobs that shook his body. 'Come on, son. Come on now. Everything's gunner be all right.'

The gentleness of his expression and tone touched Hannah. Kneeling, she wrapped her arms around them both and though she tried to hold back, she wept with Hal. Tom placed the side of his chin against her temple and she felt more than heard the harshness of his breathing. His obvious effort not to join them in their physical grief made her cry harder. His arm tightened around her, holding her and Hal close to his chest. She felt the beating of his heart, his warm breath in her hair as he made the 'sh sh sh' noises he used to soothe Janet and Allie when they were babies. Feeling the sinewy strength of him, understanding now why they were comforted to sleep, she relaxed into him. Her sobs faded to slow breathing with an occasional catch in her throat.

The harshness of Hal's cries lessened, then stopped. His heavy leaning on Tom gradually switched to a sideways lean against her. She was being pushed even closer to Tom and he felt hard and unbending. He pushed back, and though she knew he was just resisting being thrust flat out backwards, she felt as though he was trying to shove her away. Not wanting her so close. Not willing for them to fit together as they once had. Nothing like Claude, who loved to hold her, who wanted her to lean on him in more ways than one.

She tried to pull away. Tom held on until she felt suffocated enough to struggle.

'Right now, that's enough, the both of you,' he said, dropping his arm from around Hannah. 'Youse will make yerselves sick and what's the good of that?'

Hannah took a deep breath, then another as that first one caught halfway through. Sitting back on her heels, she lowered her head, wondering why she suddenly felt a shyness. Or was it awkwardness? The comfort he had given her was no different from what she would have felt with Grandma, or Allie or Janet. They were separate now, her and Tom. Claude and Madge were wedged firmly between them.

'Are you all right?' Tom asked.

She nodded.

'Good,' he stated, looking at her, then quickly looking away. 'I should be getting back. Are you all right now, Hal me lad?'

'It . . . It's my fault,' Hal stuttered when Tom took out a handkerchief and mopped away the tears.

'It's nobody's fault. Leastways, nobody here. That's right, isn't it, Hannah?'

'Nobody here,' she agreed, knowing at that moment it was true of more than Lily's death.

Tom gave Hal's hair a quick tousle, then climbed to his feet. The movement was stiff and when he paused halfway, wincing, Hannah realised that his knees were stiff. He was working harder and longer now than he ever had and it was telling on him physically.

He must believe Madge to be worth it, she thought with a twinge of bitterness.

'Where's Colin? Can I talk to him?' Tom asked.

'It's not his fault either,' Hannah stated, just managing to keep the snap out of her tone.

Tom frowned, obviously struck by the sudden coldness in her stare.

'He's not the Colin you used to know when we were kids,' he said softly. 'He's a different bloke than that. He's killed since then, Hannah.'

'But not now. Not Lily.'

'He tell ya that?'

'He did.'

'And ya believe it?'

She stared into his eyes. 'I do.'

'Then I have to go along with ya,' Tom said, though she could read the doubt in his voice.

'It wasn't Colin who hurt her, Dad. Not Colin,' Hal cried out.

'Ask him yourself,' Hannah said.

Tom nodded, gently pushing Hal towards Hannah when the boy began to cry again.

'Colin?' Tom knocked on his door. 'I want to talk to ya.'

'Nick off,' came the muffled answer.

'I want to talk to ya,' Tom said again, turning the door handle. 'He's got it locked,' he told Hannah.

She shook her head. 'There's no lock on any of the inside doors, you know that.'

Tom turned the handle again and pushed. 'Then he's got a chair under the knob.'

'Let us in, Colin,' Hannah called.

'Nick off.'

'Hal, call to him,' Hannah whispered.

Hal laid his forehead against the door. 'It's me. It's Hal.'

'Go away, bugger ya,' Colin mumbled. 'I don't feel too good.'

'Leave the man be,' Grandma said from behind them. 'He's not going to let anyone in until he's good and ready. And Hal, stop that caterwauling.'

'Lily my mother is killed,' he said as tears oozed down his cheeks.

'I don't know why you're so upset, she never did you any good,' Grandma told him sternly. 'And crying don't change anything. Now get yourselves into the kitchen and have some breakfast. You too, Tom.'

'She's right you know,' Hannah said, grateful for the interruption. 'Come on, Hal. Tom. We'll talk about it when Colin comes out.'

'I'm thinking the detectives will be here soon asking questions and Hal don't need that just now. How about I take him round to the bakery for breakfast?' Tom asked.

Hannah shook her head. 'All they know at the moment is that I found Lily. I promised to go to the station and give a full statement later today. Until then, they won't come here.'

Not until I tell them about Colin, she could have said but refrained. She didn't want to go into long explanations with Tom, especially when he seemed to doubt Colin already.

'Well I think it's a good idea,' Grandma said. 'Get Hal away from all this for a little while and he'll be able to handle it better when the coppers do come.'

Hannah looked down at Hal. 'What do you think? We can put off talking about Lily your mother until later?'

Hal hesitated for a moment, then took Tom's hand. It seemed that talking about her was the last thing he wanted to do.

Wanting to Help

Allie was first through the hospital doors the moment they opened. Janet didn't seem too pleased to see her, but Allie decided that was because she was still feeling guilty, and probably tired from the loss of so much blood.

'I won't stay long,' she assured her sister. 'I just wanted to tell you what happened last night. It's about Lily Gatley.'

'I heard about it on that lady's wireless.' Janet pointed to a mantel radio sitting on the floor between her bed and the next one along. 'Have they arrested anybody? Was she after Hal again?'

Sitting on the edge of the bed, Allie told as much as she knew, ending with, 'And people are coming from all over the place to see where she died. Australia Street's like a circus.'

'So what's happening now? The wireless didn't tell much.'

'Not much to tell. The police wouldn't have had time to find out anything. But home's pretty miserable. Colin won't come out of his room, even though Mum says he has to make a statement to the police.'

'Do you think he did it, Allie?'

'Not Colin. He wouldn't. But Grandma reckons he'll be the main suspect when the police find out he's been saying he'd kill her if she came after Hal again. Of course that won't matter when they find the real killer, but until then, they might put Colin in gaol. Grandma reckons he couldn't handle that.' She hesitated. 'Dad said the same thing. Threatening to kill her, I mean.'

'Nobody would suspect Dad,' Janet said dismissively.

'And Mum's been crying a lot. Seems her and Lily were best friends when they were kids and even though Lily turned out rotten, you know, with Hal and everything, Mum's really upset. And everyone knows about her and Claude Macy now.'

'Who do you think it was, Allie?'

Allie thought for a moment. 'Maybe some bloke we don't know. Maybe Lily owed money to some big nob and he was after her.'

'That sounds like something out of a whodunit novel,' Janet snorted. 'Would be good though. Leaves all our lot out of it.'

'Anyway, Colin will have to go see the cops soon or they'll bust his door down. That's what Mum yelled at him from the hall. She says he's got a chair stuck under the door knob so no one can open it. And he won't talk to anyone, not even Hal. But what about you? What's happening with you?'

'They're letting me out tomorrow,' Janet said slowly, 'and I'm not sure where I'll go or what to do.'

'Why don't you come home until you decide?'

'Home? Where's that, Grandma's? And sleep where?'

'We'll find somewhere. I'll bunk in with Hal for a while.'

'That won't work. It's not fair to Hal, or to you. Maybe I can talk Grandma into letting me stay in the veranda room.'

'I'd talk to her but she doesn't listen to a word I say. I'd probably ruin any chance you had. We might have to think of something else.'

'We? It's not your problem, Allie.'

'Course it is.'

'Things are better between us, little sister, but that doesn't mean ya can start poking ya nose into my business.'

'I just want to help,' Allie protested. 'You have to go somewhere.'

Janet stared up at a point on the ceiling. 'As a matter of fact, Johnny's going to see about getting me work at a guesthouse where some of his friends live. Not yet though. I might have to come home until I'm feeling stronger. I'll tell Grandma I just need the room for a few weeks.'

'You don't mean Johnny Lawson!'

'He came last night not long after you left.'

'You have to be kidding, Janet.'

She glanced at Allie, then looked away. 'When he got home to the guesthouse, they told him about the ambulance and everything and he was worried.'

'That's why you're wearing make-up, because you're expecting him back. I can't believe you'd want him anywhere near you.'

'He hasn't really done anything wrong, has he?' Janet said, trying without much success to sound casual.

'Either I'm mad or you are,' Allie stated. 'You can't let him back in your life after what he's done.'

'What's he done, Allie? He didn't force me to have sex, and he didn't make me go to Mrs Bowrie.' She looked Allie in the face. 'He didn't make you do anything you didn't want to do.'

'But you lost your baby because of him.'

Janet's stare grew intense.

'Because you knew he was no good,' Allie finished.

'It's not that he's no good, that's your opinion. The truth is, he just isn't what you want him to be.' Janet grimaced. 'Like Dad.'

'You can't compare him to Dad!'

'Just leave it alone, Allie. None of us are perfect.'

'But you're forgetting what you said last night.'

'I was angry then, and feeling guilty about . . . Well that was last night.'

'But the baby! You were so heartbroken. I don't understand you.'

Janet heaved a sudden gusty sigh. 'I guess you'll find out soon enough so I might as well tell ya now. 'I didn't lose the baby.'

Allie stood. 'What?'

'I lost a lot of blood and I'm going to have to be very careful for the next few months. No lifting. No heavy work. Just concentrate on getting this baby growing.' Janet's face lit with a smile that glowed. 'That's what they told me. Oh Allie, I've got another chance. How much of a miracle is that?'

Allie shook her head as though there was something wrong with her hearing.

'I have to see a doctor every week for a while, but I didn't lose her. The doctors here, they stopped the bleeding and they saved her. I'm so glad to be telling ya.' Janet jigged around on the bed, halfway between laughing and crying. 'If I'd held it in any longer, I woulda burst. I want to tell the whole wide world! She's a tough little bugger, like all us Gordons. And it seems Mrs Bowrie doesn't really know what she's doing. I'll be thanking God every minute of every day for that. But I'm babbling. I know I'm babbling. I'm so happy. Don't just stand there looking at me. Say something. Say how glad ya are that God or nature or whoever decides about these things has given me another go.'

Allie shook her head again, then turned and walked towards the door.

'You'll have a niece, Allie. Or could be a nephew I suppose, though I'm hoping for a girl,' Janet said softly. 'Be happy for me.'

Allie swung around. Ignoring the watching eyes from every bed in the room, she said, 'Did you know this when I was here last night?'

'They told me just after ya left. Johnny was here. He was angry at first, angry I didn't tell him about the baby. And don't shout at me from halfway across the room. Ya waking everybody up. Come back here.'

Allie walked back. 'Did you tell him what you'd tried to do?'

'I couldn't do that. He was over the moon at the thought of being a dad. He's had a pretty lonely life, ya know. No family but his mum and dad and he thinks they don't care all that much about him.'

'Can't say I blame them,' Allie snapped.

'I love him, Allie.'

'I thought I loved him too, but I got over it once I saw what he's really like.'

Janet shook her head. 'You never loved him. Ya can't turn love off like a tap when it doesn't suit ya any more. Ya just wanted him. You and a heap of other girls. He just tried to give ya what ya wanted like all the rest. What's wrong with that? He didn't mention marriage or living together happy ever after, did he?'

'He said he loved me!'

'He told ya what ya wanted to hear to make ya feel good.'

'So I'd have sex with him, you mean.'

'Well, wasn't that what ya wanted?'

'I can't believe you let me think the baby was . . . was gone. Why didn't you tell me straight away?'

'Because ya think ya know it all, Allie. You think ya can tell me what to do. You're always poking yer nose into my business and it's got nothing to do with you. Johnny and me, how I feel about him, what we're going to do. None of it's got anything to do with you.'

Allie turned away to hide her pain. She wanted to feel angry that Janet held back the news about the baby, and perhaps wasn't going to tell her until she told the rest of the family, but the hurt smothered everything else. 'I'm getting out of here before we start fighting again,' she said.

'Please don't say anything at home. I have to tell them meself. I'll have to go back for a while till I'm better. I won't be able to work and look after meself, maybe till after the baby. So I have to be the one to tell them. Mum and Grandma. Dad too.'

Allie kept her back turned. 'I won't say anything.'

'And Allie, that's not all. You're gunner hate me more than ya already do. Look at me please. Let me say it to yer face.'

Allie swung around and stared down into her sister's eyes.

'You know and I know that Mum can't afford to keep both of us. She doesn't earn enough, and we can't expect Grandma to do it. She wouldn't anyway. And we've got Buckley's of getting anything from Dad.'

'What are you trying to say?' Allie demanded, but she knew. She knew exactly how it had to be. She would have to get a full-time job. She'd have to work for a couple of years to help Janet, then it would be another three or four years at least before she could go to uni. She felt her dreams slipping away. Everything she'd ever wanted would have to be sacrificed for this baby.

'It's not fair!' she cried out.

'I know. I know,' Janet wailed. 'But it's not for forever, Allie.'

'You don't understand!'

'I didn't before but I do now,' Janet said, not once turning her eyes away from Allie's face. 'I know what it means to want something so bad that ya feel life's not worth living without it. That's how I felt when I thought I'd killed me baby.'

'Oh Janet.'

'I know. And I'm sorrier than I can say.' Janet clasped her hands together, as if in prayer. 'But truly, Allie, it's not for forever. Soon as I can, I'll get back to work and I'll help ya save up for university. Every penny I can afford. I promise.'

'It'll take years! It'll be too late! You don't understand.' And she knew Janet did not understand. They were working class, the poorer working class, and as such, they went out to work as soon as the government allowed them to leave school. That's the way it was supposed to be. Janet had always accepted that. She'd never understood Allie's ambitions.

Janet took her hand, the first time she'd done that voluntarily. 'Don't hate me too much, sis.'

'I don't.' Allie swallowed back a sob. 'I just don't like you very much at the moment.'

A cheeky smile. Probably forced, but it stopped the flow of tears that were brimming in both their eyes. 'That's okay, you're gunner love my baby.'

'But not her father. Though if you want to stuff up your life, then like you say, it's your business.'

'Exactly.' Janet glanced towards the door. 'Do me a favour and be nice, okay? Or just go right now.'

'I hope you two aren't arguing again.'

Allie knew the voice. She didn't need to look.

'You don't know anything about us,' she said brusquely. 'I don't know how you've got the hide to show your face.'

'Your sister's forgiven me.' He walked past her to the bed, bent and kissed Janet on the lips, a slow, tender kiss, before turning back to Allie. 'So why can't you?'

'Because I'm not the idiot she is,' Allie snapped.

'Be happy for me, Allie, or stay away,' Janet warned.

'Like you always say, it's your life,' Allie shot back.

'And don't say anything to the family, not until I've had a chance to tell them myself.'

'Can I tell them where you'll be?'

Johnny held out a folded piece of paper. 'I've booked a room for Jan in this guesthouse where a few of my friends stay. She'll be there until she decides what she's going to do next.'

'And what are the choices?' Allie asked as she took the paper.

Janet interrupted. 'I'll let ya know when I let Mum and Dad know. I have a lot of thinking to do.'

Stepping around Johnny, Allie moved back to the bed. The sisters stared into each others faces until Janet repeated, 'Be happy for me, Allie,' in the softest of voices.

'I am. I truly am. At least, I will be.'

'Auntie Allie,' Janet said again in the same soft voice, and held out her arms.

Their hug was hard and fierce. Allie broke away first.

'I'll wait to hear from you then,' she told Janet, and walked out, glancing back once as she turned into the hall. Johnny was watching her, still smiling. Remembering that smile when he'd seen her beside his car window that night, she realised he'd guessed why she was there.

'But it'll never happen. Not on your Nellie,' she said to his lovely black Oldsmobile as she passed it on the street, borrowing one of Grandma's favourite expressions, and after glancing around to make sure no one watched, she took a coin out of her purse and ran the edge along the shiny black paint.

'That's childish and spiteful,' she said, but couldn't make herself give a damn. As she made her way home she recalled that bright silver smear along the side of the car and pictured Johnny Lawson's reaction when he saw it, feeling a sense of smug satisfaction. It disappeared the moment she stepped off the tram and remembered last night – Lily's murder, the chaos and tears, but most of all, Hal's silence. He'd always been a quiet kid, but this was more than just quietness. He had been awake when she woke this morning, just lying there in bed with the covers up around his neck as though he was too afraid to get up. But what was he scared of?

'Where's Hal?' she asked her mother the moment she walked into the house. 'He's all right, isn't he?'

'He went with your dad.'

'And you let him go?'

'Your dad thought Hal would be better away from Australia Street while the police are all over the place and I agreed with him. He'll be bringing him back any minute now. The police have gone at last.'

'I noticed.' Allie shuddered. 'But I wouldn't go up there. Who's going to clean up the . . . You know.'

'The blood, Allie,' Grandma put in. 'It's blood.'

Allie didn't try to hide her scowl. Damn old curmudgeon. If you'd been a nicer person and not a God-blathering, narrow-minded old sourpuss forever preaching and nagging, Janet would never have gone to Mrs Bowrie, she thought. She also thought about saying it, but she'd promised Janet to keep quiet. Instead, she said, 'I don't care what she did, Lily didn't deserve to die because of it.'

Grandma's eyes flashed. 'Of course I'm not glad, you miserable little chit. Lily was your great-aunt's grand-daughter. Florrie's in there mourning for her, but you haven't bothered to go in and see if she's all right, have you?'

Allie felt a pang of guilt. No, she hadn't, and she should have. Great-Aunt Florrie was the peacemaker in this house. Many times she'd stood between Grandma's sharp tongue and Allie. But she was so quiet, so unobtrusive that everyone seemed to forget she lived here too. Until they needed her.

'I'll go see her now,' she said, and strode away before Grandma could object. 'Great-Aunt, can I come in?' she asked, poking her head around the door.

The bedroom was cramped with too much furniture, too many little ornaments crowded into every available space, too many crocheted runners covered the furniture, and the smell of potpourri was much too strong. Too much of everything. Even the bedspread on the large and bumpy bed had too many squares. Three of its edges overlapped onto the floor and the edge covering a mound of pillows beside the bedhead had been doubled over twice. The floor had an overlapping of rugs, the walls held too many photographs.

Allie recognised all of it, the furniture, the ornaments, the photographs, as a record of the lives and times of two very different women nearing the end of those lives. That thought caused a momentary stutter of her heartbeat. She realised, for the first time, that she loved this rope-thin old lady in a way she loved no one else. Perhaps because Great-Aunt Florrie was so open and generous with her love. She could calm even Grandma with a smile. Her one vice was a love of gossip, though she never repeated it. If asked, she would say it made up for the monotony of her own life. Her best friend, apart from Grandma of course, was Mrs Paterson.

Right now she was sitting on the side of the bed holding a handkerchief against her eyes. 'I'm afraid I'm not very good company right now, Allie. What can I do for you?' she asked.

'I just wanted to see if there's anything I can do for you.'

'Well that's very kind of you, but I can't think of a thing.'

Allie sat on the end of the bed. 'I guess I've been so busy thinking about Hal and, well, you know, I forgot about Lily being your granddaughter.'

'She was the prettiest baby ever born, and sweeter than sugar when she was small.' Great-Aunt Florrie heaved a sigh that seemed to come up from the depths of her body. 'But she became . . .' Another sigh. 'Not nice.'

A bloody horror, Allie thought, but kept the thought to herself.

'You shouldn't cry so much, you'll make yourself sick,' she said.

'Everyone deserves someone to cry over them when they're gone,' was the quietly spoken answer.

'I didn't mean anything,' Allie said hastily.

'I know that. You're trying to comfort me. But I can't be comforted right now. Not over Lily's terrible death, not over her terrible life. Which I might have done something to change if I'd had the courage.' Leaning forward, she patted Allie's hand. 'So if you don't mind, I'd like you to leave me to my grieving. Actually, I think I'll take a little walk.' She forced a smile. 'I'll sneak out the back way so no one will see me and offer their company. If your grandmother asks, tell her I'll be back in time for dinner tonight. I promise. She'll understand. All right?'

Allie nodded and stood.

'And please, Allie, even when she seems to be deliberately provoking you, please remember that your grandmother loves you dearly.'

Allie remembered last night.

'I know.'

Bending over her great-aunt's bowed head, she planted a soft kiss on the grey hair.

Losing Marbles

'Hey hey, what's going on here?' Tom shouted as he leapt down the back steps.

Bobby Lenahan and Hal were locked together, rolling around in the dirt, their grimaces highlighted by a sheen of sweat. Ignoring Tom, Bobby got one hand free and managed a right uppercut to Hal's cheek. Hampered by the ground, it was too short to do any damage. Hal's yell was more anger than pain as he head-butted Bobby's nose. It began to leak blood as he rolled over, dragging Hal underneath him, and tried to get a hand free for another punch.

'Enough now!' Tom grabbed handfuls of shirts and pulled them apart. 'What's this all about?'

'He's come to take you away,' Bobby said tearfully.

'That's not true for a start,' Tom said.

Wiping a smattering of Bobby's blood off his face with a shirt sleeve, Hal spoke up. 'He said I'm just like Lily my mother and I'm not.'

'Why would you say a thing like that, eh Bobby?'

'Cause he's gonner take you away and we won't have no one and Mum will start crying and . . . and . . .' The babble was cut off as Bobby burst into tears.

So it's not actually me he'd be missing, Tom thought. It's the knowing his mum can't cope on her own. That's a bit of a blow to the old ego.

Squatting down and pulling the boys into him, one on either side, he said, 'I'm not leaving here, I promise youse that. And hear me good, Bobby, when and if I ever do leave, it'll be after I've taught ya mum to look after herself and all you boys. You understand that?'

As Bobby nodded slowly, Hal pulled away. Dragging him back, Tom added, 'Hal's got his mum to look after him, and she can do it better than I ever could. It's hard when families break up but ya have to learn to go with it. In the long run, what it really does is make even bigger families. Leastways, it will when we teach our families to pull together. And I'm telling ya, I need both of youse to help me with that. Youse have to work on yer mums for a start. Slowly but, yer don't go rushing this sort of thing. And if you two play together without any fighting, that's a good start because youse are showing yer mums that yer can. Do yer see that? Hal? Bobby?'

There was a pause as the boys stared at each other, then, heads hanging, they both nodded.

Tom smiled. 'Good on youse. Now I gotter take Hal back to Grandma's or I'll be getting into trouble. Best you two go in and wash up before anybody sees ya. I'm not gunner ask youse to shake hands, just to think about what I've been saying. Okay?'

Another pause. More nods, and the boys headed for the steps side by side. There was a bit of push and shove as they entered the house, but their exchange of shy grins put Tom's mind at rest.

They'll sort it out and do the right thing. Most kids do if they're shown how, he thought.

Twenty minutes later, Tom and Hal were on their way, taking a roundabout route so Tom had time to reinforce what he'd said earlier. He found it wasn't necessary for, thanks mainly to talks with Colin, Hal had already reached the conclusion that now Tom was living with the Lenahans, Hal was related to them, and kin had to watch out for each other.

'It was Bobby who wanted to fight,' he told Tom.

'Yeah, well, I reckon that won't happen again. I'll have to thank Colin for showing you the proper way to look at things.'

They had almost reached the Golden Barley and Tom was fighting an urge to go in for a drink, just one wouldn't hurt, when Hal spoke again.

'Lily my mother is really dead, isn't she, Dad?' he asked.

No sense in telling the kid a pack of lies, Tom thought. He was old enough and tough enough to have the uncoloured truth.

'Yeah, mate, she's gone,' he answered. 'Gone where she can't hurt anyone any more. And don't start crying,' he added when he saw the look on Hal's face. 'Believe me, mate, she isn't worth yer tears. She never did anyone a good turn in her whole life. Especially not you.'

'And Colin won't get into trouble, will he, Dad?'

Tom's answer was cut off by a babble of men's voices coming from inside the pub. One voice shouted the others down.

'I tell you he killed her! I know he did. Colin Gatley killed my Maisie and he's got to pay!'

'That's Fred Peters,' Tom said. 'The bloke's lost his marbles. Why would Colin want to kill his Maisie?'

'Now, mate, yer talking nonsense.'

That was Gus Markham.

'Don't you go doing nothing stupid,' Shorty warned.

'Why's Mr Peters saying that about Colin?' Hal asked.

'I dunno. He's nuts. Come on, Hal. We'd better get to Grandma's in a hurry and let Colin know what's going on.'

Tom strode on, pulling Hal with him, going as fast as the boy's shorter legs would allow, until they reached Australia Street. They were outside Clara Paterson's house when Hal looked back, then jerked on Tom's trouser leg.

'Dad, look. It's Mr Peters coming down the street.'

'Bloody hell!'

Tom stopped, looked down at Hal, then opened Clara's gate. Leaping up the steps, dragging Hal with him, he banged on the door with a closed fist.

'Mrs Paterson, are you there? It's me, Tom Gordon.'

'Door's not locked, come on in,' she called.

As Tom opened the door, Fred Peters ran past the house.

'Jesus wept, he's got hisself a iron bar,' Tom said, and shoved Hal into the hallway. 'You stay here, son,' he ordered. 'And best tell Mrs Paterson to get herself up to the shop and call the coppers.'

Turning, he grabbed an old wooden chair off the porch, and ran.

Oh, Colin

'When I went in to see Great-Aunt Florrie, I had the distinct impression she wanted to be alone,' Hannah said as Allie entered the older women's bedroom and closed the door behind her.

'And so she does,' Grandma agreed, 'but she needs to know we're thinking of her.'

Just when I'm thinking the worst of you, you say something considerate, Hannah thought. You can be so bitchy at times, yet so caring.

'Why are you looking at me like that?' Grandma demanded.

'Like what?'

'Like I'm some kind of oddity.'

'I was thinking of Great-Aunt Florrie and the way she's taking Lily's death so hard.'

'Poor Florrie,' Grandma said softly. 'She feels guilty.'

'Why would she feel guilt?'

'Because she chose to live with me, to comfort and keep me company after your grandfather died. Now she's thinking she should have moved in with her daughter. Perhaps she would have been able to help Lily and none of this would have happened.'

'Do you think that?'

'It's possible,' Grandma conceded. 'Florrie would influence anyone for the better. If anyone could have stopped Lily from turning evil, she could.'

'Is there really any such thing?'

'You're asking me if there's evil in this world? Oh, yes. Be sure of that. There is a God, there is a devil.'

'So where does that leave Hal?' Hannah asked.

'He's a sweet boy, nothing like his mother,' Grandma said firmly. 'Perhaps he takes after his father, whoever that may be.'

'Maybe we should try to find out. His name could be on Hal's birth certificate.'

'If he'd wanted anything to do with Hal, we'd have known by now.'

'Perhaps whoever it is doesn't know about him.'

'Why do you need to know?'

Hannah gestured helplessly. 'I don't. I just thought . . .' Her voice trailed when Grandma stared at her.

'Are you worried for Hal or for yourself? No, don't look at me like that, Hannah. I know Lily claimed Tom for the father. I don't believe it, but it would make no difference to me if it was true. Can you say the same?'

'I don't really know,' Hannah answered honestly.

'If you found out that Hal was part of Tom with Lily, would that affect the way you feel about the boy? If so, you disappoint me greatly. I would never have brought him to you in the first place.'

'So you think I shouldn't care if Tom was disloyal?'

'I think you shouldn't blame Hal if that was the case.'

'I don't,' Hannah cried out, and turned aside, not wanting to continue this conversation. She was grateful when Allie strolled into the kitchen and filled the kettle.

'A cup of tea. Good idea,' she said.

'I hardly think there's a need for it. We've just finished lunch,' Grandma said. 'And speaking of lunch, Allie, you're not normally home until an hour after it. Why are you so early?'

Allie stared at her, obviously contemplating a lie. Knowing that Grandma could pick them a block away, she decided against it. 'I didn't go to work.'

'Why not? And don't tell me it was because of Lily. You didn't know her.'

'I went to see Janet.'

'You saw her last night. Have you and her suddenly become best friends?'

Allie stared down at her shoes.

'I thought not.'

'I'm not answerable to you, Grandma. I don't have to tell you every move I make.'

'That's enough, Allie,' Hannah warned.

'Why don't you tell *her* that's enough?'

'You'll give respect to your elders, missy,' Grandma snapped.

Before Allie could point out that respect had to be earned, not given, Hannah interrupted. 'Allie's right, Grandma. She isn't answerable to you, though she is to me.' She turned to Allie. 'You were with Janet last night and if you missed work to go there again this morning, something must be wrong.'

Allie hesitated before saying, 'She's been sick but she didn't want you to know. She says you've got enough to worry about without her adding to it.'

Grandma cut in. 'Janet always was a thoughtful girl.'

Allie clamped her lips shut.

Hannah frowned. 'How sick?'

'Mum, she told me not to say anything. If you want to know more, you'd better ask her. She's quit her job and I don't think she knows what she's going to do. Maybe come home for a while until she . . . Until she finds another job or something.'

'What's going on with her, Allie? I want the truth now.'

'Then you'd better wait until you can ask her.'

'Leave it, Grandma.' Hannah held up a hand as Grandma was about to speak. 'It looks as though Janet has made Allie promise to keep quiet until she gets a chance to tell us herself, so we'll respect her wishes and wait. And don't look at me like that. I'm not back answering you.'

Grandma's eyes darkened to the sinkhole green colour and Hannah knew a tirade was about to begin. The only way to avoid it was to leave. 'Come on, Allie. We'll fetch Hal from your dad,' she said, grabbing her daughter's arm and pulling her away.

They hadn't gone more than two paces when the gate clanged loudly, as though it had been thrown shut. Grandma joined Hannah and Allie in the hall as the front door crashed open. Fred Peters charged towards them brandishing a length of steel pipe.

'Come out here, Colin,' he shouted. 'Come out and face me. I know it was you and I'm going to do to you what you did to them.'

'How dare you break into my house,' Grandma began.

'Get out of my way!' he shouted.

'Grandma, wait.' Hannah stepped in front of her. 'What's this about, Fred?' she asked, not quite succeeding in keeping the quaver out of her voice. 'Calm down now. You're frightening us.'

As Hannah spoke, Tom strode down the hallway, rearing back and thrusting out a chair when Fred turned suddenly and swung the pipe at him. The chair, old and made fragile by years out in the weather, disintegrated as the length of pipe smashed into it.

'Stay back. Stay back!' Fred roared. His face was brick red in colour, his lips almost purple. The veins in his face and throat looked as though they were about to burst.

'Hey now, you wouldn't want to hit anyone with that bar,' Tom soothed. 'You wouldn't want to hit me. We've been mates for too long.'

'It's Colin I've come to get. He did it. I know he did it.'

'Look, mate, that was just pub talk,' Tom said persuasively. Darting a warning glance at Hannah, he added, 'Just blokes talking, making guesses. They don't know nothing.' He moved closer. 'You know Colin. He wouldn't hurt a flea.'

'He killed that woman. That harlot. I know what she was.'

Grandma stepped around Hannah. 'If you know that, why are you . . .'

Fred Peters swung towards her, lashing out with the pipe. Hannah shoved her aside a fraction of a second too late for the pipe to miss entirely. It caught the sleeve of Hannah's dress, dragging her off balance. She staggered and fell, grabbing at Allie as she went. They hit the floor together. Fred raised the pipe again and Allie scrambled forward, covering Grandma's body with her own.

Tom slapped his hands together as loudly as he could, once, twice, shouting, 'Hey now, Fred! Hey, mate!'

'Stay back. Stay. I know what you're trying to do. I know you're looking out for that mangy killer. But I'll go through the lot of you.'

Tom screwed his face into an expression of deep hurt. 'You wouldn't harm these women, would you, Fred? You've known them all your life. That's Hannah, Grandma and Allie lying on the floor and I'm telling them to stay where they are. Hannah and Allie, you've known them forever. We lived next door, remember that, hey, Fred? They're best mates with your Franny. She wouldn't like what you're doing, your Fran wouldn't. Come on, mate, give me that before yer do something you'll hate yourself for.'

'Please, Fred,' Hannah begged. 'Don't hurt Grandma. Don't hurt my Allie. She was one of Maisie's best friends, her and Janet. Maisie wouldn't like to think you'd hurt any of us.'

'My Maisie would never walk away from us and not come back. I know she wouldn't do something like that.' Saliva ran from the corners of Fred's mouth and flecked the air as he spoke. 'He killed her like he killed that harlot. He killed my Maisie, that's why she's never come back to us. Now I'm gunner see how he likes being bashed.'

'You can't do that,' Hannah cried out.

'No, Fred. You're wrong. Shut up, Hannah,' Tom shouted, and lunged. As he did, Fred turned and swung out again, catching Tom across the side of the head.

'You won't stop me,' Fred snarled as Tom fell. 'None of youse will.'

He swung in a circle, made awkward by his wooden leg, lashing out with the pipe as he went. It hit the wall and wrenched out of his hand. Hannah made a dive for it, grabbed it, but the strength of her dive cannoned her into the wall. She took the force of the hit on her shoulder, saving her face. The top of her arm and her elbow bounced against the wall, jerking the pipe from her hold.

Shoving her to one side, Fred gripped the weapon and spun around towards Colin's door.

'Colin, don't open your door!' Hannah screamed.

'Coward! Coward!' Fred roared and shoulder-charged the door. 'Hiding away in there.' He charged it again. 'Coward!'

Gus Markham raced down the hallway and grabbed the arm holding the pipe. Shorty was right behind him. Together they swung Fred sideways and pinned him against the wall.

'It's all right, we got him,' Shorty said when Allie screamed.

Hannah struggled to a sitting position. 'Tom, are you all right?'

Tom groaned and opened his eyes. 'Dunno. Think so. Bloody hell, Fred. What's going on with you?'

'I have to get that Colin,' Fred said, and arched his back when Gus gave his arm a vicious upward twist.

Hannah breathed easier seeing Tom talking now and gingerly rubbing the side of his head. 'We're your friends, Fred. All of us here. We'd never hurt your Maisie,' she said softly.

Fred turned his head and stared down at her. 'I've been looking after you,' he whispered. 'All the girls and women. Walking them home when they go out at night. Making them safe.'

'That was the right thing to do,' Hannah agreed. 'And Maisie will come home one day soon, you'll see.'

Shorty cut in. 'The barmaid called the cops. They shouldn't be too far away.'

Hannah climbed slowly to her feet. 'They're here,' she said thankfully as she looked along the hall and saw a police wagon pull up outside.

'Here. In here,' Allie shouted, heaving a grateful sigh when they climbed out of their car.

'About bloody time. Put this ratbag where he belongs,' Shorty said. 'As if Colin would kill anyone. Wouldn't hurt a frigging fly that bloke. He seen too much of it in the war. Where is he anyway?'

'He can't have slept through all that racket,' Grandma said.

Hannah frowned. 'He was pretty drunk last night.'

'He killed my Maisie,' Fred said, but scratchily, as though he didn't really believe it himself any more.

'Shut up, you bloody fruitcake,' Gus snarled.

'Don't do that,' Hannah shouted as he slammed Fred's head against the wall.

Fred spun sideways, out of Gus's grip, shoved him hard, then shoulder-charged the door again. It splintered open and hung on one hinge as a chair skidded across the room. Shorty grabbed him and hung on.

'Gus, help me,' he shouted. 'And bloody well hang on to him this time.'

'Mum, Grandma's hurt,' Allie said.

'I'm all right, girl. Don't fuss,' Grandma said as she climbed groggily to her feet, clinging to Allie while being led to a chair.

'Colin, what's wrong? Are you all right?' Hannah asked, looking past the broken door at Colin sprawled out across the bed, his head thrown back, one leg dangling over the side as though he'd tried to get up but failed. Hannah stood in the doorway, afraid to go in as she noted the stillness of his body, the empty medicine vial on the bedside cupboard, the empty glass on the floor.

'What seems to be the trouble here,' a constable asked as he reached Shorty and Gus. 'Why are you holding that man?'

'Because he did that.' Shorty pointed to Tom. 'Clouted him with that iron bar, I reckon. The bloody bloke's gone berserk.'

'Dad, stay still. Don't try to get up,' Allie told him.

Tom had stood, but didn't last. Sliding down the wall, he sat heavily, legs bent, head resting on his knees.

'Colin, get out here,' Hannah ordered, refusing to believe what her eyes could see. Striding across the room, she grabbed his arm. 'Come on, get up. Oh please, Colin.' Straightening, she stared down at him, then bent and placed the tips of her fingers against what should have been a pulse on his throat.

'Colin?' Her fingers moved upwards, stroking the side of his face. Kneeling, she lay her cheek against his shoulder.

'Oh, Colin.'

Nobody Can Go Back

Tom hunched down, pushing his face into his knees. The noise was killing him. His head throbbed. The pain was worse than a hangover. He felt groggy. He was having trouble focussing. It seemed to him that everybody was talking at once with none of them making much sense.

He looked up, wishing he had the guts to yell at them all to shut their gobs and let his ears have a rest. But he knew if he yelled his head would fall off.

One copper had taken out his notebook and was asking Fred questions with the speed of a Bren gun. Too bloody fast for Fred to get in a word, Tom wanted to say. And anyway, Fred was too busy trying to get into Colin's room while Gus stood in his way and kept shoving him back. Shorty was in there, just staring down as if he expected Colin to put out a hand to shake at any time now. Hannah was kneeling beside the bed, head bent, bawling her eyes out. Allie was fussing over Grandma, who ignored her to argue with the other copper.

'A person could've been murdered and in their grave by the time you lot got around to answering a call for help,' she said.

The constable walked away from her and stood looking down at Tom.

'Are you all right, mate?'

'Course I'm not bloody all right. Fred clobbered me with an iron bar,' Tom said hoarsely, and turned away so the copper wouldn't talk to him again. His head hurt too much to listen.

His vision wavered as he watched the second policeman trying to talk to Allie, who waved him away, saying, 'I don't know. Ask Mum.' She was too busy fussing over Grandma to answer questions.

Funny thing that, Tom thought. I always reckoned she didn't care much for Grandma. Just goes to show.

Gus grabbed Tom's attention by shouting at Shorty, 'What is it, mate? What's up with Hollywood?'

'Oh shit. Shit shit shit,' was Shorty's answer.

No need for that, mate, there's ladies present, Tom tried to say, but the words wouldn't form. And he was trying to decide whether Shorty was swearing because of Fred or because of Colin just lying there, not moving, not talking. And not breathing by the look of things.

'Poor bugger.' Gus sounded as though he might burst out howling at any minute.

Allie called something Tom couldn't quite make out, and when he managed to turn his head and look over at her again, Grandma clutched her dress and hung on. 'Stay with me, Allie. You don't want to see,' she ordered.

'He's been dead an hour or two, I reckon,' Shorty said, and cleared his throat loudly, obviously trying to hide his emotions.

Men aren't supposed to shed tears in company, but Shorty was close to Colin, Tom thought. They've been mates from when they were kids. Gus too. Look at Gus, he won't even go into Colin's room.

He could hear Allie talking and talking, saying the same things over and over, asking questions nobody could answer. At least, nobody did. Hannah was still sobbing. The men's voices were all going at once. The coppers trying to get answers. Gus and Shorty making sure that wouldn't happen. They hated coppers, did Gus and Shorty. Everything was about Colin. Fred must have done him in with that bar. Poor bloody Colin. Poor bloody Fred. Lost his Maisie and now his marbles.

'Let me go. Let me see,' Fred yelled suddenly. 'He's playing possum, I tell yer.'

Tom shook his head, trying to clear his vision, and immediately wished he hadn't.

'This is your doing.' Gus looked straight at Grandma as he walked back into the room.

What did she do?

'Some of her stuff out there in the shed. She must have given it to him,' Gus answered, even though Tom could have sworn he hadn't asked the question out loud. He meant to tell Gus that Grandma didn't keep anything poisonous in the shed, but when he opened his mouth, all he could manage was a groan.

'Jesus, Colin.' That was Shorty. 'It had to be you that done Lily in. Why else would yer do this to yerself?'

'He killed my Maisie,' Fred Peters roared.

Tom watched Fred shove the two coppers out of his way. Legs and arms and fists started flying, bodies thumping against walls and bouncing off while the coppers tried to grab hold of him. Which wasn't easy. Fred was a fair-sized bloke, wideways at least, and his bout of madness was making him as strong as a bull. And the swearing would have done a soldier proud.

Pulling his legs closer to his chest, Tom continued to watch the melee, blinking appreciation at every scoring punch as though he were seeing something far removed from Australia Street. Something on a movie screen. Grandma had enough sense to grab Allie and hang on to her. He couldn't see Hannah now. The coppers were standing back to back in front of Colin's room, throwing punches at anyone who came near them. Seemed like Fred just wanted to connect with a few and didn't care who it was he hit. Gus and Shorty were using the situation to score a few paybacks, pretending to be trying to grab Fred while they got in a few elbows and kicks at the coppers. Police had a bad habit of grabbing blokes wandering home after a few too many at the Golden Barley. No warning. Just a grab, a heave into the paddy wagon, then a night in the drunk tank. Complain and you earn yourself a thumping. Tom had been on the receiving end a time or two. Gus a lot. Aggressive drunk, was Gus.

A minute or two later, couldn't have been longer, Fred looked to be out cold on the floor, but that wasn't stopping the others. Not until Hannah stuck her two bob's worth in. 'Stop it. Stop it!' she screamed, and they did. They all looked a bit sheepish when she started telling them where they got off.

'Can you hear me, Tom? I want to know about Hal,' Grandma shouted in his ear as though he were deaf and not just half knocked out. 'Tommy, where's Hal? Have you forgotten him?'

If she doesn't stop shaking my arm, I'll thump her one, he thought. And she knows I don't like being called Tommy. A baby name, that is.

'With Mrs Paterson,' he mumbled.

'What about you? Are you all right?'

'Sure, Grandma,' he said, remembering not to nod. 'You?'

'I'm fit enough, but I'll be black and blue come morning. Come on, love,' she said, putting her arm around Allie. 'We'll make everyone a cup of tea. No, leave your mother be. Let her do her crying. You should be doing a bit of that too. And you stay put, Tom. Those coppers rung for the ambulance. One for you and one for Colin.'

Her voice had grown ragged. She cleared her throat with a great hawking cough that made him shudder. Not what you'd call ladylike. But then, Grandma never was.

'I reckon you've got concussion. A night in hospital is what you'll get,' she continued when she could talk again. 'The nurses will look after you. I'm not able. Not feeling too good. But I can make that tea.'

She's gone, thank Christ, Tom thought as she bustled away. Fussing old bugger. Hard as nails on the outside, marshmallow on the inner, and thinks a flaming cup of tea can cure all ills. No, I remember her saying it was the making of it and the sitting down to drink was what mattered. Gives people time to calm down. Just as well I left Hal with Mrs Paterson. Wouldn't want him to see none of this. Just as well I was right behind Fred. Christ knows what he'd have done. Just as well Gus and Shorty followed me. Christ, my head's hurting.

Hannah knelt in front of him, red-faced and red-eyed. 'Are you all right?'

'Head's a bit sore is all.'

'You've been bleeding but it's stopped now. Grandma says you have concussion.'

'Yeah. Had it in Darwin too. Gets better after a few days. What's been going on?'

'He's dead, Tom. Colin's gone. Oh, Tom, he's gone.'

'There, there, let it out, me love.' Tom brought up his legs as she collapsed onto his lap. Wrapping his arms around her, he rocked her back and forth, muttering nonsense words, letting her hear his voice while she sobbed onto his shoulder. Loud sometimes, sometimes just gasps for air. Taking it hard. Saying Colin's name over and over. Her voice breaking up.

Sounds like her whole body's breaking up, he thought. Feels like it too. The softness is gone. She's turned into all angles and hard lines. They were thick as thieves as kids, her and Colin. Always together until she started going out with me. Then he took off out bush. Maybe that's why she let me have her, paying him back for taking off even though he wouldn't have known about it at the time. Women do funny things like that. Paying him back but only in her head. No logic at all. Maybe it was Colin all along. Maybe that's why her and me couldn't make it. No, that's not right. Nothing to do with Colin. I reckon it was her getting the taste for freedom while I was away at war.

'Tom. Hannah. The ambulance is here.'

Grandma again. Always looking out for everybody.

'Hannah, did ya hear?'

She nodded and pulled back from him, slid off his lap and climbed wearily to her feet.

Yeah, bet your life that's what it was. She's always been tied down. Could always look after herself, could Hannah, and she found that out. Not like Madge. They're as different as can be. We're different too, me and Hannah. We don't fit any more. Maybe we never did.

'We're never getting back together, are we, Hannah?'

He hadn't meant to say it out loud but he must have because she answered.

'No, Tom, we can't go back.' Her sigh was more a sob. 'Nobody can ever go back.'

He'd expected that answer. It didn't hurt as much as he thought it would. He loved Hannah. Always would, no doubt of that. But he loved Madge too. He knew that now. Don't let anyone say you can't love two women because that just isn't true. You can love whole streets of people if you got enough loving in you.

'Are you going to stay with Madge, Tom?'

He made sure not to nod. 'Yeah.'

By the look on her face, she'd expected that answer. Wasn't too put out about it neither.

'Looks like we've finally got things settled between us,' she said.

The arrival of two ambulance officers stopped Tom from answering. Not that he could think of an answer anyway.

'Name's Don,' the shorter one said, giving Hannah's shoulder a pat before turning to Tom. 'That's a nasty knock you've had there, mate. How'd that happen?'

'Iron bar,' Tom explained.

Don nodded. 'Do it every time. Don't think you should walk, matey. I'll get the stretcher.'

'I can walk if ya give us a hand.'

'Okay then, come on. Take the other side, Bert.'

Tom allowed them to take most of his weight as they hauled him erect, one on either side, and half-carried him up the hallway.

'Hang on a minute,' he said at the door, and turned back to Hannah, who had followed them. 'You be all right?'

She nodded slowly.

'Will you let Madge know?'

'I'll send Allie, and I'll get Hal from Mrs Paterson.'

'Right then. You look after my boy, won't you, Hannah?'

She gave him the strangest look before nodding a yes.

Needed

Allie stood at the front door, watching her mother, Shorty and Gus walk up Australia Street to Mrs Paterson's house. Now that the police and the ambulances carrying Colin and her dad were gone, the silence had become a weight pressing down on her. All she could hear was a faint droning sound, like a swarm of bees at sundown as the hive settled for the night.

But there's no bees here, she thought.

Holding her nose and clamping her mouth shut, she blew out, causing her ears to pop. The humming sound disappeared. She knew it would. She'd had that sound before, when a fast drive down Victoria Pass with Johnny had caused pressure to build up in her ears. He'd taught her that way of getting rid of the pressure and the sound. She supposed she had it now because of the shock. First Fred Peters going berserk, then Colin like that. The way he was.

As she tried to avoid thoughts of him her mind slid to Janet. She couldn't decide whether to be mad at her sister or sorry for her. Thinking about her didn't help, but anything was better than thinking about Colin and the way he lay there on his bed all cold and pale and slack-looking. Great-Aunt Florrie had got back from her walk as the police were leaving. Grandma explained what happened over cups of tea, then, wonder of wonders, halfway through the explanation, Grandma started crying. Allie had never heard Grandma cry before. For some ridiculous reason, she'd thought that to be impossible. Grandma was everybody's rock and rocks don't cry.

Grandma told Great-Aunt Florrie that she thought Colin must have been planning it for a while, otherwise he wouldn't have saved the sleeping tablets.

But why? Most of the time he seemed pretty happy. Why did he have to be such a coward? What about everyone he left behind? Didn't he care what he was doing to them? To me and Mum, and most of all to Hal who loved him like . . . like . . .

'Like he was sent from heaven as a special present just for Hal. He adored Colin. How could he do this to the boy? How am I going to explain it?' Hannah had asked Grandma, and for once in her life, Grandma hadn't had a ready answer.

Thinking about Grandma, Allie turned and called, 'Will you be all right till I get back, Grandma?'

Great-Aunt Florrie stepped into the hall, a finger on her lips. 'I've managed to get her to lie down,' she whispered as she joined Allie on the front porch. 'I'm worried about her. She's not herself at all.'

Allie nodded. 'Mum's the same.'

'It's a selfish act, taking one's own life,' Great-Aunt Florrie said. 'It leaves behind an awful guilt as well as sorrow.'

'You don't believe he killed Lily, do you?'

'Heavens no. I have no idea who did, but it certainly wasn't Colin. What about you, Allie dear? What do you think? What are you thinking?'

'I'm thinking you're wondering why I'm not crying, and I can't answer that, Auntie. I don't know why. I'm worried for Dad. I'm worried about Hal. I can't think about Colin. I can't imagine why he'd do . . . That. What does Grandma think?'

'Emily isn't thinking much of anything at the moment. That fall she had and Colin's death have really shaken her. But don't look so worried, dear. Your grandmother is a strong person. She'll be her old self in no time. I'll take good care of her while you run that message for your mum.' Giving Allie a shoulder pat of reassurance, Great-Aunt Florrie turned back inside.

Her way of sending me away, Allie thought. She knows I don't want to go. I'd rather go with Mum to fetch Hal. Although no, maybe I wouldn't. His reaction when he hears about Colin is something I can do without right now. What I'd like to do is get angry. It would be easier to handle than this feeling that somebody's slashed my chest open and has their fist clamped around my insides.

Minutes later, with her mind still swinging pendulum-like between too many emotions to sift one from the other, she stood at the bakery gate. She agreed with her mother. Mrs Lenahan deserved to be told about Dad going to hospital. But she still felt bitterness rise up in her every time she thought of Madge Lenahan. She couldn't bear the thought of being nice to her.

'Blow it,' she muttered. 'Let her find out for herself.'

She turned, about to leave when the front door opened and Madge Lenahan walked down the steps.

'Allie, wait. Wait up,' she called. 'Don't go away without coming in. Your dad isn't here at the moment, but he'll be back in a tick. Please come inside and wait for him. Or we can sit here on the porch if you'd rather.'

At first loud and fast, her voice trickled to a slow almost-whisper as Allie looked above her, aside, to the front door – anywhere but into her face.

'I thought . . . I thought your father must have told you and you'd come here to be friendly. To talk to me about it,' she said hesitantly.

'Told me what? That he's divorcing my mother to marry you?' Allie said coldly. Without waiting for an answer, she added, 'I came to tell you that he's been taken to hospital.'

Madge Lenahan's face paled and her body seemed to go out of balance. Staggering a few steps sideways, she clung to the fence for support. Her mouth opened and closed but no words emerged.

'It's all right. Really,' Allie assured her, jolted by her reaction. 'It's concussion. He'll be all right by tomorrow but Mum thought you should know in case, you know, in case you were worried about where he'd got to.'

'I thought you'd come to tell me he was dead,' Madge said, her voice so low that Allie had to move closer and bend forward to hear her. 'I've been expecting it, you see. That he'd be taken away like Bob . . .'

Staggering backwards, she sagged onto the top step. Her voice trailed into ragged breathing as she buried her face in her hands.

Allie stared at her. 'Why would you think that?'

'At first I thought he'd leave after a while but when that didn't happen . . .'

She means it, Allie thought. She's not putting it on for effect. All this time she's been expecting Dad to leave or maybe even die.

'He came here the day Bob died because he felt sorry for me, then he stayed,' Madge Lenahan said in that same breathless way. 'I don't know why he stayed and I didn't ask, even though I knew I had no right to him. But everything fell apart you see, when Bob died like that. I'm not making myself very clear, am I?'

'I think I see what you're getting at,' Allie said hesitantly.

'I needed someone to tell me what to do, to look after me and my boys, and your dad needed something too.'

Allie frowned, waiting for Madge to continue. When she didn't, Allie said, 'Needed what?'

'He needed to be strong, you see? Needed someone to need him.'

'I needed him. So did Hal. And Janet.'

'Your mother looked after you all very well. I've always envied her.' Madge stood, still a little shaky but in control. 'Now, please, tell me what happened to Tom.'

'Mr Peters hit him with an iron bar and he's got concussion.'

'Why would Fred do a thing like that?'

'He just went off his head. It's a long story. Dad will be all right but the ambulance men thought he should be in hospital tonight so the nurses could keep an eye on him.'

'Yes. Yes, of course. Did your mother go with him?'

Allie saw the fear in her eyes and was tempted to lie. But 'People are who they are' was one of Grandma's favourite sayings, and Allie could see the sense of that now. Her mum could fend for herself. Allie hoped to be like her one day. But Mrs Lenahan was a needer and that wasn't her fault.

'No, she didn't go. She thought you might like to.'

'Thank you, Allie.'

'That's okay.' Allie nodded slowly. 'You said earlier that Dad had told me something but it wasn't about him and Mum.'

'He'll tell you. If you don't mind, I'd like to go to him now.'

A picture flashed through Allie's mind of this woman running into the hospital room and throwing herself on the bed and Tom holding her, cuddling, kissing.

'Please yourself,' she said abruptly, and turned away again.

'Charlie doesn't want to be a teacher,' Madge said, holding out a staying hand. 'He wants to join the navy. He wants me to give your father the money I'd put aside so you can go to university instead of him. He thinks we owe Tom that.' She nodded as Allie's eyes widened. 'I think so too.'

'I couldn't,' Allie stuttered. 'I don't think Mum would let me.'

'Couldn't accept my money? It isn't mine, Allie. You could say it's Charlie's, but that's not right either. Your father earned it. He's hardly taken any money at all from the business since he saved it. And he did save it. I couldn't have carried on by myself.'

'What . . . What about Larry and Bobby?'

'Larry wants to be a policeman. That's his dream as university is yours. Bobby will take over the bakery one day. You go home and think about it. Talk to Hannah about it. I'm going to the hospital.'

'Yeah. Sure. See you later,' Allie said, still dazed, still trying to sort the mixture of emotions.

'And Allie?' Madge Lenahan paused in the doorway.

Allie looked up.

'I love your father,' she said, and disappeared into the hall.

'Are you okay, Allie?' Charlie asked from the doorway just as Allie turned away again.

'Yes, I just came to tell your mother about Dad.'

'I heard. I'm sure he'll be all right. He's a tough bloke.' He joined her at the gate. 'I heard Mum tell you about the money and uni and that. I thought you'd be pleased.' He grimaced. 'Matter of fact, I thought you'd be over the moon.'

'I am. It's just . . . Unexpected, that's all.'

'Yeah.' He nodded. 'What I came down to tell you is that I'll be leaving next week. Already signed up.'

She felt dazed. 'Next week?'

'Yeah. The Albatross down south at Nowra. I'll be training there.' She could feel his eyes searching her face as he added, 'I'm hoping you'll miss me.'

'Of course I will. And Charlie, I'm sorry for acting like an idiot. You know, over your mum and my dad. I think even Mum's realising it's probably for the best. It was an ego thing, her getting so pee'd off. Her and Claude Macy are . . . you know.'

'Everybody knows,' he said dryly, 'just as they know about Mum and Tom.'

'Then I guess he's not still sleeping out on the veranda.'

'Does it worry you?'

'A bit.'

He nodded. 'Me too. That's one of the reasons I wanted to go soon as possible. Not that I blame them,' he added hastily. 'It's just hard to see someone in my dad's place.'

It was her turn to nod.

'I'm glad we're mates again, Allie.'

'Me too. Will you write?'

'Sure. And we'll probably see each other when I'm home on leave, though I know you'll be belle of the ball at uni.'

'Oh yeah, sure.' She felt herself blushing. 'I'll be there to study, not socialise.'

'From what I hear about uni, you won't be able to help it.'

'We'll see. But anyway, I'll always have time for you.'

He pulled her into a hug and they stayed that way until his mother called, 'Charlie? Come and get ready. You'll need to change that shirt.'

As Allie stepped back she slid her cheek against his, then turned aside. She knew he watched her walking away but she didn't turn back. She knew that their lives would separate now and would rarely come together again. Perhaps at first, but not for long. They wanted different things.

Not one minute's thought was needed about whether or not to accept the chance of going to university. It had been her dream for too long. And it was obviously meant to be. Just hours ago she'd thought she'd have to put if off for years, maybe forever. She would thank Charlie properly when she got her head around being able to go next year. At the moment, nothing was sinking in. And she'd thank her father, but as she thought of Madge Lenahan, of Dad sleeping in her bed, the woman was mad if she thought she'd get a thank you.

Mad. As mad as Colin.

The thought entered her mind without invitation. He hadn't been far from her thoughts since she'd seen him sprawled across his bed.

Mad. That's what they'll say. They'll say Colin killed himself and only mad people do that. But he wasn't mad. He was lots of things, but mad wasn't one of them. Not the sort of madness they mean.

She again pictured him lying on the bed, the empty tablet bottle, the empty glass on the floor. The pallor of his skin. The stillness of his body. The twisted, open-mouth expression on his face. An expression she couldn't describe, but she knew as she pictured it, as she saw it as clearly as though she was looking at him right now, she knew he had not killed himself. His mouth was open in a scream of anger. Anger that he was about to die. He would have felt the pain, felt his heart giving out. He knew he was going to die and he didn't want it. She knew that as sure as she knew he had not killed Lily Gatley.

Her legs forgot to hold her up and she fell into a squat and rolled back until she was sitting, knees up, kneecaps pushed into her eyes in much the same way her father had sat in Grandma's hallway. She continued to picture Colin's face and her heart rate doubled. Her breath shortened to sips for air. She rocked backwards and forwards as the sobs came, harsh and rasping, shuddering up from the pit of her stomach.

Bird and the Wall

Hannah slowed as she reached number 19 and thought about going in to talk to Claude. But what was there to say? He would try to comfort her and she could not be comforted. Averting her eyes so he would know, if he were looking through a window, that she didn't want to stop, she quickened her pace, leaving Shorty and Gus lagging behind. They were still discussing what had happened and she didn't want to hear their guesswork. Gus continually harped on the fact that he believed Colin had found some kind of poisonous substance amongst Grandma's herbs. Didn't he listen when Hannah swore that anything dangerous was kept under lock and key, and didn't he see the empty bottle of sleeping tablets?

'Enough, for heaven's sake!' she shouted at them, and when they stared at her as though she had suddenly become a Fred Peters, she strode into Clara Paterson's house without knocking.

'I'm sorry for barging in like this,' she said at the kitchen doorway. Clara and Hal were seated at the table, her with a cup of tea, he with a glass of lemon drink. 'Your front door was open but I know I should have knocked. Those idiots were driving me crazy.' She pointed towards the street. 'Gus and Shorty. And I'm being rude. How are you, Clara? Thanks for keeping an eye on Hal. Hello, Hal darling.'

He stared at her, and she guessed he could read in her eyes that something was wrong for he slid off the chair, still staring at her, and stood poker straight, one hand on the corner of the table for support. His knees trembled, and he gave the impression that he was about to either fall down or run.

'Where's my dad?' he asked tremulously.

Clara rubbed his hand. 'You have arrived in time for a cup of tea,

Hannah. I've just made the pot. Now sit yourself down while I pour, then you can tell us what happened. We saw the police car and ambulance and we've been rather worried, haven't we, Hal?'

'Of course you have. I should have come sooner but I . . . I,' Hannah paused to take in a few deep breaths to stop herself from bursting into tears again.

'Where's my dad?' Hal demanded again. 'Has Mr Peters hurt my dad?'

The words 'My dad' jolted Hannah. She remembered Tom saying, 'Look after my boy.' After a wary start, they had grown close over the years, Hal and Tom, and they looked so alike. The same sandy hair, the same shaped eyes.

'What's happened to my dad?' Hal cried out.

'He's all right, I promise,' Hannah said quickly, and knelt, holding out her arms to him. He ran into them, almost knocking her over, and she held him tightly, breathing in the boy smell of him, rubbing the back of his head when he buried his face in her shoulder.

'We know he went after Fred Peters,' Clara stated quietly. 'And Fred was carrying what appeared to be some kind of weapon.'

'A bar. An iron bar,' Hal said.

'And your dad came to Grandma's house and made everybody safe,' Hannah said, holding him back to look into his face. 'I have to tell you that Mr Peters hit him with the bar and the ambulance men have taken him to hospital. But he's tough, your dad, and he'll be back home tomorrow. They took him to hospital just to keep a check on him for a while, okay?'

'But he's not hurt bad, is he, Mum?'

'He's not hurt bad,' Hannah confirmed.

'Are you sure?'

'I'll take you to the hospital later and you can see for yourself.'

'What of Fred?' Clara asked. 'Has he been charged?'

'I'm not sure. There was so much happening. Colin . . .' She paused, looking from one to the other, not sure how to say it without breaking down again. That wouldn't help Hal.

'You've had a terrible time of it,' Clara said softly. 'I can see you are distraught. So many questions with so few answers. Why don't you sit up at the table and drink your tea while Hal answers one of those questions. The most important one in fact. He told me all about it while we were waiting for Tom to return. I'm very good at listening, aren't I, Hal?' She smiled at him. 'We had an excellent heart-to-heart talk. Now it's time to tell your mother what you told me.'

Hannah felt his body tense. 'What is it, Hal? What do you have to tell me?'

'It was me,' he said in a strangled voice. 'Me and Bird and the wall. But I didn't know she was killed.'

'Bird and the wall? What do you mean?'

Hal looked imploringly at Clara Paterson.

'It seems that Lily came after Hal last night,' she said. 'She went into the house. Into the room where he sleeps.'

'Into the house? How did she get in?'

'You didn't lock the door,' Hal said. 'I heard Grandma say not to. Then I was nearly asleep when Lily my mother came in.'

'Oh God! I let her in.'

'No, she came in by herself after Grandma said not to lock the door,' Hal insisted. 'And she said in my ear that she'd hurt Allie if I called out to her or Grandma or Great-Auntie Florrie. So I had to go with her.'

'She knew who was in the house,' Hannah said. 'She must have been outside, watching. I thought I saw someone but . . . I should have checked properly.'

'Something you would only do in hindsight, dear. Who would expect Lily to come so late at night?' Clara asked.

Darting a grateful glance at her, Hannah stroked Hal's cheek.

'Where was Allie?'

'Asleep.'

'Didn't Grandma call out?'

'I think she was asleep too and we were creeping.'

'And what happened after you got outside?'

'Lily my mother was very rude. She went to the toilet on Grandma's porch. She said that was her calling card. She was sick. You know, like Dad when he gets sick from drinking too much beer. She couldn't walk properly.'

Hannah closed her eyes, remembering that fetid smell. How like Lily to do something so disgusting. No doubt it was a hint as to what she intended for Hal, something hateful and crude, something to stir fear and agony in me, she thought. But it's done the opposite. I won't mourn for her now.

'Mum, are you listening?' Hal asked.

'Of course I am, darling.' Hannah opened her eyes. 'I was thinking about what you just said. I know what Lily your mother meant when she did such a rude thing. She wanted to upset everyone in Grandma's house. We won't think about that now. Tell me what happened next.'

'She made me go with her up the street.'

'You promised us you'd fight if she tried to take you again.' Hannah kissed his cheek. 'Remember that?'

'I did fight. I did. I called out to Bird. My mother Lily didn't tell me not to call for Bird. So I called him.'

Sure she knew what was coming next, Hannah tightened her arm around him. 'You were out the front of our old house then, weren't you? Claude's house?'

She knew. She'd heard the rooster's cry.

Hal nodded. His breathing became short, shallow gasps. His body shook. He was struggling not to cry as he remembered.

'Bird came out. He was really mad. He flew up. His beak went into Lily my mother's neck. Here.' He pointed to his throat. 'The blood came. It was spurting. And she . . . And she fell against the wall. I didn't know she was killed. I thought she was just hurt. I thought she'd get up again so I ran hard as I could, me and Bird.'

So that's why he cried so much when we told him Lily had died, Hannah thought. It was guilt, and fear of what would happen to him and Bird when the truth came out.

'Don't. Don't,' Hannah soothed, pulling him close and taking his weight as he sagged against her. 'It's all right. I can guess what happened.'

Clara cut in with, 'I'd say she didn't know what it was flying at her out of the dark and it terrified her.'

'She threw herself backwards to get away,' Hannah said softly. 'And she hit the back of her head against the wall.'

'With enough force to bounce her off,' Clara agreed. 'When she fell, probably already unconscious, the side of her head hit the edge of the gutter. At least, that is my guess from what Hal's told me.'

'Bird was just trying to help,' Hal said earnestly.

Clara nodded. 'Of course he was. And you were afraid of what might happen to Bird if you told.'

'I think the main problem will be getting the police to believe it,' Hannah said ruefully.

'Perhaps we should introduce them to the bird and let them see for themselves,' Clara suggested dryly.

Hal gave her a reproachful look. 'Mrs Paterson doesn't like Bird.'

'No, I'm afraid I don't, Hal. And you and I have already talked about what will happen to your rooster once the police know the full story.'

Hal's eyes filled with tears. 'They'll want to chop off his head like Mum and Grandma does with the chooks,' he said in a choked voice.

Knowing she couldn't make a promise that the rooster wouldn't be put down, Hannah said, 'First thing tomorrow we'll give Bird a thank you party for saving you. Then we'll go to the police and tell them everything we know.'

'A party with cake?' Hal asked.

'With chocolate cake,' Hannah agreed. 'It wasn't Bird's fault really. It was that blasted wall, wasn't it?'

Hal nodded into her neck. 'You're not cranky with me for not telling you last night?'

Hannah thought of Colin and wanted to cry again.

'No, darling, I'm not cranky. Sad maybe. I should have thought to ask. But I love you very much and nothing or no one, not Lily your mother or whoever your father is, will ever change that.'

And she knew it was true.

But now she had to tell him about Colin.

Not Bad Sad

Allie knew Hannah had told Hal, knew it the moment she walked into the kitchen and saw him sitting on a chair, an untouched glass of milk and two of his favourite biscuits on the table in front of him. His face was pale, his eyes red and swollen. She knew she looked pretty much the same.

When he glanced up at her, his lips began to tremble. 'Colin,' was all he could manage to say.

'I know, but you're not to cry. We have to be happy for him.'

All eyes turned to her – Grandma, Great-Aunt Florrie and Hannah.

'You remember how he talked about his mates in the prison camp?' she added, not looking away from Hal.

He nodded.

'Remember that first night he had the nightmare and we were under the bed with him? Remember what he told us?'

Hal slowly shook his head.

'He said that every time one of them died, he wanted to go too. He said he should be there with them. Well, now he is.'

'I want him to be here,' Hal said in a choked voice.

'We all do. But that's us. We have to be happy for Colin,' Allie said firmly.

'And we will be after a while,' Hannah said. 'But it's just going to take a while. Do you understand that, Hal?'

A knock on the door and a shouted, 'It's me, Shorty. Got something for youse,' halted his answer.

'I'll get it,' Allie said, and retreated up the hall. 'What is it?' she asked Shorty.

'We had a whip around at the pub. Didn't get a lot, but there'll be more when we've had a chance to walk and talk around the neighbourhood. Thought I'd drop this orf in case it was needed. You know, deposit for the funeral and that. We'd like to know if ya got any idea when it might be. Lots of people to tell, ya know. Return Soldiers' League for a start. They'll get someone to play taps and make sure there's a good turnout to see Colin orf. Anyhow, we got this to start.'

'That's good of you, Shorty. Why don't you take it down to Mum and she can fill you in on what we know.'

Shooting a nervous look towards Colin's room, he nodded. 'Right you are.'

Allie watched him shamble away before turning to stare into Colin's room. She couldn't get Colin's final expression out of her mind. She'd seen him through his nightmares often enough. Along with Hal and sometimes her mother, she'd held him, rocked him until he fell into a dream-free sleep. The opposite of that was the look he'd worn the last time she saw him. In death, he had the face of his nightmares. A mixture of fear and anger.

Someone had righted the door, but it still sagged on one hinge and resisted when she tried to push it open. Using her shoulder, she shoved hard and it grated across the floor. Deciding that the empty pill bottle and glass were enough proof that Colin had suicided, the police hadn't touched anything. The room was as it always had been: clean to the point of obsession, a bed, wardrobe, dressing table and old wooden chair, the only ornamentation a jar of Californian Poppy hair oil, a comb and a brush aligned side by side on the dressing table. The bed had been straightened. Nothing was out of place.

Her mother once described this room as a copy of Colin's life as it was then. Scrubbed and polished, austere enough to be sad. But that's just her imagination, Allie thought as she stared around the room, looking for something, anything. She found it almost immediately. There, up high on top of his wardrobe where children couldn't reach, a cardboard shoe box. Using the chair as a ladder, she climbed up and lifted the box down. Inside were a few letters, his dog tags, a large yellow envelope that probably held his discharge papers, two rolls of bandages, a roll of sticking plaster, a packet of aspirin and three bottles of pharmacy medication.

One half-full bottle contained his pain-killers. Another could have been medicine to control high blood pressure. The third, not yet opened, the seal unbroken, contained his sleeping tablets. She stared down at them and the tears came again.

'Allie, what is it?'

Allie looked up. Her mother, Grandma, Hal and Great-Aunt Florrie were crowded in the doorway with Shorty standing behind them, towering over them all.

'We heard the door,' Hannah added. 'What have you got there?'

'Colin's last bottle of sleeping tablets. It hasn't been opened.'

They all stared at her.

'That empty bottle held the last of the tablets from his old prescription,' Allie said. 'I remember seeing them the last time I was in this room after Colin had one of his nightmares. There was just two tablets left. This is the bottle Grandma got for him about a month ago.' She cleared her throat, then continued, speaking slowly and clearly to make sure they understood. 'I remember him telling me that he didn't want to get hooked on sleeping pills, and he was sleeping all right so he didn't need them anyway. He didn't want to take them. Not till last night. But then he took just two to help him sleep because of what happened to Lily. Those last two pills were in the bottle we saw on the floor. The one the police confiscated. This bottle is still full, so that means he didn't take anything to . . .' She glanced down at Hal. 'To hurt himself. This proves it. It had to be his heart. Because of what he'd seen, and drinking too much and all that, his heart gave up. That's why he looked the way he did.'

Possibles and Probables

Hannah's interview with the detectives, which she had put off until mid-afternoon, turned out to be more of an ordeal than she'd thought it would be. She told them everything Hal had told her and, as she'd suspected, they took a while to convince.

'Murder by chook,' one of them said, and laughed loud and long. He could only be convinced it was possible when a constable confirmed that a list of complaints had been made about vicious attacks by that very bird. Finally, he conceded that Bird was the probable cause of Lily's death when the same constable reminded him of the wound in her throat. When he came to the same conclusion as Clara Paterson, that Lily had struck her head on the wall, then the gutter, Hannah led the applause at his marvellous powers of deduction. Anything for peace, and to bring an end to the relentless questioning.

She had no doubt that the detective had at first thought she was the guilty party making up a rather unbelievable story. So she decided to wait a day or two before telling them about Colin. Again, they would need convincing. She wouldn't be able to do that without breaking down. Every time she thought of Colin, she felt as though her chest had been slashed. The wound was deep and abiding, and she knew a long time would pass before it would begin to heal. The past year of seeing him daily had reawakened the bond between them. She knew that would have strengthened over time and he'd be her closest friend again. The pain of losing him for the second time was unbearable. She determined not to think about him. At least, not more than she could help, and not until she sorted out the problem of Hal's rooster. 'It's a danger to the public and has to be put down,' the detective had told her. She'd cajoled them into leaving that up to her. Learning that the rooster was a child's pet had persuaded them.

Still recovering from her ordeal with the detectives, and wanting a little time and space for herself, Hannah decided to fortify herself with a drink on the way home. Keeping her head down and her face turned aside as she passed the bakery, though she thought the Lenahans would probably be at the hospital with Tom by now, she headed for the Golden Barley.

The ladies' lounge was full, as was usual on a Saturday afternoon, but she knew better than to walk into the no-woman's-land of the bar. Head still down, face turned to the wall, she skirted around the tables to a bar that was hardly more than a bench in a corner of the room with a servery behind it opening into the men's bar. Here the ladies were served when they had no men to fetch drinks for them. She ordered a scotch on the rocks and was pretending not to feel the eyes boring into her back when she heard the voices. Mainly Gus Markham, who was loudly aggressive. It was impossible not to hear him. Shorty was trying to placate him.

'I heard young Allie saying it.' Shorty spoke doggedly, so it wasn't hard to guess that he'd already said it more than once.

'What does she know? She's just a bit of a kid,' Gus blustered. 'I'm telling yer, that old woman went out and got those pills for him. Didn't yer just say so?'

'Yair, I heard someone say that Mrs Ade got 'em. But the full one was still there, so Hollywood couldn't have took no bottle of pills.' The same dogged tone. 'I reckon he just had a turn like he did here one night. You remember, when he blacked out and fell off the stool but wouldn't let us call the ambulance. But this time he didn't come out of whatever it was made him fall. Colin was in a bloody war camp. If he was gunner do himself in he'd have done it then. Or soon after.'

'If it wasn't the pills, then she gave him something out of that shed of hers where she keeps all her stuff,' Gus said, sounding even more aggressive.

'Ar, that's a load of codswallop.' Shorty sounded thoroughly disgusted. 'I reckon his wonky ticker give out from all the excitement about his cousin Lily, that's what happened. And I'm going home because you're being a bloody pain in the arse and I don't wanna hear any more about it.'

Hannah had heard enough. She was tempted to go in and tell Gus what she thought of him, but as Grandma so often said, you can't argue with a man who's been drinking. You leave them alone until they've sobered up, and that's what she'd do. Wait until tomorrow, then visit Gus, tell him exactly what she thought of him. In fact she'd threaten to report him to the police for making threats against an old woman.

Paying for the whisky, she finished it in a couple of gulps and turned to leave.

'Hey there, Hannah,' a woman's voice called.

Hannah looked around the room. A few men, but mostly women. Some she recognised as old school friends.

'Me, it's me, Hannah. Lottie Nelson. Over here.'

A hand waved. A small blonde woman stood.

'I was just leaving, Lottie. Got to get home to Hal,' Hannah called back.

Lottie nodded. 'Yeah, I know. But I heard about Colin and just wanted to give me condolences. And ask you to pass them on to your Auntie Florrie and Grandma Ade.'

'That goes from all of us here,' another woman called.

'He was a good bloke.'

'A right good bloke. Always handing out a laugh.'

'We'll miss him.'

'Yeah,' was a ragged chorus. 'We'll miss him.'

Hannah felt tears rising within her, seeming to come from deep down. She took in a long breath and, not daring to try speaking, waved a yes to Lottie.

An older woman reached out and touched Hannah's arm. 'Hang on a bit.'

'I'm sorry, I have to go,' Hannah said huskily, pulling away.

'I know, and I know why. I can see it in your face,' the woman said softly. 'I just want to ask you to tell Florrie and Emily how we feel. Ask if they'd mind letting us know when the funeral will be. Colin was a friend to everyone here.'

A brief nod, a wave, and Hannah strode from the room. She heard the buzz of conversation behind her and though she couldn't make out the words, she realised by the tone and softness that it was sympathetic.

As she hurried along the footpath past the main bar, she heard Gus's voice, even louder than before.

'I'm telling ya, I just know!'

The threat of a crying jag was over-ridden by a flash of anger. She paused, again tempted to go in and tell him off.

Then, a woman's voice screeching, 'For heaven's sake, Gus, give yer other end a go.'

A second woman. 'Yair, if youse blokes don't shut him up, we'll come into the bar and shut him up for ya.'

'Good on you,' Hannah thought, smiling now, and walked on.

Nothing More to be Said

To Hal, hospital was a place for desperately ill people. No matter how many times Hannah vowed that Tom would be home tomorrow, Hal fretted. How hard had Mr Peters hit him, was he bleeding, was he knocked out, was his head hurting real bad, why can't he come home right away? The only way to appease him was to take him to the hospital and let him see for himself.

They were in the hallway now, her, Allie and Hal, after a long walk and a short tram trip where everyone in their section had joined in a game of 'I-spy'. Funny how people who traditionally disliked anyone entering their space, physical or mental, could be induced into playing a silly game by a small boy with sad eyes and an infectious grin. Eight women and five men had spent most of the trip calling out their guesses to 'Something beginning with B'. The enthusiastic shouts had turned to groans when Hal jumped down at their stop and called back his answer of, 'It's breaths. You know, breaths from your mouth.'

'But you can't see breaths,' one of the women protested.

'You can when it's really cold,' Hal said, and was running along the footpath before the woman had a chance to protest again.

Which is a form of cheating and he knows it, Hannah thought, and was about to tell Hal so when he was grabbed from behind by two arms wrapping around him.

'How's me boy?' Janet asked as she gave him her usual smacking kiss.

'Dad got hit with a iron bar,' he told her.

'I know.'

Knowing Hannah's reluctance for demonstrations of affection in public, Janet contented herself with rubbing her mother's arm. 'I phoned

Claude to tell you I was coming over and he told me about Dad, so I thought I'd make sure he was okay. He is, isn't he?'

'As far as I know,' Hannah said. 'Are you and your sister not speaking? What's going on with you two?'

Janet shrugged. 'Nothing.'

Hannah looked from one to the other. She could tell by Allie's carefully blank expression, the one she always used when she was trying not to show emotion, and Janet's belligerent look – Janet would never suffer from illnesses caused by suppressed emotion – that something was wrong. She decided not to ask. No doubt they'd tell her in their own good time.

'So where's your manners?' she asked.

'Good-day, Allie, how the hell are ya?' Janet asked, and her tone was definitely a prod.

'Yeah. Hello, Janet.'

'Well, now all the hugging and kissing's over we'd better go in and see your father,' Hannah said dryly.

'Where did you phone Claude from?' Allie asked.

'You're asking where I'm staying and ya know the answer to that. It's none of your business. I told ya, Allie. Ya gotter stop trying to live my life. Go get a life of yer own.'

'What all this about?' Hannah asked. 'Why aren't you still at the guesthouse, Janet?'

'She got kicked out because . . .' Allie paused. 'Because of her boyfriend.'

Hannah gave Janet a searching look. 'You have a boyfriend? Why haven't we met him?'

'That's a good question,' Allie said, and her look was sly. 'Answer that one, Janet.'

'You're poking ya nose in where it doesn't belong again. I came to see Dad, not to let you get away with having a go at me so ya can just shut up,' she shot back.

'Ha!' Allie sneered.

'Stop fighting. Come on.' Hal pulled at Hannah's hand. 'Make them stop fighting so we can see Dad.'

'As a matter of fact I'm engaged,' Janet said into Allie's sneer.

'Oh yeah. Where's the ring then?'

A moment's pause, then, 'I don't want to wear it until everyone's met Johnny.'

'You came to see Dad and you knew we were here and you didn't want to show everybody? You know as well as I do that Johnny Lawson would never get engaged to you, no matter what.'

Hannah bit back a question. She wanted to know what this was all about but she knew if she asked, both girls would clam up. 'Shhh,' she warned Hal softly when she realised he was about to protest again. Slumping against her leg, he placed both hands over his ears and stared down at the ground.

'You'll never understand, Allie. Not in a million years,' Janet said, but her voice had softened now, as though for some reason Hannah couldn't fathom, she actually felt sorry for her younger sister.

Tears shone in Allie's eyes and her tone was a plea. 'You'll just get hurt again.'

Janet rubbed Allie's arm in the same way she had rubbed Hannah's a few minutes ago. 'Let me worry about that, all right?' She gestured a dismissal with the other hand. 'I believe he loves me, Allie. I'm not as smart or as pretty as you, but him and me, well, we just seem to match. I know him, he knows me and we feel at ease with each other. Do ya understand that?'

Allie thought of herself and Charlie Lenahan. She nodded slowly.

'If ya forget about how he acted with you, you'll see he's changed,' Janet continued. 'Ya will, Allie. If ya look hard enough. At least promise me you'll try.'

The silence seemed to thicken the air as Allie stared into Janet's face for long moments. Janet gave a half smile that was more an apologetic grimace and Allie reached out, rubbing her sister's arm in that same gentle way, and again nodded slowly.

Hannah's throat choked up as she looked from one to the other. For the first time as far back as she could remember, her two daughters' expressions showed the fondness for each other that sisters should have.

'Is someone going to tell me what's going on?' she asked.

'I will, Mum. I will later,' Janet promised. 'I'll bring Johnny to meet you all in a few days time and I'll tell ya everything.' She glanced at Allie. 'Well, almost. The things that matter now anyway. Big things, Mum.'

Allie shook her head. 'He'll never come.'

'If he does, will you be nice?'

'Depends what you mean by nice.' Allie's tone was innocent enough but her grin could only be called wicked.

'You'll keep,' Janet promised, and shoved her, but returned the grin.

'Now can we go see Dad?' Hal asked.

'We can,' Hannah said, and couldn't help smiling when he shot the girls a reproving look and raced through the doorway.

The smile faded when she entered the eight-bed ward to find Madge Lenahan and her three sons surrounding Tom, Madge sitting on the bed and holding his hand as though she owned it. If not for Hal's whoop of delight and his charge across the room ending in a leap into Tom's arms, she might have walked out. Yet she managed to retrieve half the smile and paste it back on when all the Lenahans, including Madge, stepped aside for her.

'No, no, stay where you are,' she insisted, knowing she sounded false but not able to stop herself.

Allie had no problem striding past them. Wrapping her arms around Tom, she held him tightly for a few seconds, then pulled back and stared into his face as though she could read his state of health printed there.

'Are you all right, Dad?' she asked.

'Me head copped the iron bar and that's the hardest part of me. Bloody thing bounced off. I'll be home tomorrow,' Tom responded.

Hannah waited for Allie to ask, 'Whose home, ours or theirs,' as she would have done just days ago. Instead, she murmured, 'Hello, Larry, Bobby, Mrs Lenahan,' before backing off and joining Hannah at the foot of the bed. 'G'day, Charlie,' she added softly, and Hannah couldn't help noticing the look that passed between them.

Well, well, she thought, seems they've patched things up. I guess that explains the civility to his mother and brothers. I wonder when that happened. Perhaps when she went to tell them about Tom. How come nobody's telling me anything these days?

'Hey, Dad, how are ya?' Janet said as she walked forward and gave her father a quick peck on the cheek.

'I'm right as rain,' was his smiling answer. 'And what about you?'

'Doing okay.'

'What's this I hear about ya going into a pub. You with a bloke, was ya?'

Janet shot a glare at Charlie. 'Someone's got a big mouth.'

'I didn't know it was a secret,' he protested. 'Though I should've when you made out you didn't see me.'

'Caught out,' Tom said, and snorted laughter when Janet's face crimsoned.

'And it looks like it's serious enough to bring on a blush,' Madge Lenahan said. 'Although now you've dobbed Janet in to her mother, Tom. Under-age drinking.'

Hannah had to turn aside to hide a smile as Janet's head lifted. Her expression could only be called haughty as she looked from her father to Madge and sniffed.

That's something new, Hannah thought. New to Janet anyway. I can't wait to meet this boyfriend of hers. But still, I want to know more about this pub business. Although knowing how Janet feels about alcohol, she'd have been drinking squash. Tom thinks so too or he wouldn't have mentioned it.

'I didn't come here to talk about me private life. I came to see if me father was all right,' Janet said stiffly. 'And seeing as he is, I'm out of here.'

Turning abruptly, she strode away, stopping just long enough to call, 'Hey, Allie.'

When Allie turned to her, Janet closed a hand on something hanging around her neck on a chain. She held it out as far as the chain would allow, though still not revealing what the something was. A smile, a wink and she was gone.

Tom looked searchingly at Allie. 'What's all that about?'

Seeing the three Lenahan boys' discomfort, and their mother's avid expression, Hannah cut in before Allie had a chance to answer.

'Family business to be discussed later,' she said, and was grateful to Hal when he climbed up on the bed and asked, 'When are you going home, hey, Dad?'

'First thing tomorrow, and I'll be round to see you second thing.'

So home is definitely at the bakery now, and Hal knows it, Hannah thought.

Hal nodded, satisfied, and turned to grin at Allie. The following silence was strained, and Madge must have thought it lasted a little too long. She coughed loudly, then said, 'I was just telling Tom about Colin. You'd wonder why he'd do such a dreadful thing.'

Hannah stared at her, appalled at her lack of sensitivity.

'Not in front of the boy,' Tom chided, shooting Hannah an apologetic look.

'We're allowed to be sad, but not bad sad,' Hal said sombrely, 'because he's gone to be with his mates. The ones from the war.'

'I'm glad you're not bad sad, son.' Tom lay a hand across Hal's cheek. 'Colin wouldn't want that. Though I'm sure he wouldn't mind a few tears because we're missing him.'

'Will you cry, hey, Dad?'

'Later, when everyone's gone and I can do it in peace and quiet.'

'To change the subject onto a more cheerful note,' Madge said brightly, 'have you had a chance to talk about university with your mother yet, Allie?'

'Um, no, not yet.' Allie's grimaced. 'There's been, you know, too much happening.'

'What's this about?' Hannah asked.

'Oh, it's good news. For Allie at least,' Madge assured her. 'Charlie insists on joining the navy, so the money saved for his higher education will go to Allie.'

'Jeez, Mum. Not now,' Charlie protested.

'I know things have been tough for you, Hannah, but I'm hoping to make up for that by using the money Madge put by for Charlie as my wages and handing it over to Allie,' Tom said. 'But there's plenty of time to talk about that.'

'Mum, don't say anything,' Allie whispered.

'That's another thing we can talk about later. We should leave. The notice outside clearly states that no more than two visitors are allowed by a patient's bed and I'd hate Tom to be embarrassed by having half of us thrown out. Meaning you, Hal and myself,' Hannah said stiffly, not able to resist the parting shot. 'Say goodbye to your dad, Hal,' she called back from halfway across the room.

'Go on with your mother,' Tom told him. 'I'll be round to see ya tomorrow first thing. Promise.'

'I don't want to discuss it now,' Hannah said through gritted teeth to Allie as they left the hospital. 'I want to know about Janet and this boyfriend. It seems you know him when the rest of us haven't even heard of him.'

'And you're not going to hear it from me,' Allie said. 'It's up to Janet to explain.'

'Explain what, Allie?'

'It's a long story, Mum, and it needs Janet to tell you. If I say anything before she's with us, she's going to be really crappy with me.'

'I can see what you mean, though I don't appreciate your way of explaining it. Okay then, we'll wait for Janet.'

'So we can talk about university and why I didn't tell you about it. I knew you wouldn't like it.'

'I need time to think about it.'

'We'll have to talk about it sooner or later,' Allie pointed out. 'And anyway, I'm going.'

'Then there's nothing more to be said, is there? Here's our tram.'

Once on the tram homeward bound, she whispered to Allie, 'Grandma will say you should put that money into the household.'

'Too bad for Grandma. She'd use it to help some of her sad women. Well, I'm a woman now, and I'll be more than sad if I can't go to uni. Especially now I've got the chance. I'll make it up to Grandma and the household when I've finished uni and I'm working.'

'Where's your pride, Allie?'

'Why should I give up on my dream because you don't like Mrs Lenahan? It's not her fault Dad left us for her.'

'Isn't it just? You don't think she did everything in her power to make him feel guilty about Bob?'

'I don't care, Mum. I'm going to uni. And anyway, you stopped loving Dad a long time ago. All you ever did was fight. Mrs Lenahan thinks the world of him. I don't know why you're acting like this.'

'Like what?' Hannah snapped.

'Like you care about Dad being with Mrs Lenahan when you've got Mr Macy.'

I guess it's an ego thing, she remembered telling Claude. She said it again now, hesitantly.

'I guess it is,' Allie said, adding quietly, 'Maybe it's the same with me.'

Hannah looked curiously at her. 'In what way?'

'Do you think you can love someone and hate them at the same time?' Allie asked in the same quiet way. 'Someone you shouldn't be even thinking about?'

'Are you talking about Charlie Lenahan? I noticed that you seem to have made up with him.'

'No, not Charlie. We're friends and I think we both know we'll never be anything more. It's someone else.' She looked around to make sure no one was listening. 'I think there's something wrong with me, Mum. There's this boy. Man,' she corrected. 'I don't like anything about him – the kind of person he is I mean. But every time I see him I want to go to bed with him even though he belongs to . . . To someone else.' When Hannah stared at her without answering, she added, 'You think I'm horrible.'

'No, no, it's just . . .' Hannah sighed. 'I forget how old you are. I was your age when your father and I . . . But that's another story.'

'Did you love him? I mean then. You know. At first.'

'Of course I did. But I've learned that there are many kinds of love. One of them is more commonly known as lust.' She bit back a smile. 'I think maybe that's what you feel for this boy. This man. And it's absolutely normal, Allie. Just be careful, that's all.'

'Oh, I'm not going to see him again. I mean, I'll have to see him because I promised . . .' She stopped abruptly and turned her face away.

Oh Lord, Hannah thought. This is what's going on between her and Janet. How could this happen? Oh Lord.

'Mum, let's leave it, okay? There's too much . . . You know, with Colin and everything. I never knew anything could hurt so much.' She glanced at Hal, who had moved along the seat and was watching people through the tram window. 'And Lily. It seems as though the whole world is turning upside down. Our world anyway.'

'We'll get through it, Allie love.'

Allie nodded and moved to sit beside Hal.

Minutes later, they were back to playing 'I-spy'. This time, with hardly anyone else on the tram, the only one to join in was the conductor.

Hannah's Moon

Hannah was the first to stir. Edging sideways, she rolled onto her back, careful not to wake Allie. She listened. No sound. Everyone must still be asleep. She glanced at the clock. Five past eight. Grandma and Great-Aunt Florrie were usually up by now. Of course today was different from every other day. Today was the day they would bury Colin. Three o'clock this afternoon.

How do you get through a day like this? Keep busy for as long as you can, that's how, Hannah told herself. Just as you've been doing for the past few days. You and the rest of the family. The house and yard have never been so clean and junk free.

The day after Colin died, they'd had visitors all day. The extended family, friends, Colin's army buddies, what was left of them, and his pub mates. But since then, nobody. Of course the idea was to leave them in peace to mourn, but peace and quiet was the last thing they needed. Even Janet had kept away.

'Because Johnny Lawson won't come with her. I told you he wouldn't,' Allie had said. 'He'd reckon that as a commitment.

Claude had handled all the funeral arrangements for Colin and Lily, bless him. Lily would be buried some time next week. The police hadn't released her body as yet.

Hannah shuddered. That would be another miserable day. God how she hated funerals.

First things first. Breakfast, then get Hal to help me catch Bird. We can't put it off any longer, and as it's going to be a miserable day anyway, we might as well get that over and done with. It might help to keep Hal's mind off Colin. We'll need to put an end to the rooster, then have a burial before Grandma calls it a waste of good meat and starts a rooster stew.

Poor Hal. The horror of his encounter with Lily, the stress of Colin dying and now his funeral, and on top of that he'll lose his precious Bird. He'll be completely devastated.

Sighing loudly, she eased herself out of bed. She'd spent yesterday afternoon cleaning the yard, replacing brick cobbles, even whitewashing the fence. Her arms and shoulders were sore, the kind of soreness that goes with hard work and sunburn. Like Chinese burns. 'One hand gripping your wrist, the other up further, then twist.' That was Lily's favourite punishment for disagreeing with anything she said when they were kids. Poor little twisted, corrupted bitch, Colin had said of her.

But she's gone now, Hannah thought, past punishment as well as redemption and I won't think of her as any of those horrible things. Just as Hal's mother, and being that, she would have to have had goodness in her. It just needed something to bring it out and maybe Hal could have done that.

'Ha!' the doubter in Hannah said, and she knew that the best way to banish Lily out of her thoughts, and to delay grieving for Colin until she could handle it a little better, was to keep busy. Not that there was anything left to do except make breakfast.

Grandma and Great-Aunt Florrie must be awake by now. Perhaps Grandma just needed to lie in for a while. Colin and Lily's deaths have really taken their toll on her. Could've knocked me over with a feather when she insisted on seeing old Doc Howe yesterday. Probably should thank Great-Aunt for that bit of commonsense. I guess they're just reluctant to start the day. Can't say I blame them.

The door to Grandma's room was open. Hannah tapped lightly, then stepped in without waiting for Grandma's usual refusal to allow anyone into her room. Two open suitcases lay open on the bed. Grandma and Great-Aunt Florrie, both dressed, were packing.

'What's this? What are you doing?' Hannah asked.

'Lily's mother sent word to say she isn't coming to Colin's funeral. Says she can't handle the two. She hasn't been well,' Grandma said. 'Will I need more than one cardigan, Florrie?'

Great-Aunt Florrie shook her head. 'You won't need two at this time of the year, Emily.'

Hannah stared from one to the other. 'Won't need them for what?'

'We're going back to Dubbo with your Aunt Ellen straight after the funeral. We'll keep her and your Aunt Martha company until it's time to come back for Lily's funeral. Meantime I might be able to help with what's making her poorly.'

'But . . . But what about here? The herbs, Grandma. There'll be people coming.'

'I've looked after these people for most of my life and what do I get for it? Nothing. They all came to pay their respects the day after Colin died, I'll give them that, but since then, not a soul. They don't give a rat's hiccup about me or anyone except themselves.'

'They probably think we want to be alone to grieve,' Hannah protested. 'I remember when Maria's mother died you said we should leave them in peace.'

'Maria's mother was a foreigner, and all those people who were there when we went to pay our respects were foreigners. I couldn't understand half the things they said.'

'Now, Emily, you're stretching the truth a little,' Great-Aunt Florrie said reprovingly. 'They all spoke English as good as you and me. You stayed away because they weren't direct family.'

'Well isn't that what you do? You call in as soon as possible, then you stay away until the funeral. That's what you do with people who aren't kin. But where are our kin? Where's all the people I've helped?'

'They did come,' Hannah said patiently. 'They'll come again today, to the funeral.'

'I'm going where I'm needed.'

'You're needed here, Grandma. You know that.'

'I'm not going to argue with you, Hannah. I'm eighty-five and I'm tired. Every muscle and bone in my body seems to be hurting me lately. I need the break. And there's no one to take over from me so people round here will have to learn to get along without help. Didn't Colin say so? And he was right. I can't go on forever. I've never had a holiday and I'm going to have one now.'

'How long will you be gone?'

'We'll come back for the funeral, and perhaps a week longer to rest up from the trip,' Great-Aunt Florrie said. 'Then we might go to see your

Aunt Elizabeth in Adelaide. Neither of us have ever been to Adelaide and we haven't seen Elizabeth for many a day.'

'Don't you believe I deserve a holiday?' Grandma asked when Hannah shook her head in bewilderment. 'Do you object to us going?'

'No, of course not. How could I? It's just . . . It won't be the same without you.'

'Thank you for that, but I'm sure you'll manage. As will all the kin.'

Hannah detected the note of bitterness but couldn't think of anything comforting to say. Not in the mood Grandma was in.

'I guess we will. We'll have to. Is there anything I can do?'

'To get rid of me as quickly as possible you mean?'

Before Hannah had time to voice a protest, Allie entered the room, her face alight with the brightest of smiles.

'Come and see,' she said, grabbing Hannah's hand and pulling her through the kitchen. 'It's like Pitt Street at knock-off time out there. I can't even get to the toilet.'

Hannah stopped at the doorway. People were pouring into the yard, men and women of all ages. Most bore food, drinks and crockery. There were no children. Children would only get in the way. No doubt a roster had been arranged, a few houses readied as creches and playrooms.

'Well, I never,' Grandma exclaimed from behind Hannah.

At the sound of her voice, all movement stopped. Fat-Auntie Jean pushed to the front of the crowd, saying, 'Hey there, Grandma, Aunt Florrie, good to see youse on yer feet. Old Doc Howe said ya would be, but we weren't too sure. We heard ya weren't too good.'

'Well, I never,' Grandma exclaimed again.

'We thought ya might need a bit of help with the wake. You know, food and stuff. Then some company if you've a mind to it.'

'But I'm going on a holiday,' Grandma said.

'That's all right, love,' Skinny-Auntie Jean called. 'Old Doc Howe told us you'd probably be going to Dubbo for a while. That'll give us time to get everything ship-shape again in time for the next herbs day. And Lily's funeral o' course.'

'It's no good, I'm tired and I can't live forever,' Grandma said. 'Might as well pack it all in now.'

Shorty threaded his way forward to stand by Fat-Auntie Jean. 'We all know what you've done for us. I know you were right about me wife, and I have to tell yer she ended up going behind me back and seeing that doc at the hospital and he's gunner fix 'er up with an operation. So I'm asking yer to have yer holiday, then come back. In the meanwhile we'll just have to do without yer.'

Great-Aunt Florrie touched Hannah's arm. 'Unless you have a better idea, Hannah.'

'I could carry on while Grandma has a decent holiday,' she agreed.

She smiled down at Hal, just out of bed and still sleepy-eyed, though the sleepiness disappeared in a hurry when he saw the gathered kin.

'With Hal's help of course,' Hannah added.

'And after that?' Great-Aunt Florrie asked.

'I'm not making any promises.' Hannah smiled down at Hal again. 'We'll just have to see what eventuates.'

Grandma leaned close so the others wouldn't hear. 'You reckon Claude Macy will wait?'

Hannah answered her with a shrug. Claude knew she didn't want to get married again. Not now anyway. Not for a while. Probably a long while. She liked being her own person. If he was willing to stay around in the hope of her changing her mind, well, she wouldn't object to that, though she was determined to be totally honest with him.

'Come on, Grandma, Great-Aunt,' she said. 'Let's finish your packing while our friends get on with it.'

'That's the spirit,' Shorty called out. 'We'll get things going here. Seeing as our mate Colin's not around to take on the foreman's job, I'm electing young Hal there. Allie can give him a hand.'

'I'll get a pencil and paper to write down who can do what,' Allie stated.

Hal nodded. 'And we'll put the jobs in order of what's to be done first. That's what Colin would do.'

Hannah smiled down at him. One thing was for sure, Colin might be gone but he'd never be forgotten.

'First to be done is breakfast,' Great-Aunt Florrie said, turning to usher Grandma, Hal and Allie into the kitchen. She nodded towards the yard. 'I believe you have a visitor, Hannah. A man bearing gifts by the look of things.'

Claude stood at the back steps, a bunch of flowers in one hand, a brown paper bag in the other.

'It's Sunday. Where did you get the flowers?' Hannah asked.

'I have connections. I've told you that umpteen times.' He smiled. 'And they're not for you, they're for Grandma Ade.'

Grandma's voice floated out of the kitchen. 'Until and if you join the family, it's Mrs Ade to you.'

'Won't you come in?' Hannah asked.

He shook his head. 'I intend to help out here while you're having breakfast.' He held out the brown paper bag. 'I came to give Mrs Ade the flowers and this to you and Hal.'

Hal appeared beside Hannah. 'What is it?' His eyes darkened. 'Is it something to do with Bird?'

'Look inside.'

Hal took the bag and tore it open. A bunch of white feathers fell out.

'Bird?' he asked.

'Yes, they belong to Bird.' Claude grinned at Hannah. 'I told you I have connections. I phoned the police station. They weren't too hard to convince that Bird should live as long as he could be contained.'

'You cut Bird's wings?' Allie appeared next to Hal. 'I can't believe you cut his wings. How did you do that?'

'With the help of thick gloves and Tom's old army coat. Tom helped by the way. Took a great deal of delight in clipping those flight feathers too.'

'Too bloody right,' Tom called from the back of the group.

Hannah stood tall to look at him. Madge was by his side. The expected flood of annoyance didn't happen. She smiled.

'And tomorrow I'm ordering a pile of chicken wire and we'll roof the fowl pen,' Claude continued. 'That should make sure of it.'

Hannah felt a sudden flood of affection for this man. She had to be by herself for a while before she could be with someone else again, but she knew now that when she was ready, Claude would be that someone else.

'I only hope you can wait,' she said softly.

He nodded, seeming to know exactly what she meant. 'I'm a patient man.'

She glanced down at the feathers. 'I don't know how to thank you.'

Claude winked. 'I'll think of a way.'

'Enough now! Breakfast.' Grandma called. 'You may join us, Mr Macy.'

'I'll pass, thanks.' He handed Hannah the flowers. 'I've been invited to help out here,' he added and turned aside.

Hannah watched him stroll over to Shorty, who was handing out orders to anyone who would listen, though most of those orders were ignored. Smiling at Claude's eagerness to be part of the community, she placed an arm around Allie and Hal, hugged them close, then gave them a gentle shove towards the kitchen.

'There's a car pulled up out front,' Hal called. 'A big black one.'

'The Oldsmobile,' Hannah heard Allie say. 'Janet's talked him into it. He's actually here. I don't believe it. It's a day of miracles.'

Just inside the doorway, Hannah stopped and looked back. The kin and friends were dividing into work groups. A few were erecting a canvas shelter in the laneway to hold the tables and chairs that were just arriving – a sign that the wake would be too large for the small house. By this afternoon, those tables would be groaning with the weight of food and drink. Nothing fancy, but it would be filling. Tea and homemade lemonade. Sandwiches, cakes, scones and pikelets. A few bottles of beer if anyone had any. Hot water and anything forgotten would be provided by the neighbours. No one in this house would be disturbed. They'd be left alone to eat breakfast in peace, to pack and to mourn. The same happening would be repeated for Lily. No effort spared.

Lifting her head to look above them, Hannah stared up at a pale blue sky devoid of cloud. There, barely visible, was the outline of a sickle moon. A new moon. She wasn't surprised.

Acknowledgements

For their unswerving encouragement and support I thank my husband Nev, my sons Danny, Andrew and Rick, and my good friend Di Bates.

For their understanding and expertise, I thank my agent Selwa Anthony, and Ali Watts and Anne Rogan at Penguin.

Also from Penguin

Burnt Sunshine

Estelle Pinney

Sydney, 1930, and Greta Osborne is a burgeoning stage star on the verge of joining the famous Palace Theatre in New York. But meeting British naval officer Andrew Flight at a New Year's Eve party changes everything. Falling in love at first sight, Greta waives aside any thoughts of sailing to New York and Andrew jumps ship. The pair flee to the tobacco town of Yunnabilla in Far North Queensland, where their relationship is viewed by the locals with pursed lips and raised eyebrows. The Great Depression brings added hardships, and circumstances push the couple further north to a remote island in Papua New Guinea where they face unexpected challenges.

Burnt Sunshine is a heart-warming and very colourful novel about two people in love who take a big chance. In spite of a world depression, a near-tragic setback, disappointments, bad times that can turn into good times, together the pair manage to laugh and love and beat the odds.

Shearwater

Andrea Mayes

'I'm in the wrong story. This was never, ever meant to happen to me . . .'

Cassie Callinan became a dutiful, front-line corporate wife, carefully preserving the safety of the status quo, and her husband's camellias. She has survived the tragedy of losing a child with her marriage intact – or so she thinks. When she discovers she has lost her husband to a younger woman, she panics. What is she supposed to do now? Where can she go? Who is she, without the familiar props of her marriage?

Fleeing her own life, Cassie finds herself amongst the eccentric inhabitants of Shearwater, an isolated coastal village. Against her will, she is gradually drawn into the life of the town, with all its dramas, joy and secrets. But then sinister gifts start arriving and it seems someone badly wants her to leave Shearwater. Who? And why?

A delicious story of self-discovery that illuminates life's infinite possibilities; a story of love, hope and human frailty that will make you laugh, and cry.

Subscribe to receive *read more*, your monthly newsletter from Penguin Australia. As a *read more* subscriber you'll receive sneak peeks of new books, be kept up to date with what's hot, have the opportunity to meet your favourite authors, download reading guides for your book club, receive special offers, be in the running to win exclusive subscriber-only prizes, plus much more.

Visit penguin.com.au to subscribe.